The Short Novels of Thomas Wolfe

THE SHORT NOVELS OF
⊂⊐ *Thomas Wolfe*

by Thomas Wolfe . . .

EDITED,
WITH AN INTRODUCTION
AND NOTES BY

C. HUGH HOLMAN

CHARLES SCRIBNER'S SONS ⊂⊐ New York

Contents

Introduction

To present a collection of the short novels of Thomas Wolfe will seem to many of his readers a quixotic or even a perverse act, for Wolfe exists in the popular fancy and even in the opinion of many of his most devoted admirers as the fury-driven author of a vast but incomplete saga of one man's pilgrimage on earth, a saga so formless that the term *novel* can be applied to its parts only with extreme caution and so monumental that it exploded the covers of four vast books in which its portions were imprisoned. Of the book upon which he embarked after *Look Homeward, Angel,* Wolfe wrote: "What I had to deal with was material which covered almost 150 years in history, demanded the action of more than 2000 characters, and would in its final design include almost every racial type and social class of American life." In a letter in 1932 he said, "The book on which I have been working for the last two or three years is not a volume but a library."

Much of the criticism of Wolfe's work has centered on its seemingly uncontrolled and formless exuberance, and it has become almost a critical truism that he possessed great talent but little control, a magnificent sense of language but a limited awareness of the demands of plot, a sensuous recall that was nearly total but an almost shocking unwillingness to subject his material to critical elision.

Yet, paradoxically, Thomas Wolfe produced some of his best work in the middle length of the short novel, the length between 15,000 and 40,000 words. Indeed, during the grueling years between the publication of his first novel in 1929 and *Of Time and the River* in 1935, his reputation was sustained and enriched by his short novels as much as it was by Sinclair Lewis's brief but telling praise for him as a "Gargantuan creature with great gusto for life" in his Nobel Prize address in 1930.

Wolfe's whole career was an endless search for a language and a form in which to communicate his vision of reality. "I believe with all my heart," he declared in *The Story of a Novel*, ". . . that each man for himself and in his own way . . . must find that way, that language, and that door—must find it for himself." This passion to find a mode of expression was coupled in Wolfe with a thoroughly organic view of art, one in which the thing to be said dictates the form in which it is uttered. He once wrote Hamilton Basso: "There is no accepted way: there are as many art forms as there are forms of art, and the artist will continue to create new ones and to enrich life with new creations as long as there is either life or art. So many of these forms that so many academic people consider as masterly and final definitions derived from the primeval source of all things beautiful or handed Apollo-wise from Mount Olympus, are really worn out already, will work no more, are already dead and stale as hell."

Look Homeward, Angel had almost automatically assumed a simple but effective narrative form. The record of childhood and youth, cast at least semi-consciously in the *bildungsroman* pattern of James Joyce's *A Portrait of the Artist as a Young Man*, had found its theme and taken its shape from the sequential flow of lyric feeling which it expressed. After its publication, Wolfe began a desperate search for another form into which to pour his materials. His letters between 1930 and 1934 are crowded with ambitious plans, nebulous projections of structure, plot, and myth, all pointed toward forming his next book. Increasingly its matter grew and the problems of the control of that matter enlarged.

By the fall of 1931 Wolfe found himself immersed in a struggle for form whose magnitude and difficulty, as well as spiritual and emotional anguish, he recorded touchingly in *The Story of a Novel*. In November, badly in need of money and in black despair over "the book," he turned to a body of materials in which he had earlier worked and began shaping them into a short novel. These materials dealt with his experiences in Cambridge and with his uncle, Henry Westall. In its finished form the short novel, *A Portrait of Bascom Hawke,* pictured an old man resigned to the death of dreams as he is seen through the eyes of a youth still half blinded by the visions of glory which the old man has given up. The two points of view, the youth's and the old man's, together gave a sense of the flow and corrosion of time. The result was a portrait in depth, done with irony, poignance, and tolerant laughter, of an eccentric who might have stepped from the pages of Dickens.

Fortunately, Wolfe had connections at this time with a publishing house which had a magazine, *Scribner's,* that was interested in the short novel as a literary form. Ludwig Lewisohn was generally correct when he asserted in 1932 that the short novel "is a form with which, in the English-speaking world, neither editors nor publishers seem ever to know what to do, trying to palm it off now as a short story and now as a novel." But in 1931 and 1932 *Scribner's Magazine* was publishing a novella in each issue, as a result of its second $5,000 Prize Short Novel contest, the announced aim of which was "to open up a field of fiction— the long-story field—which had been almost wholly neglected." In these contests, the best entries were published as they were received, and the prize was awarded to the best novel from both the published and unpublished entries. The characteristics of the short novels *Scribner's* was seeking were declared to be "adequate space for the development of character and setting, combined with precision and solidity of structure." The magazine had begun publishing short novels with James Gould Cozzen's "S. S. *San Pedro*" in August, 1930, the first of twelve long stories published as part of the first Prize Contest. Among the others were long tales by W. R. Burnett, André Maurois, and Marjorie Kinnan Rawlings. The contest was won by John Peale Bishop's *Many Thousands Gone.*

When Wolfe submitted *A Portrait of Bascom Hawke* to Maxwell Perkins in January, 1932, the second Prize Contest was nearing its February 1 closing date. Among the nine short novels published as a part of the second contest, in addition to *A*

Portrait of Bascom Hawke, were long tales by Sherwood Anderson, Edith Wharton, and Katherine Anne Porter. The judges—Burton Rascoe, William Soskin, and Edmund Wilson—declared the contest to be a tie between John Herrmann's *The Big Short Trip* and Wolfe's short novel, which was published in the April, 1932, issue of the magazine. Wolfe and Herrmann divided the $5,000 Prize between them.

A Portrait of Bascom Hawke gained considerable critical praise, such as that which Laurence Stallings gave it in *The New York Sun,* where he wrote: "Has anyone failed to admire a story in the *Scribner's Magazine* (for April) by Thomas Wolfe? There's an eddy of energy for you; and a lyrical paean to life. . . . It seems to me that Thomas Wolfe has shown in this story that his *October Fair,* announced for next fall, will be even finer than . . . *Look Homeward Angel.* . . . He seems to have all the gifts, all the talents . . . 'A Portrait of Bascom Hawke' is the book of the month."

Apparently Wolfe had been ignorant of the existence of the Short Novel Contest until he submitted *A Portrait* to Perkins in January. Learning of the contest he resolved to write another novel to enter in it, despite the fact that less than a month remained before the contest ended. It was actually Perkins who entered *A Portrait of Bascom Hawke* in the contest which it won.

As his intended entry Wolfe set to work on a short novel fashioned on his mother's endless stories of the past. During the month of January she visited him in Brooklyn, and the immediate source of *The Web of Earth* was almost certainly her conversations. The Short Novel Contest had been over more than a month before the story was finished, but *Scribner's* promptly purchased it and published it in the July, 1932, issue.

This novella, the longest of Wolfe's short novels, comes to the reader entirely through the voice of its narrator, Delia Hawke (later changed to Eliza Gant when the novel was reprinted in *From Death to Morning*). Wolfe insisted, "It is different from anything I have ever done," and added, "that story about the old woman has got everything in it, murder and cruelty, and hate and love, and greed and enormous unconscious courage, yet the whole thing is told with the stark innocence of a child." The seemingly disparate elements of the story—disjointed in temporal and logical sequence—are effectively knit together by the powerful personality of the narrator and by her obsessive search in the events of her life for the meaning of the spectral voices that spoke "Two . . . Two" and "Twenty . . . Twenty" in "the year that the locusts came."

In writing *The Web of Earth* Wolfe followed James Joyce again, as he had done in *Look Homeward, Angel.* He compared his "old woman" with Molly Bloom and seemingly felt that his short novel had a structure like that of the interior monologue at the conclusion of *Ulysses.* In her resilience, her undefeatable energy, and her vitality Eliza (or Delia) approaches "the earth goddess" and is, as Louis D. Rubin, Jr. has pointed out, reminiscent of the end of the "Anna Livia Plurabelle" sequence of *Finnegans Wake,* a sequence which was published in the little magazine *transition* about the same time. In this short novel one understands what Wolfe meant when he referred to Eliza Gant's people as "time-devouring." Thus, *The Web of Earth* becomes a fascinating counterpiece to *A Portrait of Bascom Hawke;* for each is a character sketch of an elderly person, but where Bascom Hawke is defeated and despairingly resigned, Eliza Gant is triumphant and dominant; where Bascom is the male victim of time, Eliza is the female devourer of time; where Bascom's is the vain grasp of intellect and reason in a mad and fury-driven world, Eliza's is the groping of mystery, passion, and fear in a world where reason always falls victim to the decay of time. Never did Wolfe articulate more effectively than in these two short novels the fundamental polarities of his childhood and youth.

With these two short novels successfully behind him, Wolfe next turned to organizing into short novel form blocks of the material which he had written for the still formless "big book." In the period between March, 1933, and March, 1934, he put together four long stories or short novels from these materials, finding in the limits of the novella a means of focusing matter whose organization in larger blocks still defied him.

Scribner's Magazine bought three of these long tales and published them in successive issues in the summer of 1934. "The Train and the City," a long short-story of 12,000 words, appeared in the May issue. Percy MacKaye praised this story highly, still, it lacks the unity which Wolfe had achieved in his first two short novels. *Death the Proud Brother* appeared in the June issue, and was later republished as a short novel in *From Death to Morning*. This story of 22,000 words was a skillful attempt to unify a group of seemingly disparate incidents in the city through their common themes of loneliness and death, "the proud brother of loneliness." Wolfe regarded this story very highly, saying, "It represents *important* work to me," and his novelist friend Robert Raynolds praised it highly. Although it is a successful effort to impose thematic unity upon disconnected instances of death in the city, it is less effective than Wolfe's other novellas.

The third long story was *No Door,* in its original form a short novel of 31,000 words, although it was published by *Scribner's* as two long stories, "No Door" in July, 1933, and "The House of the Far and the Lost" in August, 1934. In arranging the materials of this novel, Wolfe selected a group of intensely autobiographical incidents all centering on his sense of incommunicable loneliness and insularity, dislocated them in time, and bound them together by a group of recurring symbols arranged in *leitmotif* patterns, extending and enriching a method he had used in *Death the Proud Brother*. Through the recurring images and the repeated phrases of a prose poem used as a prologue, he knit together one portion of his life. In its concluding episode are united the themes of youth's exuberance and age's sad wisdom, which had been central to *A Portrait of Bascom Hawke,* and the enduring earth, which had been central to *The Web of Earth*.

It was in the early months of 1933 that *No Door* was completed, and by March it had been accepted by *Scribner's*. Its completion coincided with Wolfe's discovery of a plan which made work on the "big book" feasible for him again. He wrote to George Wallace: ". . . just after you left in January . . . I plunged into work and . . . I seemed suddenly to get what I had been trying to get for two years, the way to begin the book, and make it flow, and now it is all coming with a rush." Since the structure of *No Door* is essentially that of *Of Time and the River,* since the prologue to *No Door* re-appears with only minor changes as the prologue to the long novel, and since the writing of *No Door* coincides with the finding of a "way to begin the book," it is probable that the short novel was the door through which Wolfe entered *Of Time and the River.* John Hall Wheelock praised *No Door* highly, and Maxwell Perkins agreed to bring out a limited edition of the short novel in its original form. However, its absorption into *Of Time and the River* was almost complete, and it seemingly has survived as a unit only in the form of its brief first incident, published as a short story in *From Death to Morning,* where it achieved notoriety as the basis for a libel suit brought against Wolfe and Scribner's by Marjorie Dorman and her family in 1936.

Yet *No Door* represents as sure a mastery as Wolfe ever demonstrated of the subjective, autobiographical materials for which he is best known. Of the section published as "The House of the Far and the Lost," Robert Penn Warren wrote in a review almost brutally unsympathetic to *Of Time and the River*: "Only in the section dealing with the Coulson episode does Mr. Wolfe seem to have all his resources for character presentation under control. The men who room in the house . . . with the Coulsons themselves are very precise to the imagination, and are sketched in with an economy usually foreign to Mr. Wolfe. . . . Here Mr. Wolfe has managed to convey an atmosphere and to convince the reader of the reality of his characters without any of his habitual exaggerations of method and style. This section . . . possesses what is rare enough in *Of Time and the River,* a constant focus." The Coulson episode is clearly the most striking one in *No Door.* It is also an integral part of that work, and the entire short novel possesses the strong virtues that Mr. Warren here assigns to the only portion of it which survived as a unified part of the long novel.

One other short novel resulted from Wolfe's arranging of materials from the "big book" during this period. It was *Boom Town*, a story of approximately 20,000 words, portraying the real estate craze in Asheville in the satiric manner of Sinclair Lewis. This short novel was published in the *American Mercury* in May, 1934, but it had been written before *No Door*.

The discovery of an organizing principle for the "big book" brought a temporary end to Wolfe's work in the short novel form; for the next two years he devoted himself single-mindedly to *Of Time and the River*. Thus during his first period—the one of which he said, "I began to write with an intense and passionate concern with the designs and purposes of my own youth"— Thomas Wolfe produced, in addition to his two long novels, five short ones: *A Portrait of Bascom Hawke, The Web of Earth, Death the Proud Brother, Boom Town,* and *No Door*. These short novels helped to sustain his reputation, demonstrated his artistry and control of his materials, and perhaps instructed his sense of form.

When he entered the second period of his career—that of which he said, "[My] preoccupation [with my own youth] has now changed to an intense and passionate concern with the designs and purposes of life"—he found himself once more facing the problem of finding a new and adequate form in which to express his vision of experience. This search for an organic structure was complicated by his growing difficulties with his publishers and his increasing unwillingness to follow the advice of his editor, Maxwell E. Perkins. In this situation, in some respects like that of 1931, Wolfe turned his attention again to elements of his experience that lent themselves to expression in the short novel form.

In the summer of 1936 he made his last visit to Germany, a nation that he loved and that had heaped adulation upon him. On this trip he was forced to face the frightening substratum of Naziism, what he called "a picture of the Dark Ages come again

—shocking beyond belief, but true as the hell that man forever creates for himself." And he said, "I recognized at last, in all its frightful aspects, the spiritual disease which was poisoning unto death a noble and mighty people." That fall he used the short novel form to dramatize this perception of the truth about Hitler's Germany, and he elected to give his account, which he entitled "*I Have a Thing to Tell You*," the sharp intensity and the almost stark directness of the action story. At this time Wolfe had great admiration for the directness and simplicity of Ernest Hemingway's style, and in this short novel of Germany he came closest to adopting some of its characteristics. Nothing Wolfe ever wrote has greater narrative drive or more straightforward action than this novella. The simplicity and objectivity of "*I Have a Thing to Tell You*" were seldom sustained for any length of time in Wolfe's work before 1936.

This short novel also displays clearly the growing concern with the issues of the outer world which had begun to shape Wolfe's thinking. Its publication in the *New Republic* as a serial in March, 1937, despite his disclaimers of propaganda intent, indicates a marked advance in the expression of political and social concerns for Wolfe.

During much of 1937, Wolfe's energies were expended in his long and tortuous break with his publishers, Charles Scribner's Sons, certainly one of the two major emotional cataclysms of his life (the other was his earlier break with his mistress, Aline Bernstein). He was also deeply discouraged about his projected book, feeling that his long-planned and talked-of *October Fair*, often announced, was somehow being dissipated in fragments. In this despairing state, he was led by his growing sense of social injustice to attempt another experiment with a short novel as a vehicle of social criticism. He worked on this new novella, *The Party at Jack's*, during the early months of the year and spent the summer in revising and rewriting it.

Wolfe felt that he was attempting in *The Party at Jack's* "one of the most curious and difficult problems that I have been faced with in a long time," the presentation of a cross-section of society through a representation of many people, ranging from police-men, servants, and entertainers to the leaders in the literary world and the rich in the events of a single evening during which they were brought together through a party and a fire in the apart-ment house in which the party occurred. He used several devices, including the recurring quivering of the apartment house as the trains run in tunnels through its seemingly solid rock foundations and the conversations of the doormen and elevator operators, to underscore the contrast among the characters and to comment on society. Wolfe feared that readers would think this short novel to be Marxist, a charge against which he defended it, saying: ". . . there is not a word of propaganda in it. It is certainly not at all Marxian, but it is representative of the way my life has come —after deep feeling, deep thinking, and deep living and all this experience—to take its way. . . . It is in concept, at any rate, the most densely woven piece of writing that I have ever at-tempted."

The Party at Jack's is, as Wolfe asserted, free of autobiog-raphy, except in the most incidental ways. It is also in Wolfe's late, more economical style. Its taut prose and its rapid movement, together with its effective but implicit statement of social doc-trine, make it one of Wolfe's most impressive accomplishments.

Almost immediately after completing *The Party at Jack's,* Wolfe plunged into the organizing of his materials into another "big book" for his new publishers, Harper and Brothers, a task which he was prevented from completing by his death in September, 1938. He had written—in addition to a mass of manuscript out of which three later books were assembled—two novels, a num-ber of short stories, and seven short novels.

Upon these seven short novels Wolfe had expended great effort, and in them he had given the clearest demonstrations he ever made of his craftsmanship and his artistic control. Each of these seven novellas is marked in its unique way by a sharp focus and a controlling unity, and each represents a serious experiment with form. Yet they have virtually been lost from the corpus of

Wolfe's work, lost even to most of those who know that work well.

There were two reasons for these losses. In the first place Wolfe's publishers, and particularly his editor, Maxwell E. Perkins, were anxious that the long, introspective *Look Homeward, Angel* be followed by an equally impressive work. Perkins urged Wolfe to continue the Eugene Gant story and discouraged his coming before the public in a different form or manner. Wolfe at one time wanted *Look Homeward, Angel* to be followed by *No Door*, a work of less than 40,000 words, and that small book might have been followed by a volume which Wolfe described to his mother that would contain *A Portrait of Bascom Hawke, The Web of Earth*, and "another story which [he had] written," probably "The Train and the City." At this time, however, Wolfe was happy to rely on his editor's judgment, and did not trust his own.

A second reason for the loss of these short novels is the nature of Wolfe's work and his attitude toward it. All the separate parts of his writing formed for him portions of a great and eternally fragmentary whole. It was all the outgrowth of the same basic desire, the Whitmanesque attempt to put a person on record and through that person to represent America in its paradox of unity and variety, at the same time employing as his essential theme the eternal and intolerable loneliness of the individual lost in the complex currents of time. As a result, Wolfe was forever reshuffling the parts of his work and assembling them in different patterns, in a way not unlike the shifting elements of the Snopes material in Faulkner's continuing legend of Yoknapatawpha County. Thus Wolfe took the materials he had presented first as short novels and interwove them into the larger frames and subject matters of his "big books," fragmenting, expanding, and modifying them, and often destroying their separate integrity. Only two of his short novels escaped this process; and these two—*Death the Proud Brother* and *The Web of Earth*—were published in a collection of his shorter works, *From Death to Morning*, which has never received the critical attention that it deserves.

In his short novels Wolfe was dealing with limited aspects of experience, aspects that could be adequately developed in the limits of 15,000 to 40,000 words and that could be organized into what he proudly called *The Party at Jack's*, "a single thing." When later he fragmented these short novels and distributed the fragments within the larger design of the "big books," he robbed them of their own unity in order to make them a portion of a larger and more complex unity—"a single thing" of complex and multifarious parts. Indeed, Wolfe's treatment of his short novels when he incorporated them later into his long books (and there is no reason to doubt that he would have approved the use made by his editor of the longer versions of *"I Have a Thing to Tell You"* and *The Party at Jack's* in *You Can't Go Home Again*) is a key to one of Wolfe's central problems, the finding of a large form sufficient to unify his massive imaginative picture of experience. This large form that he sought would give, apparently, not the representation of a series of sharply realized dramatic moments in the life of his protagonist (and through him of America) but an actual and significant interweaving of these moments into a complex fabric of event, time, and feeling. That he struggled unceasingly for the mastery of this vast structure is obvious from his letters, from *The Story of a Novel*, and from the long books themselves. Whether he was moving toward its realization is a matter of critical debate today, as it was at the time of his death. However much one may feel that he was (and I share that belief), the fact remains that none of the published novels after *Look Homeward, Angel* succeeded in finding a clearly demonstrable unity, in being "a single thing."

The intrinsic qualities of the short novel were remarkably well adapted to Wolfe's special talents and creative methods. Although he was skilled at the revelatory vignette, in which he imprisoned a character in an instance in time, those characters and actions which were central to his effort and experience he saw in relation to the expanding pattern of life. Experience and life itself were for him, as Herbert Muller has noted, remarkably "in process." One of the distinctive aspects of Wolfe's imagination is its

tendency to see life as a thing of "becoming." He saw time—
"dark time," he called it—as being at the center of the mystery of
experience, and its representation on three complex levels was
a major concern of his work. The individual scene or person had
little value to him; it had to be put back in time to assume meaning. Wolfe was very explicit about this element of his work. In
The Story of a Novel he says: "All of this time I was being baffled
by a certain time element in the book, by a time relation which
could not be escaped, and for which I was now desperately seek-
ing some structural channel. There were three time elements inherent in the material. The first and most obvious was an element
of actual present time, an element which carried the narrative
forward, which represented characters and events as living in
the present and moving forward into an immediate future. The
second time element was of past time, one which represented these
same characters as acting and as being acted upon by all the
accumulated impact of man's experience so that each moment of
their lives was conditioned not only by what they experienced in
that moment, but by all that they had experienced up to that
moment. In addition to these two time elements, there was a
third which I conceived as being time immutable, the time of
rivers, mountains, oceans, and the earth; a kind of eternal and
unchanging universe of time against which would be projected
the transience of man's life, the bitter briefness of his day. It was
the tremendous problem of these three time elements that almost
defeated me and that cost me countless hours of anguish in the
years that were to follow."

Ultimately in the portrayal of an incident or an individual
against this complex pattern of time, that incident or individual
must be seen through a perceiving and remembering self, such
as David Hawke, the youth who can read the corrosion of time
in the contrast between his exuberance and his uncle's resignation,
in *A Portrait of Bascom Hawke*. Eliza Gant's fabric of memories
in *The Web of Earth* is a record of the impact of time on her.
The individual incidents of *No Door* assume their importance
as portions of a personal history as they are reflected in the

narrator's memory. To be fully understood, such events and people must be set against the innumerable other events and people which the perceiving self has known; it is this larger context in time which Wolfe attempts to give these short novels when he incorporates them in his longer works. We can think of an event as being an objective experience which is perceived and recalled later by the self that first knew it directly; then it, as fact and as memory, becomes a part of the totality of experience that makes the web of meaning for that self. Wolfe's short novels represent that portion of the process in which the incident is remembered, isolated, organized, and understood as incident by the self. Their later fragmentation and inclusion in the long novels represent his attempt to absorb them into his total experience and to use them in all the complexity of life as elements in his search for ultimate meaning. Hence he breaks up the sequence of actions, introduces new incidents, and frequently expands the wordage of the short novels when they are incorporated into the larger structures. These incidents thereby lose some of their artistic and inherent right to achieve unity by exclusion, and they tend to become diffuse.

Since Wolfe's success in achieving the larger unity for which he strove in the last three long novels is considerably less than total, the materials which he had organized into short novels have an integrity and a consummate craftsmanship which they seem to lack in the long books. It is for this reason that we are justified in reprinting here the five best short novels of Thomas Wolfe in the form in which he prepared them for magazine publication. In the short novel form Wolfe was a master of his craft, and these successful products of his efforts should not be forgotten.

The Short Novels of Thomas Wolfe

A Portrait of Bascom Hawke

A PORTRAIT OF BASCOM HAWKE

In the late fall of 1931, because he "needed money and had a feeling of despair over the book" on which he had been working as a second novel and for which he had been projecting elaborate and highly ambitious plans, Thomas Wolfe turned to a new field. As he wrote George McCoy, "I stopped suddenly, worked furiously for a month on a short novel and completed it." He submitted this short novel, *A Portrait of Bascom Hawke,* to Maxwell Perkins, who purchased it for *Scribner's Magazine* on January 28, 1932, for $500. It appeared in the April, 1932, issue of the magazine. Unknown to Wolfe, Perkins entered the short novel in the $5000 Prize Short Novel Contest, and it tied with John Herrmann's *The Big Short Trip* for the prize.

At the time of writing it, Wolfe did not think of *A Portrait of Bascom Hawke* as a segment of his "big book," but rather as a self-contained unit, and at least once he considered grouping it with two other short novels and making a book. As late as March, 1934, he did not regard it as a part of the work in progress, for he wrote his mother that it would be included in a collection of his stories to be published "next Winter or Spring after the big book comes out." When, however, *Of Time and the River* was finally assembled, Bascom Hawke had become Bascom Pentland and *A Portrait* had been fragmented and modified. Materials from it appeared in the novel on pages 104-111, 116-130, 132, 136-141, 141-150, 177-184, 185-186, and 192.

Wolfe accompanied the manuscript of the short novel version with a note in which he said, "I've simply tried to give you a man—as for plot, there's not any, but there's this idea which I believe is pretty plain—I've always wanted to say something about *old men* and *young men,* and that's what I've tried to do here. I hope the man seems real and living to you and that it has the unity of this feeling I spoke about."

It is "the unity of this feeling" which, indeed, controls *A Portrait of Bascom Hawke,* a developing character study whose point and poignance come through the contrast of the narrator's youth and furious exuberance with the old man's madness and despairing resignation. In these contrasting figures Wolfe found an effective method for bringing his readers a simultaneous awareness of the three levels of time: the literal present, the past as it impinges on and makes the present, and the inexorable and corrosive flow of eternity. Inevitably, the transfer of this material into *Of Time and the River,* where it became one of the aspects of reality impinging upon the young man, resulted in a shifting of the center of interest from Bascom Hawke to Eugene Gant, with a concurrent loss of "the unity of this feeling."

The version here reprinted is that of *Scribner's Magazine,* XCI (April, 1932), 193-198, 239-256.

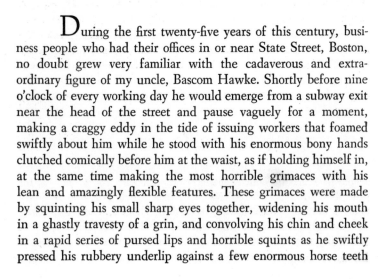

During the first twenty-five years of this century, business people who had their offices in or near State Street, Boston, no doubt grew very familiar with the cadaverous and extraordinary figure of my uncle, Bascom Hawke. Shortly before nine o'clock of every working day he would emerge from a subway exit near the head of the street and pause vaguely for a moment, making a craggy eddy in the tide of issuing workers that foamed swiftly about him while he stood with his enormous bony hands clutched comically before him at the waist, as if holding himself in, at the same time making the most horrible grimaces with his lean and amazingly flexible features. These grimaces were made by squinting his small sharp eyes together, widening his mouth in a ghastly travesty of a grin, and convolving his chin and cheek in a rapid series of pursed lips and horrible squints as he swiftly pressed his rubbery underlip against a few enormous horse teeth that decorated his upper jaw. Having completed these facial evolutions, he glanced quickly and, it must be supposed, blindly, in every direction; for he then plunged heedlessly across the street, sometimes choosing the moment when traffic had been halted, and pedestrians were hurrying across, sometimes diving into the midst of a roaring chaos of motor cars, trucks, and wagons, through which he sometimes made his way in safety, accompanied only by a scream of brake bands, a startled barking of horns, and the hearty curses of frightened drivers, or from which, howling with terror in the center of a web of traffic which he had snarled hopelessly and brought to a complete standstill, he was sometimes rescued by a red-faced and cursing young Irishman who was on point duty at that corner.

But Bascom was a fated man and he escaped. Once, it is true, a bright mindless beetle of machinery, which had no thought for fated men, had knocked him down and skinned and bruised him; again, an uninstructed wheel had passed across the soft toe-end of his shoe and held him prisoner, as if he were merely some average son of destiny—but he escaped. He escaped because he was a fated man and because the providence which guides the steps of children and the blind was kind to him; and because this same policeman whose simian upper lip had once been thick and twisted with its curses had long since run the scale from anger to wild fury, and thence to madness and despair and resignation, and had now come to have a motherly affection for this stray sheep, kept his eye peeled for its appearance every morning or, failing this, at once shrilled hard upon his whistle when he heard the well-known howl of terror and surprise, plunged to the centre of the stalled traffic snarl, plucked Bascom out to safety under curse and shout and scream of brake, and marched him tenderly to the curb, gripping his brawny hand around my uncle's arm, feeling his joints, testing his bones, massaging anxiously his sinewy carcass, and calling him "bud"—although my uncle was old enough to be his grandfather. "Are you all right, bud? You're not hurt, are you, bud? Are you O. K.?"—to which Bascom if his shock and terror had been great, could make no answer for a moment save to pant hoarsely and to howl loudly and huskily from time to time "Ow! Ow! Ow! Ow!"

At length, becoming more coherent, if not more calm, he would launch into an ecclesiastical indictment of motor cars and their drivers delivered in a high, howling, and husky voice that suggested the pronouncements of a prophet from a mountain. This voice had a quality of strange remoteness and, once heard, would never be forgotten. It actually had a howling note in it, and carried to great distances, and yet it was not loud: it was very much as if Mr. Bascom Hawke were standing on a mountain and shouting to some one in a quiet valley below—the sounds came to one plainly but as if from a great distance, and it was full of a husky, unearthly passion. It was really an ecclesiastical voice, the voice of a great preacher; one felt that it should be heard in churches, which was exactly where it once was heard, for my uncle Bascom had at various times and with great conviction, in the course of his long and remarkable life, professed and preached the faith of the Episcopalians, the Presbyterians, the Methodists, the Baptists, and the Unitarians.

Quite often, in fact, as now, when he had narrowly escaped disaster in the streets, Bascom Hawke still preached from the corner: as soon as he recovered somewhat from his shock, he would launch forth into a sermon of eloquent invective against any driver of motor cars within hearing, and if any of them entered the fray, as sometimes happened, a very interesting performance occurred.

"What happened to *you?*" the motorist might bitterly remark. "Do the keepers know you're out?"

Mr. Hawke would thereupon retort with an eloquent harangue, beginning with a few well-chosen quotations from the more violent prophets of the Old Testament, a few predictions of death, destruction and damnation for the owners of motor cars, and a few apt references to Days of Judgment and Reckoning, Chariots of Moloch, and Beasts of the Apocalypse.

"Oh, for God's sake!" the exasperated motorist might reply. "Are you *blind?* Where do you think you are? In a cow-pasture? Can't you read the signals? Didn't you see the cop put his hand up?

[6]

Don't you know when it says to 'Stop' or 'Go'? Did you ever hear of the traffic law?"

"The *traffic* law!" my uncle Bascom sneeringly exclaimed, as if the mere use of the word by the motorist evoked his profoundest contempt. His voice now had a precise and meticulous way of speech, there was something sneering and pedantical in the way he pronounced each word, biting it off with a prim, nasal and heavily accented enunciation in the manner of certain pedants and purists who suggest by their pronunciation that language in the mouths of most people is vilely and carelessly treated, that each word has a precise, subtle, and careful meaning of its own, and that they—*they* alone—understand these matters. "The *traffic* law!" he repeated again: then he squinted his eyes together, pursed his rubbery lip against the big horsy upper teeth, and laughed down his nose in a forced, sneering manner, "The *traffic* law!" he said. "Why, you pit-i-ful ig-no-*ram*-us! You il-*lit*-ter-ate ruffian! You dare to speak to me—to *me!*" he howled suddenly with an ecclesiastical lift of his voice, striking himself on his bony breast and glaring with a majestical fury as if the word of a mighty prophet had been contradicted by an upstart—"of the traffic law, when it is doubtful if you could *read* the law if you saw it,"—he sneered—"and it is obvious to anyone with the perception of a schoolboy that you would not have intelligence enough to understand it, and"—here his voice rose to a howling emphasis and he held one huge bony finger up to command attention—"*and* to interpret it, if you could read."

"Is *that* so!" the motorist heavily remarked. "A *wise* guy, eh? One of these guys who knows it all, eh? You're a *pretty* wise guy, aren't you?" the motorist continued bitterly, as if caught up in the circle of his refrain and unable to change it. "Well, let me tell *you* something. You think you're pretty smaht, don't you? Well, you're not. See? It's wise guys like you who go around looking for a good bust on the nose. See? That's how smaht you are. If you wasn't an old guy I'd give you one, too," he said, getting a moody satisfaction from the thought.

"Ow-w! Ow-w! Ow-w!" Bascom howled in sudden terror.

"If you know so much, if you're so smaht as you think you are, what *is* the traffic law?"

Then, assuredly, if there was a traffic law, the unfortunate motorist was lost, for my Uncle Bascom would deliver it to him verbatim, licking his lips with joy over all the technicalities of legal phrasing and pronouncing each phrase with a meticulous and pedantical enunciation.

"And furthermore!" he howled, holding up his big bony finger, "the Commonwealth of Massachusetts has decreed, by a statute that has been on the books since 1856, by a statute that is irrevocably, inexorably, ineluctably plain that any driver, director, governor, commander, manager, agent or conductor, or any other person who shall conduct or cause to be conducted any vehicular instrument, whether it be of two, four, six, eight or any number of wheels whatsoever, whether it be in the public service, or in the possession of a private individual, whether it be—" but by this time, the motorist, if he was wise, had had enough, and had escaped.

If, however, it had been one of his more fortunate mornings, if he had blindly but successfully threaded the peril of roaring traffic, my Uncle Bascom proceeded rapidly down State Street, still clutching his raw bony hands across his meagre waist, still contorting his remarkable face in its endless series of pursed grimaces, and presently turned in to the entrance of a large somewhat dingy-looking building of blackened stone, one of those solid, unpretending, but very valuable properties which smells and looks like the early 1900's, and which belongs to that ancient and enormously wealthy corporation which lies across the river and is known as Harvard University.

Here, my Uncle Bascom, still clutching himself together across the waist, mounted a flight of indented marble entry steps, lunged through revolving doors into a large marble corridor that was redolent with vibrating waves of hot steamy air, wet rubbers and galoshes, sanitary disinfectant, and serviceable but somewhat old-fashioned elevators and, entering one of the cars which had just plunged down abruptly, banged open its door, belched out two or three people and swallowed a dozen more, he was finally deposited with the same abruptness on the seventh floor, where he stepped out into a wide dark corridor, squinted and grimaced uncertainly to right and left as he had done for twenty-five years, and then went left along the corridor, past rows of lighted offices in which one could hear the preliminary clicking of typewriters, the rattling of crisp papers, and the sounds of people beginning their day's work. At the end of the corridor Bascom Hawke turned right along another corridor and at length paused before a door which bore this inscription across the familiar glazed glass of American business offices: The John T. Brill Realty Co.—Houses For Rent or Sale. Below this bold legend in much smaller letters was printed: Bascom Hawke—Att'y at Law—Conveyancer and Title Expert.

And now, before we enter this interesting office, let us give a closer and more particular scrutiny to the appearance of this singular man.

The appearance of this strange figure in State Street, or anywhere else, had always been sufficiently curious to attract attention and to draw comment. Bascom Hawke, if he had straightened to his full height, would have been six feet and three or four inches tall, but he had always walked with a stoop and as he grew older, the stoop had become confirmed: he presented a tall, gnarled, bony figure, cadaverous and stringy, but tough as hickory. He was of that race of men who seem never to wear out, or to grow old, or to die: they live with almost undiminished vitality to great ages, and when they die they die suddenly. There is no slow wastage and decay because there is so little to waste or decay: their mummied and stringy flesh has the durability of granite.

Bascom Hawke clothed his angular figure with an assortment of odd garments which seemed to have the same durability: they were immensely old and worn, but they also gave no signs of ever wearing out, for by their cut and general appearance of age, it seemed that his frugal soul had selected in the nineties materials which it hoped would last forever. His coat, which was originally of a dark dull pepper-and-salt gray, had gone green at the seams and pockets, and moreover it was a ridiculously short skimpy coat for a gaunt big-boned man like this: it was hardly more than a jacket, his great wristy hands burst out of it like lengths of cordwood, and the mark of his high humped narrow shoulders cut into it with a knife-like sharpness. His trousers were also tight and skimpy, of a lighter gray and of a rough woolly texture from which all fuzz and fluff had long ago been rubbed, he wore rough country brogans with raw-hide laces, and a funny little flat hat of ancient black felt, which had also gone green along the band. One understands now why the policeman called him "Bud": this great bony figure seemed ruthlessly to have been crammed into garments in which a country fledgling of the eighties might have gone to see his girl, clutching a bag of gumdrops in his large red hand. A stringy little necktie, a clean but dilapidated collar which by its bluish and softly mottled look Bascom Hawke must have laundered himself (a presumption which is quite correct since my uncle did all his own laundry work, as well as his mending, repairing, and cobbling)—this was his costume, winter and summer, and it never changed, save that in winter he supplemented it with an ancient blue sweater which he wore buttoned to the chin and whose frayed ends and cuffs projected inches below the scanty little jacket. He had never been known to wear an overcoat, not even on the coldest days of those long, raw, and formidable winters which Boston suffers.

The mark of my uncle's madness was plain upon him: intuitively men knew he was not a poor man, and the people who had seen him so many times in State Street would nudge one another, saying: "You see that old guy? You'd think he was waitin' for a handout from the Salvation Army, wouldn't you? Well, he's not. He's *got* it, brother. Believe me, he's *got* it good and plenty: he's *got* it salted away where no one ain't goin' to touch it. That guy's got a sock full of dough!"

"Jesus!" another remarks. "What good's it goin' to do an old guy like that? He can't take any of it with him, can he?"

"You said it, brother," and the conversation would become philosophical.

Bascom Hawke was himself conscious of his parsimony, and although he sometimes asserted that he was "only a poor man" he realized that his exaggerated economies could not be justified to his business associates on account of poverty: they taunted him slyly, saying, "Come on, Hawke, let's go to lunch. You can get a good meal at the Pahkeh House for a couple of bucks." Or "Say, Hawke, I know a place where they're havin' a sale of winter overcoats: I saw one there that would suit you—you can get it for sixty dollars." Or "Do you need a good laundry, Reverend? I know a couple of Chinks who do good work."

To which Bascom, with the characteristic evasiveness of parsimony, would reply, snuffling derisively down his nose: "No, sir! You won't catch me in any of their stinking restaurants. You never know what you're getting: if you could see the dirty, nasty, filthy kitchens where your food is prepared you'd lose your appetite quick enough." His parsimony had resulted in a compensating food mania: he declared that "in his young days" he "ruined his digestion by eating in restaurants," he painted the most revolting pictures of the filth of these establishments, laughing scornfully down his nose as he declared: "I suppose you think it tastes better after some dirty, nasty, stinking *nigger* has wiped his old hands all over it" (phuh-phuh-phuh-phuh-phuh!)—here he would contort his face and snuffle scornfully down his nose; and he was bitter in his denunciation of "rich foods," declaring they had "destroyed more lives than all the wars and all the armies since the beginning of time."

As he had grown older he had become more and more convinced of the healthy purity of "raw foods," and he prepared for himself at home raw revolting messes of chopped-up carrots, onions, turnips, even raw potatoes, which he devoured at table, smacking his lips with an air of keen relish, and declaring to his wife: "You may poison *yourself* on your old roasts and oysters

[11]

and turkeys if you please: you wouldn't catch *me* eating that stuff. No, sir! Not on your life! I think too much of my stomach!" But his use of the pronoun "you" was here universal rather than particular because if that lady's longevity had depended on her abstinence from "roasts and oysters and turkeys" there was no reason why she should not have lived forever.

Or again, if it were a matter of clothing, a matter of fencing in his bones and tallows against the frozen nail of Boston winter, he would howl derisively: "An overcoat! Not on your life! I wouldn't give two cents for all the old overcoats in the world! The only thing they're good for is to gather up germs and give you colds and pneumonia. I haven't worn an overcoat in thirty years, and I've never had the *vestige*—no! not the *semblance*—of a cold during all that time!"—an assertion that was not strictly accurate since he always complained bitterly of at least two or three during the course of a single winter, declaring at those times that no more hateful, treacherous, damnable climate than that of Boston had ever been known.

Similarly, if it were a question of laundries he would scornfully declare that he would not send "*his* shirts and collars to let some dirty old Chinaman spit and *hock* upon them—*yes!*" he would gleefully howl, as some new abomination of nastiness suggested itself to his teeming brain—"*Yes!* and iron it *in,* too, so you can walk around done up in old Chinaman's spit!"—(phuh-phuh-phuh-phuh-phuh!)—here he would grimace, contort his rubbery lip, and laugh down his nose in forced snarls of gratification and triumph.

This was the old man who now stood clutching his raw bony hands across his waist, before entering his office.

This was his history:

Bascom Hawke had been the scholar of his amazing family: he was a man of powerful intelligence and disordered emotions. Even in his youth, his eccentricities of dress, speech, walk, manner had made him an object of ridicule to his Southern kinsmen, but their ridicule was streaked with pride, since they accepted the impact of his personality as another proof that theirs was an extraordinary family. "He's one of 'em, all right," they said exultantly, "queerer than any of us!"

Bascom's youth, following the war between the States, had been seared by a bitter poverty: at once enriched and warped by a life that clung to the earth with a root-like tenacity, that was manual, painful, spare and stricken, and that rebuilt itself—fiercely, cruelly, and richly—from the earth. And, because there burned and blazed in him from the first a hatred of human indignity, a passionate avowal of man's highness and repose, he felt more bitterly than the others the delinquencies of his father, and the multiplication of his father's offspring, who came regularly into a world of empty cupboards.

"As each of them made its unhappy entrance into the world," he would say later, his voice tremulous with passion, "I went out into the woods, striking my head against the trees, and blaspheming God in my anger. Yes, sir," he continued, pursing his long lip rapidly against his few loose upper teeth, and speaking with an exaggerated pedantry of enunciation, "I am not ashamed to confess that I did. For we were living in conditions un-*worthy*—*unworthy*"—his voice rising to an evangelical yell, "I had almost said—of the condition of animals. And—*say*—what do you think?" —he said, with a sudden shift in manner and tone, becoming, after his episcopal declaration, matter of fact and whisperingly confidential. "Why, do you know, my boy, at one time I had to take my *own* father aside, and point out to him we were living in no way becoming decent people."—Here his voice sank to a whisper, and he tapped me on the knee with his big stiff finger, grimacing horribly and pursing his lip against his dry upper teeth.

Poverty had been the mistress of his youth and Bascom Hawke had not forgotten: poverty had burned its way into his heart. He took what education he could find in a backwoods school, read everything he could, taught, for two or three years, in a country school and, at the age of twenty-one, borrowing enough money for railway fare, went to Boston to enroll himself at Harvard. And, somehow, because of the fire that burned in him, the fierce determination of his soul, he had been admitted, secured employment waiting on tables, tutoring, and pressing every one's trousers but his own, and lived in a room with two other starved wretches on $3.50 a week, cooking, eating, sleeping, washing, and studying in the one place.

At the end of seven years he had gone through the college and the school of theology, performing brilliantly in Greek, Hebrew, and metaphysics.

Poverty, fanatical study, the sexual meagreness of his surroundings, had made of him a gaunt zealot: at thirty he was a lean fanatic, a true Yankee madman, high-boned, with gray thirsty eyes and a thick flaring sheaf of oaken hair—six feet three inches of gangling and ludicrous height, gesticulating madly and obliviously before a grinning world. But he had a grand lean head: he looked somewhat like the great Ralph Waldo Emerson— with the brakes off.

About this time, he married a young Southern woman of a good family: she was from Tennessee, her parents were both dead, in the seventies she had come north and had lived for several years with an uncle in Providence, who had been constituted guardian of her estate, amounting probably to about seventy-five thousand dollars, although her romantic memory later multiplied the sum to two hundred thousand dollars. The man squandered part of her money and stole the rest: she came, therefore, to Bascom without much dowry, but she was pretty, bright, intelligent, and had a good figure. Bascom smote the walls of his room with bloody knuckles, and fell down before God.

When Bascom met her she was a music student in Boston: she had a deep full-toned contralto voice which was wrung from her somewhat tremulously when she sang. She was a small woman, birdlike and earnest, delicately fleshed and boned, quick and active in her movements and with a crisp tart speech which still bore, curiously, traces of a Southern accent. She was a brisk, serious, lady-like little person, without much humor, and she was very much in love with her gaunt suitor. They saw each other for two years: they went to concerts, lectures, sermons; they talked of music, poetry, philosophy and of God, but they never spoke of love. But one night Bascom met her in the parlor of her boarding house on Huntington Avenue, and with a voice vibrant and portentous with the importance of the words he had to utter, began as follows: "Miss Louise!" he said carefully, gazing thoughtfully over the apex of his hands. "There comes a time when a man, having reached an age of discretion and mature judgment, must begin to consider one of the *gravest*—yes! by all means one of the most important events in human life. The event I refer to is—matrimony." He paused, a clock was beating out its punctual measured tock upon the mantel, and a horse went by with ringing hoofs upon the street. As for Louise, she sat quietly erect, with dignified and ladylike composure, but it seemed to her that the clock was beating in her own breast, and that it might cease to beat at any moment.

"For a minister of the gospel," Bascom continued, "the decision is particularly grave because, for him—once made it is *irrevocable,* once determined upon, it must be followed *inexorably, relentlessly* —aye! to the edge of the grave, to the *uttermost* gates of death, so that the possibility of an error in judgment is *fraught,*" his voice sinking to a boding whisper—"is *fraught* with the most terrible consequences. Accordingly," Uncle Bascom said in a deliberate tone, "having decided to take this step, realizing to the *full* —to the *full,* mind you—its gravity, I have searched my soul, I have questioned my heart. I have gone up into mount-ings and out into the desert and communed with my *Maker* until," his voice rose like a demon's howl, "there no longer remains an *atom* of doubt, a *particle* of uncertainty, a *vestige* of *disbelief!* Miss Louise, I have decided that the young lady best fitted in every way to be my helpmate, the partner of my joys and griefs, the confidante of my dearest hopes, the in-*spir*-a-tion of my noblest endeavors, the companion of my declining years, and the *spirit* that shall accompany me along each step of life's vexed and troubled way, sharing with me whatever God in his *inscrutable* Providence shall will, whether of wealth or poverty, grief or happiness—I have decided, Miss Louise, that that lady must be—

yourself!—and, therefore, I request," he said slowly and impressively, "the honor of your hand in mar-ri-age."

She loved him, she had hoped, prayed, and agonized for just such a moment, but now that it had come she rose immediately with lady-like dignity, and said: "Mistah Hawke: I am honuhed by this mahk of yoah esteem and affection, and I pwomise to give it my most *un*nest considahwation without delay. I wealize fully, Mistah Hawke, the gwavity of the wuhds you have just uttuhed. Foh my paht, I must tell you, Mistah Hawke, that if I accept yoah pwoposal, I shall come to you without the fawchun which was *wight*fully mine, but of which I have been depwived and defwauded by the *wascality*—yes! the *wascality* of my gahdian. I shall come to you, theahfoh, without the dow'y I had hoped to be able to contwibute to my husband's fawchuns."

"Oh, my *dear* Miss Louise! My *dear* young lady!" Uncle Bascom cried, waving his great hand through the air with a dismissing gesture. "Do not suppose—do not for one instant suppose, I beg of you!—that consideration of a monetary nature could influence my decision. Oh, not in the slightest!" he cried. "Not at all, not at all!"

"Fawchnatly," Louise continued, "my inhewitance was not *wholly* dissipated by this scoundwel. A pohtion, a vewy small pohtion, remains."

"My dear girl! My dear young lady!" Uncle Bascom cried. "It is not of the *slightest* consequence. . . . How much did he leave?" he added.

Thus they were married.

Bascom immediately got a church in the Middle West: good pay and a house. But during the course of the next twenty years he was shifted from church to church, from sect to sect—to Brooklyn, then back to the Middle West, to the Dakotas, to Jersey City, to Western Massachusetts, and finally back to the small towns surrounding Boston.

When Bascom talked, you may be sure God listened: he preached magnificently, his gaunt face glowing from the pulpit, his rather high, enormously vibrant voice, husky with emotion.

His prayers were fierce solicitations of God, so mad with fervor that his audiences felt uncomfortably they came close to blasphemy. But, unhappily, on occasions my uncle's mad eloquence grew too much for him: his voice, always too near the heart of passion, would burst in splinters, and he would fall violently forward across his lectern, his face covered by his great gaunt fingers, sobbing horribly.

This, in the Middle West, where his first church had been, does not go down so well—yet it may be successful if one weeps mellowly, joyfully—smiling bravely through the tears—at a lovely aisle processional of repentant sinners; but Bascom, who chose uncomfortable titles for his sermons, would be overcome by his powerful feelings on these occasions when his topic was "Potiphar's Wife," "Ruth, the Girl in the Corn," "The Whores of Babylon," "The Woman on the Roof," and so on.

His head was too deeply engaged with his conscience—he was in turn Episcopal, Presbyterian, Unitarian, searching through the whole roaring confusion of Protestantism for a body of doctrine with which he could agree. And, he was forever finding it, and later forever renouncing what he had found. At forty, the most liberal of Unitarians, the strains of agnosticism were piping madly through his sermons: he began to hint at his new faith in prose which he modeled on the mighty utterance of Carlyle, and in poetry, in what he deemed the manner of Matthew Arnold. His professional connection with the Unitarians, and indeed with the Baptists, Methodists, Holy Rollers, and Seventh Day Adventists, came to an abrupt ending after he read from his pulpit one morning a composition in verse entitled *The Agnostic,* which made up in concision what is lacked in melody, and which ended each stanza sadly, but very plainly, on this recurrence:

> *I do not know:*
> *It may be so.*

Thus, when he was almost fifty Bascom Hawke stopped preaching in public. There was no question where he was going. He had his family's raging lust for property. He became a "conveyancer";

he acquired enough of the law of property to convey titles; but he began to buy pieces of land in the suburbs of Boston, and to build small cheap houses, using his own somewhat extraordinary designs to save the architect's fees and, wherever possible, doing such odd jobs as laying the foundations, installing the plumbing, and painting the structure.

He regarded the price of everything as exorbitant—his furious anguish over the wages of labor was marvelous to behold: it drove him raging home, where he stamped insanely upon the floors in his fury, declaring that the Italians, Irish, Belgians, Poles, Swiss, and Yankees—or whatever unfortunate race had been represented in the last bill of charges—were infamous scoundrels, foul and dishonest cutthroats, engaged in a conspiracy to empty both his purse and his cupboard. He called upon them the entire and plenteous artillery of his abuse, his high husky voice ascending to a scream until, his own powers failing him, there flashed in him for a moment remembrance of one mightier than he, the most terribly eloquent of all earth's thunderers—his obscene and gargantuan partner, John T. Brill; and lifting his shaking hands toward Heaven, he would invoke God and Brill at the same time.

Like others in his family seared with a terrible and minute memory of war and hunger, he fled before the skeleton spectre of poverty: he was of that race which expects to avert starvation by eating sparingly.

Therefore, he mended his own shoes and wore historic clothing; he fiercely sowed and reaped the produce of his stony garden, and contrived in countless other ways to thwart the forces of organized extortion.

The small houses that he—no, he did not build them!—he went through the agonies of monstrous childbirth to produce them, he licked, nursed, and fondled them into stunted growth, and he sold them on long, but profitable terms to small Irish, Jewish, Negro, Belgian, Italian and Greek laborers and tradesmen. And at the conclusion of a sale, or after receiving from one of these men the current payment, Uncle Bascom went homeward in a delirium of joy, shouting in a loud voice, to all who might be compelled to listen, the merits of the Jews, Belgians, Irish, Swiss or Greeks.

"Finest people in the world! No question about it!"—this last being his favorite exclamation in all moments of payment or conviction.

For when they paid, he loved them. Often on Sundays they would come to pay him tramping over the frozen ground or the packed snow through street after street of smutty gray-looking houses in the flat weary-looking suburb where he lived. To this dismal heath, therefore, they came, the swarthy children of a dozen races, clad in the hard and decent blacks in which the poor pay debts and go to funerals. They would advance across the barren lands, the harsh sere earth scarred with its wastes of rust and rubbish, passing stolidly by below the blank board fences of a brick yard, crunching doggedly through the lanes of dirty rutted ice, passing before the gray besmutted fronts of wooden houses which in their stark, desolate, and unspeakable ugliness seemed to give a complete and final utterance to an architecture of weariness, sterility and horror, so overwhelming in its absolute desolation that it seemed as if the painful and indignant soul of man must sicken and die at length before it, stricken, stupefied, and strangled without a tongue to articulate the curse that once had blazed in him.

And at length they would pause before my uncle's little house —one of a street of little houses which he had built there on the barren flatlands of the suburb, and to which he had given magnificently his own name—Hawke Heights—although the only eminence in all that flat and weary waste was a stunted and almost imperceptible rise a half mile off. And here along this street which he had built, these little houses, warped, yet strong and hardy, seemed to burrow down solidly like moles for warmth into the ugly stony earth on which they were built and to cower and huddle doggedly below the immense and terrible desolation of the northern sky, with its rimy sun-hazed lights, its fierce and cruel rags and stripes of wintry red, its raw and savage harshness. And then, gripping their greasy little wads of money, as if the knowledge that all reward below these fierce and cruel skies must be wrenched painfully and minutely from a stony earth, they went in to pay my uncle. He would come up to meet them from some lower cellar-depth, swearing, muttering, and banging doors; and he would come toward them howling greetings, buttoned to his chin in the frayed and faded sweater, gnarled, stooped and frosty-looking, clutching his great hands together at his waist. Then they would wait, stiffly, clumsily, fingering their hats, while with countless squints and grimaces and pursings of the lip, he scrawled out painfully their receipt—their fractional release from debt and labor, one more hard-won step toward the freedom of possession.

At length, having pocketed their money and finished the trans-action, he would not permit them to depart at once, he would howl urgently at them an invitation to stay, he would offer long weedy-looking cigars to them, and they would sit uncomfortably, crouching on their buttock bones like stalled oxen, at the edges of chairs, shyly and dumbly staring at him, while he howled question, comment, and enthusiastic tribute at them.

"Why, my dear sir!" he would yell at Makropolos, the Greek. "You have a glorious past, a history of which any nation might well be proud!"

"Sure, sure!" said Makropolos, nodding vigorously, "Beeg Heestory!"

"The isles of Greece, the isles of Greece!" my uncle howled, "where burning Sappho loved and sung—" (phuh-phuh-phuh-phuh-phuh!)

"Sure, sure!" said Makropolos again, nodding good-naturedly but wrinkling his lowering finger's-breadth of brow in a somewhat puzzled fashion. "That's right! You got it!"

"Why, my dear sir!" Uncle Bascom cried. "It has been the ambi-tion of my lifetime to visit those hallowed scenes, to stand at sun-rise on the Acropolis, to explore the glory that was Greece, to see the magnificent ruins of the noblest of ancient civ-i-liz-a-tions!"

For the first time a dark flush, a flush of outraged patriotism, began to burn upon the swarthy yellow of Mr. Makropolos' cheek: his manner became heavy and animated, and in a moment he said with passionate conviction:

"No, no, no! No ruin! Wat you t'ink, eh! Athens fine town! We got a million pipples dere!" He struggled for a word, then cupped his hairy paws indefinitely: "*You* know? *Beeg!* O, ni-ez!" he added greasily, with a smile. "Everyt'ing good! We got everyt'ing good dere as you got here! *You* know?" he said with a confiding and painful effort. "Everyt'ing ni-ez! Not old! No, no, no!" he cried with a rising and indignant vigor. "New! de same as here? Ni-ez! You get good and cheap—everyt'ing! Beeg place, new house, dumbwaiter, elevator—wat chew like!—oh, ni-ez!" he said earnestly. "Wat chew t'ink it cost, eh? Feefateen dollar a month! Sure, sure!" he nodded with a swarthy earnestness. "I wouldn't keed you!"

"Finest people on earth!" my Uncle Bascom cried with an air of great conviction and satisfaction. "No question about it!"—and he would usher his visitor to the door howling farewell into the terrible desolation of those savage skies.

Meanwhile, my Aunt Louise, although she had not heard a word of what was said, although she had listened to nothing except the periods of Uncle Bascom's heavily accented and particular speech, kept up a constant snuffling laughter punctuated momently by faint whoops as she bent over her pots and pans in the kitchen, pausing from time to time as if to listen, and then snuffling to herself as she shook her head in pitying mirth which rose again up to the crisis of a faint crazy cackle as she scoured the pan; because, of course, during the forty-five years of her life with him thoroughly, imperceptibly, and completely, she had gone mad, and no longer knew or cared to know whether these words had just been spoken or were the echoes of lost voices long ago.

And again, she would pause to listen, with her small birdlike features uplifted gleefully in a kind of mad attentiveness as the door slammed and he stumped muttering back into the house, intent upon the secret designs of his own life, as remote and isolate from her as if they had each dwelt on separate planets, although the house they lived in was a small one.

The union of Bascom and Louise had been blessed by four children, all of whom had left their father's bed and board when they discovered how simple it is to secure an abundance of food, warmth, clothing, shelter and freedom in the generous world, whether by marriage, murder, or simply by hard labor. Of them, however, remarkable as their lives have been, it is not necessary to speak here, for he had forgotten them, they no longer touched his life: he had the power to forget, he belonged to a more ancient, a more lonely earth.

Such, briefly, had been the history of the old man who now stood before this dusty office. His life had come up from the wilderness, the buried past, the lost America. The potent mystery of old events and moments had passed around him, and the magic light of dark time fell across him.

Like all men in this land, he had been a wanderer, an exile on the immortal earth. Like all of us he had no home. Wherever great wheels carried him was home.

In the office which Bascom Hawke now entered there were two rooms, one in front and one behind, L shaped, and set in the elbow of the building, so that one might look out at the two projecting wings of the building, and see lighted layers of offices, in which the actors of a dozen enterprises "took" dictation, clattered at typewriters, walked back and forth importantly, talked into telephones or, what they did with amazing frequency, folded their palms behind their skulls, placed their feet restfully on the nearest solid object, and gazed for long periods dreamily and tenderly at the ceilings.

Through the broad and usually very dirty panes of the window in the front office one could catch a glimpse of Faneuil Hall and the magnificent and exultant activity of the markets.

These dingy offices, however, from which a corner of this rich movement might be seen and felt, were merely the unlovely counterpart of millions of others throughout the country and, in the telling phrase of Baedeker, offered "little that need detain the tourist": a few chairs, two scarred roll-top desks, a typist's table, a battered safe with a pile of thumb-worn ledgers on top of it, a set of green filing cases, an enormous green, greasy water-jar always half filled with a rusty liquid that no one drank, and two spittoons, put there because Brill was a man who chewed and spat widely in all directions—this, save for placards, each bearing several photographs of houses with their prices written below them—8 rooms, Dorchester, $6,500; 5 rooms and garage, Melrose, $4,500, etc.—completed the furniture of the room, and the second room, save for the disposition of objects, was similarly adorned.

To reach his own "office," as Bascom Hawke called the tiny cubicle in which he worked and received his clients, the old man had to traverse the inner room and open a door in a flimsy partition of varnished wood and glazed glass at the other end. This was his office: it was really a very narrow slice cut off from the larger room, and in it there was barely space for one large dirty window, an ancient dilapidated desk and swivel chair, a very small battered safe, buried under stacks of yellowed newspapers, and a small bookcase with glass doors and two small shelves on which there were a few worn volumes. An inspection of these books would have revealed four or five tattered and musty law books in their ponderous calf-skin bindings—one on *Contracts*, one on *Real Property*, one on *Titles*—a two-volume edition of the poems of Matthew Arnold, very dog-eared and thumbed over, a copy of *Sartor Resartus,* also much used, a volume of the essays of Ralph Waldo Emerson, the Iliad in Greek with minute yellowed notations in the margins, a volume of the *World Almanac* several years old, and a very worn volume of the Holy Bible, greatly used and annotated in Bascom's small, stiffly laborious, and meticulous hand.

If the old man was a little late, as sometimes happened, he might find his colleagues there before him. Miss Muriel Brill, the typist, and the eldest daughter of Mr. John T. Brill, would be seated in her typist's chair, her heavy legs crossed as she bent over to undo the metal latches of the thick galoshes she wore during the winter season. It is true there were also other seasons when Miss Brill did not wear galoshes, but so sharply and strongly do our memories connect people with certain gestures which, often for an inscrutable reason, seem characteristic of them, that any frequent visitor to these offices at this time of day would doubtless have remembered Miss Brill as always unfastening her galoshes. But the probable reason is that some people inevitably belong to seasons, and this girl's season was winter—not blizzards or howling winds, or the blind skirl and sweep of snow, but gray, grim, raw, thick, implacable winter: the endless successions of gray days and gray monotony. There was no spark of color in her, her body was somewhat thick and heavy, her face was white, dull, and thick-featured and instead of tapering downwards, it tapered up: it was small above, and thick and heavy below, and even in her speech, the words she uttered seemed to have been chosen by an automaton, and could only be remembered later by their desolate banality. One always remembered her as saying as one entered: ". . . Hello! . . . You're becoming quite a strangeh! . . . It's been some time since you was around, hasn't it? . . . I was thinkin' the otheh day it had been some time since you was around. . . . I'd begun to think you had forgotten us. . . . Well, how've you been? Lookin' the same as usual, I see. . . . Me? . . . Oh, can't complain. . . . Keepin' busy? *I'll* say! I manage to keep goin'. . . . Who you lookin' for? Father? He's in *there*. . . . Why, yeah! Go right on in."

This was Miss Brill, and at the moment that she bent to unfasten her galoshes, it is likely that Mr. Samuel Friedman would also be there in the act of rubbing his small dry hands briskly together, or of rubbing the back of one hand with the palm of the other in order to induce circulation. He was a small youngish man, a pale somewhat meager-looking little Jew with a sharp ferret face: he, too, was a person who goes to "fill in" those vast swarming masses of people along the pavements and in the subway—the mind cannot remember them or absorb the details of their individual appearance but they people the earth, they make up life. Mr. Friedman had none of the richness, color, and humor that some members of his race so abundantly possess, the succession of gray days, the grim weather seemed to have entered his soul as it enters the souls of many different races there—the Irish, the older New England stock, even the Jews—and it gives them a common touch that is prim, drab, careful, tight and sour. Mr. Friedman also wore galoshes, his clothes were neat, drab, a little worn and shiny, there was an odor of steamy thawing dampness and warm rubber about him as he rubbed his dry little hands saying: "Chee! How I hated to leave that good wahm bed this morning! When I got up I said, 'Holy Chee!' My wife says, 'Whatsa mattah?' I says, 'Holy Chee! You step out heah a moment where I am an' you'll see whatsa mattah.' 'Is it cold?' she says. 'Is it cold! I'll tell the cock-eyed wuhld!' I says. Chee! You could have cut the frost with an ax: the wateh in the pitchehs was frozen hahd; an' she has the nuhve to ask me if it's cold! 'Is it cold!' I says. 'Do you know any more funny stories?' I says. O how I do love my bed! Chee! I kept thinkin' of that guy in Braintree I got to go see today an' the more I thought about him, the less I liked him! I thought my feet would tu'n into two blocks of ice before I got the funniss stahted! 'Chee! I hope the ole bus is still workin',' I says. 'If I've got to go thaw that damned thing out,' I says, 'I'm ready to quit.' Chee! Well, suh, I neveh had a bit of trouble: she stahted right up an' the way that ole moteh was workin' is nobody's business."

During the course of this monologue Miss Brill would give ear and assent from time to time by the simple interjection: "Uh!" It was a sound she uttered frequently, it had somewhat the same meaning as "Yes," but it was more non-committal than "Yes." It seemed to render assent to the speaker, to let him know that he was being heard and understood, but it did not commit the auditor to any opinion, or to any real agreement.

The third member of this office staff, who was likely to be present at this time, was a gentleman named Stanley P. Ward. Mr. Stanley P. Ward was a neat middling figure of a man, aged fifty or thereabouts; he was plump and had a pink tender skin, a trim Vandyke, and a nice comfortable little pot of a belly which slipped snugly into the well-pressed and well-brushed garments that always fitted him so tidily. He was a bit of a fop, and it was at once evident that he was quietly but enormously pleased with himself. He carried himself very sprucely, he took short rapid steps and his neat little paunch gave his figure a movement not unlike that of a pouter pigeon. He was usually in quiet but excellent spirits, he laughed frequently and a smile—rather a subtly amused look—was generally playing about the edges of his mouth. That smile and his laugh made some people vaguely uncomfortable: there was a kind of deliberate falseness in them, as if what he really thought and felt was not to be shared with other men. He seemed, in fact, to have discovered some vital and secret power, some superior knowledge and wisdom, from which the rest of mankind was excluded, a sense that he was "chosen" above other men, and this impression of Mr. Stanley Ward would have been correct, for he was a Christian Scientist, he was a pillar of the church, and a very big church at that—for Mr. Ward, dressed in fashionable striped trousers, rubber soles, and a cutaway coat might be found somewhere under the mighty dome of the Mother Church on Huntington Avenue every Sunday suavely, noiselessly, and expertly ushering the faithful to their pews.

This completes the personnel of the first office of the John T. Brill Realty Company, and if my uncle, Bascom Hawke, arrived late, if these three people were already present, if Mr. Bascom Hawke had not been defrauded of any part of his worldly goods by some contriving rascal, of whom the world has many, if his life had not been imperilled by some speed maniac, if the damnable New England weather was not too damnable, if, in short, Bascom Hawke was in fairly good spirits he would on entering immediately howl in a high, rapid, remote and perfectly monotonous tone: "Hello, Hello, Hello! Good-morning, Good-morning, Good-morning!"—after which he would close his eyes, grimace

horribly, press his rubbery lip against his big horse teeth, and
snuffle with laughter through his nose, as if pleased by a tremendous stroke of wit. At this demonstration the other members of
the group would glance at one another with those knowing subtly
supercilious nods and winks, that look of common self-congratula-
tion and humor with which the more "normal" members of
society greet the conduct of an eccentric, and Mr. Samuel Friedman would say: "What's the matteh with you, Pop? You look
happy. Someone musta give you a shot in the ahm."

At which, a coarse powerful voice, deliberate and rich with its
intimation of immense and earthly vulgarity, might roar out of
the depth of the inner office: "No, I'll tell you what it is." Here
the great figure of Mr. John T. Brill, the head of the business,
would darken the doorway. "Don't you know what's wrong with
the Reverend? It's that widder he's been takin' around." Here,
the phlegmy burble that prefaced all of Mr. Brill's obscenities
would appear in his voice, the shadow of a lewd smile would play
around the corner of his mouth: "It's the widder. She's let him—"

At this delicate stroke of humor, the burble would burst open
in Mr. Brill's great red throat, and he would roar with that high,
choking, phlegmy laughter that is frequent among big red-faced
men. Mr. Friedman would laugh drily ("Heh, heh, heh, heh,
heh!"), Mr. Stanley Ward would laugh more heartily, but com-
placently, and Miss Brill would snicker in a coy and subdued
manner as became a modest young girl. As for Bascom Hawke,
if he was really in a good humor, he might snuffle with nosey
laughter, bend double at his meager waist, clutching his big hands
together, and stamp at the floor violently several times with one
stringy leg; he might even go so far as to take a random ecstatic
kick at objects, still stamping and snuffling with laughter, and
prod Miss Brill stiffly with two enormous bony fingers, as if he
did not wish the full point and flavor of the jest to be lost on her.

My uncle, Bascom Hawke, however, was a very complicated
person with many moods, and if Mr. Brill's fooling did not catch
him in a receptive one, he might contort his face in a pucker of
refined disgust, and mutter his disapproval, as he shook his

head rapidly from side to side. Or he might rise to great heights of moral denunciation, beginning at first in a grave low voice that showed the seriousness of the words he had to utter: "The lady to whom you refer," he would begin, "the very charming and cultivated lady whose name, sir," here his voice would rise on its howling note and he would wag his great bony forefinger, "whose name, sir, you have so foully traduced and blackened—"

"No, I wasn't, Reverend. I was only tryin' to whiten it," said Mr. Brill, beginning to burble with laughter.

"—whose name, sir, you have so foully traduced and blackened with your smutty suggestions," Bascom continued implacably, "—that lady is known to me, as you very well know, sir," he howled, wagging his great finger again, "solely and simply in a professional capacity."

"Why, hell, Reverend," said Mr. Brill innocently, "I never knew she was a professional. I thought she was an amatoor."

At this conclusive stroke, Mr. Brill would make the whole place tremble with his laughter, Mr. Friedman would laugh almost noiselessly, holding himself weakly at the stomach and bending across a desk, Mr. Ward would have short bursts and fits of laughter, as he gazed out the window, shaking his head deprecatingly from time to time, as if his more serious nature disapproved, and Miss Brill would snicker, and turn to her machine, remarking: "This conversation is getting too rough for me!"

And my uncle, if this jesting touched his complex soul at one of those moments when such profanity shocked him, would walk away, confiding into vacancy, it seemed, with his powerful and mobile features contorted in the most eloquent expression of disgust and loathing ever seen on any face, the while he muttered, in a resonant whisper that shuddered with passionate revulsion: "Oh *bad!* Oh *bad!* O *bad, bad, bad!*"—shaking his head slightly from side to side with each word.

Yet there were other times, when Brill's swinging vulgarity, the vast coarse sweep of his profanity not only found Uncle Bascom in a completely receptive mood, but they evoked from him gleeful responses, counter essays in swearing which he made slyly, craftily, snickering with pleasure and squinting around at his listeners at the sound of the words, and getting such stimulus from them as might a renegade clergyman, exulting in a feeling of depravity and abandonment for the first time.

To the other people in this office—that is, to Friedman, Ward and Muriel, the stenographer—my uncle was always an enigma; at first they had observed his pecularities of speech and dress, his eccentricity of manner, and the sudden, violent, and complicated fluctuation of his temperament, with astonishment and wonder, then with laughter and ridicule, and now, with dull, uncomprehending acceptance. Nothing he did or said surprised them any more, they had no understanding and little curiosity, they accepted him as a fact in the gray schedule of their lives. Their relation to him was habitually touched by a kind of patronizing banter—"kidding the old boy along" they would have called it—by the communication of smug superior winks and the conspiracy of feeble jests, and in this there was something base and ignoble, for my uncle was a better man than any of them.

He did not notice any of this, it is not likely he would have cared if he had, for, like most eccentrics, his thoughts were usually buried in a world of his own creating to whose every fact and feeling and motion he was the central actor. Again, as much as any of his extraordinary family, he had carried with him throughout his life the sense that he was "fated"—a sense that was strong in all of them—that his life was pivotal to all the actions of providence, that, in short, the time might be out of joint, but not himself. Nothing but death could shake his powerful egotism, and his occasional storms of fury, his railing at the world, his tirades of invective at some motorist, pedestrian, or laborer occurred only when he discovered that these people were moving in a world at cross-purposes to his own and that some action of theirs had disturbed or shaken the logic of his universe.

It was curious that, of all the people in the office, the person who had the deepest understanding and respect for my uncle was John T. Brill. Mr. Brill was a huge creature of elemental desires and passions: a river of profanity rushed from his mouth with the relentless sweep and surge of the Mississippi, he could no more have spoken without swearing than a whale could swim in a frog-pond—he swore at everything, at everyone and with every breath, casually and unconsciously, and yet when he addressed my uncle Bascom his oath was always impersonal, and tinged subtly by a feeling of respect.

Thus, he would speak to Uncle Bascom somewhat in this fashion: "Goddamn it, Hawke, did you ever look up the title for that stuff in Malden? That feller's been callin' up every day to find out about it."

"Which fellow?" my uncle Bascom asked precisely. "The man from Cambridge?"

"No," said Mr. Brill, "not him, the other— — — —, the Dor-chester feller. How the hell am I goin' to tell him anything if there's no goddamn title for the stuff?"

Profane and typical as this speech was, it was always shaded nicely with impersonality toward my uncle Bascom—conscious to the full of the distinction between "damn *it*" and "damn *you*." Toward his other colleagues, however, Mr. Brill was neither nice nor delicate.

Brill was an enormous man physically: he was six feet two or three inches tall, and his weight was close to three hundred pounds. He was totally bald, his skull was a gleaming satiny pink; above his great red moon of face, with its ponderous and pendulous jowls, it looked almost egg-shaped. And in the heavy, deliberate, and powerful timbre of his voice there was always lurking this burble of exultant, gargantuan obscenity: it was so obviously part of the structure of his life, so obviously his only and natural means of expression, that it was impossible to con-demn him. His epithet was limited and repetitive—but so, too, was Homer's, and, like Homer, he saw no reason for changing what had already been used and found good.

He was a lewd and innocent man. Like my uncle, by compari-son with these other people, he seemed to belong to some earlier, richer and grander period of the earth, and perhaps this was why there was more actual kinship and understanding between them than between any of the other members of the office. These other people—Friedman, Brill's daughter, Muriel, and Ward—belonged to the myriads of the earth, to those numberless swarms that with ceaseless pullulation fill the streets of life with their gray immemorable tides. But Brill and my Uncle Bascom were men in a thousand, a million: if one had seen them in a crowd he would have looked after them, if one had talked with them, he could never have forgotten them.

It is rare in modern life that one sees a man who can express himself with such complete and abundant certainty as Brill did —completely, and without doubt or confusion. It is true that his life expressed itself chiefly by two gestures—by profanity and by his great roar of full-throated, earth-shaking laughter, an explosive comment on existence which usually concluded and summarized his other means of expression.

Although the other people in the office laughed heartily at this soaring rhetoric of obscenity, it sometimes proved too much for Uncle Bascom. When this happened he would either leave the office immediately, or stump furiously into his own little cupboard that seemed silted over with the dust of twenty years, slamming the door behind him so violently that the thin partition rattled, and then stand for a moment pursing his lips, and convolving his features with incredible speed, and shaking his gaunt head slightly from side to side, until at length he whispered in a tone of passionate disgust and revulsion: "Oh, *bad! Bad! Bad!* By every *gesture*, by every *act*, he betrays the *boor*, the *vulgarian!* Can you imagine"—here his voice sank even lower in its scale of passionate whispering repugnance—"can you for one *moment* imagine a man of *breeding* and the social graces talking in such a way publicly?—And before his own daughter. Oh, *bad! Bad! Bad! Bad!*"

And in the silence, while my uncle stood shaking his head in its movement of downcast and convulsive distaste, we could hear, suddenly, Brill's pungent answer to all the world—and his great bellow of throaty laughter. Later on, if my uncle had to consult him on any business, he would open his door abruptly, walk out into Brill's office clutching his hands together at the waist, and with disgust still carved upon his face, say: "Well, sir, . . . If you have concluded your morning devotions," here his voice sank to a bitter snarl, "we might get down to the transaction of some of the day's business."

"Why, Reverend!" Brill roared. "You ain't heard nothin' yet!"

And the great choking bellow of laughter would burst from him again, rattling the windows with its power as he hurled his great weight backward, with complete abandon, in his creaking swivel-chair.

It was obvious that he liked to tease my uncle, and never lost an opportunity of doing so: for example, if anyone gave Uncle Bascom a cigar, Brill would exclaim with an air of innocent surprise: "Why, *Reverend,* you're not going to smoke that, are you?"

"Why, certainly," my uncle Bascom said tartly. "That is the purpose for which it was intended, isn't it?"

"Why, yes," said Brill, "but you know how they make 'em, don't you? I didn't think you'd touch it after some dirty old Spaniard has wiped his old hands all over it—yes! an' *spit* upon it, too, because that's what they do!"

"Ah!" my uncle snarled contemptuously. "You don't know what you're talking about! There is nothing cleaner than good tobacco! Finest and healthiest plant on earth! No question about it!"

"Well," said Brill, "I've learned something. We live and learn, Reverend. You've taught me somethin' worth knowing: when it's free it's clean; when you have to pay for it it stinks like hell!" He pondered heavily for a moment, and the burble began to play about in his great throat: "And, by God!" he concluded, "tobacco's not the only thing that applies to, either. Not by a damned sight!"

Again, one morning, my uncle cleared his throat portentously, coughed, and suddenly said to me: "Now, David, my boy, you are going to have lunch with me today. There's no question about it whatever!" This was astonishing news, for he had never before invited me to eat with him when I came to his office, although I had been to his house for dinner many times. "Yes, sir!" he said, with an air of decision and satisfaction. "I have thought it all over. There is a splendid establishment in the basement of this building—small, of course, but everything clean and of the highest order! It is conducted by an Irish gentleman whom I have known for many years. Finest people on earth: no question about it!'

It was an astonishing and momentous occasion; I knew how infrequently he went to a restaurant. Having made his decision, Uncle Bascom immediately stepped into the outer office, and began to discuss and publish his intentions with the greatest satisfaction.

"Yes, sir!" he said in a precise tone, smacking his lips in a ruminant fashion, and addressing himself to everyone rather than to a particular person. "We shall go in and take our seats in the regular way, and I shall then give appropriate instruction, to one of the attendants—" again he smacked his lips as he pronounced this word with such an indescribable air of relish, that immediately my mouth began to water, and the delicious pangs of appetite and hunger began to gnaw my vitals—"I shall say: 'This is my nephew, a young man now enrolled at Harvard Un-i-ver-sit-tee!' "
—here Bascom smacked his lips together again with that same maddening air of relish—" 'Yes, sir' (I shall say!)—'You are to fulfil his order without *stint*, without *delay*, and without *question*, and to the *utmost* of your ability' "—he howled, wagging his great bony forefinger through the air—"As for myself," he declared abruptly, "I shall take nothing. Good Lord, no!" he said with a scornful laugh. "I wouldn't touch a thing they had to offer. You couldn't pay me to: I shouldn't sleep for a month if I did. But you, my boy!" he howled, turning suddenly upon me, "—are to have everything your heart desires! Everything, everything, everything!" He made an inclusive gesture with his long arms; then closed his eyes, stamped at the floor, and began to snuffle with laughter.

Mr. Brill had listened to all this with his great-jowled face slack-jawed and agape with astonishment. Now, he said, heavily: "He's goin' to have everything, is he? Where are you goin' to take him to git it?"

"Why, sir!" my uncle said in an annoyed tone, "I have told you all along—we are going to the modest but excellent establishment in the basement of this very building."

"Why, Reverend," Brill said in a protesting tone. "You ain't goin' to take your nephew *there*, are you? I thought you said you was goin' to git somethin' to *eat*."

"I had supposed," my uncle said with bitter sarcasm, "that one went there for that purpose. I had not supposed that one went there to get shaved."

"Well," said Brill, "if you go there you'll git shaved, all right. You'll not only git *shaved*, you'll git *skinned* alive. But you won't git anything to eat." And he hurled himself back again, roaring with laughter.

"Pay no attention to him!" my uncle said to me in a tone of bitter repugnance. "I have long known that his low and vulgar mind attempts to make a joke of everything, even the most sacred matters. I assure you, my boy, the place is excellent in every way: —do you suppose," he said now addressing Brill and all the others, with a howl of fury—"do you suppose, if it were not, that I should for a single moment *dream* of taking him there? Do you suppose that I would for an instant *contemplate* taking my own nephew, my sister's son, to any place in which I did not repose the fullest confidence? Not on your life!" he howled. "Not on your life!"

And we departed, followed by Brill's great bellow, and a farewell invitation which he shouted after me, "Don't worry, son! When you git through with that cockroach stew, come back an' I'll take you out to lunch with *me*!"

Although Brill delighted in teasing and baiting my uncle in this fashion, there was, at the bottom of his heart, a feeling of deep humility, of genuine respect and admiration for him: he respected Uncle Bascom's intelligence, he was secretly and profoundly impressed by the fact that my uncle had been a minister of the gospel and had preached in many churches.

Moreover, in the respect and awe with which Brill greeted these evidences of my uncle's superior education, in the eagerness he showed when he boasted to visitors, as he often did, of my uncle's learning, there was a quality of pride that was profoundly touching and paternal: it was is if my uncle had been his son, and as if he wanted at every opportunity to display his talents to the world. And this, in fact, was exactly what he did want to do. Much to my uncle's annoyance, Brill was constantly speaking of his erudition to strangers who had come into the office for the first time, and constantly urging my uncle to perform for them, to "say some of them big words, Reverend." And even when my uncle answered him, as he frequently did, in terms of scorn, anger, and contempt, Brill was completely satisfied, if Uncle Bascom would only use a few of the "big words" in doing it. Thus, one day, when one of his boyhood friends, a New Hampshire man whom he had not seen in thirty-five years, had come in to renew their acquaintance Brill, in describing the accomplishments of my uncle, said with an air of solemn affirmation: "Why, hell yes, Jim! It'd take a college perfesser to know what the Reverend is talkin' about half the time! No ordinary — — — — is able to understand him! So help me God, it's true!" he swore solemnly, as Jim looked incredulous. "The Reverend knows words the average man ain't never heard. He knows words that ain't even in the dictionary. Yes, sir!—an' uses 'em, too—all the time!" he concluded triumphantly.

"Why, my dear sir!" my uncle answered in a tone of exacerbated contempt. "What on earth are you talking about? Such a man as you describe would be a monstrosity, a heinous perversion of natural law! A man so wise that no one could understand him:—so literate that he could not communicate with his fellow creatures:—so erudite that he led the inarticulate and incoherent life of a beast or a savage!"—here Uncle Bascom squinted his eyes tightly shut, and laughed sneeringly down his nose: "Phuh! phuh! phuh! phuh! phuh!—Why you con-sum-mate fool!" he sneered, "I have long known that your ignorance was bottomless —but I had never hoped to see it equalled—Nay! Surpassed!" he howled, "by your asininity."

"There you are!" said Brill exultantly to his visitor, "What did I tell you? There's one of them words, Jim: 'asserninity,' why, damn it, the Reverend's the only one who knows what that word means—you won't even find it in the dictionary!"

"Not find it in the dictionary!" my uncle yelled. "Almighty God, come down and give this ass a tongue as Thou didst once before in Balaam's time!"

Again, Brill was seated at his desk one day engaged with a client in those intimate, cautious, and confidential preliminaries that mark the consummation of a "deal" in real estate. On this occasion the prospective buyer was an Italian: the man sat awkwardly and nervously in a chair beside Brill's desk while the great man bent his huge weight ponderously and persuasively toward him. From time to time the Italian's voice, sullen, cautious, disparaging, interrupted Brill's ponderous and coaxing drone. The Italian sat stiffly, his thick, clumsy body awkwardly clad in his "good" clothes of heavy black, his thick, hairy, blunt-nailed hands cupped nervously upon his knees, his black eyes glittering with suspicion under his knitted inch of brow. At length, he shifted nervously, rubbed his paws tentatively across his knees and then, with a smile mixed of ingratiation and mistrust, said: "How mucha you want, eh?"

"How mucha we want?" Brill repeated vulgarly as the burble began to play about within his throat. "Why, how mucha you got? . . . You know we'll take every damn thing you got! It's not how mucha we want, it's how mucha you got!" And he hurled himself backward, bellowing with laughter. "By God, Reverend," he yelled as Uncle Bascom entered, "ain't that right? It's not how mucha we want, it's how mucha you got! 'od damn! We ought to take that as our motter. I've got a good mind to git it printed on our letterheads. What do you think, Reverend?"

"Hey?" howled Uncle Bascom absently, as he prepared to enter his own office.

"I say we ought to use it for our motter."

"Your *what?*" said Uncle Bascom scornfully, pausing as if he did not understand.

"Our motter," Brill said.

"Not your *motter,*" my uncle howled derisively. "The word is *not* motter," he said contemptuously. "Nobody of any refinement would say *motter. Motter* is *not* correct!" he howled finally. "Only an ig-no-*ram*-us would say *motter.* No!" he yelled with final con-clusiveness. "That is *not* the way to pronounce it! That is ab-so-lute-ly and em-phat-ic-ally *not* the way to pronounce it!"

"All right, then, Reverend," said Brill, submissively. "You're the docter. What is the word?"

"The word is *motto,*" Uncle Bascom snarled. "Of course! Any fool knows that!"

"Why, hell," Mr. Brill protested in a hurt tone. "That's what I said, ain't it?"

"No-o!" Uncle Bascom howled derisively. "No-o! By no means, by no means, by no means! You said *motter.* The word is *not* motter. The word is motto: m-o-t-t-o! M-O-T-T-O does *not* spell motter," he remarked with vicious decision.

"What does it spell?" said Mr. Brill.

"It spells *motto,*" Uncle Bascom howled. "It *has* always spelled motto! It *will* always spell motto! As it was in the beginning, is now, and ever shall be: A-a-men!" he howled huskily in his most evangelical fashion. Then, immensely pleased at his wit, he closed his eyes, stamped at the floor and snarled and snuffled down his nose with laughter.

"Well, anyway," said Brill, "no matter how you spell it, it's not how mucha we want, it's how mucha you got! That's the way we feel about it!"

And this, in fact, without concealment, without pretense, without evasion, was just how Brill did feel about it. He wanted everything that was his and, in addition, he wanted as much as he could get. And this rapacity, this brutal and unadorned gluttony, so far from making men wary of him, attracted them to him, inspired them with unshakable confidence in his integrity, his business honesty. Perhaps the reason for this was that concealment did not abide in the man: he published his intentions to the world with an oath and a roar of laughter—and the world, having seen and judged, went away with the confidence of this Italian—that Brill was "one fine-a man!" Even my uncle, who had so often turned upon his colleague the weapons of scorn, contempt, and mockery, had a curious respect for him, an acrid sunken affection: often, when we were alone, he would recall something Brill had said and his powerful and fluent features would suddenly be contorted in that familiar grimace, as he laughed his curious laugh which was forced out, with a deliberate and painful effort, through his powerful nose and his lips, barred with a few large teeth, "Phuh! phuh! phuh! phuh! phuh! . . . Of course!" he said, with a nasal rumination, as he stared over the apex of his great bony hands, clasped in meditation— "of course, he is just a poor ignorant fellow! I don't suppose— no, sir, I really do not suppose that Brill ever went to school over six months in his life!—say!" my uncle Bascom paused suddenly, turned to me abruptly with his strange fixed grin, and fastened his sharp old eyes keenly on me: in this sudden and abrupt change, this transference of his vision from his own secret and personal world, in which his thought and feeling were sunken, and which seemed to be so far away from the actual world about him, there was something impressive and disconcerting. His eyes were gray, sharp, and old, and one eyelid had a heavy droop or ptosis which, although it did not obscure his vision, gave his expression at times a sinister glint, a malevolent humor. "—Say!" here his voice sank to a deliberate and confiding whisper, "(Phuh! phuh! phuh! phuh! phuh!) Say—a man who would—he told me—O vile! vile! vile! my boy!" my uncle whispered, shutting his eyes in a kind of shuddering ecstacy as if at the memory of things too gloriously obscene to be repeated. "Can you *imagine*, can you even *dream* of such a state of affairs if he had possessed an atom, a *scintilla* of delicacy and good breeding! Yes, sir!" he said with decision. "I suppose there's no doubt about it! His beginnings were very lowly, very poor and humble, indeed! . . . Not that this is in any sense to his discredit!" Uncle Bascom said hastily, as if it had occurred to him that his words might bear some taint of snobbishness. "Oh, by no means, by no means, by no means!" he sang out, with a sweeping upward gesture of his long arm, as if he were clearing the air of wisps of smoke. "Some of our finest men—some of the nation's *leaders,* have come from just such surroundings as those. Beyond a doubt! Beyond a doubt! There's no question about it whatever! Say!"—here he turned suddenly upon me again with the ptotic and sinister intelligence of his eye. "Was *Lincoln* an aristocrat? Was he the issue of wealthy parents? Was he brought up with a silver spoon in his mouth? Was our *own* former governor, the Vice-President of the United States to-day, reared in the lap of luxury? Not on your life!" howled Uncle Bascom. "He came from frugal and thrifty Vermont farming stock, he has never deviated a *jot* from his early training, he remains to-day what he has always been—one of the simplest of men! Finest people on earth, no question about it whatever!"

Again he meditated gravely with lost stare across the apex of his great joined hands, and I noticed again, as I had noticed so often, the great dignity of his head in thought—a head that was highbrowed, lean and lonely, a head that not only in its cast of thought but even in its physical contour, and in its profound and lonely earnestness, bore an astonishing resemblance to that of Emerson—it was, at times like these, as grand a head as I had ever seen, and on it was legible the history of man's loneliness, his dignity, his grandeur and despair.

"Yes, sir!" he said, in a moment. "He is, of course, a vulgar fellow and some of the things he says at times are O! vile! vile! vile!" my uncle cried, closing his eyes and laughing. "O vile! *most* vile! . . . but (phuh-phuh-phuh!) you can't help laughing at the fellow at times because he is so . . . O, I could tell you things, my boy! . . . O *Vile! vile!*" he cried, shaking his head downwards. "What coarseness! . . . What in-*vect*-ive!" he whispered, in a kind of ecstasy.

And this invective, I know, he cherished in his secret heart so dearly that on at least one notable occasion he had invoked it, and lamented that he did not have it by him as an aid. What Uncle Bascom had said on that occasion, lifting his arms to heaven, and crying out a confession of his own inadequacy in a tone of passionate supplication, was: "O, that J. T. were here at this moment!—or that I had his tongue!—that he might aid me with his *scathing* invective!"

The occasion was this: a few years before my uncle had taken his wife to Florida for the winter, and had rented there a cottage. The place he chose was small and modest, it was several miles away from one of the larger and more fashionable towns, it was not on the coast, but set a few miles inland, and it had the advantages of a river, or peninsular inlet which rose and fell with the recurrence of the tides. This modest winter colony was so small that it could afford only one small church and one minister, himself a member of the colony. During the winter this man was taken ill: he was unable to continue his services at the church, and his little following, in looking around for a substitute, learned that Uncle Bascom had formerly been a minister. They came to him, therefore, and asked if he would serve.

"Oh, *Lord,* no!" Bascom howled derisively. "Good *heavens,* no! I shouldn't *dream* of such a thing! I shouldn't for a moment *contemplate* such a thing! I am a *total*—for twenty years I have been a *complete*—agnostic."

The flock looked at him with a dazed expression. "Wal," said one of the leading parishioners, a lean Down-Easter, "most of us here are Presbyterians, but I don't know that that would make any difference. The way I see it, we're all met here to worship the Lord, and we need a preacher no matter what his denomination is. When all's said and done," he concluded comfortably, "I don't guess there's much difference between any of us in the long run."

"Why, my dear sir!" my uncle said, with a slight sneer. "If you think there is no difference between an agnostic and a Presbyterian you had better have your head examined by a doctor without further delay. No-o!" he howled faintly. "I cannot profess belief in what I do not know! I cannot simulate conviction when I have none! I cannot preach a faith I have not got! There, sir, you have my whole position in a nut-shell!"

Here, people in the group began to stir restlessly, to mutter uneasily, and to draw away: suddenly Uncle Bascom caught the muttered word "atheist."

"No-o!" he shouted, his ptotic eye beginning to glitter with the light of combat. "By no means! By no means! You only show your ignorance when you say a thing like that. They are not the same! They are ab-so-lute-ly and em-phat-i-cal-ly not the same! An atheist is *not* an agnostic and an agnostic is *not* an atheist! Why!" he yelled, "the mere sound of the words would teach you that if you had an atom of intelligence. An atheist is a man who does not believe in God!—it is composed of the Greek prefix 'a' —meaning *not,* and the noun 'the-os,' meaning God: an atheist therefore says there is no God! Now," he continued, licking his lips for joy, "we come to the word *agnostic.* Is the sound the same? No-o! Is the meaning the same? By no means! Are the parts the same? Not on your life! The word is *agnostic*: a-g-n-o-s-t-i-c! From what language is it derived? From Greek, of course—as any fool should know! From what words? From the vowel of negation 'a' again, and from 'gnostikos'—the word for *knowing.* An agnostic therefore is what?" he demanded, glaring around at their mute faces. "Why!" he said impatiently, as no one answered, "Any schoolboy knows that much! A not-knowing man! A man who does not know! Not a man who denies! Oh, by no means!"—his great hand rose impatiently—"An *atheist* is a man who denies! An *agnostic* is simply a man who does not know!"

"I can't see there's any difference," some one muttered. "They *both* sound like a couple of godless heathen to me!"

"No difference!" Bascom howled. "My dear sir, hold your tongue before you bring down lasting shame upon your progeny! ... They are as different as night from day, as black from white,

[41]

as the sneering irreverence of the cynic from the calm, temperate, and judicial spirit of the philosopher! Why!" he declared impressively, "Some of the finest spirits of our times have been agnostics. Yes, sir! Some of the grandest people that ever lived! . . . The *great* Matthew Arnold was an agnostic!" he yelled. "Does that sound as if there was no difference? Not on your life!"

He paused, and as there was no response from his involuntary congregation, he began, after a moment, to fumble at the inside pocket of his coat with his big fingers.

"I have here a poem," he said, taking it out of his pocket, "of my own composition"—here he coughed modestly—"although it may show traces, I admit, of the influence of the great man whose name I have just mentioned, and whom I am proud to call my master: Matthew Arnold. It will, I believe, illustrate my position better than anything I could say to you." He held up his great forefinger to command attention, and then began to read.

"The title of the poem," Uncle Bascom said, "is—'My Creed'." After a short silence, he began:

> *"Is there a land beyond the stars*
> *Where we may find eternal day,*
> *Life after death, peace after wars?*
> *Is there? I cannot say.*

> *"Shall we find there a happier life,*
> *All joy that here we never know,*
> *Love in all things, an end of strife?*
> *Perhaps: it may be so."*

There were seventeen other stanzas which Uncle Bascom read to them deliberately and with telling enunciation, after which he folded the paper and looked about him with a sneer: "I think," he said, "that I have made my meaning clear. Now you know what an agnostic is."

They did. His meaning was so clear that they had no language to oppose to it: they turned, they went away like men who had been stunned. Among them, however, was one who did not yield so easily, a daughter of the Lord who had often won by persuasion and the soft violence of her beaming eye what others failed to win by harsher means. This lady was a widow, a Southern woman in her middle years: her charms were ripe, she had a gentle, loving touch, a soft and fruity unction in her voice. This lady had been able to resist few ministers and few ministers had been able to resist this lady. Now, as the others retreated, the lady advanced: she came forward with a practiced sidling movement of her hips and Uncle Bascom, who was standing triumphantly in the midst of a receding host, suddenly found himself confronted by her gentle and importunate face.

"Oh, Mr. Hawke!" she crooned sweetly, with a kind of abdominal rapture in her voice (thus, the way she pronounced his name was—Mis-tah Haw-*uk!*). "I *jus'* know that you must've been a *won*-da-ful preach-ah! I can tell by yo' face that you-ah such a *g-o-o-d* man—" Again she grunted sweetly with this ecstatic abdominal expiration.

"Why, madame! Why—" Uncle Bascom began, decidedly in a confused tone, but taking her abundance in with a sharp appraising eye.

"I was *jus'* thrilled to death all the time that you was tawkin', Mistah Haw-*uk*," the widow said. "I was a-sittin' theah an' sittin' theah, just a-drinkin' it all in, just a-*baskin'* in the rays of yo' wisdom, Mistah Haw-uk! All the time you was readin' that wonderful poem, I was just a-sayin' to myse'f: What a wonda-ful thing it is that a man like this has been chosen fo' the Suvvice of the Lawd, what a wondaful thing it is to know that this man is one o' Gawd's Suvvants!"

"Why, madame!" Bascom cried, his gaunt face flushed with pleasure. "Why, madame, I assure you I am deeply grateful . . . deeply honored to think that a lady of your obvious . . . your *undoubted* intelligence . . . should feel that way about me! But, madame!——"

"Oh, Mistah Haw-*uk!*" the widow groaned. "I jus' *love* to heah you *tawk!* I jus' *love* the way you handle langwidge! You heah

[43]

so much po' shoddy, good-fo'-nothin' tawk nowadays—all full o' slang an' bad grammah an' I don't know whatall. I don't know what fokes ah comin' to—it's a real pleasuah—yes, suh! a real sho' nuff *treat*—to heah a man who can express himse'f the way you can. The minute I saw you I said to myse'f: I jus' *know* that that man can *tawk!* I *know* it! I *know* it! I *know* it!" The widow cried, shaking her head from side to side vigorously. "Theah's a man, I said," the widow continued, "theah's a man who kin do anything he likes with me—yes, suh! just anything!—I said that just as soon as you opened yo' mouf to speak!"

"Oh, madame, madame!" cried Bascom fervently, bowing with real dignity. "I thank you. I thank you sincerely and gratefully from the bottom of my heart!"

"Yes, suh! I could just enjoy myse'f—(I said)—just a-lookin' at his haid."

"At my what?" yelled Bascom, jumping as if he had received an electric shock.

"At yo' *haid*," the widow answered.

"Oh!" howled Bascom. "At my *head!* My *head!*"—and he began to laugh foolishly.

"Yes, suh, Mistah Haw-uk," the widow continued. "I jus' thought you had the *grandest* haid I evah saw. The moment you began to read that poem I said, 'Only a man with a haid like that could a-written that poem. O thank Gawd! (I said) that he has dedicated his wondaful *haid* to the Lawd's Wuk!"

"Why, madame," Bascom cried again. "You have paid me the greatest honor! I cannot sufficiently thank you! But I am afraid— in *justice*, in *fairness*, I must admit," he said with some difficulty, "that you may not have entirely understood—that you are not quite clear—that, perhaps, I did not make the meaning, the general purpose of that poem—O! it's my own fault, I know! Beyond a doubt! Beyond a doubt!—but perhaps I did not make its meaning wholly plain!"

"Yes, you did!" the widow protested. "Every word of it was jus' as plain as day to me! I kep' sayin' to myse'f: That's *jus'* the way I've always felt, but I nevah could express myse'f befo': I nevah *met* anyone befo' that I could tawk to about it. An' now (I said), this wondaful man comes along an' puts the whole thing straight in my haid! O! (I said) if I could just sit at his feet, an' *listen* all day long, if I could jus' sit an' drink in all he had to say, if I could just *listen* to him tawk—I'd nevah ask fo' anything bettah!"

"Why, madame!" Bascom cried, deeply, genuinely moved. "I assure you I'd like nothing better! Yes, indeed! I assure you I'd be delighted! O, at any time! At any time!" he howled. "It is rare that one meets today—O, *most* rare!—a woman of your intelligence and perspicacity! We *must* have another talk!" he said. "Oh, by all means, by all means!"

"Uh-huh!" the widow grunted sweetly.

Bascom looked around craftily to see if my Aunt Louise was anywhere within sight or hearing. "Perhaps," he said, smacking his lips together, "we might meet and have a quiet walk together. Nothing is more conducive to contemplation than the tranquil peace of nature. There's no question about it."

"Uh-huh," the widow said.

"Tomorrow," Bascom whispered.

"Uh-huh," the widow crooned viscerally.

Thus, there began between Uncle Bascom and the widow a series of promenades, in which he expounded his views liberally, and in which she was able, by the harmonious adjustment of her nature, to find herself in complete agreement. Again and again, my Aunt Louise watched them depart, she peered after them through her bright mad eyes, snuffling with angry laughter, and muttering, as she had muttered many time before: "The old *fool!* . . . The *misable* old *skinflint!* . . . Too poor to buy his own wife a *dwess* . . . while he spends *faw*-chuns, *faw*-chuns on them! . . . It's in the blood . . . the blood!" she whispered hoarsely. "They're *mad* . . . *mad!* His family's *ovahsexed*, all of them!"

One evening, as Bascom and the widow were returning from one of these walks, they found themselves toward sunset a mile or so from town. It was a desolate spot: their road wound on through fringes of scrub pine and stunted palm along the edges of the inlet: the tide was out, the water lay in shallow puddles across the bed of viscous mud, a few birds wheeled with creaking eery cries above this loneliness of earth and water, and there was the smell of shelled waste, sea-scum—the potent, magical, and exultant smell of the sea in harbors. The air and the sky were sweet with incomparable clarity, with an immense delicacy of light, and the sun, which now burned like a vast orange-colored ball, without violence or heat, was resting against the lonely and desolate space of the western horizon. The widow and Bascom paused for a moment to watch this scene, and then she said triumphantly: "Now, Mistah Haw-uk, you know that *Somebody* must've *done* all that. You know it jus' didn't go an' happen by itse'f. You know, when you see a beautiful sunset like that that nobody but Gawd himse'f could've made it. Now, you know you do, Mistah Haw-uk!"

"The question of its beauty," said my uncle precisely, "is debatable. The philosopher Hegel, for example, so far from seeing beauty in a sunset, remarked that it looked to him as if the sky had small-pox!" Here Bascom closed his eyes, and snuffled with laughter.

"Oh, Mistah Haw-uk!" the widow said reproachfully. "I know *you* don't feel that way about it. A man with a *haid* like yoah's could nevah believe a thing like that!"

"Oh!" Bascom shouted, immensely tickled for some reason. "By no means! By no means!" And he stamped violently at the earth, blind with his strange forced snarl of laughter.

For a moment they were silent: a vast and exuberant elation, an exultant vitality, was alive in Uncle Bascom. He looked at the shallow waters, he looked at the setting sun, he looked at the widow, and when he tried to speak, exultant mirth possessed him, and he could not.

"Shall we?—" he began at length inquiringly, but here a whimsy of humor seized him, he stopped short, contorted his face, stamped at the earth ecstatically, and snuffled down his nose—"shall we go in *wa-ding?*" There was a deliberate, a luscious nasality in his precise enunciation of the last word.

"Oh, Mistah Haw-uk! Why-y!" the widow exclaimed fruitily. "Wading! For what?"

"For . . . oysters!" said Uncle Bascom lusciously and gently.

"For . . . *oysters!*" the widow cried. "But I didn't know there were any oysters!"

Bascom pondered this statement for a moment, and the more he considered it, the funnier it became to him. He bit his rubbery lip, closed his eyes, and began to snuffle down his nose with laughter. "O yes!" he howled. "O *my* yes! There are always . . . oysters! There are plenty of . . . oysters!"

So the widow, without much more than a half-hearted and decorous protest, and a cautious glance around to make sure that pine and palm gave shelter to no watchers, sat down beside my uncle and took off her shoes and stockings. Then, hand in hand, they advanced across the shallows and through water that rarely came above their knees, the widow tentatively, with a balancing movement and little abdominal cries of alarm, Uncle Bascom more boldly, and with confident assurances: "My dear girl!" he said, grasping her hand more tightly. "You are in no danger whatsoever! Oh, not the *slightest!*" he yelled. "You are safe as you would be in your mother's arms. Yes, sir! You may rest assured on that score! There's no question of it!"

The widow held her skirts kilted up and knotted in one hand, midway along her milky thighs, while Uncle Bascom had rolled his trousers high above his bony knees and stringy calves, which now advanced through the shallow water with a storky and tentative step. At length, about the middle of the stream, they reached a bar of hardpacked sand, and here they stood for a while looking at the setting sun, pacing along their little beach, so absorbed in their contemplation of coming dark, of solitude, and of themselves that neither noticed that the tide was coming in.

And yet the tide came in. It came steadily, urgently, imperceptibly, feathering against the fringes of the inlet, advancing, retreating, advancing, retreating, but advancing always past its last retreat until suddenly Bascom felt the shock of water at his toes: he looked down and saw that their ledge of earth and

THE SHORT NOVELS OF THOMAS WOLFE

safety was shrinking almost visibly below his glance: he yelled, first from alarm, and then for help: he shouted, but no one came; he seized the buxom widow and, by staggering effort lifted her, he tottered with her into the water. At the first step the water reached his knees, at the second, halfway up his shanks, at the third, he yelled, and dropped his cargo. She screamed, as a swirl of water caught her at the waist: she clutched him, she clung to him, she screamed, and suddenly Bascom began to curse. He shook a knotted fist at the imperturbable evening skies, he blasphemed against a deity in which he had no faith, and when a false step plunged him to his chin in water, he howled retraction of his blasphemy and begged for providential help. Neither could swim; perhaps neither was in the greatest danger, but both were terrified and shocked, the water wet their ears before they reached the shore, and when at length they tottered up on dry land again, the widow had reached the end and limit of her effort: for several moments she lay panting hoarsely, half out of water and half in, a battered half-emergent Phryne. As for Bascom, he stood on palsied limbs and with a chattering jaw for several moments: his long arms, his bony hands, his stooped shoulders, his stringy legs all bent in a common, constant drip—he was absolutely speechless, and stood there for some time chattering with fright, and dripping water. At length, the widow raised a portion of her charms, bedraggled but made undeniable by water, and moaned hoarsely, "Oh, Mistah Haw-uk! Mistah Haw-uk! Come an' git me, Mistah Haw-uk!"

At this moment Uncle Bascom's features were seized by a horrible convulsion, he opened his mouth to speak, but no words came, he raised two trembling fists toward heaven, but no words came. He tried to curse, but no words came. At length he mastered himself sufficiently to speak and, as if finding his own artillery too feeble for the occasion, he uttered slowly, with passionate conviction, the supplication already mentioned: "O that J. T. were here—that he might aid me with his *scathing* invective!"

So ended romance between Uncle Bascom and the widow.

That year I was twenty, it had been my first year in New England, and the winter had seemed very long. In the man-swarm I felt alone and lost, a desolate atom in the streets of life. That year I went to see my uncle many times.

Sometimes I would find him in his dusty little cubicle, bent over the intricacy of a legal form, painfully and carefully, with compressed lips, filling in the blank spaces with his stiff angular and laborious hand. He would speak quietly, without looking up, as I came in: "Hello, my boy. Sit down, won't you? I'll be with you in a moment." And for a time the silence would be broken only by the heavy rumble of Brill's voice outside, by the minute scratching of my uncle's pen, and by the immense and murmurous sound of time, which rose above the city, which caught up in the upper air all of the city's million noises, and yet which seemed remote, essential, imperturbable and ever-lasting—fixed and unchanging, no matter what men lived or died.

Again, I would find him staring straight before him, with his great hands folded in a bony arch, his powerful gaunt face composed in a rapt tranquillity of thought. At these times he seemed to have escaped from every particular and degrading thing in life —from the excess of absurd and eccentric speech and gesture, from all demeaning parsimonies, from niggling irascibilities, from everything that contorted his face and spirit away from its calmness and unity of thought. His face at such a time might well have been the mask of Thought, the visage of contemplation. Sometimes he would not speak for several minutes, his mind seemed to brood upon the lip and edge of time, to be remote from every dusty moment of the earth.

One day I went there and found him thus; after a few moments he lowered his great hands and, without turning toward me, sat for some time in an attitude of quiet relaxation. At length he said:

"What is man that thou art mindful of him?"

It was one of the first days of spring: the spring had come late, with a magical northern suddenness. It seemed to have burst out of the earth overnight, the air was lyrical and sang with it.

Spring came that year like a triumph and like a prophecy—it sang and shifted like a moth of light before me, but I was sure that it would bring me a glory and fulfillment I had never known.

My hunger and thirst had been immense: I was caught up for the first time in the midst of the Faustian web—there was no food that could feed me, no drink that could quench my thirst—like an insatiate and maddened animal I roamed the streets, trying to draw up mercy from the cobblestones, solace and wisdom from a million sights and faces, or prowled through endless shelves of high-piled books tortured by everything I could not see and could not know, and growing blind, weary, and desperate from what I read and saw. I wanted to know all, have all, be all—to be one and many, to have the whole riddle of this vast and swarming earth as legible, as tangible in my hand as a coin of minted gold.

Suddenly spring came, and I felt at once exultant certainty and joy. Outside my uncle's dirty window I could see the edge of Faneuil Hall, and hear the swarming and abundant activity of the markets. The deep roar of the markets came to us across the singing and lyrical air, and I drank into my lungs a thousand proud, potent, and mysterious odors which came to me like the breath of certainty, like the proof of magic, and like the revelation that all confusion had been banished—the world that I longed for won, the word that I sought for spoken, the hunger that devoured me fed and ended. And the markets, swarming with richness, joy, and abundance, thronged below me like a living evidence of fulfillment. For it seemed to me that nowhere more than here was the passionate enigma of New England felt: New England, with its harsh and stony soil, and its tragic and lonely beauty; its desolate rocky coasts and its swarming fisheries, the white, piled, frozen harshness of its winters with the magnificent jewelry of stars, the dark firwoods, and the warm little white houses at which it is impossible to look without thinking of groaning bins, hung bacon, hard cider, succulent bastings and love's warm, white, and opulent flesh.

There was the rustle of gingham by day and sober glances; then, under low eaves and starlight, the stir of the satiny thighs in feather beds, the white small bite and tigerish clasp of secret women—always the buried heart, the sunken passion, the frozen heat. And then, after the long, unendurably hard-locked harshness of the frozen winter, the coming of spring as now, like a lyrical cry, like a flicker of rain across a window glass, like the sudden and delicate noises of a spinet—the coming of spring and ecstasy, and overnight the thrum of wings, the burst of the tender buds, the ripple and dance of the roughened water, the light of flowers, the sudden, fleeting, almost captured, and exultant spring.

And here, within eighty yards of the dusty little room where my uncle Bascom had his desk, there was living evidence that this intuition was not false: the secret people, it was evident, did not subsist alone on codfish and a jug full of baked beans—they ate meat, and large chunks of it, for all day long, within the market district, the drivers of big wagons were standing to their chins in meat, boys dragged great baskets of raw meat along the pavements, red-faced butchers, aproned with gouts of blood, and wearing the battered straw hats that butchers wear, toiled through the streets below great loads of loin or haunch or rib and in chill shops with sawdust floors the beeves were hung in frozen regimental rows.

Right and left, around the central market, the old buildings stretched down to the harbor and the smell of ships: this was built-on land, in old days ships were anchored where these cobbles were, but the warehouses were also old—they had the musty, mellow, blackened air and smell of the seventies, they looked like the Victorian prints, they reeked of ancient ledgers, of "counting houses," of proud monied merchants, and the soft-spoken rumble of victorias.

By day, this district was one snarled web of chaos: a *gewirr* of deep-bodied trucks, powerful dappled horses, cursing drivers, of loading, unloading, and shipping, of dispatch and order, of the million complicated weavings of life and business.

But if one came here at evening, after the work of the day was done, if one came here at evening on one of those delicate and sudden days of spring that New England knows, if one came here as many a lonely youth had come here in the past, some boy from the inland immensity of America, some homesick lad from the South, from the marvellous hills of Old Catawba, he might be pierced again by the bitter ecstasy of youth, the ecstasy that tears him apart with a cry that has no tongue, the ecstasy that is proud, lonely, and exultant, that is fierce with joy and blind with glory, but that yet carries in it a knowledge that is born in such a moment that the intangible cannot be touched, the ungraspable cannot be grasped—the imperial and magnificent minute is gone forever which, with all its promises, its million intuitions, he wishes to clothe with the living substance of beauty. He wishes to flesh the moment with the thighs and breast and belly of a wonderful mistress, he wishes to be great and glorious and triumphant, to distill the ether of this ecstasy in a liquor, and to drink strong joy forever; and at the heart of all this is the bitter knowledge of death— death of the moment, death of the day, death of one more infrequent spring.

Perhaps the thing that really makes New England wonderful is this sense of joy, this intuition of brooding and magic fulfillment that hovers like a delicate presence in the air of one of these days. Perhaps the answer is simple: perhaps it is only that this soft and sudden spring, with its darts and flicks of evanescent joy, its sprite-like presence that is only half-believed, its sound that is the sound of something lost and elfin, and half-dreamed, half-heard, seems wonderful after the grim frozen tenacity of the winter, the beautiful and terrible desolation, the assault of the frost and ice on living flesh which resists it finally as it would resist the cruel battering of a brute antagonist, so that the tart, stingy speech, the tight gestures, the withdrawn and suspicious air, the thin lips, red pointed noses and hard prying eyes of these people are really the actions of people who, having to defend themselves harshly against nature, harshly defend themselves against all the world.

At any rate, the thing the boy feels who comes here at the day's end is not completion, weariness, and sterility, but a sense of swelling ecstasy, a note of brooding fulfillment. The air will have in it the wonderful odors of the market and the smell of the sea: as he walks over the bare cobbled pavement under the corrugated tin awnings of the warehouses and produce stores a hundred smells of the rich fecundity of the earth will assail him: the clean sharp pungency of thin crated wood and the citric nostalgia of oranges, lemons and grapefruit, the stench of a decayed cabbage and the mashed pulp of a rotten orange. There will be also the warm coarse limey smell of chickens, the strong coddy smell of cold fish and oysters; and the crisp moist cleanliness of the garden smells— of great lettuces, cabbages, new potatoes, with their delicate skins loamy with sweet earth, the wonderful sweet crispness of crated celery; and then the melons—the ripe golden melons bedded in fragrant straw—and all the warm infusions of the tropics: the bananas, the pineapples and the alligator pears.

The delicate and subtle air of spring touches all these odors with a new and delicious vitality; it draws the tar out of the pavements also, and it draws slowly, subtly, from ancient warehouses, the compacted perfumes of eighty years: the sweet thin piney scents of packing boxes, the glutinous composts of half a century, that have thickly stained old warehouse plankings, the smells of twine, tar, turpentine and hemp, and of thick molasses, ginseng, pungent vines and roots and old piled sacking; the clean ground strength of fresh coffee, brown, sultry, pungent, and exultantly fresh and clean; the smell of oats, baled hay and bran, of crated eggs and cheese and butter; and particularly the smell of meat, of frozen beeves, slick porks and veals, of brains and livers and kidneys, of haunch, paunch and jowl; of meat that is raw and of meat that is cooked, for upstairs in that richly dingy block of buildings there is a room where the butchers, side by side with the bakers, the bankers, the brokers and the Harvard boys, devour thick steaks of the best and tenderest meat, smoking hot breads, and big, jacketed potatoes.

And then there is always the sea. In dingy blocks, memoried with time and money, the buildings stretch down to the docks, and there is always the feeling that the sea was here, that this is built-on earth. A single truck will rattle over the deserted stones, and then there is the street that runs along the harbor, the dingy little clothing shops and eating places, the powerful strings of freight cars, agape and empty, odorous with their warm fatigued planking, and the smells of flanges and axles that have rolled great distances.

And finally, by the edges of the water, there are great piers and storehouses, calm and potent with their finished work: they lie there, immense, starkly ugly, yet touched with the powerful beauty of enormous works and movements; they are what they are, they have been built without a flourish for the work they do, their great sides rise in level cliffs of brick, they are pierced with tracks and can engulf great trains; and now that the day is done they breathe with the vitality of a tired but living creature. A single footfall will make remote and lonely echoes in their brooding depths, there will be the expiring clatter of a single truck, the sound of a worker's voice as he says "Good-night," and then the potent and magical silence.

And then there is the sea—the sea, beautiful and mysterious as it is only when it meets the earth in harbors, the sea that bears in swell and glut of tides the odorous savor of the earth, the sea that swings and slaps against encrusted piles, the sea that is braided with long ropes of scummy weed, the sea that brings the mast and marly scent of shelled decay. There is the sea, and there are the great ships—the freighters, the fishing schooners, the clean white one-night boats that make the New York run, now also potent and silent, a glitter of bright lights, of gleaming brasses, of opulent saloons—a token of joy and splendor in dark waters, a hint of love and the velvet belly upon dark tides—and the sight of all these things, the fusion of all these odors by the sprite of May is freighted with unspeakable memories, with unutterable intuitions for the youth: he does not know what he could utter, but glory, love, power, wealth, flight and movement and the sight of new earth in the morning, and the living corporeal fulfilment of all his ecstasy is in his wish and his conviction.

Certainly, these things can be found in New England, but perhaps the person who finds this buried joy the most is this lonely visitor—and particularly the boy from the South, for in the heart of the Southerner alone, perhaps, is this true and secret knowledge of the North: it is there in his dreams and his childhood premonition, it is there like the dark Helen, and no matter what he sees to cheat it, he will always believe in it, he will always return to it. Certainly, this was true of the gnarled and miserly old man who now sat not far from all this glory in his dingy State Street office, for my uncle Bascom Hawke, although the stranger on seeing him might have said, "There goes the very image of a hard-bitten old Down-Easter," had come, as lonely and wretched a youth as ever lived, from the earth of Old Catawba, he had known and felt these things and, in spite of his frequent bitter attacks on the people, the climate, the life, New England was the place to which he had returned to live, and for which he felt the most affection.

—"What is man that thou art *mindful* of him?"—he said again, this time with that tell-tale pedantry of emphasis which foretold a seizure of his mouthing eccentricity. "What is *man* that thou art *mindful* of him?" he repeated with yet more emphasis. The word is *mindful, mindful, mindful!*—he made the word whine like the rasp of a saw. "M-I-N-D-F-U-L! (phuh-phuh-phuh-phuh-phuh!)"

And again, his visage of calm and powerful thought was twisted by the disfiguring grimace, the inept and reasonless laughter. In a moment more, his face grew calm again, magnificently composed above his arched, gnarled hands; he spoke with eloquent deliberation. He became triumphant reasoning mind: he talked with superb and balanced judgment. And as the strange and lonely spirit of thought transformed his face, all the tumult and madness of his life was forgotten: no question of money or of self was involved.

"Beyond a doubt! Beyond a doubt!" he said deliberately. "The quality of the best writing in the books of the Old and New Testaments may take rank with the best writing that was ever done, but the amount of great writing is less than it is commonly supposed to be. There are passages—nay! *books!*"—his voice rising strangely to a husky howl—"of the vilest rubbish."

He paused a moment; then, in a remote voice—in the remote and passionate voice that had had such power to thrill men when it uttered poetry—he continued: "I am Alpha and Omega, the beginning and the end, the first and the last—the triumphant music of one of the mightiest of earth's poets, the sublime utterance of a man for whom God had opened the mysteries of heaven and hell, one of the mightiest lines, my dear boy, the most magnificent poetry that was ever written." And suddenly Bascom threw his gaunt hands before his face, and wept in strong, hoarse sobs: "Oh, my God! My God!—The beauty, the pity of it all! . . . You must excuse me," he whispered huskily after a moment, drawing his frayed and faded sleeve across his eyes. "You must excuse me. . . . It brought back . . . memories."

In spite of this ridiculous exhibition, and the absurd quality of these final words, there was something terrible and revolting about it, too: I was only twenty, and I shrank back for a moment and felt ashamed. In a moment more, however, Uncle Bascom was completely at his ease again: he acted as if nothing unusual had happened, and as if he had completely forgotten his outburst of a moment before.

After a pause, without looking at me, he said quietly, but with an unmistakable note of bitterness in his voice: "Have you seen any of my . . . children, recently?"

The question surprised me, because he rarely asked about them: most of the time he seemed to have forgotten their existence, to be wholly indifferent to them. I told him that I had seen one of his daughters the week before.

"My children—*basely* and *damnably, basely* and *damnably,* have deserted me!" he said with bitter passion. Then, quietly, indifferently, as if stating the fact more truthfully and temperately, he said: "I never see any of them any more. They never come to my house and I never go to theirs. I do not care. No, sir, I do not care. It makes no difference to me. O not the slightest! None whatever!" and he dismissed it with his big-boned hand. In a moment he added: "Their *mother* visits them, I believe. . . . Their *mother* goes, of course, whenever she gets invited."—Here again, the note of bitterness and scorn was evident, as if he held his wife guilty of some treachery in visiting her own children; but indiffer-

ence and contempt were also in his voice—he spoke of his wife
and children as if they were all strangers to him, as if their lives
touched only remotely the edges of the buried world—the world in
which he lived and moved, in which his soul wrought out its fated
destiny.

And this was true: like all of his family he had passed through
a dozen lives in living his own, he was done with his children and
done with his wife, he had forgotten them, he was indifferent to
them, he did not need them. But they, two daughters and two
sons, the youngest of whom was over thirty, the oldest more than
forty, were neither able to forget him nor forgive him. He lived in
their bitter memory; like men who are searching the causes for
some fatal catastrophic flaw which has broken the back of a mighty
bridge they went back through the painful annals of their childhood, the years of frustration and bitterness they had lived beneath his roof, the years they could not forget, escape, or deny. His
shadow fell across them: they never saw him, and they always
talked of him, aping his speech, his gesture, and his manner,
mocking him with limber tongues, but living in his life again and
secretly feeling the old fear, the old awe, because his life alone
had done what it had wished to do—warped and twisted though
it may have been, it had held the rails, it had kept its way, it had
seen new lands. For them, it sometimes seemed the years were
passing like a bitter water on one wheel of life: the wheel turned
and they got older.

And now, as if he, too, had seen them as he spoke of them, he
said: "They can all look after themselves. Everyone must look after
himself—say!" he paused suddenly, tapping his great finger on my
knee, with the inquiring and combative glitter of his eye. "Does
anyone *help* you to die? Does anyone go down into the grave with
you? Can you *do* anything for anyone? No!" he said decisively, and
in a moment he added, slowly and deliberately: "Is not my help
in *me?*"

Then, ruminant and lost, he stared across the archway of his
hands. In a moment, with what was only an apparent irrelevance,

with what was really a part of the coherent past, a light plucked from dark adyts of the brain, he said: "Who knoweth the spirit of man that goeth upward, and the spirit of the beast that goeth downward to the earth?"

He was silent and thoughtful for a moment; then he added sadly: "I am an old man. I have lived a long time. I have seen so many things. Sometimes everything seems so long ago."

Then his eye went back into the wilderness, the lost earth, the buried men.

Presently he said, "I hope you will come out on Sunday. O, by all means! By all means! I believe your aunt is expecting you. Yes, sir, I believe she said something to that effect. Or perhaps she intends to pay a visit to one of her children. I do not know, I have not the *remotest*—not the *faintest* idea of what she proposes to do," he howled. "Of course," he said impatiently and scornfully, "I never have any notion what she has in mind. No, sir, I really could not tell you. I no longer pay any attention to what she says— O! not the slightest!" he waved his great hand through the air— "*Say!*" stiffly and harshly he tapped my knee, grinning at me with the combative glitter of his ptotic eye—"*Say!* did you ever find *one* of them with whom it was possible to carry on a coherent conversation? Did you ever find one of them who would respond to the processes of reason and ordered thought? My dear boy!" he cried, "You cannot talk to them. I assure you you cannot talk to them. You might as well whistle into the wind or spit into the waters of the Nile for all the good it will do you. In his youth man will bare the riches of his spirit to them, will exhaust the rich accumulations of his genius—his wisdom, his learning, his philosophy—in an effort to make them worthy of his companionship— and in the end, what does he *always* find? Why," said Uncle Bascom bitterly, "that he has spent his powers in talking to an imbecile"—and he snarled vengefully through his nose. In a moment more, he contorted his face, and nasally whined in a grotesque and mincing parody of a woman's voice, "O, I feel *so* sick! O, deary *me*, now! I think my *time* is coming on again! O, you don't *love* me any mo-o-ore! O, I *wish* I was dead! O, I can't get *up* to-day! O, I wish you'd bring me something *nice* from *ta-own!* O, if you loved me you'd buy me a *new* hat! O, I've got nothing to *we-e-ar!*" here his voice had an added snarl of bitterness —"I'm ashamed to go out on the street with all the other wim-men!"

Then he paused broodingly for a moment more, wheeled abruptly and tapped me on the knee again: "The proper study of mankind is—say!" he said with a horrible fixed grimace and in a kind of cunning whisper—"Does the poet say—*woman*? I want to ask you: *does* he, now? Not on your life!" yelled Uncle Bascom. "The word is *man, man, man!* Nothing else but *man!*"

Again he was silent: then, with an accent of heavy sarcasm, he went on: "Your aunt likes music. You may have observed your aunt is fond of music——"

It was, in fact, the solace of her life: on a tiny gramophone which one of her daughters had given her, she played constantly the records of the great composers, particularly of Wagner, lost in the enchanted forests of the music, her spirit wandering drunkenly down vast murky aisles of sound, through which the great hoarse throats of horns were baying faintly. And occasionally, on Sundays, on one of her infrequent excursions into the world, when her daughters bought her tickets for concerts at Symphony Hall—that great gray room lined on its sides with pallid plaster shells of Greece—she would sit perched high, a sparrow held by the hypnotic serpent's eye of music—following each motif, hearing minutely each subtle entry of the mellow flutes, the horns, the spinal ecstasy of violins—until her lonely and desolate life was spun out of her into aerial fabrics of bright sound.

"—Your aunt is fond of music," Bascom said deliberately. "Perhaps you may have thought—perhaps it seemed to you that she discovered it—perhaps you thought it was your aunt's own patent and invention—but there you would be wrong! O yes! my boy!" he howled remotely.

"You may have thought so, but you would be wrong—Say!" he turned slowly with a malevolent glint of interrogation, a controlled ironic power—"was the Fifth Symphony written by a woman? Was the object of your aunt's worship, Richard Wagner, a *female?*" he snarled. "By no means! Where are their great works —their mighty symphonies, their great paintings, their epic poetry? Was it in a woman's skull that the Critique of Pure Reason was conceived? Is the gigantic work upon the ceiling of the Sistine Chapel the product of a woman's genius?—Say! Did you ever hear of a lady by the name of William Shakespeare? Was it a female of that name who wrote *King Lear?* Are you familiar with the works of a nice young lady named John Milton? Or Fräulein Goethe, a sweet German girl?" he sneered. "Perhaps you have been edified by the writings of Mademoiselle Voltaire or Miss Jonathan Swift? Phuh! Phuh! Phuh! Phuh! Phuh!"

He paused, stared deliberately across his hands, and in a moment repeated, slowly and distinctly: "The woman gave me of the tree and I did eat. Ah! that's it! There, my boy, you have it! There, in a nutshell, you have the work for which they are best fitted." And he turned upon me suddenly with a blaze of passion, his voice husky and tremulous from the stress of his emotion. "The tempter! The Bringer of Forbidden Fruit! The devil's ambassador! Since the beginning of time that has been their office—to madden the brain, to turn man's spirit from its highest purposes, to corrupt, to seduce, and to destroy! To creep and crawl, to intrude into the lonely places of man's heart and brain, to wind herself into the core of his most secret life as a worm eats its way into a healthy fruit—to do all this with the guile of a serpent, the cunning of a fox—that, my boy, is what she's here for!—and she'll never change!" And, lowering his voice to an ominous and forboding whisper, he said mysteriously, "Beware! Beware! Do not be deceived!"

In a moment more he had resumed his tone and manner of calm deliberation and, with an air of irrelevance, somewhat grudgingly, as if throwing a bone to a dog, he said, "Your aunt, of course, was a woman of considerable mentality—considerable, that is, for a female. Of course, her mind is no longer what it used to be. I never talk to her any more," he said indifferently. "I do not listen to her. I think she said something to me about your coming out on Sunday! But I do not know. No, sir, I could not tell you what her plans are. I have my own interests, and I suppose she has hers. Of course, she has her music. . . . Yes, sir, she always has her music," he said indifferently and contemptuously, and, staring across the apex of his hands, he forgot her.

Yet, he had been young, and full of pain and madness. For a space he had known all the torments any lover ever knew. So much my aunt had told me, and so much he had not troubled to deny. For bending toward me swiftly, fiercely, and abruptly in the full rich progress of a meal, her eyes ablaze with a mad and earnest light, she had suddenly muttered this ominous warning: "Take care, Dave! Take care, boy! You're one of them! Don't brood! Don't brood! You mustn't be mawbid," she whispered hoarsely, fixing the mad glitter of her bright old eyes even more intensely on me. "You're like all the rest of them—it's in the blood!" she muttered, hoarsely and fatally.

"Ah, what are you talk-ing about?" Bascom snarled in a tone of the profoundest contempt. "Scotch! English! Finest people on the face of the earth—no question about it!"

"Fugitive ideation! fugitive ideation!" she chattered like a monkey over a nut. "Mind goes off in all diwections—can't keep attention focused on anything foh five minutes! The modern decadents! Wead Nordau's book, Dave—you'll see, you'll see! You'ah all alike," she muttered. "You'ah ovah-sexed—all of you!"

"Ah," he snarled again, "you talk like a fool! Some more of your psychology, I suppose," he said with a heavy sneer. "The black magic of little minds."

He knew nothing about it, of course; occasionally he still read Kant, and he could be as deep in absolutes, categories, moments of negation, and definitions of a concept, as she with all of her complicated and extensive paraphernalia of phobias, complexes, fixations, and repressions.

Then, bending toward me once again, as if she had not heard him, she whispered: "Oh, yes! he's indifferent enough to me now —but there was a time, there was a time, I tell you!—when he was mad about me! The old fool!" she cackled suddenly and bitterly with a seeming irrelevance. Then bending forward suddenly with a resumption of her former brooding intensity she whispered: "Yes! he was mad, mad, mad! Oh, he can't deny it!" she cried. "He couldn't keep his eyes off me for a minute! He went cwazy if any other man so much as looked at me!"

"Quite true, my dear! Quite true!" my uncle said without a trace of anger or denial in his voice, with one of his sudden and astonishing changes to a mood of tender and tranquil agreement. "Oh, yes," he said again, staring reminiscently across the apex of his great folded hands. "It is all quite true—every word as she has spoken it—quite true, quite true. I had forgotten but it's all quite true." And he shook his gaunt head gently from side to side, turning his closed eyes downward, and snuffling gently, blindly, tenderly, with laughter, with a passive and indifferent memory.

For a year or two after his marriage he had been maddened by a black insanity of jealousy. It descended on his spirit like a choking and pestilence-laden cloud, it entered his veins with blackened tongues of poison, it crept along the conduits of his blood, sweltered venomously in his heart, it soaked into the convolutions of his brain until his brain was fanged with hatred, soaked in poison, stricken, maddened, and unhinged. His gaunt figure wasted until he became the picture of skeletonized emaciation, jealousy and fear ate like a vulture at his entrails, all of the vital energy, the power and intensity of his life, was fed into this poisonous and consuming fire and then, when it had almost wrecked his health, ruined his career, and destroyed his reason, it left him as suddenly as it came: his life reverted to its ancient and imbedded core of egotism, he grew weary of his wife, he thought of her indifferently, he forgot her.

And she, poor soul, was like a rabbit trapped before the fierce yellow eye, the hypnotic stare of a crouching tiger. She did not know whether he would spring, strike forth his paw to maul her, or walk off indifferently. She was dazed and stricken before the violence of his first passion, the unreasoning madness of his jealousy, and in the years that followed she was bewildered, resentful, and finally embittered by the abrupt indifference which succeeded it—an indifference so great that at times he seemed to forget her very existence for days at a time, to live with her in a little house as if he were scarcely conscious of her presence, stumping about the place in an intensity of self-absorption while he cursed and muttered to himself, banged open furnace doors, chopped up whatever combinations of raw foods his fantastic imagination might contrive, and answering her impatiently and contemptuously when she spoke to him: "What did you *say-y?* Oh, what are you talk-ing about?"—and he would stump away again, absorbed mysteriously with his own affairs. And sometimes, if he was the victim of conspiracy in the universe—if God had forsaken him and man had tricked and cheated him, he would roll upon the floor, hammer his heels against the wall, and howl his curses at oblivious heaven.

Louise, meanwhile, her children having left her, played Wagner on the gramophone, kept her small house tidy, and learned to carry on involved and animated conversations with herself, or even with her pots and pans, for when she scrubbed and cleaned them, she would talk to them: if she dropped one, she would scold it, pick it from the floor, spank it across the bottom, saying: "No, you don't! Naughty, you bad thing, you!" And often, while he stumped through the house, these solitary conversations were interspersed by fits of laughter: she would bend double over her pots snuffling with soft laughter which was faintly broken at its climax, a long high "Who-o-op." Then she would shake her head pityingly, and be off again, but at what she was laughing she could not have said.

Suddenly one night, however, she interrupted one of Bascom's stamping and howling tirades by putting on her tiny gramophone *The Ride of the Valkyries,* as recorded by the Philadelphia Symphony Orchestra. Bascom, after the first paralysis of his surprise had passed, rushed furiously toward the offending instrument that was providing such melodious but mighty competition. Then Bascom halted; for suddenly he noticed that Louise was standing beside the instrument, that she was snuffling through her nose with laughter, and that from time to time she looked craftily toward him, and broke into a high piercing cackle. Bascom also noticed that she held a large carving knife in her hand. With a loud yell he turned and fled toward his room, where he locked the door, crying out strongly in an agony of terror: "O momma! Momma! Save me!"

All this had amused Louise enormously. She played the record over time after time, forever snuffling with laughter and the high cackle: "Who-oo-oo!" She bent double with it.

The next morning after Bascom had gone furtively away to his office, Louise looked at her image in a mirror. She looked for a long time, and she said: "I wonder if I am going mad."

Her face at fifty was bloodless, birdlike, her bright eyes badly paunched and rimmed with red; her hair was dead white—all her delicate features were minutely carved with a fabric of tiny wrinkles. So she said: "I wonder if I'm going mad," and took up the study of psychology.

She read all the works of William James, and those of Professor William McDougall as often as they appeared. She subscribed to several magazines, and wrote a book herself. She called it "The Surgery of Psychic Analysis": the publishers rejected it.

"I'm a good hundred years ahead of my time," she said to one of her daughters.

Thus, Louise found the life of reason. She had found a curative for all disease: she became convinced very shortly that she was one of the very few perfectly balanced people in the world and, of course, that Bascom was utterly mad.

But sometimes, even now, the old resentment and bewilderment would return—she would remember the time of his passionate absorption in her, even the black insanity of his jealousy, with bitterness and regret.

What she had said was true. For two years after their marriage, before she had her first child, he had been like a man beset by furies. For the first time in his life his enormous egotism had been pulled away from its center: he went outside of himself, he became acutely sensitive to the world around him. Because of the fury of possession which raged in him, because the thing he possessed must be the best and dearest thing on earth, it suddenly seemed that men were united against him in an effort to take it from him. Louise was pretty and attractive: wherever she went men looked at her, and when Bascom noticed this, it almost drove him mad.

At this time he had his first church in a town in Illinois: sometimes in the middle of a sermon he would see her face below him and his own would grow livid; he would pause suddenly and lean forward gripping the edges of his lectern like a man stricken and foolish—he would recover himself and go on brokenly and indifferently, but his spirit would twist like a tortured animal, his entrails would get numb and sick, his heart seemed frozen in a ring of poison, and a thousand horrible and foolish doubts would torment him. There was no excess of fantastic possibility, no absurdity of suspicion that he did not know: his mind swarmed with poisonous fabrications, which in a second were translated into reality: he was unable to distinguish between cold fact and his delirious fancy—the moment he imagined anything he believed it to be true.

And what was the reason for this madness? He did not know, and yet he knew that he was mad. He could sit in a chair and watch the madness soak into his brain and crawl along his flesh as a man might watch the progress of a poison in his blood. It was a madness that his mind contested, that his reason knew was false, and yet it conquered him. It drove him brain-sick, heart-sick, cursing through the streets at night, it drove him stamping through the streets clutching his great hands together at the waist, and if he heard a burst of laughter in the dark, if he heard voices and the pronouns "he" and "she" he was sure the words had reference to his wife and him or to a rival, and he would turn and curse the people who had spoken. The interest of the earth and of the town he thought was fastened on his own life and his wife's: the earth was full of malevolent voices, evil whisperings—he saw himself at times as trapped, duped, tricked and mocked at by all men; he greeted his parishioners with a sick heart and a livid smile, and he searched their eyes, their faces, for a sly lurking humor, an evil and secret glee, or for some evidence that they knew the nature of his hurt, the ugly dishonor in his brain and heart, the foul color of his secret.

And it was not, it could no longer be, he felt, a secret; he felt as naked as an infant, he thought the reason for his grief was legible in every word and action, and when he went out in the streets, sometimes his spirit cowered in a dreadful kind of shame—he felt like shielding his face from sight. Shame pressed upon him from the skies, he could not escape it—and when it was not shame of his own dishonor, it was shame because he feared that he was being mocked and jeered at as a fool and cuckold by the world.

Great shapes of fear and cruelty were evoked out of immense and timeless skies, they hovered above him wherever he went, they darkened the wintry lights of desolate little towns like smears of blood: it seemed to him that there would never again be joy and confidence on earth, that the shapes of death and madness would walk in his brain forever and, having lost his faith in God, he now sought desperately for some faith in man: he dreamed of finding some earthly father, some man superior to himself in strength, wisdom, and age to whom he could confess the burden of his packed and overladen heart, from whom he might derive some wisdom, some medicine for the plague that was consuming him.

But he never found him, in his heart he knew that such a physician and confessor did not exist: he was caught in a trap, he could not confess the evil weight that lay upon his soul, he took the last full measure of man's loneliness. He could not add to his own dishonor by bringing dishonor on his wife, and always there was a censor in his brain, a core of sanity that in the darkest and evilest hours yet judged fairly, and told him he was mad.

Then it left him. When it seemed that life was no longer tolerable it left him. It guttered out as a fierce flame gutters out of the fuel it has fed upon, and it left him full of weariness, indifference, and a sense of completion: he turned from the hurt, bewildered woman into the orbit of his own remote and secret life, he went on into new lives, new places and projects, and he forgot her.

And now, as I looked at the old man, I had a sense of union with the past. It seemed to me if he would only speak, the living past, the voices of lost men, the pain, the pride, the madness and despair, the million scenes and faces of the buried life—all that an old man ever knew—would be revealed to me, would be delivered to me like a priceless treasure, as an inheritance which old men owed to young, and which should be the end and effort of all living. My savage hunger was a kind of memory: I thought if he could speak, it would be fed.

And for a moment, it seemed, I saw the visages of time, dark time, the million lock-bolts shot back in man's memory, the faces of the lost Americans, and all the million casual moments of their lives, with Bascom blazing at them from a dozen pulpits, Bascom, tortured by love and madness, walking the streets of the nation, stumping the rutted roads, muttering through darkness with clasped bony hands, a gaunt and twisted figure reeling below immense and cruel skies across the continent. Light fell upon his face and darkness crossed it:—he came up from the wilderness, from derbied men and bustled women, from all of the memories of lavish brown, and from time, dark time—from a time that was further off than Saxon thanes, all of the knights, the spearheads, and the horses.

Was all this lost?

"It was so long ago," the old man said.

Bitterly, bitterly Boston one time more: the flying leaf, the broken cloud. Was no love crying in the wilderness?

"—So long ago. I have lived so long. I have seen so much. I could tell you so many things," my uncle said huskily, with weariness and indifference. His eye was lusterless and dead, he looked for a moment tired and old.

All at once, a strange and perplexing vision, which was to return many times in the years that followed, came to me. It was this: there were a company of old men and women at dinner, seated together around a table. All of them were very old, older than my uncle; the faces of the old men and women were fragile and delicate like old yellowed china, their faces were frail and sexless, they had begun to look alike. In their youth all these people had known one another. The men had drunk, fought, whored, hated one another, and loved the women. Some had been devoured by the sterile and corrupt fear and envy that young men know. In secret their lips were twisted, their faces livid, and their hearts bitter; their eyes glittered with a reptilian hatred of another man—they dreaded his success, and they exulted in his failure, laughing with a delirious joy when they heard or read of his hurt, defeat or humiliation. They had been afraid to speak or confess what was in their hearts, they feared the mockery of their fellows; with one another their words were careful, picked, and disparaging. They gave the lie to passion and belief and they said what they knew was false. And yet along dark roads at night they had shouted out into the howling winds their great goat cries of joy, exultancy and power; they had smelled snow in thick brooding air at night, and they had watched it come, softly spitting at the window glass, numbing the footfalls of the earth with its soft silent fall, filling their hearts with a dark proud ecstasy, touching their entrails with impending prophecy. Each had a thousand dark desires and fantasies; each wanted wealth, power, fame and love, each saw himself as great, good and talented; each feared and hated rivals in business or in love—and in crowds they glared at one another with hard hostile eyes, they bristled up like crested cocks, they watched their women jealously, felt looks and glances through their shoulder blades, and hated men with white spermatic necks, amorous hair, and faces proud and insolent with female conquest.

They had been young and full of pain and combat, and now all this was dead in them: they smiled mildly, feebly, gently, they spoke in thin voices, and they looked at one another with eyes dead to desire, hostility, and passion.

[68]

As for the old women, they sat there on their yellowed and bony haunches. They were all beyond the bitter pain and ecstasy of youth—its frenzy, its hope, its sinew of bright blood and agony: they were beyond the pain and fear of anything save age and death. Here was a faithful wife, a fruitful mother; here was an adulterous and voluptuous woman, the potent mistress of a dozen men, here was her cuckold husband, who had screamed like a tortured animal when he had found her first in bed with another man, and here was the man he found her with; here was another man in whom the knowledge of his wife's infidelity had aroused only a corrupt inverted joy, he exulted in it, he urged her on into new love affairs, he besought her greedily to taunt him with it, he fed upon his pain—and now they were all old and meagre and had the look of yellowed china. They turned their mild sunken faces toward one another with looks in which there was neither hate nor love nor desire nor passion, they laughed thinly, and their memory was all of little things.

They no longer wanted to excel or to be first; they were no longer mad and jealous; they no longer hated rivals; they no longer wanted fame; they no longer cared for work or grew drunk on hope; they no longer turned into the dark and struck their bloody knuckles at the wall; they no longer writhed with shame upon their beds, cursed at the memory of defeat and desolation, or ripped the sheets between convulsive fingers. Could they not speak? Had they forgotten?

Why could not the old men speak? They had known pain, death and madness, yet all their words were stale and rusty. They had known the wilderness, the savage land; the blood of the murdered men ran down into the earth that gave no answer; and they had seen it, they had shed it. Where were the passion, pain and pride, the million living moments of their lives? Was all this lost? Were they all tongueless? It seemed to me that there was something sly and evil in their glances as they sat together, as if they hoarded some cunning and malevolent wisdom in their brains, as if the medicine to all our grief and error was in them, but as if through the evil and conspirate communication of their glance, they had resolved to keep it from us. Or were they simply devoured with satiety, with weariness and indifference? Did they refuse to speak because they could not speak, because even memory had gone lifeless in them?

Yes. Words echoed in their throat but they were tongueless. For them the past was dead: they poured into our hands a handful of dry dust and ashes.

The dry bones, the bitter dust? The living wilderness, the silent waste? The barren land?

Have no lips trembled in the wilderness? No eyes sought seaward from the rock's sharp edge for men returning home? Has no pulse beat more hot with love or hate upon the river's edge? Or where the old wheel and the rusted stock lie stogged in desert sand: by the horsehead a woman's skull. No love?

No lonely footfalls in a million streets, no heart that beat its best and bloodiest cry out against the steel and stone, no aching brain, caught in its iron ring, groping among the labyrinthine canyons? Naught in that immense and lonely land but incessant growth and ripeness and pollution, the emptiness of forests and deserts, the unhearted, harsh and metal jangle of a million tongues, crying the belly-cry for bread, or the great cat's snarl for meat and honey? All, then, all? Birth and the twenty thousand days of snarl and jangle—and no love, no love? Was no love crying in the wilderness?

It was not true. The lovers lay below the lilac bush; the laurel leaves were trembling in the wood.

Suddenly it seemed to me, that if I could put my hand upon my uncle, if I could grip my fingers in his stringy arm, my strength and youth would go into him, and I could rekindle memory like a living flame in him, I could animate for an hour his ancient heart with the exultancy, the power, the joy that pulsed in me; I could make the old man speak.

I wanted to speak to him as people never speak to one another, I wanted to say and hear the things one never says and hears. I wanted to know what his own youth beyond its grim weather of poverty, loneliness, and desperation had been like. He had been over ten years old when the war had ended, he had seen the men plod home in wreaths of dust and heard their casual voices in a room, he had breathed the air of vanished summers, he had seen cloud shadows floating on the massed green of the wilderness, the twisting of a last lone leaf upon a bough; and he had heard the desolate and stricken voices in the South long, long ago, the quiet and casual voices of lost men, a million vanished footsteps in the streets of life. And he had known the years of brown, dark lavish brown, the lost and hypocritic years, the thunder of the wheels and hooves upon the cobbles, the color of bright blood—the savagery, the hunger and the fear.

Was the memory of all this lost?

I touched him—I put my hand upon his shoulder, he did not move. Sunken in what lost world, buried in what incommunicable and tongueless past, he said—"So long ago."

Then I got up and left him and went out into the streets where the singing and lyrical air, the man-swarm passing in its million-footed weft, the glorious women and the girls compacted in a single music of belly and breasts and thighs, the sea, the earth, the proud, potent, clamorous city, all of the voices of time fused to a unity that was like a song, a token and a cry. Victoriously, I trod the neck of doubt as if it were a serpent: I was joined to the earth, a part of it, and I possessed it; I would be wasted and consumed, filled and renewed eternally; I would feel unceasingly alternate tides of life and dark oblivion; I would be emptied without weariness, replenished forever with strong joy. I had a tongue for agony, a food for hunger, a door for exile and a surfeit for insatiate desire: exultant certainty welled up in me, I thought I could possess it all, and I cried: "Yes! It will be mine!"

The Web of Earth

THE WEB OF EARTH

Early in January, 1932, Wolfe's mother visited him in Brooklyn, and for most of the visit the two of them did nothing but talk, Julia Wolfe's endless stream of reminiscences weaving itself into her son's mind. When later that month he learned of the *Scribner's Magazine* Short Novel Contest, with typical optimism, he decided to write a story and enter it, despite the fact that the closing date was February 1. The story he wrote was "about an old woman, who sits down to tell a little story," he said, "but then her octopal memory weaves back and forth across the whole fabric of her life until everything has gone into it." The story was not completed until March, over a full month beyond the deadline of the contest.

Wolfe had feared that *Scribner's* would make him "cut some of the things in it." When Perkins saw it, however, he found it to have "perfect form for all its intricacy," and told Wolfe, "Not one word of this should be changed." It was published in the July, 1932, issue of *Scribner's Magazine*.

The Web of Earth was one of his two short novels that Wolfe did not later incorporate in "the big book" (the other was *Death the Proud Brother*). He reprinted it with minor additions in the collection *From Death to Morning*. In 1932 Wolfe was trying to abandon the Gant clan and create a new protagonist, David Hawke. In the first version of *The Web of Earth* the narrator is named Delia Hawke and the other characters bear names unusual in the Wolfe canon. In the *From Death to Morning* version the narrator is Eliza Gant and the other characters are again members of a familiar clan.

Nothing Wolfe wrote has been more highly praised than this short novel. Elizabeth Nowell says, "Technically, it was the most perfect thing that Wolfe ever wrote." Wolfe reported that Perkins thought it "the best single piece of writing, the truest, the most carefully planned, and in the end the most unassailable that I've ever done."

The unifying principle in *The Web of Earth* is again character, as it had been in *A Portrait of Bascom Hawke*, but here it is character revealed through a vast web of memories, stories, and recollections that crowd in on the narrator as she talks and that stretch back seventy years. "In the telling, the story weaves back and forth like a web," Wolfe wrote, "and for that reason I have called it 'The Web of Earth.'" In working out this intricate pattern, Wolfe turned to his first literary master, James Joyce, and tried in the compulsive volubility of his narrator to draw a portrait somewhat like that of Molly Bloom in *Ulysses*. "I really believe," he asserted, "although this is a terribly boastful thing to say, that I knew this old woman better than Joyce knew that woman at the end of 'Ulysses' and furthermore that my old woman is a grander, richer, and more tremendous figure than his was."

The version here reprinted is that in *From Death to Morning* (New York: Charles Scribner's Sons, 1935), pages 212-304.

. . . In the year that the locusts came, something that happened in the year the locusts came, two voices that I heard there in that year. . . . Child! Child! It seems so long ago since the year the locusts came, and all of the trees were eaten bare: so much has happened and it seems so long ago. . . .

"What say?" I said.

Says, "Two . . . Two," says, "Twenty . . . Twenty."

"Hah? What say?"

"Two . . . Two," the first voice said; and "Twenty . . . Twenty," said the other.

"Oh, Two!" I cried out to your papa, and "Twenty . . . Twenty —can't you hear them?"

"Two . . . Two," it said again, the first voice over by the window, and "Twenty . . . Twenty" said the second, at my ear.

"Oh, don't you hear it, Mr. Gant?" I cried.

"Why, Lord, woman!" your papa said. "What on earth are you talking about? There's no one there," he said.

"Oh, yes, there is!" I said, and then I heard them once again, "Two . . . Two" and "Twenty . . . Twenty."

"There they are!" I said.

"Pshaw, Mrs. Gant," your papa said. "It's something you imagined. You fell asleep, you must have dreamed it."

"Oh, no, I didn't," I said. "It's there! It's there all right!"—because I *knew*, I *knew*: because I heard it just as plain!

"It's the condition you're in," he said. "You're tired and overwrought and you've imagined it."

Then all of the bells began to ring and he got up to go.

"Oh, don't go!" I said. "I wish you wouldn't go"—you know I had a premonition, and it worried me to see him go.

And then I heard it once again—"Two . . . Two," the first voice said, and "Twenty . . . Twenty," said the other . . . and I *know*, I *know*—why, yes! Lord God! don't I remember, boy!—the hour, the time, the very year it happened, to the day . . . because that was the year the locusts came at home and all of the trees were eaten bare.

But, say, then!—Ben—Steve—Luke—pshaw! Boy! *Gene!* I mean—I reckon Luke is thinking of me at this moment, that's why I keep calling you his name. Well, now—hah? What say?

"You started to tell me about two voices that you heard one time."

Oh, yes! That's so! Well, now, as I was—say! What was that? Hah?

"Those were the ships out on the harbor, Mama."

What say? Harbor? Ships? Oh, yes, I reckon now that's so. The harbor is yon way?

"No, Mama, it's the other way. You're turned around. It's just the other way: it's there."

Hah? *That* way? Why, no, child, surely not. . . . Are you telling me the truth? . . . Well, then, I'll vow! I *am* mixed up. I reckon comin' in that tunnel did it. But you couldn't lose me in the country; give me a landmark of some sort to go by and I'll be all right. . . . Why, boy, I'll vow! . . . There goes that thing again! Why, Lord! It sounds like some old cow! And here you are right on the edge of it! How did you ever come to such a place? Lord! Listen—do you hear it? I reckon that's a big one gettin' ready to pull out. . . . Lord, God! You're all alike: your daddy was the same—forever wantin' to be up and gone. If I'd let him he'd have been nothing but a wanderer across the face of the earth. . . . Child, child, you mustn't be a wanderer all your days. . . . It worries me to think of you away off somewheres with strange people. . . . You mustn't spend your life alone with strangers. . . . You ought to come back where your people came from. . . . Child, child, it worries me. . . . Come back again.

Well now, as I was goin' on to say, that night I heard it, the first voice—pshaw! there goes that whistle once again. Say, boy! I tell you what—it makes me want to pick right up and light out with it! Why, yes, I'm not so old! I could start out now—I tell you what, I've got a good mind to do it—I'd like to start right out and just see everything—why! all those countries: England, where all our folks came from, and France, Germany, Italy—say! I've always wanted to see Switzerland—that must certainly be a beautiful spot—as the feller says, the Wonderland of Nature. . . .

Say . . . oh, now I hear it! . . . Now I know. . . . Why, yes! It's out yon way. And where's the bridge, then, that we walked across that night?

"It's here—right at the bottom of the street. Here! Come to the window and look out. Don't you remember how we came?"

Remember! Now, boy, you ask me if I can remember! Lord, God! I reckon I remember things you never read about—the way it was, the things they never wrote about in books.

I reckon that they tried to put it down in books, all of the wars and battles, child, I guess they got that part of it all right, but Lord!—how could these fellers know the way it was when they weren't born, when they weren't there to see it: they made it seem so long ago and like it happened in some strange land—

what could they know, child, of the way it was: the way the wind blew and the way the sun was shining, the smell of the smoke out in the yard, and Mother singin', and the scalded feathers, and the way the river swelled that spring when it had rained? The way the men looked as they marched back along the river road that day, as they were comin' from the war, and the things we said, and the sound of all the voices of the people who are dead, and the way the sunlight came and went, and how it made me sad to see it, and the way the women cried as we stood there in Bob Patton's yard, and the men marched by us, and the dust rose, and we knew the war was over. Lord, God! do I remember! Those are the things that I remember, child, and that's the way things were.

I can remember all the way back to the time when I was two years old, and let me tell you, boy, there's mighty little I've forgotten since.

Why, yes!—don't I remember how they took me by the hand that day and led me down into the holler—Bob Patton and your Uncle George—and here boy-like they had constructed an effigy of Willy and Lucindy Patton out of that old black mud they had there—you could mould it in your hands just like a piece of putty —and how I screamed and all—because I *knew*, I *knew*, I'd seen them both and I remembered them—why! Willy and Lucindy were two slaves that Cap'n Patton owned—oh, Lord! the blackest African niggers you ever saw, as Father said, charcoal would 'a' left a white mark on them, their parents had been taken right out of the jungle—and those white teeth, those gleaming white teeth when they grinned—but oh! the odor! that awful odor, that old black nigger-smell that nothin' could wash out, mother couldn't stand it, it made her deathly sick, when they passed through a room they left the smell behind them—and here these two devils of boys had made this effigy with pebbles they had taken from the creek for teeth, and to think of it!—that they should tell a child of two a thing like that—*why*, that it was Willy and Lucindy Patton I was lookin' at—"Look out!" says Bob, "they're going to eat you up," he says, and how I screamed—why, I remember it all the same as yesterday!

And don't I remember taking Brother Will up to the Indian Mound—of course the story went that there were Indians buried there, that's what it was, they said—and here this brook was filled up with this old black oily stuff that came out from the mound—of course, Father always gave it as his opinion there was oil there, that's what he said, you know, that some one would make a fortune some day if they dug a well there—and Will was only two and a half years old and George told him that the old black oil was squeezed out of the corpses of the Indians and how Will screamed and hollered when he told him—"Why," Mother said, "I could wring your neck for having no more sense than to frighten a child with such a story."

And yes, now! What about it? Don't I remember that winter when the deer came boundin' down the hill across the path and stopped and looked at me not ten feet away, and I screamed because I saw its antlers? Lord! I didn't know what to make of it, I'd never heard of such an animal, and how it bounded away into the woods again and how when I told Mother she said, "Yes, you saw a deer. That was a deer you saw all right. The hunters ran it down here off the mountain" and—why, yes! wasn't it only the next spring after that when I was a big girl four years old and re-membered everything—that the Yankees began to come through there, and didn't I hear them, didn't I see them with my own eyes, the villains—those two fellers tearing along the road on two horses they had stolen, as hard as they could, as if all hell had cut loose after them—why! it's as plain in my mind to-day as it was then, the way they looked, two ragged-lookin' troopers bent down and whippin' those horses for all that they were worth, with bandanna handkerchiefs tied around their necks and the ends of them whipping back as stiff and straight as if they'd been starched and ironed—now *that* will give you some idea of how fast they were goin'—and couldn't I hear the people shoutin' and hollerin' all along the road that they were comin', and how the women-folks took on and made the men go out and hide themselves? "Oh, Lord," says Mother, wringin' her hands, "there they come!" and didn't Addie Patton come running up the hill to tell us, the poor child frightened out of her wits, you know screaming, "Oh, they've come, they've come! And Grandfather's down there all alone," she says. "They'll kill him, they'll kill him!"

Of course we didn't know then that these two Yankee stragglers were alone, we thought they were the advance guard of a whole brigade of Sherman's troopers. But Law! the rest of them never got there for a week, here these two thieving devils had broken away, and I reckon were just trying to see how much they could steal by themselves. Why, yes! Didn't all the men begin to shoot at them then as they went by and when they saw they didn't have the army with them, and didn't they jump off their horses and light out for the mountains on foot as hard as they could, then, and leave the horses? And didn't some people from way over in Bedford County come to claim the horses when the war was over? They identified them, you know, and said those same two fellers were the ones that took 'em. And Lord! didn't they tell it how Amanda Stevens set fire to the Bridge with her own hands on the other side of Sevier so that those that were comin' in from Tennessee were held up for a week before they got across—yes! and stood there laughin' at them, you know; of course they used to tell it on her that she said ("Lord!" I said, "you know she wouldn't say a thing like that!") but of course Amanda was an awful coarse talker, she didn't care what she said, and they all claimed later that's just the way she put it—"Why," she hollers to them, "you don't need a bridge to get across a little stream like that, do you? Well, you must be a pretty worthless lot, after all," she said. "Why, down here," she says, "we'd call it a pretty poor sort of man who couldn't —— across it," and, of course, the Yankees had to laugh then, that's the story that they told.

And yes! Didn't they tell it at the time how the day the Yankees marched into town they captured old man Mackery? I reckon they wanted to have some fun with him more than anything else, a great fat thing, you know, with that swarthy yeller complexion and that kinky hair, of course, the story went that he had nigger blood in him and—what about it! he admitted it, sir, he claimed it then and there in front of all the Yankees, I reckon hoping they would let him off. "All right," the Yankees said, "if you can prove that you're a nigger we'll let you go." Well, he said that he could prove it, then. "Well, how're you going to prove it?" they asked him. "I'll tell you how," this Yankee captain says, calls to one of his troopers, you know, "Run him up and down the street a few times, Jim," he says, and so they started, this soldier and old man Mackery, running up and down in that hot sun as hard as they could go. Well, when they got back, he was wringin' wet with perspiration, Mackery, you know, and the story goes the Yankee went over to him and took one good smell and then called out, "Yes, by God, he told the truth, boys. He's a nigger. Let him go!" Well, that's the way they told it, anyhow.

And yes! Don't I remember it all, yes! With the men comin' by and marchin' along that river road on their way into town to be mustered out and all of us ganged together there in the front yard of Uncle John's place to see them pass, Father and Mother and all the children and all of the Patton and Alexander and Pentland tribes and these two black African niggers that I told you John Patton owned, Willy and Lucindy Patton, and your great-grandfather, boy, old Bill Pentland that they called Bill the Hatter because he could make them of the finest felt—learned how to treat the wool with chamber lye, oh! the finest hats you ever saw, why don't I remember an old farmer coming to our house in my childhood to give a hat to Uncle Sam to be reblocked, says, "Sam, old Bill Pentland made that hat for me just twenty years ago and it's as good," he says, "as it ever was, all it needs is to be blocked and cleaned," and let me tell you, every one that knew him said that Billy Pentland was certainly a man with a remarkable mind.

Now, boy, I want to tell you, I've always said whatever ability you had came from that side of the house, there's one thing sure, Bill Pentland was a man who'd 'a' gone far if he'd had the education. Of course he had no book-learnin' but they told it, you know, how he could argue and take sides on any question, hale and hearty, mind you, right up to the hour of his death, sent word down to Sam one day to come up there to see him, says, "Sam" —of course Sam told it how he found him building his fire and singin' a hymn, at peace with the world and without a thing wrong with him—"Sam," he says, "I'm glad you've come. There are matters I want to talk over with you. Lay down on that bed," he says, "so we can talk." Well, that just suited Sam, you know, oh! the *laziest* feller that ever lived, he could spend his whole life just a-layin' round and talkin', "Why," he says, "what is it, Father? What's the matter? Aren't you feelin' good?" he says. "Oh," says Bill, "I never felt better, but I'm not goin' to be here with you much longer," he says, "I've made up my mind it's time to die, Sam, and I want to put my house in order before I go." "Why, Father," Sam says, "what are you talkin' about, what do you mean? There's nothing wrong with you." "No, not a thing," says Bill. "Why, you'll be here for years to come," says Sam. "No, Sam," the old man says, he shook his head, you know. "I've just decided that it's my time to go. I've had a Call. Now, I've lived out my full three score years and ten," he says, "with some to spare and I feel there's nothin' more I can do on earth, so I've made up my mind." "Made up your mind?" says Sam, "why, made up your mind to what?" "Why," he says, "I've made up my mind to die, Sam." "Why, Father," says Sam, "what are you talking about? You're not going to die," he says. "Yes," says Bill, "I've made up my mind to die tomorrow," says, "I've made up mind to die at ten minutes after six tomorrow afternoon, and that's the reason I sent for you." Well! they built up a roarin' big fire and stayed up all night long talkin' together, and oh! you know, talked long, long into the night, and they cooked breakfast, and Sam told it how the wind roared and howled, and how they lay around and talked some more, and they cooked dinner and talked some more and that old man was as well and strong as he'd ever been, at peace with mankind, sir, and without a worry in the world, but on the stroke of six, now, boy, I want to tell you the kind of man *he* was, on the stroke of six, he turned to Sam and said, "Get ready, Sam," and at ten minutes after six to the dot, he looked at him again and said, "Good-bye, Sam: it's my time, I'm going, son," and he turned his face to the wall, sir, and *died*—now that's the kind of man he was, that goes to show the kind of will-power and determination he had in *him*—and *let me tell you something*: we've all had it in us, that same thing, when it came our time to go, we *knew* it. Father went the same way, sir, kept wakin' up all day long to say, "Is it six o'clock, yet?"— couldn't seem to get it off his mind, you know—"Why, no, Fa- ther," I said, "it's only noon." Now, six, six, I kept a-thinkin', why does he keep asking if it's six? That *very day*, sir, as the clock was striking the last stroke of six he breathed his last, I turned to Jim and whispered, "Six": he nodded, "Yes," he said. Of course we knew.

But here he was that day—don't I remember him? Old Bill Pentland standin' there with all the rest of us to watch the troops go by, a hale and hearty old man, sir, oh! married twice and had all those children, eight by his first wife, Martha Patton, of course Father was one of *that* crowd and fourteen by that other woman—well, that's so, there *was* that other one, I reckon, that he'd had by that woman down in South Carolina, of course there was no record of the ceremony and I reckon what they said was true, but he brought that child home and sat her down at the table with all the rest of them and said to them all: "From this time on she is your sister and must be treated so," and that's the way it was all right. And here, to think of it! All these children that he had went out and had big families of their own, those that didn't die early or get killed, until now there are hundreds of them living down there in Catawba in the mountains, and in Georgia and Texas and out west in California and Oregon until now they are spread all over like a web—but that's where they came from, from that one old man, he was the only one there was to begin with, the son of that Englishman that came there back in Revolutionary days to sink those copper shafts out there in Yancey. Of course they say we've got great estates waitin' for us in England—I know Uncle Bob came to Father at the time Bill Pentland died and told him he ought to do something about it, but they decided against it, said the expense would be too great—but he was *there*, all right, Bill Pentland was there with all the rest of us the day they came back from the war. And here came all the troops, you know, and you could hear the men a-cheerin' and the women-folks a-crying, and every now and then you'd see one of the men drop out of line and then the women would start crying again, and here comes Uncle Bob—only sixteen, mind you, but he seemed like an old man to me—wearing a stovepipe hat I reckon he'd looted from some store and no shoes on, and here he comes and we all began to cry.

"Why, Lord!" says Bob, "this is a pretty homecomin' for a fact," he says, you know, trying to joke us along and cheer us up. "Why, I thought you'd be glad to see me," he says. "I didn't expect you all to bust out cryin'! Why, if that's the way you feel," he says, "I'm goin' back."

"Oh, Bob, Bob," his mother says, "you've got no shoes, poor child, you're barefooted," she says.

"No," says Bob, "I wore 'em out in my hurry to get home," he says, "I just walked them clean off my feet," he says, "but if I'd known it was going to be like this, I wouldn't have come so fast," he said, and of course that made 'em laugh.

But, child, that wasn't the reason that the women cried. So many had gone off that never would come home again and, of course, they knew it, they knew it, and then, didn't we all flock into the house, and hadn't they all been baking and cooking for a week and, let me tell you, poor as we were, that was a *meal*, no little dabs of stuff such as they give you nowadays: fried chickens—why we must have cooked two dozen of them—and boiled hams and pork and roasting ears and sweet pertaters and string beans and plates full of corn bread and hot biscuits and peach and apple dumplings and all kinds of jams and jellies and pies and cakes galore and all of the cider you could drink, and Lord! I wish you could have seen the way that Bob and Rufus Alexander and Fate Patton put that food away, why, as Mother said, you'd 'a' thought they hadn't had a square meal since they went to war and I reckon maybe she didn't miss it much either.

[85]

Why, wasn't I a big girl of five years old at the time, and saw it all, and remember it as well as I'm settin' here, yes, and things that happened long before that—and things you never heard of, boy, with all your reading out of books: why, yes, didn't we learn to do everything ourselves and to grow everything we ate and to take the wool and dye it, yes, to go out in the woods and get the sumac and the walnut bark and all the walnut hulls and elderberries for the dyes and rinse the wool in copperas water until we had a hard fast black you couldn't take the shine off—why! it beat the stuff they have today all hollow—didn't I learn to do it with my own hands and couldn't I get the finest reds and greens and yellers that you ever saw, and didn't I learn to spin the flax and bleach it and make fine shirts and sheets and tablecloths myself, why, yes, don't I remember the day—oh! that strong rank smell, you know, of scalded feathers, with Mother plucking the chicken in the yard, and the smell of the smoke, and the fresh pine chips out by the chopping block, and all (that's where you got your sense of smell from, boy!) and the wind that howled and whistled through that old coarse grass, it made me sad to listen to it (that was the year just after Sally died) and I sat there at the wheel spinning away, and I can see it all, I remember just the way it was—when here they came along the river road, and you could hear them shout and holler out "Hurrah! hurrah!" I reckon they'd all been in to town to vote. "Hurrah!" they cried: "Hurrah for Hayes!" one crowd would cry and, "Hurrah for Tilden!" cried the other.

Lord God! do I remember! I reckon that I do! I remember things you never dreamed or heard of, boy.

"But what about those voices that you heard?"

Well, now, I say—that's what I'm telling you:

"Two-two," the first voice said, and "twenty-twenty," said the other. "What say?" I said. Says, "two-two," says, "twenty-twenty." "Hah? What say?" Says, "two-two," the first voice said, says "twenty-twenty," said the other.

Well, then—say! what about it!— I was thinking about it the

other day. . . . I don't know . . . but it's pretty strange when you come to think about it, isn't it? Why, that very day, you know, the twenty-seventh of September, I remember because it was on the twenty-fifth, just two days before, that I had the talk with Ambrose Radiker, that's exactly when it was all right, about eleven o'clock in the morning, your papa was back there in his workroom lettering a tombstone he was getting ready to set up for a man out there in Beaverdam whose wife had died, when here he came, Mel Porter. Your papa said he marched right back into the work-room, sir, and stood there looking at him without sayin' a word: he just stood there shakin' his head and your papa said he certainly looked blue and depressed as if some awful calamity had befallen him, so your papa said, "What's the matter, Mel? I never saw you look so sad," he says.

"Oh, Will, Will," he says, and he just stood there shakin' his head at your papa, "if you only knew how I envy you! Here you are with a good trade you can work at and nothing to worry you: I'd give up everything I have in the world if I could just change places with you!" "Why what on earth are you talking about!" your papa said. "You're a first-class lawyer with a good practice and here you want to swap places with a stone-cutter who's got to work with his hands and never knows where his next job's comin' from," your papa said. "It's a curse and a care," your papa said, that's exactly the way he talked to him, you know the way he had of talkin', he'd come right out with a thing without mincin' words. "It's a curse and a care," he said, "and it was a bitter day for me when I first took it up: you've got to wait until they die to get a job and then their families, ingrates that they are, will give the work to one of your competitors: if I'd done the thing I was cut out for, I'd 'a' studied law like you did and gone into practice." Well, of course, they all said that, they said that Mr. Gant would certainly have made a fine lawyer, with his fluent command of language and all. "Oh, Will, Will," he said, "you can just go down on your knees and thank God that you didn't," he said. "At least you have enough to eat," he said, "and when you go home at night you can go to bed and sleep."

"Why, Mel," your papa said. "What on earth is wrong with you? Something is worryin' you, that's one thing sure." "Oh, Will," he said, shakin' his head, "it's those men. I can't sleep at night for thinkin' about them!" Well, he hadn't said *what* men, he hadn't mentioned their names, but your papa knew right away who he was talkin' about, it flashed over him all at once that he was referrin' to Ed Mears and Lawrence Wayne and those other three murderers down there in the county jail he had defended. And he had been down there to see them, he'd just come away from there, your papa said he knew exactly where he'd been the moment he looked at him, said his shoes and the bottoms of his trousers were coated with that old red-clay Niggertown dust, that's all in the world it was.

"Why, yes, Mel," your papa said, "I reckon it is pretty hard, but you've got nothin' to blame yourself for," he said. "You did all any one could expect you to do," he said; says, "You did the best you could for them," he says; says, "I don't see what you got to blame yourself about now," he says.

"Oh, Will," he says, "it's the strain, the awful strain of it," he says. "Here I've done all I could to save them," he says, "and it looks as if there's nothing else I can do," he says; says, "It looks to me as if they've got to hang," he says, "and here are their wives and childern and all of their kinfolk beggin' me to save them and," he says, "Will, I just don't know what else there is I can do," he says; says, "I've racked my brain lookin' for a way out," he says, "and it looks to me as if they've *got to swing*. I tell you what," he says, shakin' his head, and your papa said he looked mighty blue, says, "it's an awful thing when you come to think of it! What about it!" he says. "Here they've got all those little childern dependent on them who have got to grow up now with that awful stigma attached to their name of knowin' they're the childern of men who were hanged for murder. Why, it's awful, that's what it is, Will," he says; says, "I can't sleep at night for thinkin' about it."

Well, when your papa came home to dinner that day he told me all about it, says, "I tell you what, it's pretty hard on him,

[88]

isn't it? I reckon he's done all he can but he feels like he's in some way responsible for it, that maybe there's somethin' he failed to do that might have saved their lives," he says; says, "I couldn't help feelin' sorry for him," says, "he was pale as a ghost: he looked as if he hadn't been able to sleep for a week." "Hm!" I says. "Now you listen to me: there's *something mighty funny* about this *somewheres*. I've never known a lawyer yet," I says, "who wasn't able to sleep because a client was goin' to be hanged, and you can just bet your bottom dollar," I says, "that Melvin Porter isn't losin' sleep on *that* account. The only reason they'll lose sleep," I says, "is because they're afraid they're not goin' to get paid or because they're stayin' awake figgerin' how they can get the best of some one, and if he told you *any such story* as that," I says, "you can depend upon it that he wasn't tellin' you the truth—there's a nigger in the woodpile somewheres: that story *just won't wash*."

"No," your papa says, "I believe you're wrong," says, "I think you're doin' him an injustice."

"Why, pshaw, Mr. Gant!" I says. "I wouldn't be such a goose! There's not a word of truth in that story, all they've got to do is to appeal to your sympathies and you'll believe anything they tell you."

And of course that was just exactly how he was: he'd curse and rave and carry on, and then they'd tell him some big lie to get on his good side and he'd give them everything he had. Why! didn't Mel Porter's own brother, that miserable old rip, Rufus Porter—as the sayin' goes, if there's a just God in heaven he's getting today the punishment he deserves—with his old red face all stewed down like a persimmon with all the licker he'd drunk—why yes! when I was a girl didn't I see him myself march right down the aisle as big as you please, sir, that night at the meeting of the Sons of Temperance, arm in arm with Jeter Alexander to sign the pledge and Lord! as I said later if you took all the rotten old licker they'd poured down their throats since then you'd have enough to float a battleship—come to your papa and got him to sign his note and stand security for him at the bank for fourteen hundred dollars. Pshaw! when I think of it! . . . I said to your papa, *"He's* the one who ought to be hanged! I could spring the trap myself!" I said: says to your papa, in that mealy voice he had, you know, says, "Oh, it will be all right, Will." Says, "You know I wouldn't let you lose a penny," when he didn't have a dollar to his name! "I'll vow, Mr. Gant!" I said at the time. "How on earth were you ever such a fool as to do such a thing!"

"Well," he said, "he swore it was all right—said he'd go down and dig ditches before he'd let me lose a penny."

"Yes," I said, "and you were *just* fool enough to believe him, weren't you!"

"Well," your papa said, "I've learned my lesson. There's one thing sure: I'll never get stung that way again," he said.

"All right," I said, "we'll wait and see."

Well, it wasn't two years before Rufe Porter tried the very same trick on him again; he had the gall to walk right into your papa's office, sir, as big as you please, and ask him to go his note for five hundred dollars. Your papa was so mad he took him by the collar and pitched him all the way out into the square and says, "If you ever come back here again, you God-damned mountain grill," that's just the way your papa talked to him, you know the way he talked, he didn't mince words when he was mad, "I'll kill you." Why yes! wasn't old Bill Smathers the chief of police at the time standin' right there on the steps of the City Hall and saw the whole thing? and he hollered right out to your papa, "Yes, and if I'm here when he does come back, Mr. Gant, I'll help you to do it," he says; says, "you did exactly the right thing," says, "the only pity is you didn't kill him now."

When your papa came home and told me about it, I said, "Yes, and he was *exactly right!* You should have finished the job then and there. That's exactly what you should have done. It would have been good riddance," I said, you know, I reckon I was pretty bitter, to think of it—here we were with six childern to support and to think that he would go flingin' his money away on that miserable old toper: I could 'a' wrung his neck for being such a fool. "Now, you looka-here," I said. "Let this be a lesson to you: don't you ever let him have a penny again, and don't you go lendin' money out to any one without consultin' me first. You're a married man with a family of little childern to support, and your first duty is to them." Well, he promised, of course— he said he'd never do such a thing again, and I suppose I believed him.

Well, sir, it wasn't three days before he went off on a big spree, he came home roaring drunk, I remember they sent word to us from Ambrose Radiker's saloon that he was up there and that we'd better come and get him: of course, they said they couldn't do anything with him and they thought they'd better let us know. So I went myself. *Oh!* Lord! . . . Why, child! you never knew him till later when he was getting old and tired—I reckon you thought he was bad enough then, but child! child! You don't know, you don't know. You never *saw* him! . . . that nigger of Radiker's told me. . . . You know, that big old pock-marked yellow nigger that they had—*told me* that he could drink more licker than any *four* men he ever saw. . . . He *told me,* mind you, that he'd seen him stand right up at the bar and drink two quart bottles of that old rye licker without stoppin'. "Yes," I said to Ambrose Radiker, "and *you let him! You,*" I said, you know I looked him right in the eye when I said it and he looked pretty sheepish, I tell you he did! "Here you are," I said, "a man with a wife and childern of your own, and you've got no more pride nor honor than to take money out of the pocket of a man who needs it to support his family. Why, they ought to tar and feather a man like you and ride him out of town on a rail," I said. I reckon I was pretty bitter but that's just exactly the way I talked to him.

Well. . . . I reckon it stung him. He didn't say anything for a minute, but, I tell you what, his face was a study. . . . Oh! that mortified look, you know, looked as if he'd 'a' been glad if the earth had opened and swallered him up at that moment. Then, of course, he said: "Why, Eliza! *We* don't want his money! We don't need it that bad. Why, your good will would be worth more to me than that," he says. "There are plenty of people who will come in here and drink and behave themselves," he said. "You know we don't try to lure him on to get him to come in here. Why," he said, "I'd be the happiest man alive if Mr. Gant took a solemn oath never to touch another drop of licker as long as he lived—yes and lived up to it, too. Because he's one man," he says, "that ought never to touch a drop! If he'd take one drink and then go on," he said, "why, he'd be all right, but one drink's no more use to him than a drop in the eye," he says, that's just the way he put it, "he's got to drink up half a bottle before he even feels it and then," he says, oh, shaking his head, "I tell you what, he is a caution. It's just a problem to know what to do with him. You never know what he's going to do next," he says; says, "we've had some terrible times with him.

"Ah, you don't know," he says. "He can get the queerest notions in his head of any man I ever saw," he said, "you never know what's comin' next. Why, one night," he said, "he began to holler and rave about Lydia. Why," Ambrose says, "he swore that she'd come back from the grave to haunt him because of the life he'd led. 'There she is,' he hollers, 'there! . . . there! . . . Don't you see her?'—he kept a-pointin' round the room and then he said she was looking at him over my shoulder. 'Why, no,' I says, 'there's no one there, Will, you're just imaginin' all that.' 'Yes, she is,' he says, 'and damn you you're trying to shield her. Get out of the way, or I'll kill you,' he says, and with that he ups and throws a quart bottle half full of licker right at my head—why, it's a wonder," he says, "that it didn't kill me: I saw it comin' ," he says, "and ducked my head just in the nick of time but it smashed up a whole row of glasses we had settin' back behind the bar, and then," says Ambrose, "he got down on his knees and began prayin' to her and saying, 'Oh, Lydia, Lydia, say that you forgive me, baby,' and then he started talking about her eyes—'There! . . . there!' he says, 'they're glarin' at me—don't you see them?—Oh, God have mercy on me!' he hollers, 'she's come back from the grave to curse me!' It was enough to curdle your blood to hear him," Ambrose says. "Why, that nigger Dan of mine," he says, "was so scared that he lit right out of here: I didn't see hide nor hair of him for two days," he says, "you know how superstitious a nigger is," he says, "a thing like that would frighten the life out of him." "Why, of course," I says, "and let me tell you something: I'm not so sure it's nothin' but superstition, after all."

Well, he gave me a mighty funny look, I tell you what, he did, and he says, "Why, Eliza! Surely you don't think there was anything in all that?" "I wouldn't be so sure," I says. "I could tell you some mighty strange things, I could tell you of things I've seen myself," I said, "and I don't know how you're goin' to account for them unless there is, sure enough, as the saying goes, a voice beyond the grave." Well, his face was a study, I can tell you. In a moment he looked me straight in the eyes and said: *"Who* was Lydia? Did he ever know any one by that name?" "Yes," I said, "he did. That was before you knew him," I said. "Was it his other wife—the one that died?" he said. "That's who," I said. "Yes, that's exactly who it was. And he's got a lot to remember and be sorry for, too," I said. Well, I didn't say any more, I didn't tell him your papa had had two other wives, I didn't tell him that he had been married and divorced from one woman way down in the eastern part of the state before he married Lydia, of course, Lydia was the only one the folks at home knew about. I reckon I was too proud to let any one know about Maggie Efird, it was considered a disgrace in those days to have anything to do with a divorced man and as for a divorced *woman*, why, of course, she wasn't considered much better than a chippy. If I'd known about it before I married him I don't reckon I'd 'a' had anything more to do with him: I'd 'a' been too mortified at the thought of lowerin' myself in that way. But, of course, he didn't tell me! Law, no! I'd been married to him almost a year before I knew anything about it.

Of course, he told it then, he had to admit it.

Why, yes! didn't old Mrs. Mason—child! I've often thought of her, that poor old woman, to think what she went through! Here she was, of course, livin' with us about a year after we got married, just to see that he got settled once again and tryin' to restore peace in her own family: tryin' to bring John and Eller Beals together again—of course John and Lydia were her children by her first marriage, she married a man named Beals the first time, says: "Oh, Eliza, I'll help you any way I can. He'll be all right now if she just keeps away from him. If I can just keep them apart now, if I can just persuade her to go back to John and lead a decent life, I'll consider that my work in life is finished. I'll be able to die in peace," she said, oh, cryin', you know. "You don't know, you don't know," she says, "what I've lived through."

And then she told the whole story, you know, how they came to know him first, how they met him that first time down there in Sidney when he came to their house to live. Of course, he'd just come South to live: here he was workin' for John Arthur as a stonecutter, doin' all that work there on the State Penitentiary and I reckon at first he didn't have many friends; of course, he was a Yankee, and it was back in Reconstruction Days, and the feeling was still bitter.

Why, yes! Didn't he tell it himself about how bitter he was against us when he came South from Baltimore. "But my comin' was an accident," he said, "I firmly intended to go west. That was my boyhood ambition, and I'd have gone if John Arthur hadn't written me and told me to come on, that there was work to do," but, oh! he considered us nothing but a set of damned rebels and hangin' too good for us. Why! didn't they want to try Lee and Jefferson Davis as traitors—of course, his oldest brother George had been killed at Gettysburg and here he was all up in arms against us, sir—until he saw it all—and then he changed right over and cursed the government for allowin' it —why the black legislatures—there in Sidney and at that time he helped John Arthur build the penitentiary at Columbia, South Carolina—oh! some of the *blackest* niggers you ever laid your eye on, drinkin' and carousin' and squanderin' the taxpayers' money, dressed in the finest broadcloth, with big cigars in their mouth, if you please, and their feet stuck up on fine mahogany desks, the nasty stinking things—why didn't we see it all in that picture, "The Birth of the Nation" based upon Tom Dixon's book, "Yes," your papa says, "and every bit of it is true. I saw worse things than that myself." But that's the way he came, all right.

Well, he came there to their house, and they took him in, you know, as a boarder, Lydia and Old Mrs. Mason. Of course, the old woman said, she admitted it, says, "Well, we were glad to have him. We were livin' there all alone," she said, "and we needed a man around the house. We felt safer havin' him," she said. "And I tell you what," she said, "Will was certainly a good man to have about the house. I've never known his equal," she said. Well, of course, I had to admit it: you've got to give the devil his due—with all his wanderin' and goin' away, he was as good a family man as ever lived. Now, boy, I want to tell you: he could do anything about a house, he could repair and fix anything, he could make anything with his hands, and let me tell you, sir; when you went downstairs in the morning you always found a good fire burning in the range; now, you didn't have to *wait*, you didn't have to go pokin' around to get a fire. Now he liked to *eat*, and he always had a hot stove waitin' for you. Why, Lord! as I said to him, "The way you make a fire, no wonder. Why any one could make a fire the way you do," I said, "pourin' half a can of kerosene oil on it every time. Why, mercy, man!" I cried, "you'll burn us all up some day, as sure as you're born!"—child! child! that awful waste! that awful extravagance! Oh, roaring up the chimmey till the whole house shook with it, you know.

Now, boy, here's another thing: we've got to be fair, we've got to be just, and he wasn't *all the way* to blame! It wasn't *all* his fault: of course, the old woman admitted it, I said to her: "But Mrs. Mason, see here! You *must* have known something about him before he came to your house to live. Now, he'd been livin' right there in the same town with you, and surely you must have heard about him and Maggie Efird before he came to your house. Now, livin' in a little town like that, I don't see how it could have been otherwise. *You must have known!*" Well, she had to admit it then, said: "Yes, we knew about it." Said, "Of course, the story was he had to marry her, her father and brothers made him, and I reckon he hated her for it ever after. I guess that's why they got the divorce," she said.

I looked her straight in the eye: "Now," I said, "knowing that, you let me marry him, *a divorced man*, without sayin' a word! Now, why didn't you tell me about it?" I said—of course, she'd never said a word about it, if I'd waited for *her* to tell me I would never have found out. Here it was, you know, months after we got married, and it all came to light by accident. I was cleanin' out the bottom drawer of that old walnut bureau, lookin' for a place to put his shirts, and there it was—a stack of old letters and papers, you know, that he'd put away there, I reckon meaning to destroy them. Well, I picked them up, I didn't intend to look at them, I was goin' to put them in the stove and burn them up. "Now, he's left them there," I said, "intendin' to destroy them," but I had a premonition—I don't know what else you'd call it— it flashed over me all of a sudden, I reckon some providence left them there for me to read, here it was, the final papers of his divorce from Maggie Efird, and I could see it, I could read it! There it was! a-starin' me in the face.

Well, I waited for him to come home you know, I had them in my hand, said: "Here are some old letters I came across cleanin' out your bureau drawer today. Do you want them?" I didn't let on, you know, I just looked at him as innocent as you please. Well, his face was a study, I tell you what, it was. "Give me those papers," he said, and made a snatch for them. "Did you read them?" he said. I didn't say a word, I just looked at him. "Well," he said, and his face had a mighty sheepish look, I tell you what, it did, "I intended to tell you about it, but I was afraid you might not understand."

"Understand," I said, "why what is there to understand? It's all written down there as plain as the nose on your face: you are *a divorced man* and you never told me a thing about it. You let me marry you believin' you were a widower, that Lydia

[96]

was the only woman you were ever married to. I understand *that* much all right!"

"Well," he said, "that first marriage was a great mistake. I was led into it against my better judgment," he said. "I didn't want to worry you by tellin' you about it," he said. "Now," I said, "I'm going to ask you: I want to know. What was the trouble? Why were you divorced?" "Why," he said, "the decree was granted on grounds of incompatibility. She refused to live with me as my wife. She was in love with another man," he said, "and married me just to spite him. But from the moment we were married she never had anything to do with me. We never lived together for a moment as man and wife." "*Who* got the divorce," I said, "you or her?" He spoke right up quick as a flash, "I did," he said. "The decree was granted in my favor."

Well, I didn't let-on, I didn't say a word, but I knew, I *knew,* that he was lying. I had read that paper from beginning to end and the divorce had been given to *her.* Maggie Efird got the divorce, all right: I saw *that* much with my own eyes! But I didn't say anything, I just let him go on, "And you mean to say that she never lived with you as your wife?" I said.

"Not for a minute," he said, "I swear it."

Well, it was too much; that story was too fishy—here they told it on her, you know, old Mrs. Mason told me, that she was a good-lookin' girl, a high-stepper with lots of beaux before she married him, and, of course, they said that was the trouble—he *had* to marry her. I looked at him, you know, and shook my head: "No, sir," I said, "I don't believe you. There's something mighty queer about this somewhere. That story just won't wash. Now, you can't tell me that you lived with that woman eighteen months and never had anything to do with her. Now, I know *you*," I said —you know I looked him straight in the eye—"I know *you,* and I know you couldn't have kept away from her. You'd 'a' got at her somehow," I said, "if you had to bore a hole through the wall!" Well, it was too much for him; he couldn't face me, he had to look away, you know, with a sort of sheepish grin.

"Well, now," I said, "what are you going to do with these old papers? Now, surely you don't want them any more," I said. "They're no use to you that I can see." "No," he said, "I hate the sight of them. They're a curse and a care and I never want to look at them again. I'm going to burn them up."

"Yes," I said, "that's what I think, all they do is bring up memories you ought to try to forget. You ought to destroy them."

"That's what I'll do," he said. "By God, I will!"

"But still" (I said)—as I was goin' on to say, you know, I said to the old woman, Mrs. Mason—"but still, you must have known all about him when he came there to your house to live. Now, Mrs. Mason, you must have known he'd been married to Maggie Efird and divorced from her. Surely, you must have known that," I said.

"Well, yes," she said, "I guess we did"—admitted it, you know.

"Well, now, I'm going to tell you how it was," she said—and then, of course, she told the story: it all came out. Now, boy, I want to tell you: I want to show you that it wasn't *all* your daddy's fault.

Now, I'm not sayin' a word against Lydia—of course, I knew *her* before I did *him*, when they first came there to live and she opened up a little millinery shop there on that corner of Academy street where the Greenwood Hotel now stands. I reckon the first real "store" hat I ever owned I bought from her out of my savin's as a school-teacher that time I taught all winter way back there in Yancey county. I got paid twenty dollars a month and my board and room and let me tell you something: I considered myself *rich*. Why, Lord, yes! didn't I save up enough out of it to make the first payment on the first piece of property I ever owned, that corner lot there on the south side of the square where your daddy built his shop after we got married, that's exactly where it was, sir, why, yes, wasn't I only twenty-two years old at that time I bought it, and Lord! I thought I'd done something *big*, you know! Here I was a property-owner and a taxpayer like Cap'n Bob Patton and old General Alexander, and all the rest of 'em (child, child! we were so poor, we'd gone through so much hardship since the war that I reckon that's what led me on, I reckon that's what got me into it: I was determined to own something of my own); why, yes: don't I remember how I ran all the way to town the day I got my first tax-statement, $1.83, that's all in the world it was then, and the money just a-burning a hole in my pocket! Lord! what a goose I must have been! afraid they'd try to take it away from me and sell me out under the sheriff's hammer before I got there.

Well, then, as I say, I got to know Lydia before I got to know your daddy. Here she was, you know, runnin' this little millinery store there on that northeast corner, and, as I say, the first "store" hat I ever owned I got from her. That's where it was, all right. Now, boy, I'm not saying a word against Lydia: for all I know she was a good, honest, hard-working woman and till she met your daddy she was all right. Of course, she was more than ten years older than he was, and that's exactly what the trouble was, that's where the shoe pinched, all right, that was the rub. Now your daddy was not *all the way* to blame: when he came there to their house to live he was only a young man in his early twenties and Lydia was thirty-six years old. Now, if it had been some young girl he led astray you could blame him more, but you can say what you please, Lydia was old enough to know better. Of course, he was a strong fine-lookin' man and all the women were right out after him, but she should have known, a woman that age should have had too much pride and self-respect—why I'd 'a' died before I did a thing like that!—to have follered and thrown herself at him the way *she* did! Why, of course! Didn't old Mrs. Mason admit it? Didn't she *tell* me? "Oh, Lydia!" she said, "Lydia!" shakin' her head, you know. "She went clean out of her head about him."

Here she'd been a decent respectable woman all her life, runnin' a little millinery shop down there, you know, and well thought of by every one in town—and, of course, I reckon, considered sort of an old maid, and to think she'd go and behave herself like that. "Oh, it was awful," the old woman said; says, "She never gave him a moment's peace, she kept after him all the time," and, of course, that's just what happened. You know your daddy; as the sayin' goes, he didn't stop to say his prayers when there was a woman around. It was the same old story: within a year's time he'd gone and got himself all mixed up again, that woman was goin' to have a child and sayin' he'd ruined her and would have to marry her.

Well, he didn't know what to do. Told me himself, you know, admitted it, said: "I didn't want to marry her. I wasn't in love with her," he said. Well, he studied it all over and at last he decided to send her to Washington to see a doctor. So he wrote to Gil: of course Gil and your Aunt Mary were livin' there at the time—that was before Gil had follered him down South. Gil was workin' there in Washington as a plasterer, and they were brothers and he knew he could depend on him.

She went, he sent her, and I don't know just what happened, Gil never said and I didn't like to ask, but I guess it came before its time: they were riding in the day coach of a train comin' South again, some little town down there in the eastern part of the State, the conductor stopped the train and helped Gil carry her out into the station, and the next day she got up again and went on home. Now, give her her due, that woman had lots of grit: I reckon that's the way it was, all right.

Well, of course, the whole thing got found out. The story got known and your daddy had to marry her. And, I reckon, the feeling against him in the town was pretty bitter: here he was, you see, a Yankee, as the sayin' went, a damn Yankee, who'd come down there and ruined *two* of their women; of course, if there'd only been *one* it might have been different, but I reckon *two* of them was more than they could stomach. It got too hot for him; he had to leave. That was the time he decided to come to Altamont: of course Lydia had consumption and he thought the mountain air might do her good and I reckon he was afraid he had it, too—he'd been livin' with her and I guess he thought he had contracted it from her. When I first saw him he looked like a dead man, oh! as thin as a rail and that saller complexion, you know, from all the trouble and the worry he'd been through, I reckon. Well, then, Lydia sold out her stock—what little that she had—and closed her shop, and he sent her on ahead with old Mrs. Mason. Your daddy stayed behind down there a little bit, tryin' to close out what stock he had left in his marble yard, and to get what money he could, and then he came on, too, and that's how I came to know them first: when she was running that millinery shop on the corner there and he'd set up business in an old shack on the east side of the square. That's when it was, all right.

Now, boy, I was going on to tell you about that woman, Eller Beals. Up to this time, mind you, up to the time he moved up there from Sidney, she'd never had a thing to do with him. Of course, she had known him down there—she was the wife, you know, of Lydia's brother, John—but Law! they were too *fine,* you know, too *fine,* to have anything to do with your daddy, a common stone cutter who'd gone and disgraced the family like he had. Oh, they stormed and carried on about it, you know, when he got Lydia into this trouble. They wouldn't speak to him or have anything to do with him: he told me they hated the sight of him and that he hated them. And here within six months she had no more pride than to foller them all up there. Of course, she came because she had to come, I reckon: this John Beals was a shiftless good-for-nothin' sort of feller, and he couldn't support her, so she wrote Lydia and old Mrs. Mason and they told her to come on. Your daddy didn't know she was coming: they were afraid to tell him, and they thought they'd let her come and win him over afterwards. And that's just what happened: he came home one day to dinner and there she was—oh! the fine lady, if you please, all primped and powdered up and dressed to kill—that was the first he knew about it. Well, I guess it brought back bitter memories: he hated her so much he wouldn't speak to her, he picked up his hat and started to leave the house again, but she came up to him—oh, with her fine bonnet and the Langtry bang, and all: that was the way she fixed her hair, and put her arms around him, saying in that sugary voice:

"Aren't you going to kiss me, Will?"—Oh! (as I said later) to think of it! the villain! he should have wrung her neck for her then and there, it'd been a good riddance! Says, "Can't we be friends, Will?"—after the way she'd acted, if you please—honeying up to him and takin' him in right there before his own wife and his wife's mother. "Can't we let bygones be bygones?" she says, getting him to kiss her, and all—"Why it served you right," I said, "for being such a fool! A man with no better sense than that deserves anything that happens to him!" And he agreed, admitted it, you know: "You're right," he said. So that's the way she came to be there with him.

This Eller Beals was a little dark black-and-white sort of a woman: she had this white skin, and hair as black as a raven's and coal-black eyes. She had this easy sugary sleepy way of talkin', all soft and drawly—like she'd just waked up out of a good long sleep. I could a-told him the first time I laid eyes on her that she was no good: she was a bad egg if ever I saw one, a charmer out to get the men and lead them on, you know, and bleed them out of everything they owned. Of course, she was a good-looking woman, there's no denying that, she had a good figger and this creamy-white complexion without a blemish on it. "Why, yes," I said to him later when he'd begin to brag about how pretty she was to look at. "Why, yes, I reckon so, that's true, but then," I said, "a whole lot of us could be pretty if we never lifted a finger to do a lick of work. Some of the rest of us could look real nice," I said, "if we didn't have to cook and wash and bring up chil- dern." Well, he admitted it then, of course, said, "Yes, you're right."

And, here, to think of it! this villain misbehaving herself with him right under his wife's nose, sitting there primping herself and fixin' herself up pretty to entice him day after day, just livin' for him to come home and Lydia dying in that room upstairs, cough- ing her lungs out with every breath she took, and knowing about it all. Why, didn't he admit it! didn't he tell himself how Lydia said to him—of course, the poor thing knew that she was dying, says, "Will, I'm sick. I know I'm no good for you any more. I know

I haven't got long to live and, Will," she said, "you can go where
you like. You can do as you please," says, "I don't care, I'm dying,
but Will," and then he told it how she looked him in the eye,
"there's one thing I can't stand. In my *own* house! My *own*
house!" Says, "Will, *you've got to leave my brother's wife alone!*"
—Oh! he told it, admitted it, you know, says: "Ah, Lord! It's a
crime upon my soul. I reckon if there's a just God in heaven I'll
be punished for it."—And that poor old woman doing all the
work, cooking and drudging for them all, with this little powdered-
up trollop, that's all in the world she was, laying up waitin' for
him and never liftin' a hand to help, why, they should have tarred
and feathered her.

Well, as I say, when Lydia died, Eller kept right on livin'
there: she wouldn't budge. And, of course, by that time he had
lost his head about her, he was infatuated, you know, and he
wanted her to stay. And that was the time John Beals came up
to visit her, and I reckon he sized the situation up, he saw the
way things were, and I suppose it went against the grain, it was
a little more than he could stomach. Now, I always considered
him a pretty poor sort of man: a man who would wink at a thing
like that and let his wife run wild—but, give him his due, I
reckon he had some spunk left in him, after all: he was out of
work but he went down to Johnson City, Tennessee, and got him
a job there as a hotel clerk. And then he wrote back for her,
telling her to come on.

Well, she wouldn't go. She wrote him and told him she
didn't love him and would never live with him again, said she
was going to stay right where she was. Oh! she had it all fixed up
in her mind, sir, she was going to get a divorce and marry your
daddy—and him agreeing to it, if you please, like a moonstruck
fool, just a-lavishin' gifts and money on her, with that poor old
woman working like a nigger and weepin' and beggin' her to go
on back to her husband where she belonged. But you couldn't
reason with her, you couldn't budge her, oh! crazy in love with
him, mind you, determined to have him.

Well, sir, John Beals wrote to her again, and this time he meant business, he'd reached the end of the rope. "Now you can make up your mind in a hurry what you're going to do," he said, "for I'm not going to put up with you any longer. You can decide now whether you're coming by yourself or whether I'm going to have to come and take you, but I want you to understand right now that if I have to come and take you from him, I'll come prepared, and I'm going to leave a damned dead Yankee behind me in the house when I do."

Well, she didn't answer him, and let me tell you, sir, he *came*: he got on a train and came to get her. And oh! old Mrs. Mason said when she told me about it, shakin' and tremblin', you know. "Oh, I tell you, Eliza, it was awful. Here she'd locked herself in upstairs and wouldn't move, and here was John with a loaded pistol in his pocket, walkin' up and down the dining-room floor and saying, 'If she's not ready to go in half an hour I'll blow his brains out if it's the last thing I ever do,' and Will, pale as a ghost," the old woman said, "walkin' back and forth across the front porch, wringin' his hands, and her up there refusin' to go with John."

Well, they persuaded her somehow: I reckon she saw she'd have to go or there'd be bloodshed, and so she went along with him to Tennessee—but child! child! she hated it, she didn't want to go, she was bitter about it, she cursed them all. Well, that's the way it was, all right, before I married him.

And then, after we were married she kept on writing to him: the letters kept a-coming to him until finally I considered it my duty to write John Beals and inform him that his wife was misconductin' herself by writing letters to a married man, and that it was his business as her husband to stop her. Well, then, the letter came: she wrote him, you know, and I've never seen the like of it. She told him that I had written to her husband, she cursed him with every name she could think of, and she said: "If I had known you were going to marry her I'd have told her all I know about you, and you can be certain, no woman would have you if I told her all I know. Now she can have you and welcome to you; for no matter how much I may have hated her, her punishment will be greater than anything I ever wished for her."

Well, he brought it home and flung it in my face: "There you are, damn you," he said. "That's your work. Now, I want to tell you that you're setting in her place here at my table because she left me, for you can rest assured if she had never gone, you would not be here—and I want you always to remember it!"

Child! Child—I reckon I was young and proud, and it made me bitter to hear him talk that way. I got up and went out onto the porch and I wanted to go out and leave him then and there, but I was carrying my first baby around inside me, and it had rained and I could smell the flowers, the roses, and the lilies, and the honeysuckle vines, and all of the grapes a-gettin' ripe, and it was growing dark, and I could hear the people talking on their porches, and I had nowhere to go, I could not leave him, and "Lord God!" I said. "What shall I do? What shall I do?"

Well, then, of course, as I was tellin' you, he'd go up there to Ambrose Radiker's saloon, and he'd get to drinkin' and Ambrose told it on him how he'd imagine he was seeing Lydia again, and how she'd come back from the grave to haunt him. "Yes," I said, "and maybe he's not far wrong about it."

"And then," says Ambrose, "that's not all, that's not the only thing. He came in here one time and accused Dan here of being a Chinaman,"—of course, you remember that big yellow nigger Dan with all those small-pox splotches, and, of course, I reckon your daddy in his drunken way just took the notion into his head that Dan was a Chinaman. "Why, yes," says Ambrose, "he accused Dan of being a Chinaman and said he'd been sent here by somebody or other to kill him, and all such stuff as that. 'Damn you!' he says, 'I know what you're here for and I'll make an end of us both right now: God damn you!' he says, that's just the way he talked, you know, 'I'll cut your heart out,' he says, oh, laughin'," says Ambrose, "in a crazy blood-curdlin' manner, and then," he says, "he grabbed up a carving knife off the lunch counter and started round the bar to get the nigger. Why, it was awful!" he says. "It almost scared the poor darkey to death," he says; says, "Dan hadn't done anything to him," he says, "you *know*, Dan never done no harm to any one. Well, we had to do something, so we got the knife away from him, and then," he says, "I tried to reason with him. 'Why, Will,' I said, 'what have you got against Dan? Dan never did no harm to you,' I said.

"So he says, 'He's a Chinaman and I hate the sight of him'—oh, you know, he was crazy, you couldn't reason with him at all. 'Why, no, he's not,' I said. 'Now, Will, you know better than that,' I said. 'You've been comin' in here for years,' I said, 'and you know Dan, and you certainly know by now that he's no Chinaman,' I said.

" 'Why, no, sah, Mistah Gant,' says Dan, you know nigger-like, he wanted to have *his* say, 'why you know me,' he says, 'and you know I ain't no Chinaman.'

" 'Yes, he is,' he says, 'and by God I'm going to kill him.'

" 'Why, Will,' I says, 'he's not any Chinaman, and besides,' I said, 'even if he was, that wouldn't be any reason for you wanting to kill him. Now, just use your reason a little about this,' I said. 'A Chinaman's a man like any one else,' I said. 'There's one thing sure, they were put here for some purpose,' I said, 'like every one else, or they wouldn't be here. Now it wouldn't be right to go and kill a man that never did you any harm,' I said, 'just because you think he's a Chinaman, would it?'

" 'Yes, by God,' he said, 'for they're a set of fiends out of hell, they have drunk my heart's blood and now they sit there gloatin' upon my death-rattle,' he said.

"And that's not the *only* time either," said Ambrose Radiker, "that he's been that way." "What!" I said—of course, you know, I didn't let on to Ambrose I knew anything about it at all—"do you mean he's carried on that way before?" "Many's the time," he said, "I tell you what, it's a mighty peculiar thing: there's something mighty strange about it somewheres," he says. "He's got some grievance against Chinamen, at some time or other he's had trouble with them."

"No," I said, "you're wrong." I looked him straight in the eye. "Not in *this* life," I said. "Why, what do you mean?" he says, and, let me tell you, he gave me a mighty queer look.

"I can't say no more," I said, "but there are things you don't understand," I said. "Have *you* heard him talk like that?" he said.

"Yes," I said. But I wouldn't tell him any more.

I could have told him, but I got to studying it all over and "I thought I'd better not," I told your papa; says, "No, I'm glad you didn't: you did right. I'm glad you said no more." "But what is it, man? What's the reason for it?"—I tried to reason with him about it—child, child, he always had it, that awful hatred, that bitterness—"now see here, Mr. Gant, surely you must have some reason that you should feel that way against them. People don't feel that way without some cause: did one of them ever do you an injury? Did you ever know one of them?" He shook his head, says, "No. I never knew one in my life, but I've always hated the sight of them since the first time I ever saw one in my boy-hood days in the streets of Baltimore. The first thing that I saw when I came out of the ferry house at San Francisco was a Chinaman—that awful yellow skin," he said, "and I hated the place from that time on! But I don't know what the reason is— by God, I don't! It's a pretty strange thing when you come to think of it—unless," he said, and he looked at me, "I may have known them, as the saying goes, in some former life, some different reincarnation." I looked him straight in the eye: *"Yes,"* I said, "that's what I think it was, you've hit the nail on the head, all right. That's exactly what it was, it never came out of *this* world," and he looked at me, and let me tell you, sir, his face was a study.

And yes! why long years after that, you know, at the time of that Boxer Rebellion, didn't he come home one day all excited with the news! "It's come at last," he said, "as I predicted long ago: the pitcher went to the well once too often. They've declared war on China, and I'm going to enlist, by God, I will!" Oh! all up in arms against them, sir, and wantin' to leave everything, his family and business, to go out there and fight them. "No, sir, you will not!" I said. "You're a married man with a family of little childern to support and you're not going. If they need troops you let the others volunteer: your place is here. Besides," I said, "they wouldn't take you noway: they wouldn't have you, you're too old. They want the young men."

Well, I reckon it stung him, callin' him an old man like that: he flared right up, says, "I'm a better man than nine-tenths of them this minute, for we are livin' in a degenerate age, and if you think I'm not the equal of these nonentities an' nincompoops you see hangin' around the poolrooms with a cigarette stuck out of the corner of their mouths, the miserable degenerates that they are, then God help you, woman, for the truth is not in you and you are like the bird that fouls its own nest!" Says, "I can do more work right now than any four of them!"

Well, when he put it that way I had to admit he was tellin' the truth: of course, your papa was an awful strong man. Why, Lord! haven't I heard them tell it on him how they'd go back there in his shop and find him liftin' up one end of an eight hundred pound stone like it was nothin' with two big black niggers sweatin' and strainin' at the other end of it that they could hardly budge, and "Yes," I said to Wade Eliot that first time that we took him up to Hopkins, "I'll give you *my* theory now. I'll tell you what *my* diagnosis is,"—and then, of course I told him, "now my opinion is he helped to bring this trouble on by just such things as that,"—("Why, what on earth do you mean, Mr. Gant, by doin' such a thing! You're apt to strain and rupture yourself first thing you know: let the niggers do that kind of work, that's what you're paying them for." "Why, Lord!" he said, "you know I couldn't do a thing like that: if I depended on those niggers I'd never get anything done!") "But that was it, all right," I said to Doctor Eliot. "He was hastenin' his own end by just such stuff as that." "Yes," he said, "I agree with you, I think you're right. That's it exactly," he said—"But *you*," I said, "you have your family to consider, and *you're not goin'*." I put my foot right down, you know, and then, of course, he admitted I was right, he gave in, but *oh!*—child, child, you don't know what it was like—California, China, anywheres! He'd have been up and gone if I'd a-let him: a strange man.

Lord God! I never saw a man like that for wanderin'. I'll vow! a rollin' stone, a wanderer—that's all he'd a-been, oh! California, China, anywheres—forever wantin' to be up and gone, who'd never have accumulated a stick of property if I hadn't married him. Here Truman wrote to him that time from California, this same Perfesser Truman, why, yes! the father-in-law of these two murderers I'm telling you about (and how that night I got the warning, boy: "Two . . . Two—and Twenty . . . Twenty"), Ed Mears and Lawrence Wayne, who married sisters, Truman's daughters, why, yes!—but *oh!* the scholar and the gentleman, you know, no murderer to *him,* I can assure you—oh! too *fine,* too *fine,* oh! too *honorable,* you know: he wouldn't soil his hands with blood, always the finest broadcloth and the patent-leather shoes, wrote to him of course, to come on out there. Says, "The Lord has rained his blessings on this country with a prodigal hand,"—oh, the cultured gentleman with all that beautiful English and the flowery command of language, and all—says, "Come on out. This is the Wonderland of Nature, there's riches and abundance here beyond the dreams of avarice, and as yet," he says, "it's hardly been touched. If you come out now you'll be a rich man in fifteen years,"—he says—urgin' him to come, you know, says, "Sell out now. Sell everything you got and come on out." "Hm!" I says, "he's mighty anxious to get you out there, isn't he?" "Yes," says your daddy, "a new country and by God I'll do it." Then, worried-like, "What do you mean?" he says.

I didn't tell him: I just looked at him, I didn't speak. I just said, "Says come on out? And what about your wife and childern? What's to become of them?" I said. Says, "Oh, that part's all right," your papa said. "Says bring them with you, 'Sell out at once, bring Eliza and the childern with you,' your papa said. "That's what he said, all right." "I *thought* so! That's what I *thought*," I said. "What do you mean?" he said. I looked at him. I didn't tell him.

I could have told him but I didn't want to worry him. Child! I didn't tell him but I *knew*, I *knew*—that man—now boy, I want to tell you—"I've come to say good-bye," he says—and let me tell you, boy, his face was a study—why! "Oh, we're sorry to see you go!" I said, "we'll miss you." "Yes," he said, and he looked me straight in the eye—oh! that *look*, you know, "and I'll miss *you!*" He looked straight at me when he said it. "Well, now," I said, you know I thought I'd turn it off, "we'll miss you too, both Mr. Gant and I—we'll both miss you. Now," I said, you know I thought I'd jolly him along to cheer him up, "when you get out there, I hope you won't forget us. I hope you'll write us. Why, yes," I said, "if it's the wonderful place they say it is, if you can pick gold up right off the streets *I'd* like to know about it, too," I said. "Why, yes, if that's the sort of place it is, I'd like to live there too—we might pack right up and come on out," I said. "Well, now," he said, "I wish you would, there's nothin' I'd like better," and I could see, child, I could tell—why, yes! now—long years after when your papa made that trip out there. (Now, boy, that was a wild goose chase—what did he do *that* for? Why did he go out there? Why did he waste that money?) "Oh," I said, "did you see Perfesser Truman?" the first question that I asked him, you know. "Yes," he says, "I saw him," and his face was a study, I can tell you. "Well, how is he? what's he doin'?" Of course I wanted to find out, you know. I wanted to hear the news. "Say," your papa says, "what about it?" and his face was a study. "You know he did nothin' but talk about you all the time I was there. Why," he says, "I believe the damned old fool was in love with you, by God I do." Well, I didn't say anything, I didn't want to worry him, but child, I had seen it in his eyes and I *knew*, I *knew!*

I'll vow! I never saw such a man for wantin' to wander around. Pshaw! I reckon maybe old Amanda Stevens was right about them. That's what she said, you know; of course, they told it on her when all her sons went off to the Civil War—she had eight, and every last one of them went to war, sir! And, of course, all of the people were comin' around to congratulate her for sendin' them, sayin' how proud she must be, and so on. "Send nothing!" she said. "They all lit out of here in the middle of the night without sayin' a word to me about it. If I had my way I'd bring every last one of them back here where they belong, helpin' me to run this place!" "Yes," they said, "but aren't you proud of them?" they said. "Proud?" she says, "why, Lord God"—of course, you know, Amanda had an awful rough way of talkin'—"what's there to be proud of? They're all alike! I never saw a man yet that could stay where he was five minutes. Why!" she says, "all of them act as if their tails were full of turpentine," she said. Of course she was bitter to think they should all light out that way to leave her alone to run the farm without tellin' her about it.

But, I tell you what, that was *certainly* a remarkable woman; lived to be eighty-seven and hale and hearty, sir, right up to the end. Yes! and would go anywheres, you know, in the dead of winter to help out any one that was sick, and all! Of course, they told it on her at the time—whew-w! what about it?—I remember sayin', "Oh, surely she didn't say a thing like that! you must be mistaken," I said—to think that a woman would talk that way to her own daughter—"if that don't beat all!" I said: why, they told it, you know, how her daughter Clarissy that married John Burgin, this same John Burgin I've been tellin' you about all along, boy, your own distant cousin on my mother's side of the house that Ed Mears killed, as I said to your papa at the time when he came home that day tellin' me what Melvin Porter had said, I said to him: "Let them hang! they killed that man in cold-blood," I said, "a good upright man with a family of little childern that never did any harm to any one," I said, "as wicked and cold-blooded a murder as I ever heard of, and hangin's too good for them," I said. Why, they told it of course how Clarissy's first baby came seven months after she was married. Well, it was all right, of course, nobody was blamin' the girl, it never entered their minds that she had done anything wrong, but she began to scream and holler like she'd lost her mind.

"Well," the doctor says, "the baby's all right, there's nothing wrong with the baby, but if something isn't done to stop that girl from cryin' this child won't have any mother before long."

"Well, I'll stop her," Amanda says, "or know the reason why," so she marches right into the bedroom and sits right down beside the girl: "Now you look a-here," she said, "there's nothing wrong with you and I'm not going to put up with your foolishness any longer." "Oh," the girl says, "I shall die of shame! I'll never be able to hold my head up again!"—weepin' and goin' on, you know. "Why, what's the matter?" Amanda says, "what have you done," she says, "that you should feel like that?" "Oh," the girl says, "I haven't done anything but my baby came before its time!" "Why, Lord God!" the old woman says—she came right out coarse with it, you know—"is that all that's troublin' you? I thought you had more sense than to let a thing like that bother you," she said. "Oh," the girl said, "they'll all be sayin' now that I misbehaved myself before I married John!" "Why, Lord God, let them say it, then," Amanda said, "what if they do? Tell 'em your ass is your own and you can do as you please with it!" That's exactly what she said, you know, and of course they told it on her. I know when I told your papa about it, he said, "Lord! you know she didn't say a thing like that!" But that's the story that they told.

Well, I said to him, "You're *not* going." I put my foot down, you know, and when he saw I meant it, he had to give in, of course. But as I say he always had it in him, that desire to go off somewheres, California, China—why, yes, say! what about it, as long as he lived he never got over that feeling he had against them. That time, you know, long after—why yes! you must remember, you were right there with us—no, I guess that's so. You must have been away at college. That was the year before the war ended, and we all went up there with him—Luke and Ben—I tell you what, I've often thought of it, that poor child: here we were all lookin' for Mr. Gant to die at any minute, when he had five more years to live, and *Ben—Ben* was the one! We never *thought*, we never *dreamed* that *he* would be the one, would be dead and buried in the grave within a year! And to think that your daddy would behave as he did—here he was, you know, eaten up with that awful cancer—Lord! how he ever did it! with that rotten old thing consumin' him, sending out its roots, you know, all through his blood.

Wade Eliot said to me, "I don't know what's holdin' him up," he says, "I never thought I'd see him again when he went away the last time," he says; says, "it is certainly a remarkable case," he says; says, "in all my life," he says, "I've never seen the beat of it." "Well," I says, "you must have some opinion," I says. "A great doctor like you who has operated on thousands of people must know all the signs and symptoms," I says—of course, you know, I wanted to draw him out and get him to tell me what *his* theory was. "Now," I said, "surely you've some sort of notion about it, Doctor Eliot, and if you have," I said, "*I want to know!* His family has a right to know," I said, "and I want to *know the worst*. How much longer has he got to live?" I said. I looked him square in the eye.

Well, sir, he just threw back his head and laughed. "Live!" he says, "why, probably, till both you and I are in our graves," he said—and, let me tell you, he didn't miss it much! That man, here he was a fine-looking man in the prime of life, why he'd be the last one any one would expect to go, the doctor they called in for Woodrow Wilson, and all. . . . Said he'd saved thousands of lives, and here when his time comes he couldn't save his own! They did everything on earth they could to save him—as the sayin' goes, I reckon they exhausted all the resources of medical science but to no avail!—was dead and in his grave, sir, within two years after your papa died. I remember sayin' to McGuire when I read the news, "Well, it only goes to show," I said, "that when your time comes there is nothing that can save you. . . . I don't know what you'd call it," I said, "but there is some higher power, as sure as you're born, and when it calls us," I said, "we've got to go, doctors and all." "Yes," he said, "you are exactly right. There's something there," he said, "that we know nothing of"—

and here he had only a year longer to live himself, drinkin' himself to death, you know, just grievin' over the way that woman had acted. Of course, that nigger at the hospital told Luke he'd come in there late at night so drunk he'd have to get down on all-fours an' crawl upstairs like some big old bear when he had to operate the first thing in the morning, said he'd get him to put him in a tub of cold water with chunks of ice in it, said he'd seen him that way many a time and put him to bed.

"Well," says Eliot, "I don't pretend to know anything about it any more. I don't know what is keepin' him alive," he says, "but there he is, and I don't want to make any more predictions. He's not a man," he says, "he's four men, and right now," he says, "he's got more real vitality than the rest of us put together" —and of course, it was true: right up to the end he could eat a meal that would put most people in the grave, two dozen raw oysters, a whole fried chicken, an apple pie, and two or three pots of coffee, sir. Why I've seen him do it time and again! with all sorts of vegetables, corn on the cob and sweet pertaters, string beans and spinach and all such as that. Of course, Eliot was honest about it: he came right out and admitted he couldn't say. "Now here," he said, "I want you to look after him until he enters the hospital. I want him to be ready for us when he comes in here," he said, "and you see to it that he behaves himself." "Well," I said, "I think he is going to be all right. He has promised, you know, and of course we are all going to do our best. Now," I said, "what can he eat? Do we have to put him on a diet? Can he have some oysters?" I said. Well, he laughed, you know, says, "Look here, I'd call that a pretty strange diet to put a sick man on." "Well," I said, "you know he's been lookin' forward to it. He's always loved oysters," I said, "he's always remembered how he could eat them by the dozen on the half shell in his boyhood here. He's looked forward to it so much," I said, "that I hate to disappoint him." "Oh, all right," Wade Eliot says, laughin', you know, "let him have them then. You couldn't kill him noway," he said, "but look a-here!" he said, and he looked me square in the eye, "I'm not worryin' about what he eats so much as what he drinks. Now," he says, "you keep him sober. I don't want to have to get him over a drunk when he gets in here," he says. "You put the fear of God into him," he says, "I know you, and you can do it. Now, you tell him," he said, "that if he goes off on another big spree he'll never live to get home. Tell him I said so."

Well, I told him what Wade Eliot had said. "You can have the oysters," I said, "he said that would be all right, but he says you're not to touch a drop of anything to drink, or they may have to send you home in a box." "Why, Lord! Mrs. Gant," your papa said, "you know I wouldn't do a thing like that in my condition. If any one offered me a drink I'd throw it out the window. Why, the very sight of the stuff makes me sick at my stomach!" Well, he promised, of course, and I reckon we all believed him.

Well, sir, it wasn't twenty-four hours before he went off on a big spree and came home at two o'clock in the morning roaring drunk—I tell you what, I certainly felt sorry for that woman. Why! here we were all stayin' there just across from the hospital at Mrs. Barrett's, a good religious woman, you know, a big church-goer, and all, with her livin' to make and that grown-up daughter to support whose husband ran off with some other woman—and here he comes in the dead of night howlin' and hollerin' that it was nothing but a bawdy house that he was in and to bring on the women. Why, of course, you might know he waked the whole house up, they all got up to see what the trouble was, and she knocked at the door tremblin', in her night-gown and wringin' her hands. "Oh, Mrs. Gant," she says, "you'll have to get that man quiet or he'll ruin me," she says; "get him out of here," she says, "I've never had anything like that in *my* house before," she says, "and if it gets out I'm disgraced"—and her childern, you know, those two little boys she had, she sent them out on the roof and there they were perchin' up there like monkeys, and all of the people whisperin' together in the halls. Ben was so mortified and bitter to think he would behave himself like that. "By God," he said, "it'd serve him right if he did die. After the way he's acted I wouldn't care."

Well, I got hold of the bottle, I found a bottle of licker about a third full in one of his pockets, and pretty soon he began beggin' for a drink: "No, sir," I said. "Not another drop! Now you listen to me," I said. "You're a sick man: if you keep this up you'll never get home alive," I said. Well, he said he didn't care. "I'd as soon get it over with now," he says, "as go through all the torment and the agony." Well, he kept yelling for a drink, but we wouldn't let him have it—I took it and poured it out, anyway— and at last he got off to sleep. Then I took his clothes and locked them up in my trunk so he couldn't get out again.

We let him sleep it off. He slept right through until ten o'clock next morning and when he woke up he seemed to be all right, he wouldn't eat any breakfast, said it would make him sick, but I got him to drink some good hot coffee Mrs. Barrett brought up to him. She was certainly a kind, good-hearted Christian woman and your papa told her he was sorry for the way he had acted. Well, we tried to get him to get up and come with us then, none of us had had any breakfast, and we were going down the street to a lunchroom. "No," he said, "I don't feel like getting up, you go on: I want you to go on and get something to eat," he said.

Well, I knew he didn't have any more licker because I'd poured it out, and I knew he couldn't go out for any because his clothes were all locked up, so I thought it'd be all right if we left him alone for a little. Well, we went out and ate and we couldn't have been gone more than an hour, but when we came back he'd been drinkin' again, layin' up in the bed, you know, crazy-like, singin' a song to himself. "Why, Mama," Ben says, "I thought you told us you took his licker away from him and poured it out." "Why, I did," I said. "Well, he must have had another bottle that you didn't find," he said. "There's one thing sure, he's had plenty since we left him." "Well, now," I said, "if he's had anything to drink he's got it while we were away. It wasn't there in his room when we left," I said, "because I searched that place from top to bottom with a fine-tooth comb and you can just bet your bottom dollar there was no licker there." "Well, he's getting it from some one," Ben said, "and I'm going to find out who it is that's giving it to him. Let's ask Mrs. Barrett if any one has been here to see him." "Why, yes," I said, "that's the very thing."

So we all trooped downstairs and asked her if any one had been there for him. "No," she said, "no one has set foot in this house since you left it," she said, "I was on the look-out for just such a thing to happen," she said, "and if any one had been here I'd have known it." "Now there's something mighty strange about this somewheres," I said, "and I mean to get to the bottom of it. You childern come on," I said to Luke and Ben, "we're going to find out where this mystery is or know the reason why."

Well, when we got back upstairs to his room there he was, you know—and you could see it, you could tell it—he'd had something else to drink since we'd been downstairs. He was drunk as a lord. I marched right up to him: "Look a-here," I said, "you've been getting licker somewheres and I want to know who's been giving it to you." "Why, who-o? Me?" he says, in that drunken voice, "why, baby," he says, "you know me, I wouldn't touch a drop," he says—trying to hug and kiss me, you know, and all that. Well, we looked again, the children and I, we searched that place high and low, but it was no use—there was certainly nothing there, or we'd 'a' found it.

Well, I got to studyin' about it, and it flashed over me all of a sudden—I don't know why I'd never thought of it before—"Come on, childern," I said to the boys, winkin' at them, you know; "come on, we'll go downtown and see the sights. Mr. Gant, we'll be back in an hour or so," I said, "you be ready when we come," I said. "We're going to take you to the hospital at three o'clock."

Well, that just suited him, that was just what he wanted, he said, "Yes, go on,"—of course he wanted to be left alone so he could get more to drink. Well, we left him, we went right down the hall to my room and I took the childern in there and closed the door, easy-like, behind me. "Why, Mama," Luke says, "what are you talking about? We can't go off downtown and leave him alone like this while he's drinking. No," he says, "he's been getting it somewhere and I'm going to see to it that he gets no more if I have to sit there and watch him," he says. "No," I said, "you wait." "Why," he says, "what do you mean?" "Why, don't you see?" I said—pshaw! I was so mad to think I hadn't thought of it before, that miserable old toper Gus Tolly from Seneca, South Carolina, that used to stop at our house—here, he had the room right next to your papa and was waitin' to be admitted over at Hopkins with the same trouble your papa had, and here the two of them were layin' up together a-swillin' it down as hard as they could—"it's that rotten old Gus Tolly," I said, "who's been lettin' him have it." "Why, damn him," says Luke, "I'll go wring his neck for him," and he starts for the door. "No, you don't," I said, "you want a minute. I'll fix him."

Well, we waited, and sure enough, it wasn't five minutes before your papa's door opened easy-like and he came creeping out into the hall, and then we heard him knockin' at Gus Tolly's door. Well, we heard Gus Tolly say, "Have they gone yet?" and we waited a moment longer until we heard the door shut again, and then we started. I marched right up and knocked and in a moment Gus Tolly says, "Who's there?" "You open the door," I said, "and you'll find out." Well, he opened it, and his face had a mighty sheepish look, I tell you. "Why, Mrs. Gant," he says, "is that you? Why, I thought you'd all gone to town," he says. "Well now, didn't you get fooled that time?" I said. "Mr. Gant is in here," he says in that mealy voice, stickin' his old red nose out that was all covered with warts like a pickle, "we were just having a little talk together," he says. "Yes," I said, "and it looks to me you've been havin' something else besides. If it's only talk," I said, "I'd call it mighty strong talk that gets on people's breath and smells up the place till you can't bear to come near them." Oh! you know, awful, that old rank odor of rye licker, you could 'a' cut it with a knife. "Now," I says, "I've been talkin' all my life and it never had no such effect as that on me." "Yes," says Luke, "and I see you've got a whole bottle of that talk right there on the table before you."

Well, we marched right in on him then, and there he was, sir, sitting right up at the table, if you please, with a whole quart bottle of licker before him fixin' to pour himself out a drink. Well, I reckon if looks could kill we'd have all been dead, for he gave us one of the blackest and bitterest looks you ever saw, and then he began to curse and rave. Well, I got hold of the bottle and then he began to beg me to give him just one drink. "No, sir," I said, "you're going into that hospital, and what's more you're going *now*. We're not going to wait a minute longer." Of course, I knew that was the only way to handle him; I'd seen him too many times before, and I knew if we didn't take him he'd get licker somehow if he had to drill a tunnel to get to it. "Yes," said Luke, "you're going now if I have to drag you over there, and Ben will help me do it." "No," said Ben, "I'll just be damned if I do! I don't want to have anything more to do with him. He can do as he likes." "Well," said Luke, "if we let him stay here he'll drink himself to death." "Well, I don't give a damn if he does," said Ben, "if that's what he wants to do let him go right ahead. Maybe the rest of us would get some peace then if he did. He's always had his own way," he said, "he's never thought of any one but himself and I don't care what happens to him. I was lookin' forward to this trip," he said, "I thought we might all get a chance to enjoy ourselves a little and here he's gone and disgraced us all and ruined it for us. Now you can look after him if you like, but I'm done." Of course, the child was bitter: he'd been lookin' forward to comin', he'd saved up the money for the trip and had a nice new suit of clothes made before we left home, and here to think your papa would act this way, of course it was a bitter disappointment to us all. We *thought*, you know, we'd get him in the hospital and then have a little time to look around and see things for ourselves but *Law!* the way *he'd* been actin' it would have taken a whole regiment of men to look after him.

Well, he didn't want to go, of course, but he saw we meant business and he'd have to, so he went along back to his room with Luke and I got his clothes out, and we dressed him. Well, I began packin' away a few things I thought he'd need in the hospital, some nightshirts, and his bathrobe and slippers and so forth, and then I saw he had no clean shirts: the one he had on was filthy, I was ashamed to let him go in that, and I knew he'd need some clean ones after he'd begun to sit up again. "Why, where on earth are your shirts?" I said, "what have you done with them? I know that I put in six, you couldn't have lost 'em," I said, "where are they?" "Oh, they've got 'em, they've got 'em," he said in that maudlin tone, beginning to rave and carry on, you know, said, "Let 'em have them! Fiends that they are, they have impoverished and ruined me, they have drunk my hearts-blood, now they can take what's left." "Why, what are you talking about?" I said, "who do you mean?" "Why, Mama," Luke said, "it's those Chinamen that run that laundry down there. They've got his shirts," he said, "why I took them there myself," he said, "but *that* was a week ago," he said; said, "I thought he'd gone and got them by this time." "Well, we'll march right down there and get them now," I said, "he can't go to the hospital wearing that thing he's got on. We'd all be disgraced!"

Of course, that just suited him: he said, yes, go on, he'd be all ready when we came back—of course, he wanted to get rid of us so he could drink some more. I said, "No, sir, when we leave this house you're coming with us."

So we started out. He went on ahead with Luke, and Ben stayed behind to go with me. Of course, Ben was proud and he refused to help him. "I'll carry his valise and come along with Mama," he said, "but I won't be seen with him." "What's the matter?" Luke said, "he's your father as much as mine," he said, "you're not ashamed to be seen with him, are you?" "Yes, by God, I am!" said Ben—that was just the way he put it. "I don't want any one to think I know him," he said. "Now you needn't expect me to help you," he said, "I'm no damned nurse-maid," says, "I've done all I intend to do."

Well, then, we went on down the street to this laundry; it was down there a block or two below the hospital on the corner in a little old brick building and, of course, when we got there we could see them, these two Chinamen inside, just a-ironing away for all they were worth. "Well, this must be it," I said. "Yes, this is it, all right," said Luke, "this is the place." So, we all went in, and this Chinaman asked him, says, "What do you want?" "Why, God damn it," your papa says, "I want my shirt." "Well," the Chinaman says, "Tickee, tickee"—kept sayin' "tickee," you know. Well, of course, Mr. Gant had been drinkin' and he didn't understand him. He got excited, you know, says, "Tickee hell! I don't want any tickee. I want my shirt!" "Well, now, you wait," I said to your papa, "now don't you worry," I says, "*I'll* talk to him. If your shirts are here, I'll get them for you." Of course, I knew I could talk to the Chinaman and reason with him about it. "Now," I said to him, winkin', you know easy-like, "you tell *me* about it. What is it you want?" I says. "Why," he says, "tickee, tickee." Now, I thought to myself, the man's all right—I could see it, you know—he's tryin' to say something, he's tryin' to explain something to us with this tickee. "Now," I says, "do you mean you're not finished with them yet?" I thought, of course, he might not have them done—but no, I thought, that can't be, he's had a whole *week's* time to do them in. Surely, I thought, he's had time enough. "No," he said, "tickee, tickee," and then, of course, he began jabberin' to the other feller and then they both came and they both began to shout and holler at us in that awful outlandish tongue. "Well," your papa says, "I'll make an end of it all now, by God I will! Little did I reck," he says, "that it would come to this." "Now, Mr. Gant," I said, "you be quiet and I'll get to the bottom of this. If your shirts are here I'll get them." Well, these two China-men had been arguin' about it together and I reckon the other one had told him that we didn't understand because he got one of those slips of paper then that they used—as I said to Luke later, it looked exactly like it was covered by old hen tracks—and he pointed to it, you know, and said, "Tickee, tickee."

"Oh!" I cried—of course, I caught on then, it flashed over me all of a sudden, I don't know why I'd never thought of it before! "Why, of course!" I said, "he means *ticket,* that's what he's trying to say," "Yes," he says, beginning to smile and grin, you know, *he* understood that much all right, "tickee, tickee." "Why, yes," I said winkin' at him, "that's just it—tickee." Of course, I suppose, with your papa hollerin' and goin' on I'd got confused, and that was the reason I hadn't understood before. "Why, Mr. Gant," I said, "he says he gave you a laundry ticket and he wants to see it." "No, I haven't got any ticket," he says, "I want my shirt." "Why, surely, you've got a ticket," I said, "what have you done with it? Surely you haven't gone and lost it." "I never had one," he said, you know—drunken-like. "Why, yes, he has," Luke said, "I remember giving it to him now. What did you do with the laundry ticket I gave you?" he said, "where is it? Speak, speak!" he says, shakin' him—the child was excited and upset, you know, to think he'd go and do a thing like that. "Don't stand there mumbling like an idiot! God damn it, where's the ticket?" Well, sir, we searched his pockets, we went through everything he had, and there was no ticket to be found, it wasn't *there!* "Well, now," I said to the Chinaman, "Mr. Gant has mislaid that ticket somewheres but I tell you what you do: you just let us have his shirts anyway and as soon as I find the ticket I'll bring it to you myself"—you know, tryin' to humor him along. "Oh, *no!*" he says, he couldn't do anything like that, and he began to jabber away, I reckon tryin' to tell us he didn't know where the shirts were and couldn't let us have them noway until we brought the ticket. Well, sir, the trouble started then and there: your papa grabbed him by the neck and says, "God damn you, I'm goin' to kill you," hittin' at him over the counter, you know, says, "fiend that you are, you have impoverished and ruined me, you have hounded me to the gates of death," he said, "but I'll make an end of you now before I go," says, "I'll take you with me."

Well, Ben and Luke got hold of him and pulled him off, but the damage was done: the other feller had gone screamin' and hollerin' out the door and he came back now with a policeman. "What's the meaning of all this?" the policeman says, "what's going on here?" he says, sizin' us all up, you know. "They have robbed me," your papa says, "and now, fearful, awful and blood-thirsty fiends that they are, they stand there plottin' my destruction." Why, he'd 'a' ruined us all, if he'd gone on: Luke shook him, you know, says, "Now you be quiet or you'll land in jail. You've made trouble enough." "No, now, officer," I said to the policeman—of course, I knew I had to be diplomatic—"there's been a little misunderstanding, but everything's all right." "Why," he says, "what happened?" "We're takin' my husband here to the hospital," I said—of course, I thought I'd let him know your papa was a sick man—"and we just came by to get some shirts we left here to be laundered." "Why, what's the matter?" he says, "won't they let you have them?" "Well," I said, "it seems they gave Mr. Gant a laundry ticket and I reckon he's mislaid it. At least, we haven't been able to find it yet. But the shirts are here," I said, "they're bound to have them: my son here brought them himself a week ago."

Well, he began to eye Luke then, and I tell you what! That child certainly made a good appearance. Of course, he was all dressed up nice in his sailor clothes—you know he'd got leave of absence to come up there from Norfolk and as Mrs. Barrett said, says, "That is certainly a fine-looking boy. I tell you," she says, "it does you good to look at him—makes you feel that no harm can come to a country as long as it's got boys like that to defend it," she says.

"Why, yes, Captain," Luke says—you know, callin' him that, I reckon, to make him feel good—"it's all right. The shirts are here all right," he says, "because I brought them myself but I guess my father accidentally mislaid the ticket." "Well," the policeman says to me, "would you *know* the shirts if you saw them?" "Why, Lord!" I said, "you know I would! I'd know them in the dark, I'd be able to pick them out by the size of them. Why, you *know*," I said, lookin' him straight in the eye, "you can use your own reason," I said, "they wouldn't have another shirt in the house that would fit a man like that," I said. Well, he took one look at your papa, and then he began to laugh. "No," he said, "I reckon you're right. Well, I tell you what to do," he said, "you go around there yourself and pick 'em out," he said, "and I'll stay right here until you find them."

And that's exactly what he did. I marched right around behind the counter and that man stayed there until I found them. "Here they are!" I sang right out—way down at the bottom of a pile, you know, why I must have opened up fifty packages before I came to them and I tell you what! those two Chinamen didn't like it either, the looks that they gave us were oh! bitter, bitter. If that policeman hadn't been there to pertect us, I'll tell you what, I'd been alarmed, of course, there's no telling what people like that might do, especially with your papa ravin' and stormin' at them the way he did. I know I said to Luke later, after we'd taken him up and put him in the hospital, "I tell you what," I said, "I was glad to get out of that place. There was a look in the eyes of those men I didn't like; it made my flesh crawl!" "Yes," he said, "I felt the same way. Damned if I don't believe papa was right about them: I wouldn't trust one of them as far as I could throw an elephant," he said. "Well, child," I said, "he's had it a long time, that feelin', you know, and you may rest assured there's something there, something we can't understand," I said.

And, of course, that's just what I told Ambrose Radiker, that day in his saloon long, long ago! "It's something," he said, "sure enough—and he's a terror when he has it. I don't know what to do with him when he gets that way." "Well, I tell you what to do," I said, "don't sell him any licker when he asks for it. Now, the best way to keep out of trouble," I said, "is to avoid it." "That's right," he said. "Well, what do you want to put up with it for?" I said. "Now, surely, you've got strength of mind enough not to be forced into a thing against your better judgment. You've got more sense that that," I said. "Why, what can I do?" he. said. "Why, you can refuse him the next time he comes here after licker," I said, "that's exactly what you can do." "Why, Eliza," he said, "what good would that do? He'd only give that old Rufe Porter the money and send him in here to buy a bottle, and I'd rather see him spend his money on himself," he says, "than squander it on that old toper." "Why, you don't mean to tell me he ever did that," I said. "Yes," says Ambrose, "that's exactly what he's done, many a time. Rufe comes and buys the licker for him and they drink it up together over at the shop." "Well, that explains it then!" I said. "The cat's out of the bag at last!" Of course, I knew then—I could see—just how that villain had got him into his power, gettin' him to go his note, and all: he'd get him drunk, of course, an' then your daddy would do anything he told him to.

"*Yes!*" I said, that day he came home and told it how Mel Porter had been in to see him and was so upset because those men were going to hang. "Let them hang—and I wish that miserable old brother of his was going to be hanged with 'em." "Oh, you mustn't talk like that," he said, "I hate to hear you say such things." Of course, I was bitter against him. "Well," your papa says, "I couldn't help feeling sorry for Mel. I reckon he's been under a great strain and now he's all worried and grieved to think that all of them have got to hang." "Not a bit of it," I said, "if you swallered any such story as that you're more gullible than I am, you don't know Mel Porter as well as I do. Now you can mark my words," I said, "it's something else that's troublin' him." "No," he says, "I think you're wrong." "All right," I said, "you wait and see."

Well, he didn't have to wait long, either. That very night, sir, they made that break from jail. They got away scot-free, all five of them, and none of them was ever caught. "Ah-hah," I said to him, "what did I tell you? And you were just fool enough to think Mel Porter was worryin' about their bein' hanged, weren't you? You see, don't you?" "Well," he said, "I reckon you're right! I guess that's what was troublin' him. He knew about it!" "Knew about it! Why, of course!" I said. "That's just it!"—of course, we could see then that he'd known about it all along, he knew they were going to make the break that night, and in his heart he was dreadin' it—he was afraid something would go wrong and there'd be more bloodshed, for they were a set of desperate bloody men and they wouldn't have hesitated to kill any one who got in their way, and so, of course, the thought of it was weighin' on Mel Porter's conscience. "Well," your papa says, "it's an awful thing and I hate to think about it."

"What about it?" says Mr. Gant. "Dock Hensley came in to see me the other day and tried to give me two tickets for you and me to see it. To think of it!" he says, "here they were all boon companions six months ago, and now Dock is just waitin' for the moment when he springs the trap on them." "Why, yes," I said, "they were all thick as thieves together"—and, of course, that was true. Ed Mears and Lawrence Wayne and Dock Hensley had been bosom friends for twenty years—"and let me tell you something," I said, "I don't know that any of them are any worse than he is. Now," I said, "they're all tarred with the same brush: they are all violent men, and Dock Hensley has shed as much blood as any of them, and I reckon he knows it. The only difference," I said, "is that he has worn a badge and has always had the authority of the law to pertect him." Why, of course! didn't they tell it on him that time he was being tried for the murder of Reese McLendon—of course they freed him on grounds of self-defense and an officer in the performance of his duty, but I said at the time to your papa: "Now, you know as well as I do that that was nothing but a deliberate cold-blooded murder if ever there was one." Of course, Reese was an awfully strong man, and when he got drunk he was a holy terror—and, I guess, he'd killed plenty, too—but here he and Hensley were close friends, you know, had always got along fine together, and then they arrested him for bein' drunk and disturbin' the peace. Well, the story goes that he got to making so much noise that they had to take him out of the cell. Oh! they said you could hear him howlin' and hollerin' the whole way across the square, and they put him downstairs in what they called the dungeon; of course, it was nothing but an old cellar basement with a dirt floor that the city had used one time as a stable. Well, that was Hensley's defense: he said he went down there to see if he couldn't reason with him and do something to quiet him down, and of course, his story was that McLendon had picked up an old horseshoe that he'd found laying around down there and when he came in, he said, McLendon jumped on him and tried to brain him with the horseshoe.

So his claim was that it was either his life or McLendon's and he got the horseshoe out of his hand and gave him a lick across the forehead with it that killed him. Well, the rest of them told it when they tried him that he came back upstairs all covered with blood and said: "You'd better get a doctor for Reese. I'm afraid I've killed him." Well, of course, when the doctor got there he saw there was nothing he could do, said McLendon was dead, you know. Why, the doctor said it looked as if he'd hit him a hundred times with the thing, said the whole side of his head was bashed into jelly and he lay there welterin' in his blood. Oh, they said it was awful.

Your papa went to that trial and he came home and told about it: "I tell you what," he said, "in all my life I've never heard anything to equal Zeb Pentland's address to the jury to-day"— of course, your cousin Zeb was prosecutin' him—"It was a masterly effort," your papa says, "I wish you could have heard it." "Well," I said, "what are they going to do? Will they convict him?" "Why, Lord, no!" your papa said, "he'll go free. He'll get off on grounds of self-defense, but I tell you what," he said, "I wouldn't have been standing in his shoes today for a million dollars. You can mark my words," he said, "he'll never be able to forget what Pentland said to him as long as he lives. His face turned pale as he listened," he said, "and I reckon he'll carry it with him to his grave." Of course, it came out in the trial—Zeb Pentland proved it—how Dock Hensley had shot down and killed eighteen men since he had been an officer of the law, and your papa said he turned to the jury and told them, "You have given a policeman's badge, you have armed with the full authority and pertection of the law a man without mercy and without pity, to whom the shedding of human blood means no more than the killing of a fly, you have given him a loaded pistol and yet some of you," he said, "would set this mad dog free again to ravin and destroy, and take the lives of innocent and defenseless people. Look at him as he sits there before you!" he said, "cowerin' and tremblin' with the mark of Cain upon his brow and with his hands red with the blood of all his victims! The accusing fingers of dead men are pointed at him from the grave," he said, "and their blood, could it have a tongue, would cry aloud for his conviction as do the tongues of all the widows and orphans he has made—" Well, Mr. Gant said it was a powerful effort, said Hensley turned pale and trembled as if the spirits of the dead had come back to accuse him, sure enough. But of course they acquitted him like every one predicted.

But, Lord! as I said to your papa, I could never stand to go near the man after that time they had us to their house for dinner and here he was, sir—he had it on the table right where every one was going to eat!—to think of it, I said!—why, the skull of a nigger he had shot and killed—that he should have no more refinement, I said to your papa, than to do a thing like that right there with guests comin' to his house for dinner and before his own children, usin' it, mind you, as a sugar bowl! Oh, braggin' about it, you know, like he'd done something big, with the top of the skull sawed off to make a lid and a place in the forehead for the sugar to pour out where the bullet hole was. Why it was enough to turn your stomach, I couldn't touch a bite. When we got out, your papa said, "Well that's the last time I'll ever go to *his* house," he said, "I don't want to have anything to do with a man who's got no more mercy in him than that. It's enough to curdle your blood," he said, and from that day on he never set foot in his house again. Oh! he couldn't endure him, you know. But they say that's exactly why he killed himself in the end—I know Gilmer who was stayin' at the house, brought me the news, came right back to the kitchen, you know, says, "Well, it was a terrible sight." Says, "I was the first one there. I heard the explosion," he says, "right behind the new courthouse, and when I got there—there he was," he says, "all sprawled out behind a pile of brick"; says, "they couldn't tell who it was for a while, the whole top of his head blown off so they couldn't identify him. Oh, *awful,* you know."

"Well," I said, "I'm not surprised. Those who live by the sword will perish by the sword," and, of course, that's just what happened, I reckon his conscience got too much for him, he couldn't face it any longer. Why, didn't Amy tell Daisy way back there when they were both in high school together, "Oh, daddy!" she says—the child came right out with it, you know—"oh, we don't know what to do with him. We're afraid he's goin' to lose his mind," she says. "He wakes up in the middle of the night screamin' and hollerin' and we think he's goin' crazy," she said. "Ah-hah!" I said to your papa when I heard it, "you see, don't you? The guilty fleeth when no man pursueth." "Well," he said, "I reckon he's got a lot to forget. He's got all those crimes upon his soul and he can't forget them. It's the torment of a guilty conscience as sure as you're born. It wouldn't surprise me if he committed suicide some day," he said.

But, of course, for a long time there he seemed to get all right. He quit the force and became a sort of religious fanatic, a pillar of the Methodist Church, and all, right down there among them in the amen corner every Sunday and yes! what about it! in the real estate business, if you please, swellin' it around town in a big car, promotin' *Hensley Heights,* and all such stuff as that, and of course I reckon for a time there like all the rest of us he made some money or *thought* he did.

I know when I bought those lots from W. J. Bryan he told me Hensley had acted as agent in a couple of deals for him, and I reckon Bryan was feelin' pretty good about it, he began to brag about him, says: "I tell you what: Hensley is certainly a fine upright sort of man," he says. "In all my dealin's with him," he says, "I don't think I've ever heard him make use of a coarse expression, or utter a word that couldn't be spoken in the presence of a lady." Hm! I thought to myself, times have certainly changed, I thought, but of course, I didn't say anything, I just let him go on. "Yes," he says, "I've found him honest and upright in all my dealin's with him and what's more, you'll find him right in his seat in church every Sunday morning. And for a man who says he never had any schoolin'," he says, "his knowledge of the Scriptures is profound," says, "I've tried him out myself on texts from all parts of the Bible and I haven't managed to trip him up yet." Says, "It's a rare thing that you'll find a business man in this day and time with so much interest in spiritual matters," says, "he is certainly a credit to the community." "Why, yes," I said, "I reckon you're right but then there are a whole lot of things about this community you don't know, Mr. Bryan. Of course," I said, "you're a recent comer and there may have been a time when Dock Hensley wasn't such a credit as he is now." "Why, when was that?" he said. "Well," I said, of course I wasn't going to tell him anything, winkin' at him, you know, "maybe we'd better let dead dogs lie. I reckon it was a long time ago, for a fact," I said, "about the time you first began to run for President."

Well, sir, he just threw back his head and hah-hahed. "Why, yes!" he said, "I reckon that was a long time ago, sure enough. Well, maybe you'd better say no more," he said; says, "but I'll bet you if there was anything I *did* want to know," he said, "you'd remember it." "Why, yes," I said, "of course, I don't believe in any one braggin' on themselves, but I've always been considered to have a pretty good memory," I said. "Well, I should say you have," he said, "I was tellin' my wife the other day," he says, "that it was remarkable to find a person who took as keen an interest in all that's goin' on as you do. Why," he says, "I said to her I believe you remember everything that ever happened to you." "Well, no," I said, "I wouldn't go so far as that. There may be a few things that I don't remember very well before I was two years old, but there hasn't been much I've missed out on since then." "Well, I just bet there's not," he said, laughin', you know, as big as you please. But, of course then I said to him—you know I didn't want to do the man an injury, I thought I would give him credit for his good points—said, "Well, Mr. Bryan, there are things we could say against any one," I said, "for there is no one alive that hasn't got his faults. Judge not lest ye be judged," I said. "That is certainly true," he said. "We must all be charitable." "And I suppose if I wanted to," I said, "that I could tell you things about Dock Hensley that might not be exactly to his credit, but," I said, "you may rest assured on one score: he has certainly been a home-lovin' man and he has stuck to his wife and childern: no matter what else he has done he has never been guilty of no immorality or licentiousness, no one has ever been able to say that about him," and of course, that was true: they tried to prove *something* like that on him in that trial, in order to discredit his character, they tried to show that he'd gone running around after other women besides his wife, but they couldn't do it, sir—they had to give the devil his due—his morals were pure.

"Why, Dock," your papa said, "you've been good friends with those men for twenty years," says, "I don't see how you've got the heart to do it." "Yes, I know," he says, "it's an awful thing, but some one's got to do it. That's part of my job, that's what the people elected me for," he says, "and besides I believe Ed and Lawrence would rather have me do it anyway. I've talked it all over with 'em," he says—of course, they told it that he'd been goin' down there to the jail to see them, and that they were all as thick as thieves, sir, laughin' and carryin' on together—says, "they'd rather have me do it than some stranger." "Yes," Mr. Gant said, "but I should think it would trouble your conscience. I don't see how you'd be able to sleep at night after doin' such a thing." "Why, pshaw! Mr. Gant," he said, "it wouldn't bother me at all. I've done it many a time," he said, "all I've got to do is spring the trap. Why, I think no more of it than I would of wringin' a chicken's neck," he said. "What about it!" your papa says to me, "did you ever hear of such a man? Why it seems that all human feeling and mercy has been left out of him," he says.

Well, we never could find out if Dock Hensley was in on it or not—if he knew they were goin' to make that break—but if he did, it looked mighty funny that— "I tell you what," says Mr. Gant a day or two after it happened, "I believe we misjudged

Dock Hensley," he says, "I believe he knew they were goin' to make that break all along and that's the reason," he says, "he was takin' it so easy." "Well, now," I said, "there's something mighty funny about it somewhere. If he knew about it why did he come to your office with those passes? Why was he so anxious to have us come and see it?" "Well," he says, "I reckon he did it in order to turn suspicion away from him." "No, sir," I said, "I don't believe a word of it. He was just waitin' his chance to hang 'em— yes, and gloatin' about it." Well, of course, Mr. Gant didn't want to believe it of him, said he didn't like to think that any man could be so callous.

Of course, they said later that the whole thing had been arranged for weeks: that was the story, you know, that John Rand, the jailer, had been fixed, as the sayin' goes, to let them make their getaway. Now they weren't able to prove anything on the man and he *may* have been an honest all-right sort of feller— but there was something mighty queer about it somewhere: here they found him, you know, in Ed's cell all trussed up as slick as as a whistle and without a mark upon him, sir, to indicate he'd ever made the least resistance. Well, the story he told was that he'd gone in there to take Ed and Lawrence their supper and that they overpowered him and tied him up as soon as he came in, said they took his keys and unlocked the other three and skipped right out. Of course, those other three had nothing to do with Ed and Lawrence, they were just plain ordinary murderers, mountain grills, as your papa called them, down there waitin' to be hanged, and the story goes that Ed said to Lawrence, "well, we'll just turn them loose, too, while we're about it."

Well, there was something funny about John Rand's story. People didn't like the look of it. And then, within six months' time John Rand goes into business for himself, opens up a great big plumbing shop on South Main street with a stock that must have cost him thousands of dollars. "Look here," your papa said, "do you know what they're saying? They're saying that John Rand was bribed to let those men escape." "Well," I said, "they may be right. It's mighty funny," I said, "that a man who never earned over fifty dollars a month in his life gets money enough all of a sudden to start up a big business of his own. Now *where* did all that money come from: you've got to admit it looks fishy." "Yes," your daddy says, "but who bribed him? Where did the money come from?" he said. "Why," I said, "it came from Yancey County where all their kinfolk and relations live—that's exactly where it came from." "Why," he says, "are their people well-to-do?" "They've got *plenty*," I said, "plenty—and they'd 'a' spent every last penny they had to see those men go free." Of course, I knew what I was talkin' about. "Look here," I said, "I've lived here all my life and I know those people better than you do. I grew up among them," I said, "and I want to tell you they'd 'a' stopped at nothing." Why, they said the money poured in there like water, said thousands of dollars were spent in their defense, why, yes! didn't they tell it that old Judge Truman alone—the brother of this same Perfesser Truman, of course, Ed Mears and Lawrence Wayne married Perfesser Truman's daughters, they both married sisters—didn't they tell it that Judge Truman alone, one of the biggest lawyers that they had in Yancey, spent over ten thousand dollars in defendin' them, "and you can rest assured," I told your papa, "that that wasn't a drop in the bucket. Wherever they are today, they're well provided for," I said, "and you needn't waste your pity on them." "Well," he said, "I'm glad they got away. There's been enough bloodshed already. I don't see any use in adding to it."

I shook my head. "No," I said, "you're wrong. They should have been hanged and I'm sorry they didn't get what was comin' to them, but," I said, "I'm glad *we* acted as we did. I shouldn't have cared if they'd been caught, but I don't want the blood of any man, guilty or innocent, on my conscience." "No," he said, "nor do I." "But *you know*," I said, "*you know* as well as you're standin' there that those men were guilty as hell"—that's just the way I put it—why, *murder,* of course, as deliberate and cold-blooded murder as any one was ever guilty of. Here they told it at the trial that both of them walked in to that mica mine on

Saturday afternoon when they were payin' off, and they were spoilin' for a fight—that's all in the world it was. Why! I said to your papa at the time, if it had been money they were after, if they'd wanted to hold up the place, you might have seen some reason for it—but no! they were out to start a row, and they'd come ready for it. Of course, they'd both been drinkin' and when they drank they were always up to devilment. And here, of course, they began to abuse that paymaster—a decent law-abidin' man, they said—and to hinder him from payin' off and, of course, that was when John Burgin stepped into the office. "Now, boys," he said, "I don't like to see you act like this. Why don't you go on off now," he says, tryin' to reason with them, you know, "before you get yourselves in trouble?" "Why, damn you," says Lawrence Wayne, "what business is it of yours what we do?" "Why, it's no business at all," John Burgin says, "only I don't like to see you act this way. I don't want to see you get into any trouble," he said, "and I know when you wake up tomorrow morning you're goin' to regret this thing." "Well, now," says Lawrence Wayne, "don't you worry how we're goin' to feel tomorrow morning. You worry about yourself. It's people like you," he says, "who don't wake up at all. Why, damn you," he says, "I never did like your face noway. Now you'd better go on," he says, "while you're still able to walk." "All right," John said, "I'll go. I don't want to have no trouble with you. I was just tryin' to reason with you to behave yourselves for the sake of your wives and children, but if that's the way you feel about it, I'll go on." And they said he turned his back on them and was walkin' away when Ed Mears shot him, turned to Lawrence, they said, with a kind of a drunken grin, says, "Lawrence, do you reckon I can hit him?" and he shot that man down that never did him no harm, through the back of his head—and then, of course, they both cut loose on the paymaster and that man he had assistin' him—killed them all, and then skipped out. "But to think of it!" I said to your papa, "there was no excuse, no provocation as far as I can see—they were *simply out to kill*," I said, "and hangin's the only treatment

they deserve." "Yes," he said, "but I'm glad we acted as we did."
Now, boy, I want to tell you:

"Two . . . Two," the first voice said, and "Twenty . . . Twenty,"
said the other.

I know exactly when it was—I'm goin' to tell you now: it was
on the twenty-seventh day of September, sir, at twenty minutes
to ten o'clock in the evening. The reason I know is—well, that's
what I'm goin' to tell you—but it was just two days before that
on the twenty-fifth day of the month, sir—that I'd had that talk
with Ambrose Radiker in his saloon, that's exactly when it was.
That was just after Mr. Gant had been off on that spree and
they'd had to send for us to get him and bring him home. Now,
I thought, I've had as much as I can stand, I won't put up with
it any longer, and I marched right in there by myself to have it
out with him.

Well, I could see that Ambrose was telling me the truth—
that was the time of course he told me how your daddy raved
and carried on in his delirium against the Chinese and how
much trouble they'd had with him—give the devil his due, of
course—saloon-keeper though he may have been, I believe he
told the truth and was being honest with me. "Now," he said,
"I've done everything I can but if there's anything more I can do
to persuade him to stop drinkin' you tell me what it is and," he
says, "I'll do it!"—and yes! didn't he stop in to see us that very
evening on his way home, we were sitting there after supper, you
know, your daddy reading the paper to me, and all, and says,
"Will, I want you to promise me that you'll try to cut out drinkin'.
I hate to see you do it," he said, "a man with your mind and your
command of language and all—why there's nothing you couldn't
accomplish if you set yourself to it!" "Why, yes," I said, "he's
smart enough, all right. I don't believe there's a man in the community with half his natural ability," I said, "and he could go
far if it wasn't for that accursed cravin' for licker. There's one
thing sure," I said, "he never learned it from any of my people
—you know, my father, Major Pentland," I said, "never touched

a drop in his life and never allowed any one to come inside his house if he thought he drank." "Yes, I know," says Ambrose, "he is certainly a fine man and a credit to the community," he says, "and, Will," he says, "here you are with everything it takes to make a man happy—with a fine wife and a family of children and a good business and, Will, for *their* sakes," he said, "you oughtn't to do it, you ought to cut out drinkin'." Well, your papa admitted he was right and he promised, you know, said he'd never touch another drop and Ambrose went on then—that was the very night it was, all right, the twenty-seventh of September.

Well, then, I heard it! "Two . . . Two," said one, and "Twenty . . . Twenty," said the other. "Why, Lord, woman!" says Mr. Gant, "there's no one there!"—went to the window and looked out, you know, says, "It's something you imagined. You don't hear anything," he said.

"Oh, yes, I do!" I said—of course, I was as sure of it as I was sitting there—"there it is again!" I said, and of course I heard it just as plain, "Two . . . Two," the first one over by the window said, and "Twenty . . . Twenty," the other one kept whispering in my ear.

And that was the time the bell began to ring—that courthouse bell, you know, banging it out as hard and fast as it could go. "Oh, Lord!" I said, "something's happened. What do you reckon it can be?" You could hear them the whole way to the square shoutin' and hollerin' and smashing in the windows of Curtis Black's hardware store to get the guns, that's what they did, all right, and then man-like, of course, your papa wanted to be up and gone, grabs his hat, you know, says, "I think I'll go and see!"

"Oh, don't go!" I said, "don't go! I wish you wouldn't go. You oughtn't leave me while I'm in this condition," I said. "Why, Lord," he said, "I'll be back in half an hour. Why you're all right," he said, "there's nothing can happen to you." I shook my head— I had a premonition, I don't know what else you'd call it—but something *awful, awful,* some approachin' calamity. "I wish you wouldn't go," I said—but he was up and gone.

[136]

I looked at the clock as he went out the door and the minute hand stood just exactly at twenty minutes to ten o'clock.

So I waited. I felt it, you know, I didn't know what it was, but I knew that it was comin', and I listened to that old wooden clock there on the mantel—tock-tock, tock-tock, it said, ticking the minutes off, and let me tell you: that was the longest time I ever waited, each of those minutes seemed an hour. The clock struck ten.

And then I heard it—creepin' along the alley-way above our house, and then I heard the fence-wires creak outside the window, and then it dropped down on the flower-beds outside the house—and then it crept up soft and easy and began to crawl along the porch outside the sitting-room door. "Oh, Lord!" I said—it flashed over me all at once, the meaning of it—"they've come! they're here! What shall I do," I said, "left all alone here with the childern to face them, these bloody men?"

Of course, I saw it then—the meaning of that warning—"Two . . . Two," and "Twenty . . . Twenty"—they'd tried to warn me and your papa that they'd be there in twenty minutes. "He should have waited, he should have listened," I said, "that was what they were trying to tell him."

I went to the door—how on earth I ever mustered strength and courage in my condition, I don't know how I ever did it, but child! child! I must have been given strength and courage to face them by some higher power—and I flung it open. It was a pitch-black night along toward the beginning of autumn. It had been raining but the rain had stopped and Lord! it seemed that you could cut the darkness with an axe, everything still and heavy, frosty-like—that was the reason we could hear them all so plain up on the square, but not a sound, sir! not a word now!

"All right!" I sang right out into the dark, you know, like I wasn't afraid of anything. "I know you're there, Ed! You can come on in." He didn't speak. I listened. I could hear him breathing, heavy-like. "Now, surely," I said, "you're not going to be afraid of me. I'm all alone," I said, "I'm nothing but a defenseless woman, and you've got nothing to be afraid of"—of course, I knew that that would aggervate him.

Well, it stung his pride, he got right up and walked into the room: "I'm not afraid of any one," he said, "man nor woman." "Well, no," I said, "I reckon you're not. At least they all said you weren't afraid of John Burgin when you shot him in the back when he was walkin' away from you and surely," I said, "a man who's killed as many people as you have is not going to be afraid of one lone woman who's been left alone in the house without pertection. Now I know better than that," I said, "I know you're not afraid of *me*."

"No, Eliza," he said, "I'm not, and that's the reason that I'm here," he said. "You've got nothing to fear from me," he said, "I came here because I knew that I could trust you and you wouldn't give me away. I need your help," he said. Well, I reckon the look of the feller was too much for me, he looked like a hunted animal and *let me tell you,* I never want to see no such look in any one's eyes as I saw in his that night: if he'd been to hell and back it couldn't have been worse. It was too much for me, I couldn't have told on him then no matter what he'd done. "It's all right, Ed. You've nothing to fear from me, I won't give you away. And you can tell Lawrence," I said, "to come on in. I know he's out there."

Well, he gave me a mighty funny look. "Why, what do you mean?" he said, "Lawrence isn't here. He's not with me." "Yes, he is," I said. "I *know* he's there. I'm *sure* of it. And you can tell him so, and to come on in." "Why, how do you *know* he's there?" he said, worried, "What makes you so *sure* of it?" "Well, I tell you," I said, "I was *warned* about it, Ed. I knew that you were both coming." "Warned?" he said, beginning to get excited, you know, "Why, who warned you? Has any one been here? How did any one know?" he said. "No," I said, "you needn't get excited, Ed. Some one was here to warn me, all right, that you and Lawrence were coming, but it's no one you've got to be afraid of in *this* world. The next world is a different matter, of course," I said, "I can't tell you about that. You'll have to face that for yourself." Well, he looked at me and his eyes were sticking out of his head. *"Spirits?"* he said. "Yes," I said, "that's what they were, all right! Now I don't know *who* they were, but they came here to warn me, whisperin' in my ear, and they said you and Lawrence were on your way and would be here in twenty minutes."

Well, his face was a study, and at last he said: "No, Eliza, you're wrong. I don't want to alarm you," he said, "but if they were here they came here to warn you about something else. It wasn't me and Lawrence," he said, "I'll swear to that!" "Why, what do you mean?" I said. "I've told you," he said, "Lawrence isn't with me. We parted company outside the jail; we decided that was best and he lit out toward South Carolina. I'm going across the mountain," he said, "and if we get away we hope to meet again out West." "You look me in the eye," I said, "are you telling me the truth?" Well, he looked straight at me: "Yes," he said, "so help me God, it's true!"

Well, I looked at him and I saw, of course, that he was telling me the truth. "Well," I said, "it was something else, then, what it is I don't yet know, but I'll find out. Now," I said, "why did you come here to my house? What do you want?" I said. "Why," he said, "Eliza, I've got to get away across those mountains tonight, and I've got no shoes, I'm barefooted," he said. And then, of course, I saw, I reckon I'd been too excited to notice before, but there he was, ragged and bleeding, in his bare feet, and let me tell you he was a sight to behold and marvel at: here he was with no shoes and no coat and nothing to wear but an old ragged pair of pants that looked as if he'd been sleeping in them all the time he'd been in jail, and a dirty old flannel shirt that had been all ripped out beneath the shoulder, and here his hair was all matted and tangled up like a bird's nest, hanging down over his eyes and he must have had a six weeks' growth of beard upon his face—why it looked as if he hadn't had a shave or haircut since he went to jail, the very sight of him was enough to scare the life out of a grizzly bear. Why, as I told your papa later, they'd thought of everything to help him make his get-away except the things he needed most: here they'd given him a pistol and cartridges to kill people with—as if he hadn't killed enough already—but they didn't have sense enough to give him shoes to walk in or a coat to keep him warm. "If that don't beat all I ever heard of!" I told your papa.

"I've got to get them somehow," he said. "If I don't I'll cut my feet to pieces going across the mountains and then," he said, "if I can't walk, I'm done for. They'll catch me sure." "Why, of course," I said. "Well," he said, "that's why I came here to see you, Eliza. I knew you wouldn't give me up and I could depend on you to help me. Now," he says, "you can see for yourself I've got an awful big foot and the only man I know," he says, "who wears a shoe that would fit me is Mr. Gant. Now if you'll only let me have a pair of his old shoes—anything you've got—I'll pay you for them. I've got plenty of money," he said, and he pulled out a big roll of bills, he had certainly come well heeled, "and I'll pay you anything you say they're worth." "No, Ed," I shook my head, "I don't want your money"—of course, I couldn't have touched it, it'd been like taking blood money—"but I'll give you the shoes." So I went to the closet and got them out, a fine new pair, sir, that your daddy had bought only a couple of months before, in good condition, for he certainly took good care of all his clothes. "Here they are," I said, "and I hope you'll be able to use them." Well, he put them on then and there, and they fitted him, sir, as if they'd been made for him. Well, you know, murderer that he was, he showed he still had feeling left in him, he took my hand and began to cry, says: "I'll never forget what you've done as long as I live. If there's ever anything I can do to pay you for it," he says, "I'll do it." "Well, you can do something," I said, "and you can do it here and now." "What is it?" he said. "I don't want your money," I said, "I wouldn't touch it. You can have the shoes, Ed, and I hope they help you to escape—you need the shoes," I said, "but you don't need that pistol you're carryin' in your hip pocket." I could see it, you know, making a big bulge when he walked. "Now you've shed enough blood already," I said, "and come what may, whether you escape or not, I never want to hear that you've shed another drop of blood. You give that gun to me," I said, "and go on. If they catch you it won't do you any good."

Well, he looked at me a moment as if he couldn't make up his mind, and then he gave it to me. "All right," he said, "I reckon you're right. I don't suppose it'd do me much good noway and besides, if they do catch me I don't care. I've committed so many crimes in my life," he said, "that I don't care what happens to me now. I'd just as soon be out of it," he said. "No," I said, "I don't like to hear you talk like that. You've got a wife who's stuck by you through thick and thin and little childern, and now," I said, "you must begin to think of them. Go on off somewheres," I said, "where no one knows you and make a fresh start, and when you are ready, send for her and I *know* her," I said—I looked him in the eye—"I *know* her, and she'll come."

Well, it was too much for him. He couldn't speak, he turned his head away, said, "All right. I'll try!" "Now, you go on," I said. "I don't want them to find you here," I said, "and I hope that all goes well with you." "Good-bye," he said, "I'm going to try to lead a different life hereafter." "Yes, that's what you've got to do. You've got to try to atone for all the harm you've done. Go," I said, "and sin no more."

Well, he went. I heard the fence wires creak and I saw him going up the street, I reckon toward the mountain. He got away, all right. I never saw him again.

Well, he hadn't been gone ten minutes when here he came, you know, your daddy, all excited with the news he *thought* he had to tell.

"Well," he said, "they got away, all five of them. Hensley and a big mob have smashed the windows of Black's hardware store to get guns and he's out after them now with a posse."

"Yes," I said, "and you had to run all the way to town to find *that* out, didn't you? The next time you go chasing off like that bring me back something I don't know about." "Why," he said, "how did you hear? Do you know about it?" he said. "Know about it!" I said, "why I know more about it than you'll ever know," I said. "I got my information at first hand," I said, "and I didn't have to stir out of this house to get it, either." "Why," he says, "how was that? What do you mean?" "I've had a caller since you went away," I said. "Who was it?" he says. I looked at him. "Ed Mears was here," I said. "Good God!" your papa says, "do you mean to tell me that murderer was here—in my house? Have you given the alarm?" he says, "have you told the neighbors?" "No," I said. "Well, I'm going to," he says, "this very minute." And he started to go again. I stopped him. "No," I said, "you'll do no such thing. You'll stay here. Now, I gave him my promise not to give him away, and we're going to stick to it. You keep quiet." He studied about it for a moment. "Well," he said, "I reckon you're right. Maybe it's the best way, after all. But that's the strangest thing I ever heard about," he said. "By God it is!"

Well, they got away, all right. None of them were ever caught. Of course, years later when your daddy made that trip to California, Truman told him that both Ed and Lawrence had come to his house in Colorado when he was living there and, of course, the girls both follered them within six months or so. Lawrence's wife, who was Mary Truman, died out there in Colorado of consumption a year or two later, and I don't know for certain what ever became of Lawrence. The story went that he settled down in Kansas and got married again and had a big family of children and is living there right now, sir, a well-to-do man and highly respected in his community.

Of course, we *know* what happened to Ed Mears. I got the whole story from Dock Hensley. Truman told your papa that Ed had come out there to Colorado and went up into the mountains to some mining camp to work, and, of course, when he was ready he sent for Addie, and she follered him. Well, Truman said, she lived with him up there a year or so and then she came down to her father's house again. Oh! he told it, you know! Said it was awful, she couldn't stand no more of it, said Ed was going crazy and would go out of his mind sometimes screaming and raving that the spirits of the dead men he had killed had come back from the grave to haunt and torment him. "You see, don't you," I said to your papa when he told it, "you see what happens, don't you? I've never known it to fail," I said. "The guilty fleeth when no man pursueth." "Yes," he said, "that's it. A guilty conscience as sure as you're born," he said. "So I took her away from him," said Truman. "I sent her back East where she would never see him any more. Of course," he said, "he threatened me—but he threatened my life, but I could see that the man was goin' crazy, and I wouldn't let her go back to him," he said.

Well, Addie came home again and got a divorce: of course, Cash Jeter took the case for her—that was long before he got elected to the Senate, he was nothing but a practising attorney at the time—and the story goes, in the course of the proceedings he fell in love with her, and marries her, if you please, within a month's time after she got the final papers. "Well, they didn't wait long, did they?" I said to your papa! "Now it does seem to me," I said, "that they might have waited a decent length of time." "Ah, Lord!" your papa says, "the funeral baked meats did coldly furnish forth the marriage tables. 'Twas thrift Horatio with a vengeance," he says. "That's so," I said, "that's what it was, all right."

Well, then, they sent Dock Hensley West to get a man who'd killed some one, and, of course, when he came back he told it how he had run into Ed Mears in Mexico. Said he was on a boat somewheres going from Texas into Mexico follerin' on the trail of this murderer he'd been sent to get, I reckon, when here he saw him, face to face—Ed Mears. Dock said he'd grown a beard, but said he'd recognized him, "but I want to tell you," he says, "he's changed a lot. He's not the same man that you knew," he says. Dock said he looked like a dead man, said he was nothing but a shader of his former self. "Why," he said, "he was only a bundle of skin and bone, he didn't have no more meat on him than a squirrel," he says. "Well," I said, "did he know you? Did he speak to you?"—of course, you know, I wanted to hear the story. "Why, Lord, yes!" Hensley said. "We roomed together for four days down there, hail-fellow-well-met and boon companions," he says. Then, he went on to say, you know, "Of course," he says, "when he first saw me on the boat he thought that I had come for him, he stepped right up," he said, "to surrender himself." "All right, Dock," he says, "I know you came down here to take me back and," he says, "I'm ready to go." "Why, no, Ed," I says, "you're wrong. I'm here for some one else. You're not the man I'm lookin' for," I said, "I don't want you—and besides," I said, "even if I did I've got no authority to arrest you, I've got no warrant for you." "Well," he said, "I'm comin' back anyway some day. I've one more killing to do yet before I die," he said, "and then they can take me and do what they like with me." "Why, who's that?" Dock says—asks him, "who do you want to kill?" he says. "Cash Jeter," he says. And then Dock told it how bitter he hated him for getting the divorce and marrying his wife.

So Dock said that before he left for home again Ed handed him a letter and asked him to deliver it to Jeter when he got back—and he said he *saw* that letter with his own eyes, mind you, and that in all *his* life he never read the like of it: "I may have been a murderer," Ed wrote, "and I've got many a crime upon my soul to atone for but in all my days I have never sunk so low as to steal a man's wife away from him. Now," he said, "you can set your house in order and get ready for me because I'm coming back. It may be a month, or it may be a year, or it may be ten years, but I'll *be* there," he said. "I've got a score to settle with you, and you get ready." Well, Dock said when he handed that letter to Jeter he opened it and read it and Dock said his face turned pale and you could see him tremble and I suppose, of course, his life was hell on earth from that day on until the news got back to them that Ed was dead—because, of course, Ed never lived to get there, the story went that he got killed in a saloon in Mexico. But you can rest assured that he'd 'a' come.

Well, that's the way it was, all right: that's just what happened.

But still and all—the thing was puzzlin' me, you know—"Two ... Two," and "Twenty ... Twenty"—what could it mean?

"Why, Lord," your papa said, "it didn't mean a thing! It never happened anyway," he said, "it's something you imagined."

"You wait," I said, "you wait and see."

It wasn't long. We didn't have long to wait.

It started in along some time before dinner, about one o'clock. Oh, Lord! it felt like something had tore loose inside me. And he was there, he'd come home early, here he was, you know, out in the backyard rendering the lard out of some hogs he'd bought. "Why, what on earth!" I cried. "What ever made you buy them?" Child, child! that awful waste, that awful extravagance! Why, as I told him, if it hadn't been for me he'd have spent every penny he earned featherin' the nests of the butchers and the farmers and the saloon-keepers—he couldn't resist 'em, you know. "Why, man alive!" I said, "what ever persuaded you to go and do a thing like that!" Here we were with hams and bacon in the pantry that he'd bought, six smoked hams, if you please, and here he comes with this whole hog. "Why, man, you'll kill us all with all this hog meat!" I said—yes! with lots of chickens of our own and a twelve-pound roast he'd sent down from the market—"Why, we'll get down sick," I said, "you'll have the childern all in bed! So much meat isn't good for people." To think of it! the waste, you know—child, child, many's the time I've sat down and cried about it, to think he'd go and squander away his money in that way. "Why, Lord!" I said, "I never saw such a glutton in my life!" I thought I'd appeal to his pride, you know. "Why, all you think of is your belly! Now stop here and consider for a moment: how do you ever expect to accumulate any property if everything you earn goes rolling down your gullet to feed your gut? Why, I'll vow! man! I believe all of your brains are in your belly!" Why, yes! he'd meet up with some old farmer who had a whole wagon load of stuff he wanted to get rid of so he could get out of town and hike for home again, and he'd buy him out, sir. Why, didn't I tell you! What about it! to think that he could be such a dunce—the time he sent this man home with forty dozen eggs—Lord! I could have thrown them at him I was so aggervated!—when here we had hens of our own layin' us fresh ones every day as hard as they could. "Why, what ever prompted you to do such a trick as that?" I said. "Well," he says, sheepish-like, "he let me have the lot at seven cents a dozen. It was such a bargain," he says, "it seemed a pity not to buy them." "Why I don't care," I said, "if he let you have them for two cents a dozen, it was money thrown away," I said, "we'll never use them." "Oh, we can use them," he said. "We'll give 'em to the childern." "Why, Lord, man, how you talk!" I said, "you'll get the childern so sick of eggs they'll never look one in the face again. They'll never eat 'em," I said, "they'll all go bad!" And he looked pretty sheepish about it, I tell you what he did! "Well," he says, "I thought I was actin' for the best. I guess I was mistaken," he said.

And yes! Didn't he come home one time with a whole load of cantaloupes and watermelons—twenty-seven watermelons, if you please, and the Lord knows how many cantaloupes, hundreds of 'em, I reckon. "To think you had no better sense than that!" I said. "Oh, we'll eat 'em, we'll eat 'em," he said. "The childern will eat 'em up," he says. Yes, didn't Luke get down sick from eating them, "and there's a doctor bill to pay," I told him . . . and all the other times he'd come with wagon loads of roastin' ears and termaters and string beans and sweet pertaters and onions and radishes and beets and turnips and all kinds of garden vegetables and all sorts of fruit, peaches and pears and apples and plums, when here we had a big orchard and garden right behind the house growin' everything we needed. Why, it kept me busy thinkin' up ways to keep it all from goin' to waste, said, "how do you ever expect me to look after the children if you keep dumping this stuff in here on me?"—here I was in that condition, you know, putting up preserves for all I was worth and him out there rendering the lard out. Oh! the smell of it, that old strong smell of fat, you know—right up to the very time, four hundred and thirty-seven jars of preserved cherries, peaches, apple, grape, and plum jelly, quince honey, preserved pears, termater ketchup, chow chow, pickled cucumbers, and all such stuff as that, why you couldn't get into the pantry, it was stacked up to the ceiling, and *let me tell you, now,* he could *eat:* now I've seen some good eaters in my day and time but I've never seen any one who could poke it away the way *he* could. I reckon he got it from that crowd he came from up there, told it you know how they'd come in from the fields in his boyhood and sit down to a meal that would stall an ox. Why didn't I see the old woman myself, when we were up there that time, eat a whole chicken and three big hunks of pie—says to Augusta, you know, "Daughter, fill my plate again," she says, and she was in her seventies then—that's exactly how she got her death, sir. "To think of it!" I said when I heard the news—in her ninety-sixth year and fell out of her chair and broke her leg while reachin' for an ear of corn: of course it killed her, she was too old to recover from the injury, her bones wouldn't knit together again, "but if that don't beat all!" I said.

Why, I'll vow! It's a wonder his constitution stood it as long as it did—brains and eggs and bacon and fried steak and oatmeal and hot biscuits and sausage and two or three cups of coffee for his breakfast, and two or three different kinds of meat, liver and roast beef and pork and fish and chicken, and a half dozen different vegetables, beans and mashed pertaters and succotash and turnip greens and preserved peaches and pie, and all such as that, for dinner and supper. "Why," I said to Wade Eliot, "I belive that's what helped bring on this trouble. He's been diggin' his grave with his teeth." "Well," he said, "he's been diggin' a long time, hasn't he?" and, of course, I had to admit it, but I'll vow! I sometimes think he might be alive today if he'd only used more judgment!

Well, then, I say, it hit me, those awful stabbing pains. I went to the window and called out to him, "Come! come quick!" And let me tell you, he didn't *wait*: he came a-running.

"Oh, it can't be!" I said. "There hasn't been time enough."

"That's what I think it is," he said. "I'm going for the doctor." And he went.

That was the year the locusts came: it seems so long ago since the year that the locusts came, and all the earth was eaten bare, it seems so long ago. But no (I thought) the thing kept puzzlin' me, you know—it can't be that, there hasn't been time enough for that, it was only the year before in January—Lord! Lord! I often think of all that I've been through, and wonder that I'm here to tell it. I reckon for a fact I had the power of Nature in me; why! no more trouble than the earth takes bearing corn, all of the childern, the eight who lived, and all the others that you never heard about—all of the childern and less married life than any woman that I knew—and oh! to think of it, to think that he should say the things he did—cursin' and tauntin' me and runnin' wild with other women, when he had done it all, and like a devil when he saw what he had done. Lord! Lord! he was a strange man, a wild and savage man; sometimes it seemed I never got to know him: there was a devil in him somewhere, something wild and strange we never got to know about—the things he did and said were more than I could stand, they made me bitter and I prayed that God would punish him, but Lord! it was so long ago since the year that the locusts came, and I think of it all, the orange trees, the fig trees, and the singin' and all of the times we knew together. Oh! the good, the bad times, all of the happiness and bitter weepin', and there is something now that can't be said, I tried to hate him but now I have no words to say against him: he was a strange man but where he was no one was ever cold, no one was ever hungry, there was enough for all, and now when I remember him it seems so long ago since the year when the locusts came, and there's something that I want to say that can't be spoken.

That year—it was the year the childern had the typhoid and

Steve and Daisy were just gettin' well again and I had taken
them—Lord! how did I ever do it all alone—down to St. Augus-
tine—and he came, he couldn't stay, of course, he follered us,
and began to drink—I tried to find it but he got Steve to hide
it in the sand up underneath the house—and to curse and rave
when he had seen me, says, "Damn you! if you bring it back with
you I'll kill you both!" And child, to think that he should talk
like that, it made me bitter and I didn't stop to think: I walked
the floor, I walked the floor and then I went out on the porch
and leaned against a post—we were livin' in a cottage that I'd
rented from some Northern people—and there was no rail—there
was nothin' but that old loose sand there anyway, and I knew the
childern wouldn't hurt themselves if they fell off—and Lord!
What shall I do! What shall I do! I thought. . . .

The next day he had sobered up again and was all right and
so toward sunset of that day we took the childern with us and
set out for old Fort Marion, the Spanish Fort, down by the Ponce
de Leon, and here were all the people in their finery and the
soldiers' band a-playin' and then you heard the gun and the
bugle blowin' as the flag came down—yes—Toodle-oo! Toodle-oo!
—that was the way the bugle blew and all the little childern put
their hands up to their mouths to see if they could do it too, and
the birds flyin', the palm trees and the music and the smell of
water and the orange blossoms, and that old black fort—why
Lord! the walls were fourteen feet in places—with the sun goin'
down behind it like some big orange, and the people listenin' to
the music. In January of that year the locusts came at home, and
then I felt as if the whole thing had torn loose inside me.

"Come on," I said. "We've got to go," and says, "What is it?"
"Oh, Lord!" I told him, "it's tearin' me in two. Oh, Lord! We'll
never get there! Come!"—and we went, the childern and all, and
my feet slippin' and sinkin' in the sand, until I thought I'd never
get there, and that great hunk of a thing tearing away at me,
and he picked me up and carried me the last part of the way into
the house, and I said, "You see, don't you? You see what you've
done. That's your work!" and he was frightened and his face

turned pale and he trembled as he looked and he said, "My God! My God! What have I done!" and he walked the floor, and it got dark, and I lay there, and all of the childern were asleep around me, and he went out into the yard, and we had a fig tree there, and I lay there in the dark listenin' to people comin' by, and I could hear music playin' somewheres and hear their voices laughin' and singin', and smell all of the blossoms—oh! the magnolias and the lilies and the roses, the poinsettias, and all the other flowers they had there and the orange trees and all, and the little childern sleepin' in the house, you know, and see the sky all full of stars and Lord God! I thought, what shall I do, what shall I do?—and that was the year the locusts came at home and now it seems so long ago.

But Lord! I reckon Nelson got it right that time, said, "You've got the power of nature in you for a fact. I've never seen the like of it," he said. Why, yes! didn't I have them all, and couldn't I make things grow by touchin' them, and wasn't it that way ever since I was a child—termaters and flowers and corn and vegetables—and all kinds of fruit. Why Lord! it seemed that all I had to do was stick my fingers in the earth and they'd come up for me. "Oh," says old man Shumaker, workin', you know to all hours in his garden till it looked like a checkerboard, everything standin' up straight and neat without a weed among it, like I reckon he'd been taught to do in Germany, says, "Oh! you mustn't let your garden go that way. You've got to weed it out or things will never grow." "You wait," I said, "you wait and see! They'll grow," I said, "they'll grow for me, and I'll have things as good as yours for all your work and grubbin'." And didn't I have onions and radishes and lettuce and termaters that beat him out of sight—why Lord! you could see them poppin' from the earth! and let me tell you, if the worst comes to the worst, I wouldn't starve, if I didn't have a penny I could live, I'd make the earth produce for me. I've done it and I could do it yet.

Why, yes! didn't I go in to the Catawba Coal Company here one day last winter to pay my bill and talk to him just two days before he dropped dead from that heart attack, and see him, you know, Miller Wright, not a day over seventy, pale as a ghost and trembling and shaking all over like a leaf? "Why, Miller," I said, "it worries me to see you in this condition. What is it? What's the matter?" "Oh," he says, trembling and shaking, "Eliza, it's the worry, the awful worry! I can't sleep no more for thinkin' of it." "Why, what is it?" I said; says, "Oh, Eliza, everything I ever had is gone! I'm penniless. Most of it went in real estate," he says, "and now that miserable bank has closed its doors. What am I going to do?" he said. "Do?" I said, "why you're going to do the same as me—profit by your mistakes and start all over." "Oh, but Eliza, Eliza," he said, shakin' his head at me, "it's too late—we're both past seventy and we're too old, too old," he said. "Old!" I said, "why, Lord God, I could start right out tomorrow and earn my living with the best of them." "Yes," he said, "but Eliza, what are you going to do?" "Do!" I said, "why, I tell you," I said, "I'm going to pitch right in and work hard till I'm eighty and then," I says, winkin' at him, you know, "I'm goin' to cut loose and *just raise hell*," I said—that's exactly what I said, you know, I thought I'd jolly him up a bit and, of course, he had to laugh then, says, "Well, I reckon that's as good a plan as any." "Now, look here, Miller," I said, "you ought to know better than to give in like this. We've both been through the mill, and we've seen some mighty rough times—why, these people that they've got today don't know anything about it, they don't know what hardship is" —why, didn't we both grow old within five miles of each other and don't I remember it all, yes! every minute of it like it was today, the men marchin', and the women cryin', the way the dust rose, the times we went through and the way we had to work, the wool, the flax, the wheel, the things we grew and the things we had to make, and a thousand things you never dreamed or heard of, boy, the summertime, the river and the singin', the poverty, the sorrow, and the pain—we saw and had to do it all— "And *you!*" I said to Miller Wright. "You! You did it, too," I said, "and you remember!"

Well, he had to admit it then, you know, says, "Yes, you're

right, I remember. But," he says—you know, he brightened up a bit, "could you do it *now?*" "Do it?" I said. "Why, I could do it like a flash. Now, Miller," I said, "suppose we did lose out. We're in the boat with lots of others. We all thought we were doing the right thing and I reckon we lost our heads," I said. "We allowed ourselves to be swept off our feet against our better judgment"—pshaw! when I think of it! I had my mind all made up. . . . If I'd only known. . . . Why, I was just going to make another trade or two and then get out. Pshaw! I'll vow, I believe if it hadn't been for all these sharks and New York Jews and easy-money grafters that came in there over-night . . . *that* was the time I should have sold if I'd only had the sense to see it . . . and as for all that stuff we bought in Florida, I believe we'd have been all right today if that hurricane hadn't come along and hit us like it did, and then on top of it these lying villains out in California spread that story about the Mediterranean fruit-fly down in Florida. Why, Lord, there was no more fruit-fly there than at the North Pole—it was all part of a lying story they put out to ruin and injure Florida because they couldn't stand to see us get ahead of them, and Hoover and all his crowd playin' right along with them and abettin' them in their villainy because *he* came from California, if you please—that's all in the world it was, but Florida will come back in spite of all the lies they told about her, you can't down Florida!—"And Miller," I said, "the banks haven't got everything," I said. "They may think they have, but now," I said, winkin' at him, "I've got a secret that I'm goin' to tell you. I've still got a little patch of land out in the country that no one knows about and if the worst comes to worst," I said, "I won't starve. I'll go out there and grow my food and I'll have plenty. And if you go broke you can come on out," I said. "You won't go hungry, I can make things grow." "Oh, but Eliza," he said, "it's too late, too late. We're both too old to start again, and we've lost everything." "No," I said, "not everything. There's something left." "What is it?" he said. "We've got the earth," I said. "We've always got the earth. We'll stand upon it and it will save us. It's never gone back on nobody yet."

Well, here they came, you know, tearing along for all they were worth, your papa and Old Doctor Nelson. I lay there with those awful pains rending me as if they were going to tear me in two.

"But no," I said to Doctor Nelson. "It can't be that. I'm not ready for it yet. It's not been time, it's two weeks before my time," I said.

"No matter about that," he said. "*you're* ready. It's *your* time," he said. "It's *your* time, sure enough."

And, sure enough, it was. Why! that was it, of course!—that's what I've been telling you, boy!—that explained it all.

"Two . . . Two," the first voice said, and "Twenty . . . Twenty" said the other:—

Twenty days later from that evening that Ed Mears came there to our hourse, to the minute, at twenty minutes to ten o'clock on the seventeenth day of October, *twins* were born—Ben and Grover were both born that night.

The next day as I lay there thinkin', it flashed over me, the meaning of it, of course I saw it all. The mystery was explained.

And that's the story, sir, that's just the way it happened.

"Two . . . Two," the first voice said, and "Twenty . . . Twenty," said the other.

I've told you now.

"What do you think of that?" I said to Mr. Gant. "You see, don't you?"

His face was a study. "It's pretty strange when you come to think of it," he said. "By God, it is!"

Lord, boy! What's that I hear now on the harbor? Hah? What say? A ship!—Now it will soon be April, and I must be going home again: out in my garden where I work, the early flowers and blossoms will be comin' out, the peach trees and the cherry trees, the dogwood and the laurel and the lilacs. I have an apple tree and it is full of all the birds there are in June: the flower-tree you planted as a child is blooming by the window where you planted it. (My dear child, eat good food and watch and guard your health: it worries me to think of you alone with strangers.) The hills are beautiful and soon it will be spring once more. (It worries me to think of you like this, alone and far away: child, child, come home again!)

O listen! . . .

Hah? What is it? . . .

Hah? What say? . . .

(Lord God! A race of wanderers!)

Child, child! . . . what is it?

Ships again!

No Door

A STORY OF TIME AND THE WANDERER

NO DOOR · A Story of Time and the Wanderer

After the publication of *A Portrait of Bascom Hawke* and *The Web of Earth*, Wolfe set to work organizing materials out of the "big book," into short novel form. Three long stories, published in consecutive issues of *Scribner's Magazine* in the summer of 1933, resulted from this effort. They were "The Train and the City," *Death the Proud Brother*, and *No Door*. "The Train and the City" Wolfe distributed in short fragments over his last three long books. *Death the Proud Brother* he reprinted as a short novel in *From Death to Morning*. *No Door*, in many respects his most interesting work, has never been published before as a unit in its original form, although Wolfe wished to publish it as a small book in the spring of 1934 and Scribner's temporarily agreed to bring it out.

Wolfe wrote *No Door* as an interpretation of one aspect of his personal experience. He wrote to his sister: "If you have time and are interested in knowing anything about my own life for the last ten or fifteen years, you might look at [*No Door*]." In it Wolfe used a thematic organization, with recurring symbols functioning in *leit-motif* patterns and with a conscious violation of the simple chronology of the events, in order to present a picture of loneliness and insularity. "The habit of loneliness," he wrote his sister, when describing *No Door*, "once formed, grows on a man from year to year and he wanders across the face of the earth and has no home and is an exile, and he is never able to break out of the prison of his own loneliness again, no matter how much he wants to."

Scribner's found the original *No Door* too long to publish in one issue; so Wolfe cut it to 19,000 words, the big cut being the long episode of the narrator's adventure in the Coulson house in England. This section was published as a 12,000 word story in *Scribner's* in August, 1934, under the title, "The House of the Far and the Lost." Of it Wolfe said to Robert Raynolds: "I wrote it seven or eight months ago as part of . . . 'No Door,' and . . . we cut [it] out of the magazine as being something that could go."

The material of *No Door* underwent major changes in Wolfe's books. Its opening episode appears as a short story, "No Door," in *From Death to Morning;* versions of the remainder appear in *Of Time and the River*, pages 2, 90-93, 327-334, 601-608, 611-613, and in *You Can't Go Home Again*, pages 37-44. "The House of the Far and the Lost" appears virtually unchanged in *Of Time and the River*, pages 619-627, and 637-652. Quite obviously the tight thematic structure of the short novel was lost in this process, as it had been lost in the magazine publication as two separate stories.

The version here printed assembles the original text, as prepared for magazine publication, for the first time. It is a reprinting of *No Door* from *Scribner's Magazine*, XCIV (July, 1933), pages 7-12, 46-56, with "The House of the Far and the Lost," from *Scribner's Magazine*, XCVI (August, 1934), pages 71-81, inserted between section III and section IV of the magazine version of *No Door*.

     . . . of wandering forever and the earth again . . . of seed-time, bloom, and the mellow-dropping harvest. And of the big flowers, the rich flowers, the strange unknown flowers.

Where shall the weary rest? When shall the lonely of heart come home? What doors are open for the wanderer, and in what place, and in what land, and in what time?

Where? Where the weary of heart can abide forever, where the weary of wandering can find peace, where the tumult, the fever, and the fret shall be forever stilled.

Who owns the earth? Did we want the earth that we should wander on it? Did we need the earth that we were never still upon it? Whoever needs the earth shall have the earth: he shall be still upon it, he shall rest within a little place, he shall dwell in one small room forever.

Did he feel the need of a thousand tongues that he sought thus through the moil and horror of ten thousand furious streets? He shall need a tongue no longer, he shall need no tongue for silence and the earth: he shall speak no word through the rooted lips, the snake's cold eye will peer for him through sockets of the brain, there will be no cry out of the heart where wells the vine.

The dead tongue withers and the dead heart rots, blind mouths crawl tunnels through the buried flesh, but the earth will endure forever; hair grows like April on the buried breast and from the sockets of the brain the death flowers grow and will not perish.

O flower of love whose strong lips drink us downward into death, in all things far and fleeting, enchantress of our twenty thousand days, the brain will madden and the heart be twisted, broken by her kiss, but glory, glory, glory, she remains: Immortal love, alone and aching in the wilderness, we cried to you: You were not absent from our loneliness.

I. OCTOBER: 1931

It is wonderful with what warm enthusiasm well-kept people who have never been alone in all their life can congratulate you on the joys of solitude. I know whereof I speak. I have been alone a great deal in my life—more than any one I know—and I also knew, for one short period, a few of these well-kept people. And their passionate longing for the life of loneliness is astonishing. In the evening they are driven out to their fine house in the country where their wives and children eagerly await them; or to their magnificent apartments in the city where their lovely wife or charming mistress is waiting for them with a tender smile, a perfumed, anointed, and seductive body, and the embrace of love. And all of this is as a handful of cold dust and ashes, and a little dross.

Sometimes one of them invites you out to dinner: your host is a pleasant gentleman of forty-six, a little bald, healthily plump, well-nourished-looking, and yet with nothing gross and sensual about him. Indeed he is a most æsthetic-looking millionaire, his features, although large and generous, are full of sensitive intelligence, his manners are gentle, quietly subdued, his smile a little sad, touched faintly with a whimsy of ironic humor, as of one who has passed through all the anguish, hope, and tortured fury youth can know, and now knows what to expect from life and whose "eye-lids are a little weary," patiently resigned, and not too bitter about it.

Yet life has not dealt over-harshly with our host: the evidence of his interest in un-monied, precious things is quietly, expensively, all around him. He lives in a pent-house apartment near the East River: the place is furnished with all the discrimination of a quiet but distinguished taste, he has several of Jacob Epstein's heads and figures, including one of himself which the sculptor made "two years ago when I was over there," and he also has a choice collection of rare books and first editions, and after admiring these treasures appreciatively, you all step out upon the roof for a moment to admire the view you get there of the river.

Evening is coming fast, and the tall frosted glasses in your hands make a thin but pleasant tinkling, and the great city is blazing there in your vision in its terrific frontal sweep and curtain of star-flung towers, now sown with the diamond pollen of a million lights, and the sun has set behind them, and the red light of fading day is painted upon the river—and you see the boats, the tugs, the barges passing, and the winglike swoop of bridges with exultant joy—and night has come, and there are ships there—there are ships—and a wild intolerable longing in you that you cannot utter.

When you go back into the room again, you feel very far away from Brooklyn, where you live, and everything you felt about the city as a child, before you ever saw or knew it, now seems not only possible, but about to happen.

The great vision of the city is burning in your heart in all its enchanted colors just as it did when you were twelve years old and thought about it. You think that some glorious happiness of fortune, fame, and triumph will be yours at any minute, that you are about to take your place among great men and lovely women in a life more fortunate and happy than any you have ever known—that it is all here, somehow, waiting for you and only an inch away if you will touch it, only a word away if you will speak it, only a wall, a door, a stride from you if you only knew the place where you may enter.

And somehow the old wild wordless hope awakes again that you will find it—the door that you can enter—that this man is going to tell you. The very air you breathe now is filled with the thrilling menace of some impossible good fortune. Again you want to ask him what the magic secret is that has given his life such power, authority, and ease, and made all the brutal struggle, pain, and ugliness of life, the fury, hunger, and the wandering, seem so far away, and you think he is going to tell you—to give this magic secret to you—but he tells you nothing.

Then, for a moment the old unsearchable mystery of time and the city returns to overwhelm your spirit with the horrible sensations of defeat and drowning. You see this man, his mistress, and all the other city people you have known, in shapes of deathless brightness, and yet their life and time are stranger to you than a dream, and you think that you are doomed to walk among them always as a phantom who can never grasp their life or make their time your own. It seems to you now that you are living in a world of creatures who have learned to live without weariness or agony of the soul, in a life which you can never touch, approach or apprehend; a strange city-race who have never lived in a dimension of time that is like your own, and that can be measured in minutes, hours, days, and years, but in dimensions of fathomless and immemorable sensation; who can be remembered only at some moment in their lives nine thousand enthusiasms back, twenty thousand nights in drunkenness ago, eight hundred parties, four million cruelties, nine thousand treacheries or fidelities, two hundred love affairs gone by—and whose lives therefore take on a fabulous and horrible age of sensation, that has never known youth or remembered innocence and that induces in you the sensation of drowning in a sea of horror, a sea of blind, dateless, and immemorable time. There is no door.

But now your host, with his faintly bitter and ironic smile, has poured himself out another good stiff drink of honest rye into a tall thin glass that has some ice in it, and smacked his lips around it with an air of rumination, and, after two or three reflective swallows, begins to get a trifle sorrowful about the life harsh destiny has picked out for him.

While his mistress sits prettily upon the fat edge of an upholstered chair, stroking her cool and delicate fingers gently over his knit brows, and while his good man Ponsonby or Kato is quietly "laying out his things" for dinner, he stares gloomily ahead, and with a bitter smile congratulates you on the blessed luck that has permitted you to live alone in the Armenian section of South Brooklyn.

Well, you say, living alone in South Brooklyn has its drawbacks. The place you live in is shaped just like a pullman car, except that it is not so long and has only one window at each end. There are bars over the front window that your landlady has put there to keep the thugs in that sweet neighborhood from breaking in; in winter the place is cold and dark, and sweats with clammy water, in summer you do all the sweating yourself, but you do plenty of it, quite enough for any one; the place gets hot as hell.

Moreover—and here you really begin to warm up to your work—when you get up in the morning the sweet aroma of the old Gowanus Canal gets into your nostrils, into your mouth, into your lungs, into everything you do, or think, or say! It is, you say, one huge gigantic Stink, a symphonic Smell, a vast organ-note of stupefying odor, cunningly contrived, compacted, and composted of eighty-seven separate several putrefactions; and with a rich and mounting enthusiasm, you name them all for him. There is in it, you say, the smell of melted glue and of burned rubber. It has in it the fragrance of deceased, decaying cats, the odor of rotten cabbage, prehistoric eggs, and old tomatoes; the smell of burning rags and putrefying offal, mixed with the fragrance of a boneyard horse, now dead, the hide of a skunk, and the noisome stenches of a stagnant sewer; it has as well the——

But at this moment your host throws his head back and, with a look of rapture on his face, draws in upon the air the long full respiration of ecstatic satisfaction, as if, in this great panoply of smells, he really had found the breath of life itself, and then cries:

"Wonderful! Wonderful! Oh, simply *swell! Marvellous!*" he cries and then throws back his head again, with a shout of exultant laughter.

"Oh, John!" his lady says at this point with a troubled look upon her lovely face, "I don't think you'd like a place like that at *all*. It sounds simply *dreadful!* I don't like to hear of it," she says, with a pretty little shudder of distaste. "I think it's simply terrible that they let people live in places like that!"

"Oh!" he says, "it's wonderful! The power, the richness, and the beauty of it all!" he cries.

Well, you agree, it's wonderful enough. And it's got power and richness—sure enough! As to the beauty—that's a different matter: You are not so sure of that—but even as you say this you remember many things. You remember a powerful big horse, slow-footed, shaggy in the hoof, with big dappled spots of iron gray upon it that stood one brutal day in August by the curb. Its driver had unhitched it from the wagon and it stood there with its great patient head bent down in an infinite and quiet sorrow, and a little boy with black eyes and a dark face was standing by it holding some sugar in his hand, and its driver, a man who had the tough seamed face of the city, stepped in on the horse with a bucket full of water which he threw against the horse's side. For a second, the great flanks shuddered gratefully and began to smoke, the man stepped back on to the curb and began to look the animal over with a keen deliberate glance, and the boy stood there, rubbing his hand quietly into the horse's muzzle, and talking softly to it all the time.

Then you remember how a tree that leaned over into the narrow little alley where you lived had come to life that year, and how you watched it day by day as it came into its moment's glory of young magic green. And you remember a raw, rusty street along the waterfront, with its naked and brutal life, its agglomeration of shacks, tenements, and slums and huge grimy piers, its unspeakable ugliness and beauty, and you remember how you came along this street one day at sunset, and saw all of the colors of the sun and harbor, flashing, blazing, shifting in swarming motes, in an iridescent web of light and color for an instant on the blazing side of a proud white ship.

And you start to tell your host what it was like and how the evening looked and felt—of the thrilling smell and savor of the huge deserted pier, of the fading light upon old rusty brick of shambling houses, and of the blazing beauty of that swarming web of light and color on the ship's great prow, but when you start to tell about it, you cannot, nor ever recapture the feeling of mystery, exultancy, and wild sorrow that you felt then.

Yes, there has been beauty enough—enough to burst the heart, madden the brain, and tear the sinews of your life asunder—but what is there to say? You remember all these things, and then ten thousand others, but when you start to tell the man about them, you cannot.

Instead you just tell him about the place you live in: of how dark and hot it is in summer, how clammy cold in winter, and of how hard it is to get anything good to eat. You tell him about your landlady who is a hardbitten ex-reporter. You tell him what a good and liberal-hearted woman she is; how rough and ready, full of life and energy, how she likes drinking and the fellowship of drinking men, and knows all the rough and seamy side of life which a newspaper reporter gets to know.

You tell how she has been with murderers before their execution, got the story from them or their mothers, climbed over sides of ships to get a story, forced herself in at funerals, followed burials to the graveyard, trampled upon every painful, decent, sorrowful emotion of mankind—all to get that story; and still remains a decent woman, an immensely good, generous, and lusty-living person, and yet an old maid, and a puritan, somehow, to the roots of her soul.

You tell how she went mad several years before, and spent two years in an asylum; you tell how moments of this madness still come back to her, and of how you went home one night several months before, to find her stretched out on your bed, only to rise and greet you as the great lover of her dreams—Doctor Eustace McNamee, a name, a person, and a love she had invented for herself. Then you tell of her fantastic family, her three sisters and her father, all touched with the same madness, but without her energy, power, and high ability; and of how she has kept the whole crowd going since her eighteenth year.

You tell about the old man who is an inventor who does not invent; of how he invented a corkscrew with the cork attached that would not cork; an unlockable lock; an unbreakable looking-glass that wouldn't look. And you tell how the year before, he inherited $120,000—the first money he had ever had—and promptly took it down to Wall Street where he was as promptly shorn of it, meanwhile sending his wife and daughters to Europe in the nuptial suite of a palatial liner and cabling them when they wanted to come back: "Push on to Rome, my children! Push on, push on! Your father's making millions!"

Yes, all this, and a hundred other things about this incredible, mad, fantastic, and yet high-hearted family which I had found in a dingy alleyway in Brooklyn I could tell my host. And I could tell him a thousand other things about the people all about me—of the Armenians, Spaniards, Irishmen in the alley who came home on week days and turned on the radio, until the whole place was yelling with a hundred dissonances, and who came home on Saturday to get drunk and beat their wives—the whole intimate course and progress of their lives published nakedly from a hundred open windows with laugh, shout, scream, and curse.

I could tell him how they fought, got drunk, and murdered; how they robbed, held up, and blackjacked, how they whored and stole and killed—all of which was part of the orderly and decent course of life for them—and yet, how they could howl with outraged modesty, complain to the police, and send a delegation to us when the young nephew of my landlady lay for an hour upon our patch of backyard grass clad only in his bathing trunks.

[165]

"Yuh gotta nekkid man out deh!" they said, in tones of hushed accusatory horror.

Yes, we—good sir, who are so fond of irony—we, old Whittaker, the inventor, and Mad Maude, his oldest daughter, who would grumble at a broken saucer, and then stuff lavish breakfasts down your throat, who would patiently water twenty little feet of back-yard earth from April until August, and until the grass grew beautifully, and then would turn twenty skinny, swarthy, and half-naked urchins loose into it to stamp it into muddy ruin in twenty minutes while she played the hose upon their grimy little bodies; we, this old man, his daughters, and his grandson, three bank clerks, a cartoonist, two young fellows who worked for Hearst, and myself; we, good sir, who sometimes brought a girl into our rooms, got drunk, wept, confessed sinful and unworthy lives, read Shakespeare, Milton, Whitman, Donne, the Bible—and the sport-ing columns—we, young, foolish, old, mad, and bewildered as we were, but who had never murdered, robbed, or knocked the teeth out of a woman; we, who were fairly decent, kind, and liberal-hearted people as the world goes, were the pariahs of Balcony Square—called so because there was neither square nor balconies, but just a little narrow alleyway.

Yes, we were suspect, enemies to order and the public morals, shameless partakers in an open and indecent infamy, and our neighbors looked at us with all the shuddering reprehension of their mistrustful eyes as they beat their wives like loving husbands, cut one another's throats with civic pride, and went about their honest toil of murder, robbery, and assault like the self-respecting citizens they were.

Meanwhile a man was murdered, with his head bashed in, upon the step of a house three doors below me; and a drunken woman got out of an automobile one night at two o'clock, scream-ing indictments of her escort to the whole neighborhood.

"Yuh gotta pay me, ya big bum!" she yelled. "Yuh gotta pay me now! Give me my t'ree dollehs, or I'll go home an' make my hus-band beat it out of yuh!"

"Staht actin' like a lady!" said the man in lower tones. "I won't

pay yuh till yuh staht actin' like a lady! Yuh gotta staht actin'
like a lady!" he insisted, with a touching devotion to the rules of
gallantry.

And this had continued until he had started the engine of his
car and driven off at furious speed, leaving her to wander up and
down the alleyway for hours, screaming and sobbing, cursing
foully and calling down the vengeance of her husband on this
suitor who had thus misused her—an indictment that had continued unmolested until three young ambitious thugs had seized
the opportunity to go out and rob her; they passed my window
running, in the middle of the night, one fearful and withdrawing,
saying, "Jeez! I'm sick! I don't feel good! Wait a minute! Youse
guys go on an' do it by yourself! I want a cup of coffee!"—And the
others snarling savagely:

"Come on! Come on, yuh yellah bastad! If yuh don't come on,
I'll moiduh yuh!" And they had gone, their quick feet scamper-
ing nimbly in the dark, while the woman's drunken and demented howls came faintly from the other end, and then had
ceased.

Your host has been enchanted by that savage chronicle. He
smites himself upon the brow with rapture, crying, "Oh, grand!
Grand! What a lucky fellow you are! If I were in your place I'd
be the happiest man alive!"

You take a look about you and say nothing.

"To be free! To go about and see these things!" he cries. "To
live among real people! To see life as it is, in the raw—the *real*
stuff, not like this!" he says with a weary look at all the suave
furnishings of illusion that surround him. "And above all else to
be *alone!*"

You ask him if he has ever been alone, if he knows what loneliness is like. You try to tell him, but he knows about this too. He
smiles faintly, ironically, and dismisses it and you, with a wise
man's weary tolerance of youth: "I know! I know!!" he sighs. "But
all of us are lonely, and after all, my boy, the real loneliness for
most of us is *here*"—and he taps himself a trifle to the left of the
third shirt-stud, in the presumptive region of his heart. "But you!

Free, young, and footloose, with the whole world to explore— You have a fine life! What more, in God's name, could a man desire?"

Well, what is there to say? For a moment, the blood is pounding at your temples, a hot retort springs sharp and bitter to your lips, and you feel that you could tell him many things. You could tell him, and not be very nice or dainty with it, that there's a hell of a lot more that a man desires: good food and wonderful companions, comfort, ease, security, a lovely woman like the one who sits beside him now, and an end to loneliness—but what is there to say?

For you are what you are, you know what you know, and there are no words for loneliness, black, bitter, aching loneliness, that gnaws the roots of silence in the night.

So what is there to say? There has been life enough, and power, grandeur, joy enough, and there has also been beauty enough, and God knows there has been squalor and filth and misery and madness and despair enough; murder and cruelty and hate enough, and loneliness enough to fill your bowels with the substance of gray horror, and to crust your lips with its hard and acrid taste of desolation.

And oh, there has been time enough, even in Brooklyn there is time enough, strange time, dark secret time enough, dark million-visaged time enough, forever flowing by you like a river, even in cellar-depths in Brooklyn there is time enough, but when you try to tell the man about it you cannot, for what is there to say?

For suddenly you remember how the tragic light of evening falls even on the huge and rusty jungle of the earth that is known as Brooklyn and on the faces of all the men with dead eyes and with flesh of tallow gray, and of how even in Brooklyn they lean upon the sills of evening in that sad hushed light. And you remember how you lay one evening on your couch in your cool cellar depth in Brooklyn, and listened to the sounds of evening and to the dying birdsong in your tree; and you remember how two windows were thrown up, and you heard two voices—a woman's and a man's—begin to speak in that soft tragic light. And the memory of their words came back to you, like the haunting refrain of some old song—as it was heard and lost in Brooklyn.

"Yuh musta been away," said one, in that sad light.

"Yeah, I been away. I just got back," the other said.

"Yeah? Dat's just what I was t'inkin'," said the other. "I'd been t'inkin' dat yuh musta been away."

"Yeah, I been away on my vacation. I just got back."

"Oh, yeah? Dat's what I t'ought meself. I was t'inkin' just duh oddeh day dat I hadn't seen yuh f'r some time, 'I guess she's gone away,' I says."

And then for seconds there was silence—save for the dying birdsong, voices in the street, faint sounds and shouts and broken calls, and something hushed in evening, far, immense, and murmurous in the air.

"Well, wat's t' noos sinct I been gone?" the voice went out in quietness in soft tragic light. "Has anyt'ing happened sinct I was away?"

"Nah! Nuttin's happened," the other made reply. "About duh same as usual—*you* know?" it said with difficult constraint, inviting intuitions for the spare painfulness of barren tongues.

"Yeah, I know," the other answered with a tranquil resignation —and there was silence then in Brooklyn.

"I guess Fatheh Grogan died sinct you was gone," a voice began.

"Oh, yeah?" the other voice replied with tranquil interest.

"Yeah."

And for a waiting moment there was silence.

"Say, dat's too bad, isn't it?" the quiet voice then said with comfortless regret.

"Yeah. He died on Sattiday. When he went home on Friday night, he was O. K."

"Oh, yeah?"

"Yeah."

And for a moment they were balanced in strong silence.

"Gee, dat was tough, wasn't it?"

"Yeah. Dey didn't find him till duh next day at ten o'clock.

When dey went to look for him he was lyin' stretched out on duh bat' room floeh."

"Oh, yeah?"

"Yeah. Dey found him lyin' deh," it said.

And for a moment more the voices hung in balanced silence.

"Gee, dat's too bad. . . . I guess I was away when all dat happened."

"Yeah. Yuh musta been away."

"Yeah, dat was it, I guess. I musta been away. Oddehwise I woulda hoid. I was away."

"Well, so long, kid. . . . I'll be seein' yuh."

"Well, so long!"

A window closed, and there was silence; evening and far sounds and broken cries in Brooklyn, Brooklyn, in the formless, rusty, and unnumbered wilderness of life.

And now the old red light fades swiftly from the old red brick of rusty houses, and there are voices in the air, and somewhere music, and we are lying there, blind atoms in our cellar-depths, gray voiceless atoms on the manswarm desolation of the earth, and our fame is lost, our names forgotten, our powers are wasting from us like mined earth, while we lie here at evening and the river flows . . . and dark time is feeding like a vulture on our entrails, and we know that we are lost, and cannot stir . . . and there are ships there! there are ships! . . . and Christ! we are all dying in the darkness! . . . and yuh musta been away . . . yuh musta been away. . . .

And that is a moment of dark time, that is one of strange million-visaged time's dark faces.

II. OCTOBER: 1923

My life, more than the life of any one I know, has been spent in solitude and wandering. Why this is true, or how it happened, I have never known; yet it is so. From my fifteenth year—

save for a single interval—I have lived about as solitary a life as a modern man can have. I mean by this that the number of hours, days, months, and years—the actual time that I have spent alone—has been immense and extraordinary.

And this fact is all the more astonishing because I never seemed to seek out solitude, nor did I shrink from life, or seek to build myself into a wall away from all the fury and the turmoil of the earth. Rather, I loved life so dearly that I was driven mad by the thirst and hunger which I felt for it.

At college, I would prowl the stacks of the great library at night pulling books out of a thousand shelves and reading in them like a mad man. The thought of these vast stacks of books would drive me mad; the more I read, the less I seemed to know; the greater the number of the books I read, the greater the immense uncountable number of those which I could never read would seem to be. Within a period of ten years I read at least twenty thousand volumes—deliberately I have set the number low—and opened the pages and looked through many times that number. If this seems unbelievable, I am sorry for it, but it happened. Yet all this terrific orgy of the books brought me no comfort, peace, or wisdom of the mind and heart. Instead, my fury and despair increased from what it fed upon, my hunger mounted with the food it ate.

And it was the same with everything I did.

For this fury which drove me on to read so many books had nothing to do with scholarship, nothing to do with academic honors, nothing to do with formal learning. I was not in any way a scholar and did not want to be one. I simply wanted to know about everything on earth; I wanted to devour the earth, and it drove me mad when I saw I could not do this. In the midst of a furious burst of reading in the enormous library, the thought of the streets outside and the great city all around me would drive through my body like a sword. It would now seem to me that every second that I passed among the books was being wasted—that at this moment something priceless, irrecoverable was happening in the streets, and that if I could only get to it in time and see it, I would somehow get the knowledge of the whole thing in me—the source, the well, the spring from which all men and words and actions, and every design upon this earth proceed.

And I would rush out in the streets to find it, be hurled through the tunnel into Boston and then spend hours in driving myself savagely through a hundred streets, looking into the faces of a million people, trying to get an instant and conclusive picture of all they did and said and were, of all their million destinies. And I would search the furious streets until bone and brain and blood could stand no more—until every sinew of my life and spirit was wrung, trembling, and exhausted, and my heart sank down beneath its weight of despair and desolation.

Yet a furious hope, a wild extravagant belief, was burning in me all the time. I would write down enormous charts and plans and projects of all that I proposed to do in life—a program of work and living which would have exhausted the energies of ten thousand men. I would get up in the middle of the night to scrawl down insane catalogs of all that I had seen and done: the number of books I had read, the number of miles I had travelled, the number of people I had known, the number of women I had slept with, the number of meals I had eaten, the number of towns I had visited, the number of states I had been in.

And at one moment I would gloat and chuckle over these stupendous lists like a miser gloating over his hoard, only to groan bitterly with despair the next moment, and to beat my head against the wall, as I remembered the overwhelming amount of all I had not seen or done, or known. Then I would begin another list filled with enormous catalogs of all the books I had not read, all the food I had not eaten, all the women that I had not slept with, all the states I had not been in, all the towns I had not visited. Then I would write down plans and programs whereby all these things must be accomplished, how many years it would take to do it all, and how old I would be when I had finished. An enormous wave of hope and joy would surge up in me, because it now looked easy, and I had no doubt at all that I could do it.

I never asked myself how I was going to live while this was going on, where I was going to get the money for this gigantic adventure, and what I was going to do to make it possible. Although I had a good mind in some respects, I was no better than a child when it came to things like this; the fact that to explore and devour the world, as I was going to do, would require the fortune of a millionaire had no meaning to me at all. If I thought about it, it seemed to have no importance or reality whatever—I just dismissed it impatiently, or with a conviction that some old man would die and leave me a fortune; that I was going to pick up a purse containing hundreds of thousands of dollars while walking in the Fenway, and that the reward would be enough to keep me going; or that a beautiful and rich young widow, true-hearted, tender, loving and voluptuous, who had carrot-colored hair, little freckles on her face, a snub nose and luminous gray-green eyes with something wicked, yet loving and faithful, in them, and one gold filling in her solid little teeth, was going to fall in love with me, marry me, and be forever true and faithful to me while I went reading, eating, drinking, whoring, and devouring my way around the world; or finally that I would write a book or play every year or so, which would be a great success, and yield me fifteen or twenty thousand dollars at a crack.

Thus, I went storming away at the whole earth about me, sometimes mad with despair, weariness, and bewilderment; and sometimes wild with a jubilant and exultant joy and certitude as the conviction came to me that everything would happen as I wished. Then at night I would hear the vast sounds and silence of the earth and of the city, I would begin to think of the dark sleeping earth and of the continent of night, until it seemed to me it all was spread before me like a map—rivers, plains, and mountains and ten thousand sleeping towns; it seemed to me that I saw everything at once.

Then I would think about the State of Kansas, of Wyoming, Colorado, or some other place where I had never been, and I could sleep no more, and I would twist about in bed, and tear the sheets, get up and smoke, and walk around the room. I would feel an intolerable desire to go and see these places, to hear the voices of the people, to step out of the train upon the earth, and it seemed to me if I could do this only for five minutes I would be satisfied. I would become obsessed with the notion that the earth of these places would look and feel different from anything I had ever known, that it had a quality and texture of its own, a kind of elastic quality so that the foot would spring upon it, and also a feeling of depth and solidity which the earth in the East did not have. And I felt that I could never rest in peace again until I had stepped upon this earth, and tested it.

Meanwhile, the great antagonists of fixity and everlasting change, of wandering forever and return, of weariness intolerable and insatiate thirst, of certitude and peace and no desire and everlasting torment of the soul, had begun to wage perpetual warfare in me. And now I hardly ever thought of home. Rather, like a man held captive in some green land of sorcery, who does not know the years are passing while he dreams his life away, the enormous plant of time, desire, and memory flowered and fed forever with a cancerous growth through all the tissues of my life until the earth I came from, and the life that I had known seemed remote and buried as the sunken cities of Atlantis.

Then, one day I awoke at morning and thought of home. A lock-bolt was shot back in my memory and a door was opened. Suddenly, as if a curtain of dark sorcery had been lifted from my vision, I saw the earth I came from, and all the people I had known in shapes of deathless brightness. And instantly an intolerable desire to see them all again began to burn in me. I said: "I must go home again!" And this, too, all men who ever wandered on the earth have said.

Three years had passed by like a dream. During this time my father had died. That year I went home for the last time in October.

October had come again, and that year it was sharp and soon: frost was early, burning the thick green on the mountain sides to massed brilliant hues of blazing colors, painting the air with sharpness, sorrow, and delight. Sometimes, and often, there was warmth by day, an ancient drowsy light, a golden warmth and pollenated haze in afternoon, but over all the earth there was the premonitory breath of frost, an exultancy for all the men who were returning, a haunting sorrow for the buried men, and for all those who were gone and would not come again.

My father was dead, and now it seemed to me that I had never found him. He was dead, and yet I sought him everywhere, and could not believe that he was dead, and was sure that I would find him. It was October and that year, after years of absence and of wandering, I had come home again.

I could not think that he had died, but I had come home in October, and all the life that I had known there was strange and sorrowful as dreams. And yet I saw it all in shapes of deathless brightness—the town, the streets, the magic hills, and the plain prognathous faces of the people I had known as if I had revisited the shores of this great earth with a heart of fire, a cry of pain and ecstasy, a memory of intolerable longing and regret for all that glorious and exultant life which I must visit now forever as a fleshless ghost, never to touch, to hold, to have its palpable warmth and substance for my own again. I had come home again, and yet I could not believe that he was dead, and I thought I heard his great voice ringing in the street again, and that I would see him striding toward me across the Square with his gaunt earth-devouring stride, or find him waiting every time I turned the corner, or lunging toward the house bearing the tremendous provender of his food and meat, bringing to us all the deathless security of his strength and power and passion, bringing to us all again the roaring message of his fires that shook the firefull chimney throat with their terrific blast, giving to us all again the exultant knowledge that the good days, the magic days, the golden weather of our lives would come again, and that this dream-like and phantasmal world in which I found myself would waken instantly, as it had once, to all the palpable warmth and glory of the earth, if only my father would come back to make it live, to give us life, again.

Therefore, I could not think that he was dead. And at night, in my mother's house, I would lie in my bed in the dark, hearing the wind that rattled dry leaves along the empty pavement, hearing far-off across the wind, the barking of a dog, feeling dark time, strange time, dark secret time, as it flowed on around me, remembering my life, this house, and all the million strange and secret visages of time, dark time, thinking, feeling, thinking:

"October has come again, has come again. . . . I have come home again, and found my father dead . . . and that was time . . . time . . . time. . . . Where shall I go now? What shall I do? For October has come again, but there has gone some richness from the life we knew, and we are lost."

Storm shook the house at night—the old house, my mother's house—where I had seen my brother die. The old doors swung and creaked in darkness, darkness pressed against the house, the darkness filled us, filled the house at night, it moved about us soft and secret, palpable, filled with a thousand secret presences of sorrowful time and memory, moving about me as I lay below my brother's room in darkness, while storm shook the house and something creaked and rattled in the wind's strong blast.

Wind beat at us with burly shoulders in the night. The darkness moved there in the house like something silent, palpable—a spirit breathing in my mother's house, a demon and a friend—speaking to me its silent and intolerable prophecy of flight, of secrecy and of storm, moving about me constantly, prowling about the edges of my life, ever beside me, in me, whispering:

"Child, child—come with me—come with me to your brother's grave tonight. Come with me to the places where the young men lie whose bodies have long since been buried in the earth. Come with me where they walk and move again tonight, and you shall see your brother's face again, and hear his voice, and see again, as they march toward you from their graves, the company of the young men who died, as he did, in October, speaking to you their messages of flight, of triumph, and the all-exultant darkness, telling you that all will be again as it was once."

And I would lie there thinking:

"October has come again—has come again"—feeling the dark around me, not believing that my father could be dead, thinking:

"The strange and lonely years have come again. . . . I have come home again . . . come home again . . . and will it not be with us as it has been again?"—feeling darkness as it moved about me, thinking, "Is it not the same darkness that I knew in childhood, and have I not lain here in bed before, and felt this darkness moving all about me? . . . Did we not hear dogs that barked in darkness, in October," I then thought. "Were not their howls far broken by the wind? . . . And hear dry leaves that scampered on the streets at night . . . and the huge and burly rushes of the wind . . . and hear limbs that stiffly creak in the remote demented howlings of the wind . . . and something creaking in the wind at night . . . and think, then, as we think now, of all the men who have gone and never will come back again, and of our friends and brothers who lie buried in the earth? . . . Oh, has not October now come back again," I cried, "as always—as it always was?"—and hearing the great darkness softly prowling in my mother's house at night, and thinking, feeling, thinking, as I lay there in the dark:

"Now October has come again which in our land is different from October in the other lands. The ripe, the golden month has come again, and in Virginia the chinkapins are falling. Frost sharps the middle music of the seasons, and all things living on the earth turn home again. The country is so big you cannot say the country has the same October. In Maine, the frost comes sharp and quick as driven nails, just for a week or so the woods, all of the bright and bitter leaves, flare up: the maples turn a blazing bitter red, and other leaves turn yellow like a living light, falling about you as you walk the woods, falling about you like small pieces of the sun, so that you cannot say where sunlight shakes and flutters on the ground, and where the leaves.

"Meanwhile the Palisades are melting in massed molten colors, the season swings along the nation, and a little later in the South dense woodings on the hill begin to glow and soften, and when they smell the burning woodsmoke in Ohio children say: 'I'll bet that there's a forest fire in Michigan.' And the mountaineer goes hunting down in North Carolina, he stays out late with mournful flop-eared hounds, a rind of moon comes up across the rude lift of the hills: what do his friends say to him when he stays out late? Full of hoarse innocence and laughter, they will say: 'Mister, yore ole woman's goin' to whup ye if ye don't go home.' "

Oh, return, return!

"October is the richest of the seasons: the fields are cut, the granaries are full, the bins are loaded to the brim with fatness, and from the cider-press the rich brown oozings of the York Imperials run. The bee bores to the belly of the yellowed grape, the fly gets old and fat and blue, he buzzes loud, crawls slow, creeps heavily to death on sill and ceiling, the sun goes down in blood and pollen across the bronzed and mown fields of old October.

"The corn is shocked: it sticks out in hard yellow rows upon dried ears, fit now for great red barns in Pennsylvania, and the big stained teeth of crunching horses. The indolent hoofs kick swiftly at the boards, the barn is sweet with hay and leather, wood and apples. This, and the clean dry crunching of the teeth, is all: the sweat, the labor, and the plow are over. The late pears mellow on a sunny shelf; smoked hams hang to the warped barn rafters; the pantry shelves are loaded with three hundred jars of fruit. Meanwhile the leaves are turning, turning up in Maine, the chestnut burrs plop thickly to the earth in gusts of wind, and in Virginia the chinkapins are falling.

"There is a smell of burning in small towns in afternoon, and men with buckles on their arms are raking leaves in yards as boys come by with straps slung back across their shoulders. The oak leaves, big and brown, are bedded deep in yard and gutter: they make deep wadings to the knee for children in the streets. The fire will snap and crackle like a whip, sharp acrid smoke will sting the eyes, in mown fields the little vipers of the flame eat past the black coarse edges of burnt stubble like a line of locusts. Fire drives a thorn of memory in the heart.

"The bladed grass, a forest of small spears of ice, is thawed by noon: summer is over but the sun is warm again, and there are days throughout the land of gold and russet. But summer is dead and gone, the earth is waiting, suspense and ecstasy are gnawing at the hearts of men, the brooding prescience of frost is there. The sun flames red and bloody as it sets, there are old red glintings on the battered pails, the great barn gets the ancient light as the boy slops homeward with warm foaming milk. Great shadows lengthen in the fields, the old red light dies swiftly, and the sunset barking of the hounds is faint and far and full of frost: there are shrewd whistles to the dogs of frost and silence—this is all. Wind scuffs and rattles at the old brown leaves, and through the night the great oak leaves keep falling.

"Trains cross the continent in a swirl of dust and thunder, the leaves fly down the tracks behind them: the great trains cleave through gulch and gulley, they rumble with spoked thunder of the bridges over the powerful brown wash of mighty rivers, they toil through hills, they skirt the rough brown stubble of shorn fields, they whip past empty stations in the little towns and their great stride pounds its even pulse across America. Field and hill and lift and gulch and hollow, mountain and plain and river, a wilderness with fallen trees across it, a thicket of bedded brown and twisted undergrowth, a plain, a desert, and a plantation, a mighty landscape with no fenced niceness, an immensity of fold and convolution that can never be remembered, that can never be forgotten, that has never been described—weary with harvest, potent with every fruit and ore, the immeasurable richness embrowned with autumn, rank, crude, unharnessed, careless of scars or beauty, everlasting and magnificent, a cry, a space, an ecstasy!— American earth in old October.

"And the great winds howl and swoop across the land: they make a distant roaring in great trees, and boys in bed will stir in ecstasy, thinking of demons and vast swoopings through the earth. All through the night there is the clean, the bitter rain of acorns, and the chestnut burrs are plopping to the ground.

"And often in the night there is only the living silence, the distant frosty barking of a dog, the small clumsy stir and feathery stumble of the chickens on limed roosts, and the moon, the low and heavy moon of autumn, now barred behind the leafless poles of pines, now at the pinewood's brooding edge and summit, now falling with ghost's dawn of milky light upon rimed clods of fields and on the frosty scurf on pumpkins, now whiter, smaller, brighter, hanging against the church spire's slope, hanging the same way in a million streets, steeping all the earth in frost and silence.

"Then a chime of frost-cold bells may peal out on the brooding air, and people lying in their beds will listen. They will not speak or stir, silence will gnaw the darkness like a rat, but they will whisper in their hearts:

" 'Summer has come and gone, has come and gone. And now —?' But they will say no more, they will have no more to say: they will wait listening, silent and brooding as the frost, to time, strange ticking time, dark time that haunts us with the briefness of our days. They will think of men long dead, of men now buried in the earth, of frost and silence long ago, of a forgotten face and moment of lost time, and they will think of things they have no words to utter.

"And in the night, in the dark, in the living sleeping silence of the towns, the million streets, they will hear the thunder of the fast express, the whistles of great ships upon the river.

"What will they say then? What will they say?"

Only the darkness moved about me as I lay there thinking; feeling in the darkness: a door creaked softly in the house.

"October is the season for returning: the bowels of youth are yearning with lost love. Their mouths are dry and bitter with desire: their hearts are torn with the thorns of Spring. For lovely April, cruel and flowerful, will tear them with sharp joy and word-less lust. Spring has no language but a cry; but crueller than April is the asp of time.

"All things on earth point home in old October: Sailors to sea, travellers to walls and fences, hunters to field and hollow and the long voice of the hounds, the lover to the love he has forsaken— all things that live upon this earth return, return: Father, will you not, too, come back again?

"Where are you now, when all things on the earth come back again? For have not all these things been here before, have we not seen them, heard them, known them, and will they not live again for us as they did once, if only you come back again?

"Father, in the night time, in the dark, I have heard the thunder of the fast express. In the night, in the dark, I have heard the howling of the winds among great trees, and the sharp and windy raining of the acorns. In the night, in the dark, I have heard the feet of rain upon the roofs, the glut and gurgle of the gutter spouts, and the soaking gulping throat of all the mighty earth, drinking its thirst out in the month of May—and heard the sorrowful silence of the river in October. The hill-streams foam and welter in a steady plunge, the mined clay drops and melts and eddies in the night, the snake coils cool and glistening under dripping ferns, the water roars down past the mill in one sheer sheet-like plunge, making a steady noise like wind, and in the night, in the dark, the river flows by us to the sea.

"The great maw slowly drinks the land as we lie sleeping: the mined banks cave and crumble in the dark, the dark earth melts and drops into its tide, great horns are baying in the gulf of night, great boats are baying at the river's mouth. Thus, thick with the wastes of earth, dark with our stains, and heavied with our dumpings, rich, rank, beautiful and unending as all life, all living, the river, the dark immortal river, full of strange tragic time, is flowing by us—by us—by us—to the sea.

"All this has been upon the earth, and will abide forever. But you are gone, our lives are ruined and broken in the night, our lives are mined below us by the river, are whirled away into the sea and darkness, and we are lost unless you come to give us life again.

"Come to us, father, in the watches of the night, come to us as you always came, bringing to us the invincible sustenance of your strength, the limitless treasure of your bounty, the tremendous structure of your life that will shape all lost and broken things on earth again into a golden pattern of exultancy and joy. Come to us, father, while the winds howl in the darkness, for October has come again bringing with it huge prophecies of death and life and the great cargo of the men who will return. For we are ruined, lost, and broken if you do not come, and our lives, like rotten chips, are whirled about us onward in the darkness to the sea."

So, thinking, feeling, speaking, I lay there in my mother's house, but there was nothing in the house but silence and the moving darkness: storm shook the house and huge winds rushed upon us, and I knew then that my father would not come again, and that all the life that I had known was now lost and broken as a dream.

Suddenly I knew that every man who ever lived has looked, is looking, for his father, and that even when his father dies, his son will still search furiously the streets of life to find him, and that he never loses hope but always feels that some day he will see his father's face again. I had come home again in October and there were no doors, there were no doors for me to enter and I knew now that I could never make this life my own again. Yet, in all the huge unrest that was goading me to flight I had no place or door or dwelling-place on earth to go, and yet must make for myself a life different from the one my father made for me or die myself.

Storm shook the house at night and there was something calling in the wind. It spoke to me and filled my heart with the exultant prophecies of flight, darkness, and discovery, saying with a demon's whisper of unbodied joy:

"Away! Away! Away! There are new lands, morning, and a shining city! Child, child, go find the earth again!"

III. OCTOBER: 1926

Smoke-gold by day, the numb exultant secrecies of fog, a fog-numb air filled with the solemn joy of nameless and impending prophecy, an ancient yellow light, the old smoke-ochre of the morning, never coming to an open brightness—such was October in England that year. Sometimes by night in stormy skies there was the wild, the driven moon, sometimes the naked time-far loneliness, the most—oh most—familiar blazing of the stars that shine on men forever, their nameless, passionate dilemma of strong joy and empty desolation, hope and terror, home and hunger, the huge twin tyranny of their bitter governance—wandering forever and the earth again.

They are still-burning, homely particles of night that light the huge tent of the dark with their remembered fire, recalling the familiar hill, the native earth from which we came, from which we could have laid our finger on them, and making the great earth and home seem near, most near, to wanderers; and filling them with naked desolations of doorless, houseless, timeless, and unmeasured vacancy.

And everywhere that year there was something secret, lonely, and immense that waited, that impended, that was still. Something that promised numbly, hugely, in the fog-numb air, and that never broke to any open sharpness, and that was almost keen and frosty October in remembered hills—oh, there was something there incredibly near and most familiar, only a word, a stride, a room, a door away—only a door away and never opened, only a door away and never found.

At night, in the lounging rooms of the old inn, crackling fires were blazing cheerfully, and people sat together drinking small cups of the black bitter liquid mud that they called coffee.

The people were mostly family groups who had come to visit their son or brother in the university. They were the most extraordinary, ugly, and distinguished looking people I had ever seen. There was the father, often the best looking of the lot: a man with a ruddy weathered face, a cropped white mustache, iron gray hair—an open, driving, bull-dog look of the country carried with tremendous style. The mother was very ugly with a long horse face and grimly weathered cheek flanks that seemed to have the tough consistency of well-tanned leather. Her grim bared smile shone in her weathered face and was nailed forever round the gauntness of her grinning teeth. She had a neighing voice, a shapeless figure, distinguished by the bony and angular width of the hip structure, clothed with fantastic dowdiness—fantastic because the men were dressed so well, and because everything they wore, no matter how old and used it might be, seemed beautiful and right.

The daughter had the mother's look: a tall gawky girl with a bony, weathered face and a toothy mouth, she wore an ill-fitting evening or party dress of a light unpleasant blue, with a big meaningless rosette of ruffles at the waist. She had big feet, bony legs and arms, and she was wearing pumps of dreary gray and gray silk stockings.

The son was a little fellow with ruddy apple-cheeks, crisp, fair, curly hair, and baggy gray trousers; and there was another youth, one of his college friends, of the same cut and quality, who paid a dutiful but cold attention to the daughter, which she repaid in kind, and with which every one was completely satisfied.

They had to be seen to be believed, but even then, one could only say, like the man who saw the giraffe: "I don't believe it." The young men sat stiffly on the edges of their chairs, holding their little cups of coffee in their hands, bent forward in an attitude of cold but respectful attentiveness, and the conversation that went on among them was incredible. For their manner was impregnable, they were cold, remote, and formal almost to the point of military curtness, and yet one felt among them constantly an utter familiarity of affection, a strange secret warmth, past words or spoken vows, that burned in them like glacial fire.

When you got ten or fifteen feet away from them their language could not have been more indecipherable if they had spoken in Chinese; but it was fascinating just to listen to the sounds. For there would be long mounting horse-like neighs, and then there would be reedy flute-like notes, and incisive cold finalities and clipped ejaculations and sometimes a lovely and most musical speech. But the horse-like neighs and clipped ejaculations would predominate; and suddenly I understood how strange these people seemed to other races, and why Frenchmen, Germans, and Italians would sometimes stare at them with gape-mouthed stupefaction when they heard them talking.

Once when I passed by them they had the family vicar or some clergyman of their acquaintance with them. He was a mountain of a man, and he too, was hardly credible: the huge creature was at least six and a half feet tall, and he must have weighed three hundred pounds. He had a flaming moon of face and jowl, at once most animal and delicate, and he peered out keenly with luminous smoke-gray eyes beneath a bushy hedge-growth of gray brows. He was dressed in the clerical garb and his bulging grossly sensual calves were encased in buttoned gaiters. As I went by, he was leaning forward with his little cup of muddy coffee held delicately in the huge mutton of his hand, peering keenly out beneath his beetling bush of brow at the young man who was the brother's friend.

"Did you ever read—that is, in recent yöhs—the concluding chaptahs in 'The Vicah of Wakefield'?" Carefully he set the little cup down in its saucer. "I was reading it again the other day. It's an extraordinary thing!" he said.

It was impossible to reproduce the sound of these simple words, or the effect they wrought upon my senses.

For first, the words "Did you ever" were delivered in a delicate rising-and-falling neigh, the word "read" really came out with a long reedy sound, the words "that is in recent yöhs," in a parenthesis of sweetly gentle benevolence, the phrase "the concluding chaptahs in 'The Vicah of Wakefield,'" in full, deliberate, satisfied tones of titular respect, the phrase "I was reading it again the other day," thoughtfully, reedily, with a subdued, gentle, and mellow reminiscence, and the final decisive phrase, "It's an extraordinary thing," with passionate conviction and sincerity that passed at the end into such an unction of worshipful admiration that the words "extraordinary thing" were not spoken, but breathed out passionately, and had the sound "'strawd'n'ry thing!"

"Ow!" the young man answered distantly, and in a rather surprised tone, with an air of coldly startled interest. "Now! I can't say that I have—not since my nursery days, at any rate!" He laughed metallically.

"You should read it again," the mountainous creature breathed unctuously. "A 'strawd'n'ry thing! A 'strawd'n'ry thing." Delicately he lifted the little cup of muddy black in his huge hand again and put it to his lips.

"But *frightfully* sentimental, down't you think?" the girl neighed sharply at this point. "I mean all the lovely woman-stoops-to-folly sawt of thing, you now. After all, it is a bit thick to expect people to swallow *that* nowadays," she neighed, "particularly after all that's happened in the last twenty yöhs. I suppose it mattuhed in the eighteenth centureh but after all," she neighed with an impatient scorn, "who cares today? Who cares," she went on recklessly, "*what* lovely woman stoops to? I can't see that it makes the *slightest* difference. It's not as if it mattuhed any longah! No one cares!"

"Ow!" the young man said with his air of coldly startled interest. "Yes, I think I follow you, but I don't entirely agree. How can we be certain what *is* sentimental and what's not?"

"But it seems to me he misses the whole point!" the girl exclaimed with one full mouth-like rush. "After all," she went on scornfully, "no one is interested in woman's folly any longah— the ruined-maiden broken-vows sawt of thing. If that was what she got she should have jolly well known what she wanted to begin with! *I'll* not waste any pity on her," she said grimly. "The greatest folly is not knowin' what you want to do! The whole point today is to live as cleveleh as possible! That's the only thing that mattahs! If you know what you want and go about it cleveleh, the rest of it will take care of itself."

"Um," the mother now remarked, her gaunt bare smile set grimly, formidably, on her weathered face. "That takes a bit of doin', *doesn't* it?" And as she spoke these quiet words her grim smile never faltered for an instant and there was a hard, an obdurate, an almost savage irony in her intonation, which left them all completely unperturbed.

"Oh, a '*strawd'n'ry* thing! A '*strawd'n'ry* thing!" the huge clerical creature whispered dreamily at this point, as if he had not heard them. And delicately he set his little cup back on the saucer.

One's first impulse when he saw and heard them was to shout with an astounded laughter—and yet, somehow, one never laughed. They had a formidable and impregnable quality that silenced laughter: a quality that was so assured in its own sense of inevitable rightness that it saw no other way except its own, and was so invincibly sure in its own way that it was indifferent to all others. It could be taken among strange lands and alien faces, and to the farthest and most savage colonies on earth, and would never change or alter by a jot.

Yes, they had found a way, a door, a room to enter, and there were walls about them now, and the way was theirs. The mark of dark time and the architecture of unnumbered centuries of years were on them, and had made them what they were, and what they were, they were, and would not change.

I did not know if their way was a good way, but I knew it was not mine. Their door was one I could not enter. And suddenly the naked empty desolation filled my life again, and I was walking on beneath the timeless sky, and had no wall at which to hurl my strength, no door to enter by, and no purpose for the furious unemployment of my soul. And now the worm was eating at my heart again. I felt the slow interminable waste and wear of gray time all about me and my life was passing in the darkness, and all the time a voice kept saying: "Why? Why am I here now? And where shall I go?"

When I got out into the High Street after dinner, the dark air would be thronging with the music of great bells, and there would be a smell of fog and smoke and old October in the air, the premonitory thrill and menace of some intolerable and nameless joy. Often at night, the visage of the sky would by some magic be released from the thick grayness that had covered it by day, and would shine forth barely, blazing with flashing and magnificent stars.

And, as the old bells thronged through the smoky air, the students would be passing along the street, singly or in groups of two or three, briskly, and with the eager haste that told of meetings to come, appointments to be kept, or the expectation of some good fortune, happiness, or pleasure toward which they hurried on.

The soft glow of lights would shine from the ancient windows of the colleges, and one could hear the faint sounds of voices, laughter, sometimes music.

Then I would go to different pubs and drink until the closing time. Sometimes the proctors would come into a pub where I was drinking, speak amicably to every one, and in a moment more go out again.

Somehow I always hoped that they would take me for a student. I could see them stepping up to me, as I stood there at the bar, saying courteously, yet gravely and sternly:

"Your name and college, sir?"

Then I could see the look of astonished disbelief on their grim red faces when I told them I was not a student, and at last, when I had convinced them, I could hear their crestfallen muttered-out apologies, and would graciously excuse them.

But the proctors never spoke to me, and the bar-man, seeing me look at them as they went out one night, misunderstood the look, and laughed with cheerful reassurance:

"You've nothing at all to worry about, sir. They won't bother you. It's only the gentlemen at the University they're after."

"How do they know I'm not there?"

"That I couldn't tell you, sir," he answered cheerfully, "but they 'ave a way of knowin'! Ah, yes!" he said with satisfaction, slapping a wet cloth down upon the bar. "They 'ave a way of knowin', right enough! They're a clever lot, those chaps. A very clever lot, sir, and they always 'ave a way of knowin' when you're not." And smiling cheerfully, he made a vigorous parting swipe across the wood, and put the cloth away below the counter.

My glass was almost empty and I looked at it, and wondered if I ought to have another. I thought they made them very small, and kept thinking of the governors of North and South Carolina. It was a fine, warm, open sort of pub, and there was a big fire-place just behind me, crackling smartly with a fire of blazing coals: I could feel the warmth upon my back. Outside, in the fog-numb air, people came by with lonely, rapid footsteps and were lost in fog-numb air again.

At this moment the bar-maid, who had bronze-red hair and the shrewd, witty visage of a parrot, turned and called out in a cheerful, crisply peremptory tone: "Time please, gentlemen. Closing time."

I put the glass down empty. I wondered what the way of knowing was.

It was October, about the middle of the month, at the opening of the Michaelmas term. Everywhere there was the exultant thrill and bustle of returning, of a new life, beginning in an ancient and beautiful place that was itself enriched by the countless lives and adventures of hundreds of years. In the morning there was the numb excitement of the foggy air, a smell of good tobacco, beer, grilled kidneys, ham and sausages, and grilled tomatoes, a faint nostalgic smell of tea, and incredibly, somehow, in that foggy old-gold light, a smell of coffee—a maddening, false, delusive smell, for when one went to find the coffee it would not be there: it was black liquid mud, bitter, lifeless, and undrinkable.

Everything was very expensive and yet it made you feel rich yourself just to look at it. The little shops, the wine shops with their bay windows of small leaded glass, and the crusty opulence of the bottles of old port and sherry and the burgundies, the mellow homely warmth and quietness of the interior, the tailor shops, the tobacco shops with their selected grades of fine tobacco stored in ancient crocks, the little bell that tinkled thinly as you went in from the street, the decorous, courteous, yet suavely good-natured proprietor behind the counter, who had the ruddy cheeks, the flowing brown mustache and the wing-collar of the shopkeeper of solid substance, and who would hold the crock below your nose to let you smell the moist fragrance of a rare tobacco before you bought, and would offer you one of his best cigarettes before you left—all of this gave somehow to the simplest acts of life and business a ritualistic warmth and sanctity, and made you feel wealthy and secure.

And everywhere around me in the morning there was the feeling of an immanent recovery, a recapture of a life that had always been my own. This familiar look kept shining at me through the faces of the people. It was in the faces of tradesmen—people in butcher shops, wine shops, clothing stores—and sometimes it was in the faces of women, at once common, fine, familiar, curiously delicate and serene, going to the markets, in the foggy old-bronze light of morning, and of men who passed by wearing derby hats and wing collars. It was in the faces of a man and his son, good-humored little red-faced bullocks, packed with life, who ran a pub in the Cowley Road near the house where, later, I went to live.

It was a look round, full, ruddy, and serene in its good-nature and had more openness and mellow humor in it than I had found in the faces of the people in New England. It was more like the look of country people and small-town people in the South. Sometimes it had the open tranquil ruddiness, the bovine and self-satisfied good humor of my uncle, Crockett Pentland, and sometimes it was like Mr. Bailey, the policeman, whom the negro killed one winter's night, when snow was on the ground and all the bells began to ring. And then it was full and hearty like the face of Mr. Ernest Pegram, who was the City Plumber and lived next door to my father, or it was plump, common, kindly, invincibly provincial, ignorant and domestic, like the face of Mrs. Higginson, who lived across the street, and had herself been born in England and whose common kindly face had the same animal, gentle, smoke-like delicacy of expression round the mouth that some of these men and women had.

It was a life that seemed so near to me that I could lay my hand on it and make it mine at any moment. I seemed to have returned to a room I had always known, and to have paused for a moment without any doubt or perturbation of the soul outside the door.

But I never found the door, or turned the knob, or stepped into the room. When I got there I couldn't find it. It was as near as my hand if I could only touch it, only as high as my heart and yet I could not reach it, only a hand's breadth off if I would span it, a word away if I would speak it.

I never found it. The old-smoke-gold of morning would be full of hope and joy and immanent discovery but afternoon would come and the soft gray humid skies pressed down on me with their huge numb waste and weight and weariness of intolerable time, and the empty naked desolation filled my guts.

I would walk that legendary street past all those visible and en-chanted substances of time, and see the students passing through the college gates, the unbelievable velvet green of college quads, and see the huge dark room of peace and joy that time had made, and I had no way of getting into it.

Each day I walked about the town and breathed the accursed languid softness of gray foreign air, that had no bite or sparkle in it, and went by all their fabulous age-encrusted walls of Gothic time, and wondered what in the name of God I had to do with all their walls or towers, or how I could feed my hunger on the portraits of the Spanish king, and why I was there, why I had come!

Around me was the whole structure of an enchanted life—a life hauntingly familiar—and now that I was there I had no way of getting into it. The inn itself was ancient, legendary, beautiful, elfin, like all the inns I had ever read about, and yet all of the cheer, the warmth, the joy and comfort I had dreamed of finding in an inn was lacking.

Upstairs the halls went crazily up and down at different levels, one mounted steps, went down again, got lost and turned around in the bewildering design of the ancient added-onto structure—and this was the way I had always known it would be. But the rooms were small, cold, dark, and dreary, the lights were dim and dismal, you stayed out of your room as much as possible and when you went to bed at night you crawled in trembling between clammy sheets. When you got up in the morning there was a small jug of warm water at your door with which to shave, but the jug was too small. You got out of the room and went downstairs as quickly as you could.

Downstairs it would be fine. There would be a brisk fire crack-ling in the hearth, the old smoke-gold of morning and the smell of fog, the crisp cheerful voices of the people and their ruddy competent morning look, and the cheerful smells of breakfast, always liberal and good, the best meal that they had: kidneys and ham and eggs and sausages, toast and marmalade and tea.

But at night there would come the huge boiled-flannel splendor of the dinner, the magnificent and prayerful service of the waiter, who served you with such reverent grace from heavy silver platters that you felt the food must be as good as everything looked. But it never was.

I ate at a large table in the centre of the dining-room provided by a thoughtful management for such isolated waifs and strays as myself. The food looked very good, and was, according to the genius of the nation, tasteless. How they ever did it I could never tell: everything was of the highest quality and you chewed upon it mournfully, wearily, swallowing it with the dreary patience of a man who has been condemned forever to an exclusive diet of boiled unseasoned spinach. There was a kind of evil sorcery, a desolate mystery in the way they could take the choicest meats and vegetables and extract all their succulence and native flavor from them, and serve them up to you magnificently with every atom of their former life reduced to the general character of stewed hay or well-boiled flannel.

There would be a thick heavy soup of dark mahogany, a piece of boiled fish covered with a nameless, tasteless sauce of glutinous white, roast beef that had been done to death in dish-water, and solid, perfect, lovely brussels sprouts for whose taste there was no name whatever. It might have been the taste of boiled wet ashes, or the taste of stewed green leaves, with all the bitterness left out, pressed almost dry of moisture, or simply the taste of boiled clouds and rain and fog. For dessert, there would be a pudding of some quivery yellow substance, beautifully moulded, which was surrounded by a thin sweetish fluid of a sickly pink. And at the end there would be a cup of black bitter liquid mud.

I felt as if these dreary ghosts of food would also come to life at any moment, if I could only do some single simple thing—make the gesture of an incantation, or say a prayer, or speak a magic word, a word I almost had, but couldn't quite remember.

It was the food that plagued my soul with misery, bitter disappointment, and bewilderment. For I liked to eat and they had written about food better than any one on earth. Since my childhood, there had burned in my mind a memory of the food they wrote about. It was a memory drawn from a thousand books (of which "Quentin Durward," curiously, was one), but most of all it came from that tremendous scene in "Tom Brown's School-Days" which described the boy's ride through the frosty darkness on an English stagecoach, the pause for breakfast at an inn, blazing fire, cheerful room, snowy table groaning with spiced meats, waiter reeling in with steaks, grilled kidneys, eggs and bacon, piping hot.

I could remember with a gluttonous delight the breakfast which that hungry boy had devoured. It was a memory so touched with the magic relish of frost and darkness, smoking horses, the thrill, the ecstasy of the journey and a great adventure, the cheer, the warmth, the bustle of the inn, and the delicious abundance of the food they gave the boy, that the whole thing was evoked with blazing vividness, and now it would almost drive me mad with hunger when I thought of it.

Now it seemed to me that these people had written so magnificently about good food not because they always had it, but because they had it rarely and therefore made great dreams and fantasies about it, and that this same quality—the quality of *lack* rather than of *possession,* of desire rather than fulfilment—had got into everything they did, and made them dream great dreams, and do heroic acts, and had enriched their lives unmeasurably.

They had been the greatest poets in the world because the love and substance of great poetry were so rare among them. Their poems were so full of the essential quality of sunlight because their lives had known sunlight briefly, and so shot through with the massy substance of essential gold (a matchless triumph of light and color and material in which they have beaten the whole world by every standard of comparison) because they had known so much fog and rain, so little gold. And they had spoken best of April because April was so brief with them.

Thus from the grim gray of their skies they had alchemied gold, and from their hunger, glorious food, and from the raw bleakness of their lives and weathers they had drawn magic. And what was good among them had been won sternly, sparely, bitterly from all that was ugly, dull, and painful in their lives, and, when it came, was more rare and beautiful than anything on earth.

But that, I knew, was also theirs: it was another door I could not enter.

In the fall of that year I lived out about a mile from town in a house set back from the Ventnor Road. The house was called a "farm"—Hill-top Farm, or Far-end Farm, or some such name as that—but it was really no farm at all. It was a magnificent house of the weathered gray stone they have in that country, as if in the very quality of the wet heavy air there is the soft thick gray of time itself, sternly yet beautifully soaking down forever on you—and enriching everything it touches—grass, foliage, brick, ivy, the fresh moist color of the people's faces, and old gray stone with the incomparable weathering of time.

The house was set back off the road at a distance of several hundred yards, possibly a quarter of a mile, and one reached it by means of a road bordered by rows of tall trees which arched above the road, and which made me think of home at night when the stormy wind howled in their tossed branches. On each side of the road were the rugby fields of two of the colleges and in the afternoon I could look out and down and see the fresh moist green of the playing fields, and watch young college fellows, dressed in their shorts and jerseys, and with their bare knees scurfed with grass and turf as they twisted, struggled, swayed, and scrambled for a moment in the scrimmage-circle, and then broke free, running, dodging, passing the ball as they were tackled, filling the moist air with their sharp cries of sport. They did not have the desperate, the grimly determined, the almost professional earnestness that the college teams at home have; their scurfed and muddy knees, their swaying scrambling scrimmages, the swift breaking away and running, their panting breath and crisp clear voices gave them the appearance of grown-up boys.

Once when I had come up the road in afternoon while they

were playing, the ball got away from them and came bounding out into the road before me, and I ran after it to retrieve it as we used to do when passing a field where boys were playing baseball. One of the players came over to the edge of the field and stood there waiting with his hands upon his hips while I got the ball: he was panting hard, his face was flushed, and his blond hair tousled, but when I threw the ball to him, he said "Thanks very much!" crisply and courteously—getting the same sound into the word *"very"* that they got in *"American,"* a sound that always repelled me a little because it seemed to have some scornful aloofness and patronage in it.

For a moment I watched him as he trotted briskly away on to the field again: the players stood there waiting, panting, casual, their hands upon their hips; he passed the ball into the scrimmage, the pattern swayed, rocked, scrambled, and broke sharply out in open play again, and everything looked incredibly strange, near, and familiar.

I felt that I had always known it, that it had always been mine, and that it was as familiar to me as everything I had seen or known in my childhood. Even the texture of the earth looked familiar, and felt moist and firm and springy when I stepped on it, and the stormy howling of the wind in that avenue of great trees at night, was wild and desolate and demented as it had been when I was eight years old and could lie in my bed at night and hear the great oaks howling on the hill above my father's house.

The name of the people in the house was Coulson: I made arrangements with the woman at once to come and live there: she was a tall, weathered-looking woman of middle age, we talked together in the hall. The hall was made of marble flags and went directly out onto a gravelled walk.

The woman was crisp, cheerful, and worldly looking. She was still quite handsome. She wore a well-cut skirt of woollen plaid, and a silk blouse: when she talked she kept her arms folded because the air in the hall was chilly, and she held a cigarette in the fingers of one hand. A shaggy brown dog came out and nosed upward toward her hand as she was talking and she put her hand

upon its head and scratched it gently. When I told her I wanted
to move in the next day, she said briskly and cheerfully:

"Right you are! You'll find everything ready when you get
here!" Then she asked if I was at the university. I said no, and
added, with a feeling of difficulty and naked desolation, that I
was a "writer," and was coming there to work. I was twenty-four
years old.

"Then I am sure what you do will be *very, very* good!" she
said cheerfully and decisively. "We have had several Americans
in the house before and all of them were very clever! All the
Americans we have had here were very clever people," said the
woman. "I'm sure that you will like it." Then she walked to
the door with me to say good-bye. As we stood there, there was
the sound of a small motor-car coming to a halt and in a moment a
girl came swiftly across the gravel space outside and entered the
hall. She was tall, slender, very lovely, but she had the same
bright hard look in her eye the woman had, the same faint, hard
smile around the edges of her mouth.

"Edith," the woman said in her crisp, curiously incisive tone,
"this young man is an American—he is coming here tomorrow."
The girl looked at me for a moment with her hard bright glance,
thrust out a small gloved hand, and shook hands briefly, a swift
firm greeting.

"Oh! How d'ye do!" she said. "I hope you will like it here."
Then she went on down the hall, entered a room on the left, and
closed the door behind her.

Her voice had been crisp and certain like her mother's, but it
was also cool, young, and sweet, with music in it, and later as I
went down the road, I could still hear it.

That was a wonderful house, and the people there were wonderful people. Later, I could not forget them. I seemed to have
known them all my life, and to know all about their lives. They
seemed as familiar to me as my own blood and I knew them with
a knowledge that went deep below the roots of thought or memory. We did not talk together often, or tell any of our lives to

one another. It will be very hard to tell about it—the way we felt and lived together in that house—because it was one of those simple and profound experiences of life which people seem always to have known when it happens to them, but for which there is no language.

And yet, like a child's half-captured vision of some magic country he has known, and which haunts his days with strangeness and the sense of immanent, glorious re-discovery, the word that would unlock it all seems constantly to be almost on our lips, waiting just outside the gateway of our memory, just a shape, a phrase, a sound away the moment that we choose to utter it—but when we try to say the thing, something fades within our mind like fading light, and something melts within our grasp like painted smoke, and something goes forever when we try to touch it.

The nearest I could come to it was this: In that house I sometimes felt the greatest peace and solitude that I had ever known. But I always knew the other people in the house were there. I could sit in my sitting-room at night and hear nothing but the stormy moaning of the wind outside in the great trees, the small gaseous flare and jet from time to time of the coal fire burning in the grate—and silence, strong living lonely silence that moved and waited in the house at night—and I would always know that they were there.

I did not have to hear them enter or go past my door, nor did I have to hear doors close or open in the house, or listen to their voices: if I had never seen them, heard them, spoken to them, it would have been the same—I should have known they were there.

It was something I had always known, and had known it would happen to me, and now it was there with all the strangeness and dark mystery of an awaited thing. I knew them, felt them, lived among them with a familiarity that had no need of sight or word or speech. And the memory of that house and of my silent fellowship with all the people there was somehow mixed with an image of dark time. It was one of those sorrowful and unchanging images which, among all the blazing stream of images that passed constantly their stream of fire across my mind, was somehow fixed, detached, and everlasting, full of a sorrow, certitude, and mystery that I could not fathom, but that wore forever on it the old sad light of waning day—a light from which all the heat, the violence, and the substance of furious dusty day had vanished, and was itself like time, unearthly-of-the-earth, remote, detached, and everlasting.

And that fixed and changeless image of dark time was this: In an old house of time I lived alone, and yet had other people all around me, and they never spoke to me, or I to them. They came and went like silence in the house, but I always knew that they were there. I would be sitting by a window in a room, and I would know then they were moving in the house, and darkness, sorrow, and strong silence dwelt within us, and our eyes were quiet, full of sorrow, peace, and knowledge, and our faces dark, our tongues silent, and we never spoke. I could not remember how their faces looked, but they were all familiar to me as my father's face, and we had known one another forever, and we lived together in the ancient house of time, dark time, and silence, sorrow, certitude, and peace were in us. Such was the image of dark time that was to haunt my life thereafter, and into which, somehow, my life among the people in that house had passed.

In the house that year there lived, besides myself and Morison, the Coulsons, the father and mother and their daughter, and three men who had taken rooms together, and who were employed in a factory where motor-cars were made, two miles from town.

I think the reason that I could never forget these people later and seemed to know them all so well was that there was in all of them something ruined, lost, or broken—some precious and irretrievable quality which had gone out of them and which they could never get back again. Perhaps that was the reason that I liked them all so much, because with ruined people it is either love or hate: there is no middle way. The ruined people that we like are those who desperately have died, and lost their lives because they loved life dearly, and had that grandeur that makes such people spent prodigally the thing they love the best, and risk and lose their lives because it is so precious to them, and die at length because the seeds of life were in them. It is only the people who love life in this way who die—and these are the ruined people that we like.

The people in the house were people who had lost their lives because they loved the earth too well, and somehow had been slain by their hunger. And for this reason I liked them all, and could not forget them later: there seemed to have been some magic which had drawn them all together to the house, as if the house itself was a magnetic centre for lost people.

Certainly, the three men who worked at the motor-car factory had been drawn together for this reason. Two were still young men in their early twenties. The third man was much older. He was a man past forty, his name was Nicholl, he had served in the army during the war and had attained the rank of captain.

He had the spare, alert, and jaunty figure that one often finds in army men, an almost professional military quality that somehow seemed to set his figure upon a horse as if he had grown there, or had spent a lifetime in the cavalry. His face also had the same lean, bitten, professional military quality: his speech, although good-natured and very friendly, was clipped, incisive, jerky, and sporadic, his lean weather-beaten face was deeply, sharply scarred and sunken in the flanks, and he wore a small cropped mustache, and displayed long frontal teeth when he smiled—a spare, gaunt, toothy, yet attractive smile.

His left arm was withered, shrunken, almost useless, part of his hand and two of the fingers had been torn away by the blast or explosion which had destroyed his arm, but it was not this mutilation of the flesh that gave one the sense of a life that had been ruined, lost, and broken irretrievably. In fact, one quickly forgot his physical injury: his figure looked so spare, lean, jaunty, well-conditioned in its energetic fitness that one never thought of him as a cripple, nor pitied him for any disability. No: the ruin that one felt in him was never of the flesh, but of the spirit. Something seemed to have been exploded from his life—it was not the nerve-centres of his arm, but of his soul, that had been destroyed. There was in the man somewhere a terrible dead vacancy and emptiness, and that spare, lean figure that he carried so well seemed only to surround this vacancy like a kind of shell.

He was always smartly dressed in well-cut clothes that set well on his trim spruce figure. He was always in good spirits, immensely friendly in his clipped spare way, and he laughed frequently—a rather metallic cackle which came suddenly and ended as swiftly as it had begun. He seemed, somehow, to have locked the door upon dark care and worry, and to have flung the key away—to have lost, at the same time that he lost more precious things, all the fretful doubts and perturbations of the conscience most men know.

Now, in fact, he seemed to have only one serious project in his life. This was to keep himself amused, to keep himself constantly amused, to get from his life somehow the last atom of entertainment it could possibly yield, and in this project the two young men who lived with him joined in with an energy and earnestness which suggested that their employment in the motor-car factory was just a necessary evil which must be borne patiently because it yielded them the means with which to carry on a more important business, the only one in which their lives were interested—the pursuit of pleasure.

And in the way in which they conducted this pursuit, there was an element of deliberate calculation, concentrated earnestness, and focal intensity of purpose that was astounding, grotesque, and unbelievable, and that left in the mind of one who saw it a formidable and disquieting memory because there was in it almost the madness of desperation, the deliberate intent of men to cover up or seek oblivion at any cost of effort from some hideous emptiness of the soul.

Captain Nicholl and his two young companions had a little motor-car so small that it scuttled up the road, shot around and stopped in the gravel by the door with the abruptness of a wound-up toy. It was astonishing that three men could wedge themselves into this midget of a car, but wedge themselves they

[200]

did, and used it to the end of its capacity, scuttling away to work in it in the morning, and scuttling back again when work was done, and scuttling away to London every Saturday, as if they were determined to wrest from this small motor, too, the last ounce of pleasure to be got from it.

Finally, Captain Nicholl and his two companions had made up an orchestra among them, and this they played in every night when they got home. One of the young men, who was a tall fellow with blond hair which went back in even corrugated waves across his head as if it had been marcelled, played the piano, the other, who was slight and dark, and had black hair, performed upon a saxophone, and Captain Nicholl himself took turns at thrumming furiously on a banjo, or rattling a tattoo upon the complex arrangement of trap drums, bass drums, and clashing cymbals that surrounded him.

They played nothing but American jazz music or sobbing crooner's rhapsodies or nigger blues. Their performance was astonishing. Although it was contrived solely for their own amusement, they hurled themselves into it with all the industrious earnestness of professional musicians employed by a night-club or a dance hall to furnish dance music for the patrons. The little dark fellow who played the saxophone would bend and weave prayerfully with his grotesque instrument, as the fat gloating notes came from its unctuous throat, and from time to time he would sway in a half circle, or get up and prance forward and back in rhythm to the music as the saxophone players in dance orchestras sometimes do.

Meanwhile the tall blond fellow at the piano would sway and bend above the keys, glancing around from time to time with little nods and smiles as if he were encouraging an orchestra of forty pieces or beaming happily and in an encouraging fashion at a dance floor crowded with paying customers.

While this was going on, Captain Nicholl would be thrumming madly on the strings of a banjo. He kept the instrument gripped somehow below his withered arm, fingering the end strings with his two good fingers, knocking the tune out with his good right hand, and keeping time with a beating foot. Then with a sudden violent movement he would put the banjo down, snatch up the sticks of the trap drum, and begin to rattle out a furious accompaniment, beating the bass drum with his foot meanwhile, and reaching over to smash cymbals, chimes, and metal rings from time to time. He played with a kind of desperate fury, his mouth fixed in a strange set grin, his bright eyes burning with a sharp wild glint of madness.

They sang as they played, bursting suddenly into the refrain of some popular song with the same calculated spontaneity and spurious enthusiasm of the professional orchestra, mouthing the words of Negro blues and jazz with an obvious satisfaction, with an accent which was remarkably good, and yet which had something foreign and inept in it, which made the familiar phrases of American music sound almost as strange in their mouths as if an orchestra of skilful patient Japanese were singing them.

They sang:

> *"Yes, sir! That's my baby*
> *Yes, sir! Don't mean maybe*
> *Yes, sir! That's my baby now!"*

or:

> *"Oh, it aint gonna rain no more, no more*
> *It aint gonna rain no more"*

or:

> *"I got dose blu-u-ues"*—

the young fellow at the piano rolling his eyes around in a ridiculous fashion, and mouthing out the word "blues" extravagantly as he sang it, the little dark fellow bending forward in an unctuous sweep as the note came gloating fatly from the horn, and Captain Nicholl swaying sideways in his chair as he strummed upon the banjo strings, and improvising a mournful accompaniment of his own, somewhat as follows: "I got dose blu-u-ues! Yes, suh! Oh! I got dose blues! Yes, suh! I sure have got 'em—dose

blu-u-ues—blu-u-es—blu-u-ues!"—his mouth never relaxing from
its strange fixed grin, nor his eyes from their bright set stare of
madness as he swayed and strummed and sang the words that came
so strangely from his lips.

It was a weird scene, an incredible performance, and somehow
it pierced the heart with a wild nameless pity, an infinite sorrow
and regret.

Something precious, irrecoverable had gone out of them, and
they knew it. They fought the emptiness in them with this deliberate, formidable, and mad intensity of a calculated gaiety, a terrifying mimicry of mirth, and the storm wind howled around us in
dark trees, and I felt that I had known them forever, and had no
words to say to them—and no door.

There were four in the Coulson family: the father, a man of
fifty years, the mother, somewhere in the middle forties, a son, and
a daughter, Edith, a girl of twenty-two who lived in the house
with her parents. I never met the son: he had completed his
course at Oxford a year or two before, and had gone down to
London where he was now employed. During the time I lived
there the son did not come home.

They were a ruined family. How that ruin had fallen on them,
what it was, I never knew, for no one ever spoke to me about them.
But the sense of their disgrace, of a shameful inexpiable dishonor,
for which there was no pardon, from which there could never be
redemption, was overwhelming. In the most astonishing way I
found out about it right away, and yet I did not know what they
had done, and no one ever spoke a word against them.

Rather, the mention of their name brought silence, and in that
silence there was something merciless and final, something that
belonged to the temper of the country, and that was far more
terrible than any open word of scorn, contempt, or bitter judgment
could have been, more savage than a million strident, whispering,
or abusive tongues could be, because the silence was unarguable,
irrevocable, complete, as if a great door had been shut against
their lives forever.

Everywhere I went in town, the people knew about them, and said nothing—saying everything—when I spoke their names. I found this final, closed, relentless silence everywhere—in tobacco, wine, and tailor shops, in book stores, food stores, haberdashery stores—wherever I bought anything and gave the clerk the address to which it was to be delivered, they responded instantly with this shut finality of silence, writing the name down gravely, sometimes saying briefly "Oh! Coulson's!" when I gave them the address, but more often saying nothing.

But whether they spoke or simply wrote the name down without a word, there was always this quality of instant recognition, this obdurate, contemptuous finality of silence, as if a door had been shut—a door that could never again be opened. Somehow I disliked them more for this silence than if they had spoken evilly: there was in it something ugly, sly, knowing, and triumphant that was far more evil than any slyly whispering confidence of slander, or any open vituperation of abuse, could be. It seemed somehow to come from all the evil and uncountable small maggotry of the earth, the cautious little hatreds of a million nameless ciphers, each puny, pallid, trivial in himself, but formidable because he added his tiny beetle's ball of dung to the mountainous accumulation of ten million others of his breed.

It was uncanny how these clerk-like faces grave and quiet, that never spoke a word, or gave a sign, or altered their expression by a jot, when I gave them the address, could suddenly be alive with something secret, foul, and sly, could be more closed and secret than a door, and yet instantly reveal the naked, shameful, and iniquitous filth that welled up from some depthless source. I could not phrase it, give a name to it, or even see a certain sign that it was there, no more than I could put my hand upon a wisp of fading smoke, but I always knew when it was there, and somehow when I saw it my heart went hard and cold against the people who revealed it, and turned with warmth and strong affection toward the Coulson family.

There was, finally, among these grave clerk-like faces one face that I could never forget thereafter, a face that seemed to resume

into its sly suave surfaces all of the nameless abomination of evil
in the world for which I had no name, for which there was no
handle I could grasp, no familiar places or edges I could get my
hands upon, which slid phantasmally, oilily, and smokily away
whenever I tried to get my hands upon it. But it was to haunt my
life for years in dreams of hatred, madness, and despair that found
no frontal wall for their attack, no word for their vituperation, no
door for the shoulder of my hate—an evil world of phantoms,
shapes, and whispers that was yet as real as death, as ever-present
as man's treachery, but that slid away from me like smoke whenever I tried to meet, or curse, or strangle it.

This face was the face of a man in a tailor shop, a fitter there,
and I could have battered that foul face into a bloody pulp, distilled the filthy refuse of his ugly life out of his fat swelling neck
and through the murderous grip of my fingers if I could only
have found a cause, a logic, and an act for doing it. And yet I never
saw the man but twice, and briefly, and there had been nothing in
his suave, sly careful speech to give offense.

Edith Coulson had sent me to the tailor's shop: I needed a suit
and when I asked her where to go to have it made, she had sent
me to this place because her brother had his suits made there and
liked it. The fitter was a heavy shambling man in his late
thirties: he had receding hair, which he brushed back flat in a
thick pompadour, yellowish, somewhat bulging eyes, a coarse
heavy face, loose-featured, red, and sensual, a sloping meaty jaw,
and large discolored buck-teeth which showed unpleasantly in
a mouth that was always half open. It was, in fact, the mouth
that gave his face its sensual, sly, and ugly look, for a loose and
vulgar smile seemed constantly to hover about its thick coarse
edges, to be deliberately, slyly restrained, but about to burst at any
moment in an open, evil, foully sensual laugh. There was always
this ugly suggestion of a loose, corrupt, and evilly jubilant mirth
about his mouth, and yet he never laughed or smiled.

The man's speech had this same quality. It was suave and courteous, but even in its most urbane assurances, there was something
non-committal, sly, and jeering, something that slid away from

THE SHORT NOVELS OF THOMAS WOLFE

you, and was never to be grasped, a quality that was faithless, tricky, and unwholesome. When I came for the final fitting it was obvious that he had done as cheap and shoddy a job as he could do; the suit was vilely botched and skimped, sufficient cloth had not been put into it, and now it was too late to remedy the defect.

Yet, the fitter gravely pulled the vest-down till it met the trousers, tugged at the coat, and pulled the thing together where it stayed until I took a breath or moved a muscle, when it would all come apart again, the collar bulging outward from the shoulder, the skimpy coat and vest crawling backward from the trousers, leaving a hiatus of shirt and belly that could not be remedied now by any means.

Then, gravely he would pull the thing together again, and in his suave, yet oily, sly, and non-committal phrases, say:

"Um! Seems to fit you very well."

I was choking with exasperation, and knew that I had been done, because I had foolishly paid them half the bill already, and now knew no way out of it except to lose what I had paid, and get nothing for it, or take the thing, and pay the balance. I was caught in a trap, but even as I jerked at the coat and vest speechlessly, seized my shirt, and thrust the gaping collar in his face, the man said smoothly,

"Um! Yes! The collar. Should think all that will be all right. Still needs a little alteration." He made some chalk marks on me. "Should think you'll find it fits you very well when the tailor makes the alterations."

"When will the suit be ready?"

"Um. Should think you ought to have it by next Tuesday. Yes. I think you'll find it ready by Tuesday."

The sly words slid away from me like oil: there was nothing to pin him to or grasp him by, the yellowed eyes looked casually away and would not look at me, the sensual face was suavely grave, the discolored buck-teeth shone obscenely through the coarse loose mouth, and the suggestion of the foul loose smile was so pronounced now that it seemed that at any moment he would have to turn away with heavy trembling shoulders, and stifle the evil jeering laugh that was welling up in him. But he remained suavely grave and non-committal to the end, and when I asked him if I should come again to try it on, he said, in the same oily tone, never looking at me:

"Um. Shouldn't think that would be necessary. Could have it delivered to you when it's ready. What is your address?"

"The Far-end Farm—it's on the Ventnor Road."

"Oh! Coulson's!" He never altered his expression, but the suggestion of the obscene smile was so pronounced that now it seemed he had to out with it. Instead, he only said:

"Um. Yes. Should think it could be delivered to you there on Tuesday. If you'll just wait a moment I'll ask the tailor."

Gravely, suavely, he took the coat from me and walked back toward the tailor's room with the coat across his arm. In a moment, I heard sly voices whispering, laughing slyly, then the tailor saying:

"Where does he live?"

"Coulson's!" said the fitter chokingly, and now the foul awaited laugh did come—high, wet, slimy, it came out of that loose mouth, and choked and whispered wordlessly, and choked again, and mingled then with the tailor's voice in sly, choking, whispering intimacy, and then gasped faintly, and was silent. When he came out again his coarse face was red and swollen with foul secret merriment, his heavy shoulders trembled slightly, he took out his handkerchief and wiped it once across his loose half-opened mouth, and with that gesture wiped the slime of laughter from his lips. Then he came toward me suave, grave, and courteous, evilly composed, as he said smoothly:

"Should think we'll have that for you by next Tuesday, sir."

"Can the tailor fix it so it's going to fit?"

"Um. Should think you'll find that everything's all right. You ought to have it Tuesday afternoon."

He was not looking at me: the yellowish bulging eyes were staring casually, indefinitely, away, and his words again had slid away from me like oil. He could not be touched, approached, or handled: there was nothing to hold him by, he had the impregnability of smoke or a ball of mercury.

As I went out the door, he began to speak to another man in the shop, I heard low words and whispered voices, then, gasping, the word "Coulson's!" and the slimy, choking, smothered laughter as the street door closed behind me. I never saw him again. I never forgot his face.

That was a fine house: the people in it were exiled, lost, and ruined people, and I liked them all. Later, I never knew why I felt so close to them, or remembered them with such warmth and strong affection.

I did not see the Coulsons often and rarely talked to them. Yet I felt as familiar and friendly with them all as if I had known them all my life. The house was wonderful as no other house I had ever known because we all seemed to be living in it together with this strange speechless knowledge, warmth, and familiarity, and yet each was as private, secret, and secure in his own room as if he occupied the house alone.

Coulson himself I saw least of all: we sometimes passed each other going in or out the door, or in the hall: he would grunt "Morning," or "Good Day," in a curt blunt manner, and go on, and yet he always left me with a curious sense of warmth and friendliness. He was a stocky well-set man with iron-gray hair, bushy eyebrows, and a red weathered face which wore the open color of the country on it, but also had the hard dull flush of the steady heavy drinker.

I never saw him drunk, and yet I think that he was never sober: he was one of those men who have drunk themselves past any hope of drunkenness, who are soaked through to the bone with alcohol, saturated, tanned, weathered in it so completely that it could never be distilled out of their blood again. Yet, even in this terrible excess one felt a kind of grim control—the control of a man who is enslaved by the very thing that he controls, the control of the opium eater who cannot leave his drug but measures out his dose with a cold calculation, and finds the limit of his capacity, and stops there, day by day.

But somehow this very sense of control, this blunt ruddy style of the country gentleman which distinguished his speech, his manner, and his dress, made the ruin of his life, the desperate intemperance of drink that smouldered in him like a slow fire, steadily, nakedly apparent. It was as if, having lost everything, he still held grimly to the outer forms of a lost standard, a ruined state, when the inner substance was destroyed.

And it was this way with all of them—with Mrs. Coulson and the girl, as well: their crisp, clipped friendly speech never deviated into intimacy, and never hinted at any melting into confidence and admission. Upon the woman's weathered face there hovered, when she talked, the same faint set grin that Captain Nicholl had, and her eyes were bright and hard, a little mad, impenetrable, as were his. And the girl, although young and very lovely, sometimes had this same look when she greeted any one or paused to talk. In that look there was nothing truculent, bitter, or defiant: it was just the look of three people who had gone down together, and who felt for one another neither bitterness nor hate, but that strange companionship of a common disgrace, from which love has vanished, but which is more secret, silent, and impassively resigned to its fatal unity than love itself could be.

And that hard bright look also said this plainly to the world: "We ask for nothing from you now, we want nothing that you offer us. What is ours is ours, what we are we are, you'll not intrude nor come closer than we let you see!"

Coulson might have been a man who had been dishonored and destroyed by his women, and who took it stolidly, saying nothing, and drank steadily from morning until night, and had nothing for it now but drink and silence and acceptance. Yet I never knew for certain that this was so, it just seemed inescapable, and seemed somehow legible not only in the slow smouldering fire that burned out through his rugged weathered face, but also in the hard bright armor of the women's eyes, the fixed set grin around their lips when they were talking—a grin that was like armor, too. And

Morison, who had referred to Coulson, chuckling, as a real "bottle-a-day-man," had added quietly, casually, in his brief, indefinite, but blurted-out suggestiveness of speech:

"I think the old girl's been a bit of a bitch in her day. . . . Don't know, of course, but has the look, hasn't she?" In a moment he said quietly, "Have you talked to the daughter yet?"

"Once or twice. Not for long."

"Ran into a chap at Magdalen other day who knows her," he said casually. "He used to come out here to see her." He glanced swiftly, slyly at me, his face reddening a little with laughter. "Pretty hot, I gather," he said quietly, smiling, and looked away. It was night: the fire burned cheerfully in the grate, the hot coals spurting in small gaseous flares from time to time. The house was very quiet all around us. Outside we could hear the stormy wind in the trees along the road. Morison flicked his cigarette into the fire, poured out a drink of whiskey into a glass, saying as he did so: "I say, old chap, you don't mind if I take a spot of this before I go to bed, do you?" Then he shot some seltzer in the glass, and drank. And I sat there, without a word, staring sullenly into the fire, dumbly conscious of the flood of sick pain and horror which the casual foulness of the man's suggestion had aroused, stubbornly trying to deny now that I was thinking of the girl all the time.

One night, as I was coming home along the dark road that went up past the playing field to the house, and that was bordered on each side by grand trees whose branches seemed to hold at night all the mysterious and demented cadences of storm, I came upon her suddenly standing in the shadow of a tree. It was one of the grand wild nights that seemed to come so often in the autumn of that year: the air was full of a fine stinging moisture, not quite rain, and above the stormy branches of the trees I could see the sky, wild, broken, full of scudding clouds through which at times the moon drove in and out with a kind of haggard loneliness. By that faint, wild, and broken light, I could see the small white oval of the girl's face—somehow even more lovely now just because I could not see it plainly. And I could see as well the rough gleaming bark of the tree against which she leaned.

[210]

As I approached, I saw her thrust her hand into the pocket of her overcoat, a match flared, and for a moment I saw Edith plainly, the small flower of her face framed in the wavering light as she lowered her head to light her cigarette.

The light went out, I saw the small respiring glow of her cigarette before the white blur of her face, I passed her swiftly, head bent, without speaking, my heart filled with the sense of strangeness and wonder which the family had roused in me.

Then I walked on up the road, muttering to myself. The house was dark when I got there, but when I entered my sitting-room the place was still warmly and softly luminous with the glow of hot coals in the grate. I turned the lights on, shut the door behind me, and hurled several lumps of coal upon the bedded coals. In a moment the fire was blazing and crackling cheerfully, and getting a kind of comfort and satisfaction from this activity, I flung off my coat, went over to the sideboard, poured out a stiff drink of scotch from a bottle there, and coming back to the fire, flung myself into a chair, and began to stare sullenly into the dancing flames.

How long I sat there in the stupor of sullen and nameless fury, I did not know, but I was sharply roused at length by footsteps light and rapid on the gravel, shocked into a start of surprise by a figure that appeared suddenly at one of the French windows that opened directly from my sitting-room to the level sward of velvet lawn before the house.

I peered through the glass for a moment with an astonished stare before I recognized the face of Edith Coulson. I opened the doors at once, she came in quickly, smiling at my surprise, and at the glass which I was holding foolishly, half-raised in my hand.

I continued to look at her with an expression of gape-mouthed astonishment and in a moment became conscious of her smiling glance, the cool sweet assurance of her young voice.

"I say!" she was saying cheerfully. "What a lucky thing to find you up! I came away without any key—I should have had to wake the whole house up—so when I saw your light—" she concluded briskly, "—what luck! I hope you don't mind."

"Why no-o, no," I stammered foolishly, still staring dumbly at her. "No—no-o—not at all," I blundered on. Then suddenly coming to myself with a burst of galvanic energy, I shut the windows, pushed another chair before the fire, and said:

"Won't you sit down and have a drink before you go?"

"Thanks," she said crisply. "I will—yes. What a jolly fire you have." As she talked she took off her coat and hat swiftly and put them on a chair. Her face was flushed and rosy, beaded with small particles of rain, and for a moment she stood before the mirror arranging her hair, which had been tousled by the wind.

The girl was slender, tall, and very lovely with the kind of beauty they have when they are beautiful—a beauty so fresh, fair, and delicate that it seems to be given to just a few of them to compensate for all the grimly weathered ugliness of the rest. Her voice was also lovely, sweet, and musical, and when she talked all the notes of tenderness and love were in it. But she had the same hard bright look in her eye that her mother had, the faint set smile around her mouth: as we stood there talking she was standing very close to me, and I could smell the fragrance of her hair, and felt an intolerable desire to put my hand upon hers and was almost certain she would not draw away. But the hard bright look was in her eye, the faint set smile around her mouth, and I did nothing.

"What'll you have?" I said. "Whiskey?"

"Yes, thank you," she said with the same sweet crisp assurance with which she always spoke, "and a splash of soda." I struck a match and held it for her while she lit the cigarette she was holding in her hand, and in a moment returned to her with the drink. Then she sat down, crossed her legs, and for a moment puffed thoughtfully at her cigarette, as she stared into the fire. The storm wind moaned in the great trees along the road, and near the house, and suddenly a swirl of rain and wind struck the windows with a rattling blast. The girl stirred a little in her chair, restlessly, shivered:

"Listen!" she said. "What a night! Horrible weather we have here, isn't it?"

"I don't know. I don't like the fog and rain so well. But this —the way it is tonight—" I nodded toward the window—"I like it."

She looked at me for a moment.

"Oh," she said non-committally. "You do." Then, as she sipped her drink, she looked curiously about the room, her reflective glance finally resting on my table where there was a great stack of the ledgers in which I wrote.

"I say," she cried again. "What are you doing with all those big books there?"

"I write in them."

"Really?" she said, in a surprised tone. "I should think it'd be an awful bother carrying them around when you travel?"

"It is. But it's the best way I've found of keeping what I do together."

"Oh," she said, as before, and continued to stare curiously at me with her fair, lovely young face, the curiously hard, bright, and unrevealing glance of her eye. "I see. . . . But why do you come to such a place as this to write?" she said presently. "Do you like it here?"

"I do. As well as any place I've ever known."

"Oh! . . . I should think a writer would want a different kind of place."

"What kind?"

"Oh—I don't know—Paris—London—some place like that where there is lots of life—people—fun—I should think you'd work better in a place like that."

"I work better here."

"But don't you get awfully fed up sitting in here all day long and writing in those enormous books?"

"I do, yes."

"I should think you would . . . I should think you'd want to get away from it sometime."

"Yes I do want to—every day—almost all the time."

"Then why don't you?" she said crisply. "Why don't you go

off some week-end for a little spree. I should thing it'd buck you up no end."

"It would—yes. Where should I go?"

"Oh, Paris, I suppose. . . . Or London! London!" she cried. "London is quite jolly if you know it."

"I'm afraid I don't know it."

"But you've *been* to London," she said in a surprised tone.

"Oh, yes. I lived there for several months."

"Then you know London," she said impatiently. "Of course you do."

"I'm afraid I don't know it very well. I don't know many people there—and after all, that's the thing that counts, isn't it?"

She looked at me curiously for a moment with the faint hard smile around the edges of her lovely mouth.

"—should think that might be arranged," she said with a quiet, an enigmatic humor. Then, more directly, she added: "That shouldn't be difficult at all. Perhaps I could introduce you to some people."

"That would be fine. Do you know many people there?"

"Not many," she said. "I go there—whenever I can." She got up with a swift decisive movement, put her glass down on the mantel and cast her cigarette into the fire. Then she faced me, looking at me with a curiously bold, an almost defiant directness of her hard bright eyes, and she fixed me with this glance for a full moment before she spoke.

"Good-night," she said. "Thanks awfully for letting me in— and for the drink."

"Good-night," I said, and she was gone before I could say more, and I had closed the door behind her, and I could hear her light swift footsteps going down the hall and up the steps. And then there was nothing in the house but sleep and silence, and storm and darkness in the world around me.

Mrs. Coulson came into my room just once or twice while I was there. One morning she came in, spoke crisply and cheerfully, and walked over to the window looking out upon the velvet lawn and at the dreary, impenetrable gray of foggy air. Although the room was warm, and there was a good fire burning in the grate, she clasped her arms together as she looked and shivered a little:

"Wretched weather, isn't it?" she said in her crisp tones, her gaunt weathered face and toothy mouth touched by the faint fixed grin as she looked out with her bright hard stare. "Don't you find it frightfully depressing? Most Americans do," she said, getting the sharp disquieting sound into the word.

"Yes. I do, a little. We don't have this kind of weather very often. But this is the time of year you get it here, isn't it? I suppose you're used to it by now?"

"Used to it?" she said crisply turning her hard bright gaze upon me. "Not at all. I've known it all my life but I'll never get used to it. It is a wretched climate."

"Still, you wouldn't feel at home anywhere else, would you? You wouldn't want to live outside of England."

"No?" she said, staring at me with the faint set grin around her toothy mouth. "Why do you think so?"

"Because your home is here."

"My home? My home is where they have fine days, and where the sun is always shining."

"I wouldn't like that. I'd get tired of sunlight all the time. I'd want some gray days and some fog and snow."

"Yes, I suppose you would. But then, you've been used to having fine days all your life, haven't you? With us, it's different. I'm so fed up with fog and rain that I could do without it nicely, thank you, if I never saw it again. . . . I don't think you could ever understand how much the sunlight means to us," she said slowly. She turned, and for a moment looked out the window with her hard bright stare, the faint set grin about her mouth. "Sunlight—warmth—fine days forever! Warmth everywhere—in the earth, the sky, in the lives of the people all around you nothing but warmth and sunlight and fine days!"

"And where would you go to find all that? Does it exist?"

"Oh, of course!" she said crisply and good-naturedly turning to me again. "There's only one place to live—only one country where I want to live."

"Where is that?"

"Italy," she said. "That's my real home. . . . I'd live the rest of my life there if I could." For a moment longer she looked out the window, then turned briskly, saying:

"Why don't you run over to Paris some week-end? After all, it's only seven hours from London: if you left here in the morning you'd be there in time for dinner. It would be a good change for you. I should think a little trip like that would buck you up tremendously."

Her words gave me a wonderful feeling of confidence and hope: I think she had travelled a great deal, and she had the casual, assured way of speaking of a voyage that made it seem very easy, and filled one with a sense of joy and adventure when she spoke about it. When I tried to think of Paris by myself it had seemed very far away and hard to reach: London stood between it and me, and when I thought of the huge smoky web of London, the soft gray skies above me, and the enormous weight of lives that were hidden somewhere in that impenetrable fog, gray desolation and weariness of the spirit filled me. It seemed to me that I must draw each breath of that soft gray air with heavy weary effort, and that every mile of my journey would be a ghastly struggle through some viscous and material substance of soft heavy gray, that weighted down my steps, and filled my heart with desolation.

But when Mrs. Coulson spoke to me about it, suddenly it all seemed wonderfully easy and good. England was magically small, the channel to be taken in a stride, and all the thrill, the joy, the mystery of Paris mine again—the moment that I chose to make it mine.

I looked at her gaunt weathered face, her toothy mouth with the faint fixed grin, the hard bright armor of her eyes, and wondered how anything so clear, so sharp, so crisp, and so incisive could have been shaped and grown underneath these soft and humid skies that numbed me, mind and heart and body, with their thick numb substance of gray weariness and desolation.

A day or two before I left, Edith came into my room one afternoon bearing a tray with tea and jam and buttered bread. I was sitting in my chair before the fire, and had my coat off: when she came in I scrambled to my feet, reached for the coat and started to put it on. In her young crisp voice she told me not to, and put the tray down on the table, saying that the maid was having her afternoon away.

Then for a moment she stood looking at me with her faint and enigmatic smile.

"So you're leaving us?" she said presently.

"Yes. Tomorrow."

"And where will you go from here?" she said.

"To Germany, I think. Just for a short time—two or three weeks."

"And after that?"

"I'm going home."

"Home?"

"Back to America."

"Oh," she said slowly. "I see." In a moment, she added, "We shall miss you."

I wanted to talk to her more than I had ever wanted to talk to any one in my life, but when I spoke all that I could say, lamely, muttering, was:

"I'll miss you, too."

"Will you?" She spoke so quietly that I could scarcely hear her. "I wonder for how long?" she said.

"Forever," I said, flushing miserably at the sound of the word, and yet not knowing any other word to say.

The faint hard smile about her mouth was a little deeper when she spoke again.

"Forever? That's a long time, when one is young as you," she said.

"I mean it. I'll never forget you as long as I live."

"We shall remember you," she said quietly. "And I hope you think of us sometime—back here buried, lost, in all the fog and rain and ruin of England. How good it must be to know that you are young in a young country—where nothing that you did yes-terday matters very much. How wonderful it must be to know that none of the failure of the past can pull you down—that there will always be another day for you—a new beginning. I wonder if you Americans will ever know how fortunate you are," the girl said.

"And yet you could not leave all this?" I said with a kind of desperate hope. "This old country you've lived in, known all your life. A girl like you could never leave a place like this to live the kind of life we have in America."

"*Couldn't* I?" she said with a quiet, but unmistakable passion of conviction. "There's nothing I'd like better."

I stared at her blindly, dumbly for a moment; suddenly all that I wanted to say, and had not been able to say, found release in a movement of my hands. I gripped her by the shoulders and pulled her to me, and began to plead with her:

"Then why don't you? I'll take you there!—Look here—" my words were crazy and I knew it, but as I spoke them, I believed all I said—"Look here! I haven't got much money—but in America you can make it if you want to! I'm going back there. You come, too—I'll take you when I go!"

She had not tried to free herself; she just stood there passive, unresisting, as I poured that frenzied proposal in her ears. Now, with the same passive and unyielding movement, the bright armor of her young eyes, she stepped away, and stood looking at me silently for a moment, the faint, hard smile at the edges of her mouth. Then slowly, with an almost imperceptible movement, she shook her head. "Oh, you'll forget about us all," she said quietly. "You'll forget about our lives here—buried in fog—and rain—and failure—and defeat."

"Failure and defeat won't last forever."

"Sometimes they do," she said with a quiet finality that froze my heart.

"Not for you—they won't!" I said, and took her by the hand again with desperate entreaty. "Listen to me—" I blundered on in-coherently, with the old feeling of nameless shame and horror.

"You don't need to tell me what it is—I don't want to know—but whatever it is for you—it doesn't matter—you can get the best of it."

She said nothing, but just looked at me through that hard bright armor of her eyes, the obdurate finality of her smile.

"Good-bye," she said, "I'll not forget you either." She looked at me for a moment curiously before she spoke again. "I wonder," she said slowly, "if you'll ever understand just what it was you did for me by coming here."

"What was it?"

"You opened a door that I thought had been closed forever," she said, "a door that let me look in on a world I thought I should never see again—a new bright world, a new life and a new beginning—for us all. And I thought that was something which would never happen to any one in this house again."

"It will to you," I said, and took her hand again with desperate eagerness. "It can happen to you whenever you want it to. It's yours, I'll swear it to you, if you'll only speak."

She looked at me with her direct hard glance, an almost imperceptible movement of her head.

"I tell you I know what I'm talking about."

Again she shook her head.

"You don't know," she said. "You're young. You're an American. There are some things you'll never be old enough to know.—For some of us there's no return.—Go back," she said, "go back to the life you know—the life you understand—where there can always be a new beginning—a new life."

"And you—" I said dumbly, miserably.

"Good-bye, my dear," she said so low and gently I could scarcely hear her. "Think of me sometime, won't you—I'll not forget you." And before I could speak she kissed me once and was gone, so light and swift that I did not know it, until the door had closed behind her. And for some time, like a man in a stupor, I stood there looking out the window at the gray wet light of England.

The next day I went away, and never saw any of them again, but I could not forget them. Although I had never passed beyond the armor of their hard bright eyes, or breached the wall of their crisp, friendly, and impersonal speech, or found out anything about them, I always thought of them with warmth, with a deep and tender affection, as if I had always known them—as if, somehow, I could have lived with them or made their lives my own if only I had said a word, or turned the handle of a door— a word I never knew, a door I never found.

IV. LATE APRIL: 1928

Before me, all that Spring, in the broad window of the dingy storage house across the street, a man sat, in a posture that had never changed, looking out the window. It was an old building with a bleak and ugly front of a rusty, indurated brown, a harsh webbing of fire escapes, and a battered old wooden sign which stretched across the whole width of the façade, and on which in faded letters was inscribed this legend: The Security Distributing Corporation. I did not know what a Distributing Corporation was, nor the purport of its business, but every day since I had come into this street to live, enormous motor vans and powerful horse-drawn trucks had driven up before this dingy building, had backed cleanly and snugly against the floor of old, worn planking that ended with a sharp, sheared emptiness three feet above the sidewalk pavement. And instantly the quiet and musty depths of the old building would burst into a furious energy of work: the drivers and their helpers would leap from their seats to the pavements, and the air would be filled with the harsh, constricted cries and shouts of the city:

"Back it up, deh! Back it up! Cuh-*mahn!* Cuh-*mahn!* Givvus a hand, youse guys! Hey-y! *You! Lightnin'!*" They looked at one another with hard smiling faces of derision, quietly saying, "Jesus!" They stood surlily upon their rights, defending truculently the narrow frontier of their duty: "Wadda I care where it goes? Dat's *yoeh* lookout! Wat t'hell 'sit got to do wit me!" And they worked furiously, unamiably, with high exacerbated voices, spurred and goaded by their harsh unrest. They worked with speed and power and splendid aptness, shouting: "Hey-y! Youse guys! D'yuth t'ink all we got to do is run aroun' with youse all night? . . . Back it up, deh! Back it up!"

They had the tough, seamed face, the thick, dry skin without a hue of freshness or of color, the constricted speech, the hard assurance of men born and nurtured from the city's iron breast, and yet there was a bitter savour to them, too. Born to a world of brick and stone and savage conflict, torn from their mother's womb into a world of crowded tenements and swarming streets, stunned into sleep at childhood beneath the sudden, slamming racket of the elevated trains, taught to fight, to menace, and to struggle in a world of savage violence and incessant din, the qualities of that world had been stamped into their flesh and movements, written into their tongue and brain and vision, distilled through all the tissues of their flesh until their lives, schooled in the city's life, had taken on its special tones and qualities. Its harsh metallic clangours sounded from their strident tongues, the savage speed and violence of its movement were communicated to their acts and gestures, the rhythm of its furious dissonance, its vertical heights and canyoned narrowness, and the vast illusion of its swarming repetitions, had yielded them the few words and oaths and gestures, the perfect, constant, catlike balance that they needed, and stunned their senses to a competent and undaunted tonelessness, cutting the pattern of their lives sparely into its furious and special groove.

The city was their stony-hearted mother and they had drawn a harsh nurture from its breast. Surly of act, and ready in an instant with a curse, their pulse beat with the furious rhythm of the city's stroke, their tongues were bitter with its strident and abusive languages, and their hearts were filled with an immense and secret pride, a dark, unspoken tenderness when they thought of it.

Their souls were like the implacable asphalt visage of a city street: each day the movement of a furious life, a thousand new and alien pageantries, the violent colors of a thousand new sensations swept across the visage of that soul, and each day all sound and sight and fury were erased from its unyielding surfaces. Ten thousand furious days had passed about them, and they had no memory: they lived like creatures born full-grown into present time, shedding the whole accumulation of the past with every step they took, with every breath they drew, and their lives were written in the passing of each moment of dark time.

And they were sure and certain, forever wrong, but always confident; and they had no hesitation, they confessed no ignorance, nor error, and they knew no doubt. They began each morning with a jibe, a shout, an oath of harsh impatience; eager for the tumult of the day, they sat strongly in their seats at furious noon, and through fumes of oil and hot machinery addressed their curses to the public at the tricks and strategies of cunning rivals, the tyranny of the police, the stupidity of the pedestrian, and the errors of less skilful men than they. Each day they faced the million perils and confusions of the streets with as calm a heart as if they were alone upon a country road. Each day, with an undaunted and untroubled mind, they embarked upon an adventure at which the hearts of men bred only to the wilderness would have recoiled in horror and desolation.

The power and precision with which they worked stirred in me a strong and deep emotion of respect, and it also touched in me a sense of regret and humility. For whenever I saw it, my own life, with its tormented desires, its fury of love and madness, its wild and uncertain projects and designs, its labors begun in hope and confidence and ended in despair and incompletion, its obscure purposes and bewilderment, by a cruel comparison with the lives of these men who had learned to use their strength and talents perfectly in a life demanding manual skill, and mastery of sensuous materials, seemed blind, faltering, baffled, still lost in clouds and chaos and confusion.

Five times a week at night, the mighty vans were lined up at the curb in an immense and waiting caravan. Their huge bulk was covered now with great bolts of canvas, on each side a small green lamp was burning, and the drivers, their faces faintly lit with

small, respiring points of red tobacco ash, were talking quietly in
the shadow of their great machines. Once I had asked one of the
drivers the destination of these nightly journeys, and the man had
told me that they went to Philadelphia, and would return again
by morning.

That spring the picture of these great vans at night, immense,
sombre, and yet alive with a powerful and silent expectancy, the
small green glow of the drivers waiting for the word to start, had
given me a sense of mystery and joy. I could not have said what
emotion the scene evoked in me, but in it was something of the
cruel loveliness of April, the immense space and loneliness of the
land at night, the lilac dark, sown with its glittering panoply of
stars, and the drivers moving in their great dark vans through sleeping towns, and out into the fragrant country-side again, and into
first light, cities, April, and the birdsong in the morning.

They were a part of that great company of men throughout the
earth who love the night, and I felt a sense of union with them.
For I had loved the night more dearly than the day. The energies
of my life had risen to their greatest strength at night, and at the
centre of my life had always been the secret and exultant heart
of darkness.

I knew the joys and labors of such men as these, who drove
their huge vans through the country in the night. I could see and
feel with the literal concreteness of an experience in which I had
shared all hours and movements of their journey. I could see the
dark processional of vans lumbering through the sleeping towns,
and feel the darkness, the cool fragrance of the country on my
face again. I could see the quiet, seamed faces of the drivers dimly
lit by lantern flares, and I knew the places where they stopped to
eat, the little all-night lunch rooms or the lunch wagon warm
with greasy light, now empty, save for the dozing authority of the
soiled night-time Greek, and now filled with the heavy shuffle
of the drivers' feet, the hard and casual intrusions of their voices.

I could smell the pungent solace of strong, fragrant fresh tobacco, the plain, priceless, and uncostly joy of the first cigarette
lit between the cupped flame of a hard hand and a strong-

seamed mouth, in slow fumes a deep-drawn luxury from the nostrils of a tired man. Then I could smell the sultry excellent excitement of black boiling coffee, the clean hungry spur and savor of the frying eggs and onions, and the male and meaty relish of strong frying hamburgers. I could see and smell and taste the strong coarse pats of forcemeat red, smacked by a greasy hand upon the blackened sheet of frying plate, turning, in a coil of pungent smoke, from ground, spicy, sanguinary beef into a browned and blackened succulence, crisp on its surface, juicy at the core with the good raw grain of meat.

They ate coarsely, thrusting at plate and cup with strong, hoarse gulpings, goatily, with jungle lust, with the full sharp relish of male hunger and the pleasant weariness of a strong fatigue. They ate with bestial concentration, grained to the teeth with coarse spicy meat, coating their sandwiched hamburgers with the liberal unction of the thick tomato ketchup, and rending with hard blackened fingers soft yielding slabs of fragrant baker's bread.

Oh, I was with them, of them, for them, blood brother of their joy and hunger to the last hard gulping of the craw, the last deep ease and glow of strong hungry bellies, the last slow coil of pungent blue expiring from the bellows of their grateful lungs.

Their lives seemed glorious to me in the magic of dark and April. They swept strongly, invincibly, into the heart of desolation, through all the fury, pain and madness of my soul, speaking to me again their exultant prophecies of new lands, triumph and discovery, the morning of new joy upon the earth again, the resurrection of man's ancient, deathless, and triumphant labor of creation, saying to me again with an invincible contention that we who were dead should live again, we who were lost be found, and that the secret, wild, and lonely heart of man was young and living in the darkness, and could never die.

All that Spring in the window of the warehouse, the man sat at a desk, staring out into the street. I had seen this man three hundred times, and yet I had never seen him do anything but look out the window with a fixed abstracted stare. At first, the man had seemed so natural and unobtrusive a part of his surroundings that his personality had faded quietly into them, as much a part of the old warehouse building as its dusty brick and dingy planking, and he had gone unnoticed.

Then Esther, with her merry, quick, and sharp observance, had caught and fixed him in her memory, had looked quietly at him day by day and then, one day, with laughter, had pointed to him, saying, "There's our friend in the Distributing Corp. again! What do you suppose he distributes? I've never seen him do anything but look out the window! Have you noticed him? Hah?" she said eagerly and merrily clapping her small hand to her ear. "God! It's the strangest thing I ever saw! He sits there day by day and he does nothing!" she cried with a rich laugh of astonishment. "Have you seen him? He spends all his time looking out the window." She paused, making a slight movement of bewildered protest. "Isn't it queer?" she said, after a moment, with serious wonder. "What do you suppose a man like that can do? What do you suppose he's thinking of?"

"Oh, I don't know," I said indifferently. "Of nothing, I suppose."

And yet from that moment the man's face had been fixed in my memory. For several weeks thereafter when she came in every day, she would look across the street and cry out in a jolly voice, that had in it the affectionate satisfaction and assurance that people have when they see some familiar and comforting object of their memory.

"Well, I see our old friend, The Distributing Corp., is still looking out his window! I wonder what he's thinking of today." And she would turn away, laughing, her face flushed with merriment and good humor. Then, for a moment, with the childlike fascination which words and rhythms had for her, she meditated their strange beat with an abstracted gravity, silently framing and pronouncing with her lips a series of meaningless sounds such as "Corp—Borp—Forp—Dorp—Torp—," and at length singing out in an earnest and gleeful chant, and with an air of triumphant discovery: "The Distributing Corp, The Distributing Corp, He sits all day and he does no Worp!" And, in spite of my protest that her rhyme had neither sense nor reason in it, she cast back her encrimsoned face, and roared with laughter, a rich full woman's yell of delight and triumph.

Then we had laughed no more about the man. For, incredible, comical as his indolence had been when we first noticed it, as obscure and mysterious as his employment seemed, there came to be something formidable, immense, and impressive in the quality of that fixed stare. Day by day a thronging traffic of life and business passed before him in the street. Day by day, the great vans and wagons came, the drivers, handlers, packers swarmed before his eyes, filling the air with their harsh cries, irritably intent with driving labor, but the man in the window never wavered in his fixed abstracted stare.

That man's face remained forever in my memory. It was fixed there like one of those unforgettable images that a man remembers from his whole city life, and became for me a timeless image of fixity and judgment, the impartial, immutable censor of all the blind confusion and oblivion of a thousand city days, and of the tortured madness and unrest of my own life.

For night would come, and I would see the night's dark face again, and live again the crowded century of darkness that stretched from light to light, from midnight until morning.

From the meditation of a half-heard phrase, the hard mockery of a scornful eye, a young thug's burst of jeering laughter as he passed below my window with his comrades, or from some incident remembered, the inflection of a tone, the protraction of a smile, the hideous distortion of any casual act or word or circumstance, or from no visible cause whatever, the tidal flood of madness, hatred, and despair would awake with evil magic, poisoning me bone, brain, and blood, swarming through every tissue of my life the foul corruption of its malignant taint, becoming the instant and conclusive proof of the faithlessness and treachery of my mistress.

[226]

Then I would call the woman on the phone, and if she answered me, I would curse and taunt her foully, ask her where her lover was, and if she had him with her at that moment, and believe I heard him whispering and snickering behind her even when she swore no one was there. Feeling even as I cursed at her a rending anguish of inexpiable regret, I would tell her never to come back, rip the phone out of its moorings in the wall, hurl it on the floor, and smash and trample it to fragments underneath my feet, as if the instrument itself had been the evil agent of my ruin.

I would drain the bottle to its last raw drop, feel for a moment its fatal, brief, and spurious illusions of deliberation and control, and then rush out into the streets of night to curse and fight with people, with the city, with all life. Into the tremendous fugue of all-receiving night was packed a century of living, the death, despair and ruin of a hundred lives. Night would reel about me lividly the huge steps of its demented dance, and day would come incredibly like birth, like hope, like joy again, and I would be rescued out of madness to find myself upon the Bridge again, walking home across the Bridge, and with morning, bright, shining morning, blazing incredibly again upon the terrific frontal cliff and wall of the great city.

I would come home into my street at morning, and find the living stillness of my rooms that had been waiting to receive me, and see again, after all the madness, death, and million blind confusions of the night, the stolid, fixed, unchanging judgment of that face set in the warehouse window, staring out into the street forever with its look of sorrow, stern repose, and tranquil prophecy, its immutable judgment of dark time.

That man's thick white face, fixed there like the symbol of some permanence among the blind rush and sweep of all the million things that pass, the furious and immeasurable erosions of time, was connected somehow with another image which came to me that Spring among all the blazing stream of visions that passed constantly, a train of fire, across my brain and this one, unlike the others, was wordless and inexplicable, and neither dream nor fantasy.

And that image which was to haunt me sorrowfully, was this:
In an old house at the end of day, a man was sitting by the window. Without violence or heat the last rays of the sun fell on the warm brick of the house, and painted it with a sad unearthly light. In the window the man sat always looking out. He never spoke, he never wavered in his gaze, and his face was neither the face of the man in the warehouse window, nor any other face that I had ever seen, but it looked at me quietly, and the immutable exile of an imprisoned spirit was legible upon it, and it was the calmest and the most sorrowful face that I had ever seen.

That man's face became for me the face of darkness and of time. It was fixed above the memory of that Spring like some dark judge or destiny, some sorrowful and yet impassive witness of all the fury and anguish in the lives of men.

It never spoke a word to me that I could hear, its mouth was closed, its language was unspeakable—and yet what it said to me was more plain and inevitable than any spoken word could ever be. It was a voice that seemed to have the whole earth in it, and to resume into itself that murmurous and everlasting sound of time that, day and night, hovers forever above the earth, and all the furious streets of life, unchanging and eternal in its sustenance, no matter what men live or die.

It was the voice of evening and of night, and in it were all the million tongues of all those men who have passed through the heat and fury of the day, and who now lean quietly upon the sills at evening. In it was the whole vast hush and weariness that seemed to come upon the city at the hour of dusk, when the blind and savage chaos of another day is ended—and when everything, streets, buildings, and ten million men and women seem to breathe slowly with a sorrowful and weary joy.

The knowledge of their million tongues was in that single tongueless voice, the wisdom of man's life of labor, fury and despair, spoke to me from it in the hour of evening, and remained with me in all the madness and despair that I would know at night. And what that tongueless image said to me, was this:

"Child, child," it said. "Have patience and belief, for life is many days and all this present grief and madness of your life will pass away. Son, son, you have been mad and drunken, furious and wild, filled with hatred and despair, and all the dark confusions of the soul—but so have we. Your thirst and hunger were so great you thought that you could eat and drink the earth but it has been this way with all men dead or living in their youth. You found the earth too great for your one life, you found your brain and sinew smaller than the hunger and desire that fed on them—but, child, this is the chronicle of the earth and of all life. And now because you have known madness and despair, because you will grow mad and desperate again before this night is over, we, made of your earth and quality, men who have known all of the madness, anguish, and despair that youth can know, we who have stormed the ramparts of the furious earth and been hurled back, we who have been maddened by the unknowable and bitter mystery of love, the passion of hatred and desire, of faith and jealousy, grief and longing, we who now lean quietly on the sills of evening, watching the tumult, pain, and frenzy of this life, now call upon you to take heart and hope again, for we can swear to you that these things pass, and we can tell you there are things that never change and are the same forever:

"Because we shall not go into the dark again, nor suffer madness, nor admit despair; because we have found doors—Because we shall build walls about us now, and find a place, and see a few things clearly, letting millions pass. . . .

"Because we have known so many things, we have seen so many things, we have lived so long and lived alone so much and thought so many things; and because there is a little wisdom in us now; because, belly and back and bone and blood, we have made our own a few things now, and we know what we know, we have what we have, we are what we are. . . .

"We shall not strike against the wall at night and cry, 'No

more!'; we shall not hear the clocks of time strike out on foreign air, we shall not wake at morning in some foreign land to think of home, nor hear the hoof and wheel come down the streets of memory again; because we shall not go again, we shall not go again, because our wandering is over and our hunger fed—O brother, son and comrade, famished youth, over the dust and fury of ten thousand days, over all the madness of our hunger and unrest, we had a vision of the things that never change, we had a vision of the things that last forever, and we made this song for you:

"Some things will never change. Some things will always be the same. Lean down your ear upon the earth, and remember there are things that last forever. Behold: because we have been set here in the shift and glitter of so many fashions, because we have seen so many things that come and go, so many words forgotten, so many fames that flared and were destroyed; because our brains were bent and sick and driven by the rush, the jar, the million shocks of multitude and number, because we were a grain of dust, a cellulate and dying atom, a dwarfed wanderer among the horror of immense architectures, a stranger whose footfalls had not worn away the millionth part of an inch from the million streets of life; a sinew of bright blood and agony staggering under the weight of its desire, exploded by its everlasting hunger; and because our proudest songs were lost in all the snarl of voices, our vision broken and bewildered by the buildings, because we thought men so much less than mortar, our hearts grew mad and desperate, and we had no hope.

"But we know that the vanished step is better than the stone it walked upon, that one lost word will live when all the towers have fallen down, we know that the vanished men, the dead that they motored to swift burials and at once forgot, the cry that was wasted, the gesture that was half remembered, the forgotten moments of a million obscure lives will live here when these pavements are forgotten, and the dust of the buried lovers will outlast the city's dust. Lift up your heart, then, as you look at those proud towers: for we tell you that they are less than blade and leaf, for the blade and leaf will last forever.

"Some things will never change. Some things will always be the same. The tarantula, the adder, and the asp will always be the same. The sound of the hoof in the street will never change, the glitter of sunlight on the roughened water will always be the same, and the leaf that strains there in the wind upon the boughs will always be the same. April again! Patches of sudden green, the feathery blur and smoky buddings of young boughs, and something there that comes and goes and never can be captured, the thorn of Spring, the sharp, the tongueless cry! These things will always be the same.

"The voice of forest water in the night, the silence of the earth that lives forever, the glory of the proud and deathless stars, a woman's laughter in the dark—and a cry! a cry!—these things will always be the same.

"Hunger and pain and death will never change, the lids of dark, the innocence of morning, the clean hard rattle of raked gravel, the cricketing stitch of mid-day in hot meadows, the stir and feathery stumble of the hens upon the roost, the smell of the sea in harbors, and the delicate web of children's voices in bright air, these things will always be the same.

"All things belonging to the earth will never change—the leaf, the blade, the flower, the wind that cries and sleeps, and wakes again, the trees whose stiff arms clash and tremble in the dark, and the dust of lovers long since buried in the earth—all things proceeding from the earth to seasons, all things that lapse and change and come again upon the earth—these things will always be the same, for they come up from the earth that never changes, they go back into the earth that lasts forever; only the earth endures, but it endures forever.

"Under the pavements trembling like a pulse, under the buildings trembling like a cry, under the waste of time, the hoof of the beast again above the broken bones of cities, there will be something growing like a flower, forever bursting from the earth, forever deathless, faithful, coming into life again like April."

"I Have a Thing to Tell You"

NUN WILL ICH IHNEN 'WAS SAGEN

"I HAVE A THING TO TELL YOU"
(Nun Will Ich Ihnen 'Was Sagen)

In the summer of 1936 Wolfe made his last visit to Germany, a land which he felt was in many ways his spiritual home. But that summer the horrors hidden behind the mask of Naziism revealed themselves and were crystallized in an incident on the train from Berlin to Paris in which a frightened little Jew had given Wolfe a handful of coins to keep for him just before he was dragged back into the Nazi terror at the border. That incident Wolfe made the center of a short novel, which he first called *I Have Them Yet,* in reference to the coins, but later named *"I Have a Thing to Tell You."* In September he wrote his agent from Paris: "I've written a good piece over here—I'm afraid it may mean that I can't come back to the place where I am liked best and have the most friends, but I've decided to publish it." Yet months of work, re-writing and refining the story, were to take place before it was finally ready for publication in the *New Republic* in three installments on March 10, 17, and 24, 1937. His prophecy was true; his books were immediately banned in Germany.

In *"I Have a Thing to Tell You"* Wolfe returned to the short novel form as the one in which to recount the truth he discerned about Germany. He wrote to Dixon Wecter: ". . . the story wrote itself. It was the truth as I could see it, and I decided that a man's own self-respect and integrity is worth more than his comfort or material advantage."

Yet Wolfe did not regard this short novel as propaganda. When he was asked to allow it to be translated into Yiddish, he feared that it would be used for propaganda purposes, and said: "And frankly I do not think the story ought to be used in that way. It is a straight story; so far as I know, it has no propaganda in it save what the reader wishes to supply for himself by inference, and its greatest value, it seems to me, lies in that fact—that I wrote it as I wrote all my other stories about a human situation and living characters."

"I Have a Thing to Tell You" is an objective, rapid, straight-

forward narrative, centered sharply in its revelation of the state of Germany. When it was incorporated in *You Can't Go Home Again*, where it appears in greatly expanded form on pages 634-640, 641-651, 655, 663-704, and 743, its emphasis was shifted so that it became one of several incidents in George Webber's German experience. Perhaps the greatest violence ever done a passage by Wolfe was that done the concluding paragraphs of *"I Have a Thing to Tell You"* when they were transferred to the last page of the novel and set in a totally new context, so that they appear to be a prophecy of his approaching death.

The version here reprinted is that of *The New Republic*, LXXXX (March 10, 17, 24, 1937), pages 132-136, 159-164, 202-207.

CE

At seven o'clock the phone beside my bed rang quietly. I stirred, then roused sharply, from that fitful and uneasy sleep which a man experiences when he has gone to bed late knowing he has got to get up early. It was the porter.

"It is seven o'clock," he said.

I answered: "All right. Thank you. I'm awake."

Then I got up, still fighting dismally with a stale fatigue which begged for sleep and with a gnawing tension of anxiety which called for action. One look about the room assured me. My old leather trunk lay packed and ready on the baggage rest. Now there was very little more to do except to shave and dress and drive to the station. The train was not due until half-past eight, and the station was not three minutes distant. I thrust my feet into my slippers, walked over to the windows, tugged the cord and pulled up the heavy blinds.

It was a gray morning. Below me, save for an occasional taxicab or motor car, the quiet thrum of a bicycle, or some one walking briskly to his work, with a lean, spare clack of early morning, the Kurfürstendamm was bare and silent. In the center of the street, above the tram tracks, the fine trees had already lost their summer freshness—that deep intensity of German green which is the greenest green on earth and which gives to all their foliage a kind of forest darkness, a legendary sense of magic and of time. The leaves looked faded now and dusty. They were already touched here and there by the yellowing tinge of autumn. A tram, cream-yellow, spotless, shining as a perfect toy, slid past, with a kind of hissing sound upon the rails and at the contacts of the trolley. Except for this the tram made no noise. Like everything they made, the tram was perfect in its function. Even the little cobblestones that paved the tramway were spotless as if each of them had just been gone over thoroughly with a whisk broom, and the strips of grass on either side were as green and velvety as Oxford sward.

On both sides of the street the great restaurants, cafes and terraces of the Kurfürstendamm were also bare and empty. Chairs were racked upon the tables, and everything was clean and still. Three blocks away, at the head of the street, the clock on the Gedächtnis-Kirche struck seven times. I could see the great bleak masses of the church, and in the trees a few birds sang.

Some one knocked upon the door. I turned and crossed and opened it. The waiter stood there with his breakfast tray. He was a boy of fifteen years, a blond-haired solemn child with fresh pink face. He wore a boiled shirt and a waiter's uniform that was spotless-clean, but that, I think, had been sawed off and shortened down a little from the costume of some more mature inhabitant to fit its present owner. He marched in solemnly, stolidly uttering, in a gutteral and toneless voice, his three phrases of English, which were: "Good morning, sir," as I opened the door; "If you bleeze, sir," as he set the tray down upon the table; and "Sank you very much, sir," as he marched out, turned and closed the door behind him.

For six weeks the formula had not varied by an atom, and now as he marched out again I felt a feeling of affection and regret. I told him to wait a moment, got my trousers, took some money and gave it to him. His pink face reddened into happiness. I shook hands with him, and then the boy said: "Sank you very much, sir." And then, very quietly and earnestly: *"Gute Reise."* He clicked his heels together and bowed formally; and then closed the door. And I stood there for a moment, with that nameless feeling of affection and regret, knowing that I should never see him again.

Then I went back to the table and poured out a cup of the hot rich chocolate, broke a crusty roll, buttered it, spread it with strawberry jam and ate it. The pot was still half full of chocolate, the dish still piled with little scrolls of creamy butter. There was enough of the delicious jam, the crusty rolls and flaky croissants to make a half-dozen breakfasts, but I had eaten all I wanted. I brushed my teeth and shaved myself, put shaving brush and tooth-brush, all the other things, together in a little leather case, and put it away in the old trunk. Then I dressed. By seven-twenty I was ready.

Hartmann came in as I was ringing for the porter. He began to laugh as he saw me, closing his eyes, contorting his features and snuffling with laughter through his sourly puckered lips as if he had just eaten a half-ripe persimmon. Then he looked anxiously at me and said: "You are ready, then? You are going?"

I nodded. "Yes. Everything's all ready. How do you feel, Franz?"

He laughed suddenly, took off his spectacles and began to polish them. Without his glasses, his small face had a tired and worn look, and his weak eyes were bloodshot and weary from the night before. "Oh, Gott!" he cried with a kind of gleeful desperation. "I feel perfectly *dret-ful!* I have not efen been to bett! May I tell you something?" he said, and peered at me with the serious intensity with which he always uttered these words, "I feel like hell—I really do."

He spoke good English. He had lived and worked in London for a year or two and since then his knowledge of the language had made his services extremely useful to the exporting firm that employed him. He rarely made an actual mistake in accent or pronunciation, yet one was instantly aware that he was speaking in a foreign tongue. It is not easy to describe—it was, more than anything else, perhaps, a certain intonation of the voice—a voice that spoke familiar words with the latent rhythm of another speech. He spoke without difficulty—there was occasionally a certain awkwardness in tense, an unsure exercise of idiom, a Germanic transposition of the English words—but his speech was always fluent, and his meaning clear. Yet, even when he spoke such simple words as "You are ready, then?" one was aware of a certain carefulness with "then," as of one who had been schooled to say the word correctly. Or again, when he used such phrases as "Now, I may tell you something"—an expression that he used habitually, one felt a sense of strangeness not so much from the way he spoke the words (he spoke them very well, with a slight tendency toward the lisp, almost as if he were saying "thumthing") as from the rather curious use he put them to. Thus, if one asked a casual question—where to buy a shirt, or where to get a bus, or whether there had been a call upon the telephone—Hartmann would turn with an air of almost startled earnestness and say: "Now I may tell you something—someone *did* call, yes."

I looked at him a moment as he put his spectacles back on.

"Then you've had no sleep at all?" I said.

"Oh, yes," he said wearily. "I have slept an hour. I came back home. My girl was asleep—I did not want to wake her up. So I laid down upon the couch. I did not efen take off my clothes. I was afraid I would be coming too late to see you at the station. And that," he said peering at me most earnestly again, "would be *too* dret-ful!"

"Why don't you go back home and sleep today after the train goes? I don't think you'll be able to do much at the office, feeling as you do. Wouldn't it be better if you took the day off and caught up on your sleep?"

"Well, then," said Hartmann abruptly, yet rather indifferently, "I will tell you something. It does not matter. It really does not matter. I will take something—some coffee or something"—he shrugged his shoulders—"it will not be too bad. But, Gott!" again the desperately gleeful laugh, "how I shall sleep tonight! After that I shall try to know my girl again."

"I hope so, Franz. I'm afraid she hasn't seen much of you the last month or so."

"Well, then," said Hartmann, as before, "I will tell you something—it does not matter. It really does not matter. She is a good girl—she knows about these things—you like her, yes?—you think she is nice?"

"Yes, I think she's very nice."

"Well, then," said Hartmann, "I may tell you: she *is* very nice. We get along together very well. I hope they will let me keep her," he said quietly.

"They? Who do you man by 'they,' Franz?"

"Oh," he said, wearily, "these people—these stupid people— that you know about."

"But, good Lord, Franz! Surely they have not yet forbidden *that,* have they? Why you can step right out on the Kurfürstendamm and get a dozen girls before you've walked a block."

"Oh," said Hartmann, "you mean the little whores. Yes, you may still go to the little whores. That is quite all right. You see, my dear shap"—here Hartmann's small face puckered in a look of impish malice and he began to speak in that tone of exaggerated and mincing refinement that characterized some of his more vicious utterances—"I will now tell you something. Under the Dritte Reich we are all so happy, everything is so fine and healthy that it is perfectly God damn dret-ful," he sneered. "You may go to the little whores in the Kurfürstendamm. But you cannot have a girl. If you have a girl you must marry her and—may I tell you?" he said frankly—"I cannot marry. I do not make enough money. It would be *quite* impossible!" he said decisively. "And may I tell you this?" he continued, pacing nervously up and down the room, taking rapid puffs at his cigarette. "If you have a girl, then you most have two rooms. And that also is quite impossible! I have not efen money enough to afford two rooms."

"You mean, if you are living with a girl you are compelled by law to have two rooms?"

"It is the law, yes," said Hartmann, nodding with the air of finality with which a German states established custom. "You must. If you are living with a girl, she must have a room. Then you can say," he went on seriously "you are not living with each other. You may sleep together every night. But then, you see, you will be good. You will not do some things against the Party. . . . Gott!" he cried, and lifting his impish face, he laughed again. "It is all quite dret-ful."

"But if they find, Franz, that you're living with her in a single room?"

"Well, then," he said quietly, "I may tell you she will have to go." And then, wearily, with the tone of bitter indifference that had become so marked in one short year: "It does not matter. I do not care. I pay no attention to these stupid people. I have my work. I have my girl. If they let me keep them that is all that matters."

But now the porter had come in and was busy adjusting the straps of the leather trunk. I packed my briefcase with the letters, books and manuscript that had accumulated and gave it to the man. He dragged the baggage out into the hall and told us he would wait for us below.

I looked at my watch, found that it still lacked three-quarters of an hour until train time, and then asked Hartmann if we should go immediately to the station or wait at the hotel.

"Well, then," he said, "I may tell you that we can be waiting here. If you wait here another half an hour I should imagine there would still be time."

He offered me a cigarette. I struck a match for him. Then we sat down, myself at the table, Hartmann upon the couch against the wall. And for a moment more we smoked in silence.

"Well, then," said Hartmann, "this time, it really is to be good-bye. . . . This time you really will be going," he said, peering at me sharply with his earnest, anxious look.

"Yes, Franz. I've got to go this time. I've missed two boats already. I can't miss another one."

We smoked in silence for a moment, and then suddenly, earnestly, as before, "Well, then, may I tell you something? I am sorry."

"And I, too, Franz."

"We will all be terribly missing you," he said.

And again we smoked in troubled silence.

"You will come back, of course," said Hartmann presently. And then, most emphatically, "You must, of course. We like you here"—and in a moment, very simply, quietly, "you know, we do so love you."

I did not say anything, but something tightened in my throat. And he, peering at me anxiously again, continued: "And you like it here? You like us? Yes!" he cried, in answer to his own question. "Of course you do!"

"Of course, Franz."

"Then you must come back," he said quietly. "It would be quite dret-ful if you did not."

I did not speak, but again I noticed, as I had so often done before, the deep and tragic resonance of his quiet voice, a voice touched somehow, for an American, with unfathomed depths of living, with a resignation that had long since passed despair, a fortitude that had gone far past both pride and hope. He looked at me searchingly again, but I said nothing. In a moment Hartmann said: "And I—I too shall hope that we shall meet again."

"I hope so, Franz. I believe we shall, some day." And then, trying to throw off the sadness that had fallen on us, I said strongly: "Of course we shall! I will come back, and we shall sit together talking just the same as we are now."

He did not answer, but for a moment his face was contorted by the look of bitter humor I had seen so often.

"You think so," he said and smiled his wry and bitter smile.

"I'm sure of it!" I said more positively than ever. "We'll sit together drinking, we'll have parties, we'll stay up all night and dance around the trees and go to Aenna Maentz at three o'clock for chicken soup. All of it will be the same."

"Well, then," he said quietly, "I hope that you are right. I am not too sure," said Hartmann, "I may not be here."

"You!" I said, and laughed derisively. "Franz, you know you will be here as long as Karl is here. You couldn't get along without each other. You'll always be together. Besides, the firm has got to have you for the English trade."

"I am not so sure," he said. He was silent a moment longer, puffing at his cigarette, and then he continued, rather hesitantly: "You see—there are these fools—these stupid people!" He ground his cigarette out viciously in the ashtray and, his face contorted in a wry smile of defiant, lacerated pride, he cried angrily: "Myself —I do not care. I do not worry for myself. I have my little life!" cried Hartmann—"my little chob—my little girl—my little room. These people—these fools!" he cried—"I do not notice them. I do not see them! It does not bother me!" he cried. And now indeed his face was bitter as a grotesque mask. "I shall always get along," said Hartmann. "If they run me out—well, then, I may tell you that I do not care! There are other places!" he cried bitterly. "I have lived in England and Vienna. If they take my chob, my girl"—he cried scornfully and waved his hand impatiently—"may I tell you that it does not matter? And if these fools—these stupid people—if they take this little life of mine, I do not think that is so terrible. You think so? Yes?"

"Yes, I think so, Franz. I should not like to die."

"Well, then," said Hartmann quietly, "with you it is a different matter. You are American. With us, it cannot be the same. I have seen men shot, in Munich, in Vienna—I do not think it is too bad"—he turned and looked searchingly at me again, "no, I should imagine it is not too bad," he said.

"Oh, hell, you're talking like an idiot now! No one's going to shoot you. No one's going to take your job or girl away."

Hartmann did not answer for a moment. Presently he said, abruptly: "Now I think that I may tell you something. In the last year here these fools—these stupid people—have become quite dret-ful. All the Chews have been taken from their work, they have nothing to do any more. These people come around— some stupid people in their uniforms," he said contemptuously— "and they say that everyone must be an Aryan man—this wonderful plue-eyed person eight feet tall who is being Aryan in his family since 1820. If there is a little Chew back there—then I

[243]

should imagine it will be a pity." Hartmann jeered. "This man can no more work—he is no more in the Cherman spirit. It is all quite stupid." He smoked in silence for a moment, then continued. "This last year these big fools are coming round to Karl and me. They demand to know who I am, where I am from—whether I am porn or not. They say I must be proving to them that I am an Aryan man. Otherwise I can no longer hold my chob."

"But, my God, Franz!" I cried, and stared at him in stupefaction. "You don't mean to tell me that—why *you're* not a Jew! *Are* you?"

"Oh, *Gott,* no! Hartmann cried, with a sudden shout of gleeful desperation. "My dear shap, I am so God damn Cherman it is simply dret-ful."

"Well, then," I demanded, puzzled, "why should they bother you? Why do they worry about your being Aryan if you're German?"

Hartmann was silent a moment longer before he answered, and the look of wounded humor in his face had deepened perceptibly before he spoke again. "My dear Paul," he said, "now I may tell you something. I am completely Cherman, it is true. Only, my poor dear mother—I do love her so, of course—but, Gott!" He laughed again through a closed mouth, with a kind of bitter merriment in his face, as if he were laughing with an unripe persimmon in his mouth. "Gott! She is such a fool. This poor lady," he said, a trifle contemptuously, "was loving my father very much, so much, in fact, that she did not go to the trouble to marry him. So these people come and ask me all these questions and say 'Where is your father?'—and of course I cannot tell them. Because, alas, my dear old shap, I am this bastard. Gott!" he cried again, seeing the look of stupefaction on my face, and, with eyes narrowed into slits, laughed through the corners of his mouth. "It is all so dret-ful—so stupid—and so horribly funny!" Hartmann cried.

"But Franz! Surely you must know who your father is—you must have heard his name?"

"My *Gott*, yes!" he cried, and laughed through his closed lips again. "That is what makes it all so funny."

"You mean you know him, then? He is living?"

"But of course!" said Hartmann. "He is living in Berlin."

"But do you ever see him?"

"But of course!" he said again. "I see him every week. We are *quite* good friends."

"But—then I don't see what the trouble is—unless they can take your job from you because you are a bastard. It's embarrassing, of course, but can't you explain it to them? Won't your father help you out?"

"I am sure he would," said Hartmann, "if I told this thing to him. Only, I cannot tell him. You see," he went on quietly, after a moment's pause, "my father and I are quite good friends. We never speak about this thing together—the way he was knowing my mother. And now, I would not ask him to help me—because it might be seeming I was taking an advantage. It might spoil everything."

"But your father—is he known here? Would these people know his name?"

"Oh, *Gott*, yes!" Hartmann cried out gleefully. "That is what makes it all so horrible—and so dret-fully amusing. They would know his name at once—perhaps they say I am this little Chew and throw me out because I am no Aryan man—and my father," Hartmann choked, bent half over in his bitter merriment—"my father is this big Nazi—this most important person in the Party!"

For a moment I looked at him and could not speak. As he sat there, smiling his embittered and disdainful smile, the whole legend of his life became plain. He had been life's tender child, so sensitive, so affectionate, so amazingly intelligent. He had been the fleeceling lamb thrust out into the cold to bear the blast and to endure the bitter strife of want and loneliness. He had been wounded cruelly. He had been warped and twisted and yet he had maintained a kind of bitter hard integrity.

"I'm so damned sorry, Franz! I never knew of this."

"Well, then," said Hartmann indifferently, "I may tell you

that it does not matter. It really does not matter." He snuffled a little through his lips, flicked the ash off his cigarette and shifted his position. "I shall do something about it—I have engaged one of these little men—what do you call them?—lawyers—oh, Gott! but they are dret-ful!" Hartmann shouted gleefully—"to make some lies for me. This little man with his papers—he will feel around until he discovers fathers, mothers, sisters, brothers—everything I need. If he cannot, if they will not believe—well, then," said Hartmann, "I must lose my chob. It does not matter.

"But these fools," he said again with an expression of disgust—"these dret-ful people! Some day, my dear Paul, you must write a bitter book. You must tell all these people just how horrible they are. Myself—I am a little man. I have no talent. I am only a little clerk. I cannot write a book. I can do nothing but admire what others do and know if it is good. But you must tell these dret-ful people what they are. I have a little fantasie," he went on with a look of impish glee—"when I feel bad—when I see all these dret-ful people sitting at the tables putting food into their mouths, walking up and down in the Kurfürstendamm, then I imagine that I have a little ma-shine gun. So I take this little ma-shine gun and go up and down and when I see one of these dret-ful people I take the little ma-shine gun and I go—ping-ping-ping-ping-ping!" As he uttered these words he took aim and hooked his finger rapidly, saying "ping-ping-ping" in a rapid, childish key. "Oh, Gott!" he cried esctatically, "I should so enchoy it if I could go around with this little ma-shine gun and use it on all these stupid fools. But I cannot. My ma-shine gun is only in imagination. With you it is different. You have a ma-shine gun you can really use. And you must use it," he said earnestly. "Some day you must write this bitter book in which you tell these fools where they belong. Only," and he turned anxiously toward me, "you must not do it yet. Or if you do, you must not say some things in your next book that will make these people angry with you here."

"What kind of things do you mean, Franz?"

"These things about"—he lowered his voice and glanced quickly toward the door—"about politics—about the Party. Things that would bring them down on you. It would be quite dret-ful if you did."

"Why would it?"

"Because," he said, "you have a name here. I don't mean with these fools, but with the people left who still read books. If you should spoil it now—if you should write some things now that they would not like—the Reichsschriftenkammer would forbid your books. And that would be a pity. We do so like you here— I mean the people who do understand. They cannot believe that they are reading a translation. They say that it must sound as if it had been written in Cherman in the beginning and—Oh, Gott!" he shouted gleefully again—"they call you this very great writer."

"That's a good deal more than they do at home, Franz."

"I know. But then, I notice, in America they love everyone a year—and then they spit upon him. Here, with many people you must have it—this name of yours," he said earnestly. "And it would be too dret-ful if you spoil it now. You will not?" he said, and again looked anxiously at me.

I did not answer for a moment, and then I said: "A man must write what he must write. A man must do what he must do."

"Then you mean if you felt you had to say some things—about politics—about these stupid fools—about—"

"What about life?" I said. "What about people?"

"You would say it?"

"Yes, I would."

"Efen if it did you harm? Efen if it spoiled you here?" And, peering anxiously at me, he waited for my answer.

"Yes, Franz, even if that happened."

He was silent a moment more and then, with apparent hesitancy, said: "Efen if you write something—if they say to you that you cannot come back?"

I too was silent now. There was much to think of. But at last I said: "Yes, even if they told me that."

He straightened sharply, with a swift intake of anger and impatience. "Then I may tell you something," he said harshly. "You are one big fool." He rose, flung his cigarette away and began to pace nervously up and down the room. "Why should you go and spoil yourself," he cried. "You are at home here. Everybody understands you. And for a little politics"—he said bitterly—"because there are these stupid fools, you would now go and spoil it all."

I made no answer. In a moment, still walking feverishly up and down he said: "Why should you do it? You are no politician. You are no propaganda Party man. You are not one of these God damn little New York *Salon-Kommunisten*." He spat the word out viciously, his pale eyes narrowed into slits. "May I now tell you something?" He paused abruptly, looking at me. "I hate these bloody little people—they are everywhere the same. You find them everywhere—in London, Paris and Vienna. They are bad enough in Europe, but in America!" Hartmann shouted, his face lighting up with impish glee—"Oh, *Gott!* If I may tell you, they are simply dret-ful! Where do you get them from? Even the European esthete says, 'My Gott! these bloody men, these awful people, these damned esthetes from the Oo Ess Ah—are dret-ful!' "

"Are you talking now of Communists?"

"Well, now, I may tell you something"—curtly and coldly, with a kind of arrogant dismissal that was becoming more and more characteristic of him—"it does not matter what they call themselves. They are all the same. They are these little *expressionissmus, surrealissmus, kommunissmus* people—but really they are all the same. I am so tired of all these belated little people," he said, and turned away with an expression of weariness and disgust. "It simply does not matter what they say. For they know nothing."

"You think then, Franz, that all of communism is like that—that all communists are just a crowd of parlor fakes?"

"Oh, *die Kommunisten*," said Hartmann wearily. "No, I do not think they are all fakes. And *Kommunissmus!*" he looked at me, shrugged his shoulders with an air of protesting agreement, and said: "Well, then, I think that it is very good. I think that some day we may live like that. Only, I do not think that you and I will see it. It is too great a dream. It is more than to expect. And these things are not for you. You are not one of these little propaganda Party people—you are a writer. It is your duty to look about you and to write about the world and people as you see them. It is not your duty to write propaganda speeches and call them books. You could not do that. It is quite impossible."

"But if by writing about the world and people as you see them you come in conflict with these propaganda Party people—what then?"

"Then," he said roughly, "you will be a great big fool. You can write about the world and people without these Party people coming down on you. You do not need to mention them. And if you do, and do not say nice things, then you cannot come back. And for what? If you were some little propaganda person in New York, you could say these things and then it would not matter. Because they can say anything they like—but they know nothing of us, and it costs them nothing. You have so much to lose. You have a name. The people admire you here!" Anxiously, earnestly, searchingly again, he looked at me and said: "And you? You do so like the people, too?"

"Enormously."

"You must, of course," he quietly replied, then added gently: "They are really a good lot. They are big fools, of course, but they are not too bad."

He was silent a moment, ground out his cigarette in the ashtray and then said, a little sadly, "Well then, you must do what you must do. But you are one big fool. Come on, old shap," he said. He looked at his watch and put his hand upon my arm. "Now it is time to go."

We paused a moment, looking at each other, then we clasped each other by the hand.

"Good-bye, Franz," I said.

"Good-bye, dear Paul," said Hartmann quietly. "We shall miss you very much."

"And I you," I answered.

Then we went out.

II.

The hour had come: along the station platform there was a flurry of excitement in the crowd, a light flashed, the porters moved along the quay. I turned and looked up the tracks. The train was sweeping down on us. It bore down swiftly, sweeping in around the edges of the Zoölogic Gardens, the huge snout of the locomotive looming bluntly, the fenders touched with trimmings of bright green. The great machine steamed hotly past and halted. The dull line of the coaches was broken vividly in the middle with the glittering red of the Mitropa dining car.

We swung to action. My porter, heaving up my heavy leather case, clambered quickly up the steps and found a seat for me. There was a blur of voices all around, an excited tumult of farewell. Hartmann shook hands hard and fast, his small and bitter face was contorted as if he were weeping, as indeed he was. With a sudden shock of recognition I saw how close together were his laughter and his grief. I heard his curiously vibrant, deep and tragic voice saying, "Good-bye, good-bye, dear Paul, *auf wiedersehen.*"

Then I climbed up into the train. The guard slammed the door. Even as I made my way down the narrow corridor toward my compartment the train started, was in motion. These forms, these faces and these lives all slid away.

Hartmann kept walking forward, waving his hat, his face still contorted with that strange grimace that was half bitter mirth, half sorrow. Then the train swept out around the curve. And he was lost.

We gathered speed. The streets and buildings of the West slipped past me—those solid ugly streets, those great solid ugly buildings of Victorian German style, that yet, with all the pleasant green of trees, the window-boxes bright with red geraniums, the air of order, substance and comfort, had always been as familiar and as pleasant to me as the quiet streets and houses of a little town. Already we were sweeping through Charlottenburg. We passed the station without halting and on the platforms, with the old and poignant feeling of loss and of regret, I saw the people waiting for the Stadtbahn trains. Upon its elevated track the great train swept on smoothly toward the West, gathering in momentum slowly. We passed the Funkturm. Almost before I knew it we were running through the western outskirts of the city, toward the open country. We passed an aviation field. I saw the hangars and a flock of shining planes. Even as I looked a great silver-bodied plane moved out, taxied along and gathered speed, lifted its tail and, as we vanished, broke slowly from the earth.

And now the city was behind us. Those familiar faces, forms and voices of just six minutes past were now remote from me as dreams, imprisoned there as in another world, a world hived of four million lives, of hope and fear and hatred, anguish and despair, of love, of cruelty and devotion, that was called Berlin.

And now the land was stroking past, the level land of Brandenburg, the lonely flatland of the north that I had always heard to be so ugly and that I had found so strange, so haunting and so beautiful. The dark solitude of the forest was around us now, the loneliness of the *kiefern* trees, tall, slender, towering and straight as sailing masts, bearing upon their tops the burden of their needled and eternal green. Their naked poles shone with that lovely gold-bronze color that is itself like the material distillation of a magic light. And all between was magic too. The forest dusk was gold-brown, also, with this magic light, the earth gold-brown and barren, the trees themselves alone and separate, a pole-like forest filled with haunting light.

And then, the light would open and the wood be gone. And we were sweeping through the level cultivated earth, tilled thriftily to the very edges of the track. And I could see the clusters of farm buildings, the red-tiled roofs, the cross-quarterings of barns and houses. Then we would find the magic of the woods again.

I opened the door of my compartment and went in and took a seat beside the door. On the other side, in a corner by the window, a young man sat and read a book. He was an elegant young man dressed most fashionably. There was a kind of foppish elegance about his costume that one felt somehow was Continental, even though one did not know from what place upon the Continent he came.

What struck me therefore with a sense of shock was the American book he was reading. Even as I pondered on this puzzling combination the door was opened and a woman and a man came in.

They were Germans. The woman was no longer young, but plump, warm, seductive-looking, with hair so blonde it was the color of bleached straw, and eyes as blue as sapphires. She spoke rapidly to the man who accompanied her, then turned to me and asked me if the other places were unoccupied. I replied that I thought so, and looked inquiringly at the young man in the corner. And he too replied, in somewhat broken German, that he believed so. The woman nodded her head in satisfaction, spoke with quick authority to her companion and he went out and presently returned with their baggage—two valises, which he arranged upon the baggage rack above their heads.

He was a tall, blond, fresh-complexioned German, who conveyed indefinably an impression of bewildered innocence. The woman, although most attractive, was obviously much the older of the two. One knew for a certainty she was in her thirties, and she might even already have attained her fortieth year. There were traces of fine wrinkles at the corners of her eyes, a kind of physical maturity and warmth which had in it the wisdom of experience, but from which some of the freshness of youth had gone.

The young fellow obviously was in his early twenties. One felt instantly, without knowing why, that there was no family relation between these two: it was completely evident that the young man could not have been a brother, but it was also evident that they were not man and wife. Again, the woman, with the seductive warmth of her appeal, had an almost shameless physical attraction, a kind of naked allure such as one often sees in people

of the theatre—in a chorus girl or in the strip woman of a bur-
lesque show. Beside her assurance, her air of practice and authority,
her sharply vivid stamp, the young man was almost countrified.
And he certainly did look nervous and uneasy in the art of
travel: I noticed that he kept his head down most of the time, and
did not speak unless she spoke to him. And when she did, he
would flush crimson with embarrassment, two wedge-shaped flags
of color deepening in his fresh pink face to beetlike red.

It was hard not to fall back upon an ancient parable—to assume
that the boy was the village hayseed in the toils of the city siren,
that she had duped him into taking her to Paris, that the fool
and his money would soon be parted. And yet, there was certainly
nothing repulsive about the blonde-haired woman. She was decidedly a most attractive and engaging creature. She even seemed
to be completely unaware of that astonishing quality of sexual
magnetism which she undoubtedly did possess, and to express
herself sensually and naturally with the innocent warmth of a
child.

While I was busy with these speculations the door of the compartment opened again and a stuffy-looking little man with a long
nose looked in, peered about truculently and rather suspiciously,
and then demanded to know if the remaining seats in the compartment were free. We all told him that we thought so. Upon
receiving this information, he too, without another word, dis-
appeared down the corridor, to reappear again with a large valise.
I helped him stow it away upon the rack above his head; although
I do not think he could have done it for himself, he accepted my
service without a word of thanks, hung up his overcoat, fidgeted
and worried about, took a newspaper from his pocket, sat down
and opened it, banged the compartment door rather viciously, and,
after peering around sourly and mistrustfully at the rest of us,
rattled his paper and began to read.

While he read his paper I had a chance to observe this sour-
looking customer from time to time. In a well known phrase of
modern parlance, he was "nothing to write home about." Not that
there was anything sinister-looking about the man—decidedly

there was not. It was just that he was a drab, stuffy, irascible-looking little fellow of the type that one is always afraid one is going to encounter on a trip but that one hopes fervently he won't meet. He looked like the kind of fellow who would always be banging down the window of the compartment without asking anyone else about it, always fidgeting and fuming about—always, in short, trying by every cranky, crusty and ill tempered means to make his traveling companions as uncomfortable as possible.

Yes, he was certainly a well known type, but aside from these unpleasant aspects he was wholly unremarkable. It was only when he had intruded himself into the intimacy of a long journey and began immediately to buzz and worry around like a troublesome hornet that he became memorable. At this moment, in fact, the elegant young gentleman in the corner by the window almost ran afoul of him. The young fellow took out an expensive-looking cigarette case, and, smiling amiably, asked the lady if she objected to his smoking. She immediately answered, with great friendliness, that she minded not at all. I myself received this welcome information with considerable relief, took a package of cigarettes from my pocket and was on the point of joining my unknown young companion in the luxury of smoke when old Fuss-And-Fidget opposite me rattled his paper viciously, glared sourly at us and then, pointing at a sign upon the wall of the compartment, croaked dismally, *"Nicht Raucher."*

Well, all of us had known that at the beginning, but we had not known that Fuss-And-Fidget was going to make an issue of it. The young fellow and I glanced at each other with a slightly startled look, grinned a little, caught the lady's eye, which was also twinkling with the comedy of the occasion, and were obedi-ently about to put our cigarettes away unsmoked when Fuss-And-Fidget looked sourly around at us a second time and then said bleakly that as far as he was concerned it was all right. He'd just wanted to point out to us that we were in a nonsmoking compartment. The implication plainly was that from this time on the crime was on our heads, that he had done what he could as a good citizen to warn us, but that if we proceeded with our guilty plot against the laws of the land it was no further concern of his. Being thus reassured, we produced our cigarettes again and lighted up.

Time passed in silence now, and presently I fell into a dozing sleep, from which I would start up from time to time to look about me, then to doze again. Again and again I started up to find old Fuss-And-Fidget's eyes fixed on me in a look of such suspicion and ill tempered sourness that the expression barely escaped malevolence. Moreover, he was so fidgety and nervous that it was almost impossible to sleep longer than for a few minutes at a time. He was always crossing and uncrossing his legs, always rattling his newspaper, always fooling with the handle of the door, half opening the door and banging it to again, as if he were afraid it was not securely closed. He was always jumping up and going out into the corridor, where he would pace up and down, look out the windows at the speeding landscape, and fidget up and down the corridor again, holding his hands behind him, twiddling his fingers nervously as he walked.

Meanwhile, the train was advancing across the country at terrific speed. Forest and land, village and farm, tilled land and pasture rushed past us with the deliberate but devouring movement of the high velocity. We slackened a moment as we crossed the Elbe but there was no halt. Two hours after our departure from Berlin we were sweeping in beneath the arched, enormous roof of the Hannover station. There was a halt of ten or fifteen minutes here. I had fallen into a doze but as the train slackened and began to come into the outskirts of the old city I awoke. But fatigue still held me. I did not get up.

The others in the compartment—everyone except myself and the elegant young gentleman in the corner—got up and went out upon the platform to get as much fresh air and exercise as our short stay allowed. Meanwhile, my companion in the corner had put down his book and, after peering out the window for a moment, turned to me and said in English, marked by a slight accent, "Where are we now?"

I told him we were at Hannover.

He sighed a little and said, "I am tired of traveling. I shall be glad when I get home."

"And where is home for you?"

"New York," he said, and seeing a look of surprise upon my face he added quickly: "Of course I am not American by birth, as you can see. But I am a naturalized American and my home is in New York."

I told him that I lived there too, and he asked me if I had been long in Germany.

"No, not recently. I came over about two months ago."

"At first, when you came in this morning, I thought you were German. But then I saw you could not be German from your accent. When I saw you reading The Paris Herald I decided that you were English or American."

"I am American, of course."

"Yes, I can see that now. I," he said, "am Polish by birth. I went to America fifteen years ago to live, but my family still live in Poland."

"And you have been to see them, naturally?"

"Yes. I have two brothers living in the country. I am coming from there now," he said. He was silent for a moment and then added with some emphasis, "But not again. Not for a long time will I visit them. I am sick of Europe," he went on. "I am tired of all this foolish business, these politics, this hate, these armies and this talk of war—the whole damn stuffy atmosphere—here"—he cried indignantly and, thrusting his hand into his breast pocket, he pulled out a paper, "Will you look at this?"

"What is it?"

"A paper—a permit—which allows me to take twenty-three marks out of Germany. Twenty-three marks!" he repeated scornfully, "—as if I want their God damn money."

"I know. You've got to get a paper every time you turn around. Look here!" I cried, and reaching in my own breast pocket I pulled out a mass of papers big enough to choke a horse. "I got all of these in two months' time."

The ice was broken now. Upon a mutual grievance we began

to warm up to each other. It quickly became evident that my new acquaintance, with the patriotic fervor of his race, was almost passionately American.

"Oh," he said, "it will be good after all this to be back there where all is Peace—where all is Friendship—where all is Love."

I had myself some reservations on this score, but I did not utter them. His fervor was so genuine and warm that it would have been unkind to try to qualify it. And besides, I too was homesick now and his words, generous and wholehearted as they were, warmed me with their pleasant glow.

For I, as he, was weary and oppressed, exhausted with these pressures, worn out with these tensions of the nerves and spirit, sickened by the cancer of these cureless hates which had not only poisoned the life of nations but had eaten in one way or another into the lives of all my frends, of almost everyone that I had known here. And so, like my new-found fellow countryman, I too felt, beneath the extravagance and intemperance of his language, a certain justice in comparison. And I felt further that it would be very good to be back home again, out of the poisonous constrictions of this atmosphere, where, whatever we might lack, we still had air to breathe in, winds to clear that air.

My new friend now told me that he was a member of a brokerage concern in Wall Street. This seemed to call for some similar identification on my part and I gave him the most truthful answer I could make, which was that I worked for a publishing house. He remarked then that he knew the family of a New York publisher. And when I asked him who these people were he answered, "The Edwards family."

I said: "I know the Edwardses. They are friends of mine and Mr. Edwards is my publisher. And you," I said, "your name is Johnnie, isn't it? I have forgotten you last name, but I have heard it—"

He nodded quickly, smiling. "Yes, Johnnie Stefanowski," he said. "And you?—what is your name?"

I told him.

He said, "Of course. I know of you."

And instantly we were shaking hands, with that kind of stunned but exuberant surprise which reduces people to the banal conclusion that "it's a small world after all."

And now indeed we had established contact at a thousand points and found we knew in common scores of people. We discussed them enthusiastically, almost joyfully. By the time the other people returned to the compartment and the train began to move again we were engaged in rapid conversation.

Our three companions looked somewhat startled to hear this rapid-fire of conversation, this evidence of acquaintanceship between two people who had apparently been strangers just ten minutes since. Our little blonde lady smiled at us and took her seat; the young man also. Old Fuss-And-Fidget, all ears now, glancing quickly, sharply, from one to the other of us, listened attentively to all we said.

The cross-fire of our talk went back and forth, from my corner of the compartment to my friend's. I felt myself a sense of embarrassment at the sudden intrusion of this intimacy in a foreign language among fellow travelers, with whom we had heretofore maintained a restrained formality. But Johnnie Stefanowski evidently was troubled not at all and smiled in a friendly fashion at our companions as if they too were parties to our conversation and could understand every word we said.

Under this engaging influence, everyone began to thaw out visibly. The little blonde lady now began to talk in an animated way to her young companion. In a few moments Fuss-And-Fidget chimed in too. In a very short time the whole compartment was humming with this rapid interplay of English and of German.

Johnnie Stefanowski now proposed that we seek out the *Speisewagen* and procure refreshment. "I am not hungry," he said indifferently. "In Poland I have had to eat too much. I am sick of food—but would you like some Polish fruits?" he said, indicating a large paper-covered package at his side. "I believe they have prepared some things for me—some fruits from my brother's estate, some chickens and some partridges. I have no appetite myself, but wouldn't you take something?"

I told him that I was not hungry yet.

He suggested thereupon that we get a drink. "I still have these marks," he said, "seventeen or eighteen of them. I no longer have any need of them. But now that I have met you I think it would be nice if we could spend them. Shall we go and see what we can find?"

To this I agreed. We arose, excused ourselves to our companions and as Stefanowski left his seat, old Fuss-And-Fidget asked him if he was willing to change seats. Indifferently the young man answered, "Yes, take my seat, of course. It does not matter to me where I sit."

We went out into the narrow corridor and, moving forward through several coaches of the hurtling train, we finally reached the *Speisewagen,* skirted the hot breath of the kitchens and seated ourselves at one of the tables in one of the beautiful, bright clean coaches of the Mitropa service. Stefanowski seemed to have a Polish gentleman's liberal capacity for drink. He tossed his brandy off at a single gulp, remarking rather plaintively: "It is very small. But it is good and does no harm. We shall have more."

Pleasantly warmed by brandy, and talking together with the ease of people who had known each other for many years, we now began to discuss our companions in our own compartment.

"The little woman—she is rather nice," said Stefanowski—"I think she is not very young, and yet, she is quite charming, isn't she? A personality."

"And the young man with her?" I inquired. "You do not think he is her husband?"

"No, of course not," replied my companion instantly. "It is most curious," he went on in a puzzled tone, "he is much younger, obviously, and not the same—he is much simpler than the lady."

"Yes. It's almost as if he were some young fellow from the country, and she—"

"Is like someone in the theatre," Stefanowski nodded. "An actress. Or perhaps some music-hall performer."

"And the other man?" I said. "The little one? The fidgety little fellow who keeps staring at us. Who is he?"

"Oh, that one," said my friend impatiently. "I do not know. I do not care. He is some stuffy little man—you always meet them on a trip—it does not matter. But shall we go back now?" he said, "and talk to them? We shall never see them after this: and it would be interesting to find out who they are."

I agreed. Accordingly, my Polish friend now called the waiter, got our bill and paid it—and still had ten or twelve marks left from what remained of the waning twenty-three. Then we got up and went back through the speeding train to our compartment.

The lady smiled at us as we came in. And our three fellow passengers all regarded us with a kind of sharpened curiosity. It was evident that during our absence we had been the subject of their speculation. Stefanowski smiled and spoke to them at once. His German was somewhat broken but coherent, and he was a man of such natural warmth and social assurance that his deficiencies did not bother him at all. Our companions responded quickly, even eagerly, to our greeting, and immediately gave free expression to their curiosity, to the speculations which our meeting, our apparent recognition of each other, had aroused.

The lady asked Stefanowski where he came from—"*Was sind sie für ein Landsmann?*" And he replied that he was an American.

"*Ach so?*"—for a moment she looked surprised, then added quickly, "but not by birth?"

"No," said Stefanowski, "I am Polish by birth. But I live in New York now. And my friend here"—he indicated me, and they all turned to stare curiously at me—"is an American by birth."

They nodded in satisfaction and, smiling with eager curiosity, the lady said—"And your friend here—he is an artist, isn't he?"

Stefanowski said I was.

"A painter?"—the lady almost gleefully pursued the confirmation of her own predictions.

"He is not a painter. He is a writer." My young Polish friend said "*Dichter,*" which means poet, which I amended quickly to "*ein schriftsteller.*"

All three of them thereupon looked at one another with nods of satisfaction, saying ah, they thought so, it was evident, etc.

Old Fuss-and-Fidget even now chimed in with a sage observation that it was apparent "from the head." The others nodded in agreement, and the lady, now turning again to Stefanowski, said, "But you—you are not an artist, are you? You do something else?"

He replied that he was a business man—a *"Gèschäftsmann"*—that his business was in Wall Street, a name which apparently had imposing connotations for them, for they all nodded in an impressed manner and said "ah" again.

We went on then and told them how we had never seen each other before that morning, but how each of us had known of the other through many mutual friends whom we had known for years. This news delighted everyone. Our little blonde lady nodded triumphantly, burst out in excited conversation with her companion and with Fuss-And-Fidget, the effect of which was, "What did I tell you? I said the same thing, didn't I? It's a small world after all, isn't it?" etc.

Now we were all really wonderfully at ease with one another, all talking eagerly and naturally, as if we had known one another for years. The little lady began to tell us all about herself. She and her husband were, she said, proprietors of a business near the Alexanderplatz. No—smiling—the young man was not her husband. He was a young artist and employed by her. In what sort of business? She laughed—one would never guess. She and her husband manufactured mannikins for window-shop display. Their business, I inferred, was quite a large one. She told us that they employed over fifty workers, and occasionally they had had almost a hundred. For this reason, she had to go to Paris once or twice a year. For, she explained, Paris set the fashion in these figures as it did in clothes.

Of course, they did not buy the Paris models. *Mein Gott!* that was impossible with the present money situation as it was. Nevertheless, hard as it was, she had to get to Paris somehow once or twice a year, just in order to keep up with "what was going on." She took this young man with her on these trips. He made designs, drew models of the late show-window modes in Paris, and duplicated them for her when he returned.

[261]

Stefanowski now remarked that he did not see how it was even possible, under present circumstances, for a German citizen to travel anywhere. It had become difficult enough for a foreigner now to travel in and out of Germany. The money complications were so confusing and so wearisome. I added to this an account of my own experiences of the summer in my brief travels—the difficulties that had attended even a short journey to the Austrian Tirol. Ruefully I displayed the pocket full of papers, permits, visas and official stamps I had accumulated in two months. Upon this common ground we all again were vociferously agreed. The lady affirmed that it was stupid, exhausting and, for a German with business out of his own country, almost impossible. She added quickly, loyally, that of course it was also necessary, but then began to give an account of her own difficulties, which went swiftly into a bewildering maze of checks and balances, and which finally ended by her waving her hand charmingly, saying, *"Ach Gott!* it is all too complicated, too confusing, to explain."

Old Fuss-And-Fidget put in here, with confirmations of his own. He was, he said, an attorney in Berlin—a *"Rechtsanwalt"*—who had formerly had extensive professional connections in France and in other portions of the Continent. He had visited America as well, he added. He had been there, in fact, as recently as 1930, when he had attended an international congress of lawyers in New York. He even spoke a little English, which he now unveiled for us, and he was going now, he told us, to another international congress of lawyers which was to open in Paris within the next day or so and which would last a week. But it was hard for a German to make a trip even of this short duration. And as for his former professional activities in other countries, they were now, alas, impossible.

He asked me if any of my books had been translated and published in Germany and I told him they had. They were all warmly curious, wanted to know the title and my name. Accordingly, I wrote out for them the German titles of the books, the name of the German publisher, my own name. The little lady put the paper away in her pocketbook and announced enthusiastically that she would buy the books on her return to Germany. And Fuss-And-Fidget, after carefully reading the paper, folded it and put it away in his wallet, remarking that he too would buy the books when he returned.

Stefanowski now picked up his bulky paper package, opened it and demanded that everyone partake. There were some splendid pears and peaches, a plump broiled chicken, some fat squabs and various other delicicies. Our companions protested that they could not deprive him of his lunch, but the young man insisted with a vigorous warmth that was obviously a characteristic of his good-hearted nature that he and I were going to the dining car for luncheon anyway, and that if they did not eat the contents of the package it would go to waste. Whereupon, they all helped themselves to fruit, which they pronounced delicious, and the lady promised she would later on investigate the chicken. Upon these assurances, with friendly greetings all around, my Polish friend and I departed for a second time.

III.

It is astonishing how short a time it takes to get acquainted on a journey. As we made our way a second time along the corridors of the speeding train I reflected that already Stefanowski and I were as accustomed to each other as if we had been friends for many years. As to the new-found friends in our compartment, we were delighted with them all. In the most extraordinary way, and in the space of fifteen minutes' time, we seemed to have entered into the lives of all these people and they in ours. Now we were not only immensely interested in the information they had given us about themselves: we were as warmly, eagerly concerned with the problems that confronted them as if their troubles were our own.

During a long and sumptuous meal—a meal that began with brandy, proceeded over a fine bottle of Bernkasteler and wound up over coffee and more brandy and a good cigar, a meal on which we were both exuberantly determined to spend the remainder of our German money, we discussed our companions again. The little woman, we agreed, was charming. And the young man, although diffident and shy, was very nice. We even had a word of praise for Fuss-And-Fidget now. After we had cracked his crusty shell the old codger was not bad. He really was quite friendly underneath.

"And it does show," said Stefanowski quietly, "how good people really are, how easy it is to get along with one another in this world, how people really like each other—if only—"

"—if only—" I said, and nodded.

"These damned politicians," Stefanowski said.

At length we called for our bill and paid it. Stefanowski dumped his marks upon the table, counted them: "You'll have to help me out," he said. "How many have you got?"

I dumped mine out. We had enough to pay the bill, to give the waiter something extra. And there was enough left over for a double jolt of brandy and a good cigar.

So, grinning with satisfaction, in which our waiter joined amiably as he read our purpose, we paid the bill, ordered the brandy and cigars, and, full of food, of drink, and of the pleasant knowledge of a job well done, we puffed contentedly on our cigars.

We were now running through the great industrial region of western Germany. The pleasant landscape had been darkened by the grime and smoke of enormous works. Now it was grim with the skeletons of enormous smelting and refining plants, disfigured with great heaps of slag, with mountainous dumps. It was a new portion of the land, one of the few I had not seen before. It was brutal, smoky, dense with life, the grimy warrens of industrial towns. But it had the brutal fascination of these places too, the thrilling power of raw, enormous works.

Stefanowski informed me that we were already almost at the border and that, since our own coach went directly through to Paris, we should have no additional need of money for porter's fees.

This made us remember the difficulties of our fellow travelers, who were Germans. We agreed that the existing law which permitted native citizens to take only ten marks from the country was, for people in the business circumstances of our little blonde companion and old Fuss-And-Fidget, a very trying one.

At this moment Stefanowski had a brilliant inspiration, the result of his own generous impulse. "But why," he said, "why can't we help them?"

"How? In what way can we help them?"

"Why," he said, "I have here a permit that allows me to take twenty-three marks out of the country. You have no permit, but everyone is allowed—"

"To take ten marks," I said and nodded. "So you mean then," I concluded, "that since each of us has spent his German money—"

"But can still take as much as is allowed out of the country—yes," he said. "So we could suggest it to them—" he went on.

"—that they give us some of their marks to keep, you mean?"

He nodded. "Yes. It is not much, of course. But it might help."

No sooner said than seized upon. We were almost jubilantly elated at this opportunity of doing some slight service for these people to whom we had taken such a liking. At this moment, even while we were smiling confirmation at each other, a man in uniform came through the car, paused at our table—which was the only one that was now occupied—and quietly but authoritatively informed us that the Pass-Control had come upon the train and that we must return at once to our compartment to await examination. We rose, knowing now we had no time to lose, hastened back along the coaches of the swaying train, entered our compartment again and immediately told our fellows that the inspection would soon begin and that the officials were on the train.

There was a flurry of excitement. Everyone began to get ready. The blonde lady took out her purse and passport and with a worried look began to count her money. Stefanowski watched her quietly for a moment and then, taking out his own certificate and showing it, remarked that he was officially allowed possession of the sum of twenty-three marks, that he had had the sum in his possession, but now had spent it. I took this as my cue and remarked that I too had spent the ten marks that the law allowed me.

Our little blonde companion looked eagerly at both of us and read the friendship of our meaning.

"Then you mean?" she said, and gleefully—"but it would be wonderful, of course, if you would!"

"Have you as much as twenty-three marks?" said Stefanowski.

"Yes," she nodded quickly, with a worried look, "I have more than that. But if you would take the twenty-three and keep them until we are past the frontier—"

He stretched out his hand. "Give them to me," he said quietly. The transfer was completed, the money in his pocket, in the wink of an eye.

In another moment Fuss-And-Fidget had taken ten marks from his pocket and without a word passed them across to me. I thrust the money in my pocket, and we all sat back, a little flushed, excited but triumphant, trying to look composed.

A few minutes later an official opened the compartment door, saluted and asked for our passports. He inspected Stefanowski's first, found everything in order, took his certificate, saw his twenty-three marks, stamped the passport and returned it to him.

Then he turned to me. I gave him my passport and the various papers certifying my possession of American currency. He thumbed through the pages of the passport, which were now almost completely covered with stamps and entries, and finally smiled quite kindly, and returned my passport to me. Then he inspected the passports of the little blonde lady, her companion and Fuss-And-Fidget. Everything, apparently, was in order, save that the lady had confessed to the possession of more than twenty marks, and the official regretfully informed her that he must take from her anything in excess of ten. It would be held at the frontier and restored to her, of course, when she returned. She smiled ruefully, shrugged her shoulders, and gave the man twelve marks. All other matters were evidently now in order, for the man saluted and withdrew.

So it was over then! We all drew a deep breath of relief, and commiserated our charming lady friend upon her loss. But I think we were all quietly jubilant, too, to know her loss had been no greater, that we had been able in some degree to lessen it. I asked Fuss-And-Fidget if I should return his money now or later on. He told me to wait until we had crossed the frontier into Belgium. At the same time, he made some casual explanation, to which none of us paid any serious attention at the time, to the effect that his ticket was good only to the frontier, and that he would utilize the fifteen minutes of our wait at Aachen, the frontier town, to buy a ticket for the remainder of the trip to Paris.

We were now, in fact, approaching Aachen. The train was slackening speed. We were going through a pleasant countryside, a smiling landscape of green fields and gentle hills, unobtrusively, mildly, somehow unmistakably European. The seared and blasted districts of the mines and factories were behind us. We were entering the outskirts of a pleasant town.

This was Aachen. In another moment the train was slowing to a halt before the station. We had reached the frontier. There was to be a wait of fifteen minutes and a change of engines. All of us got out—Fuss-And-Fidget to get a ticket, the others to stretch their legs and get a breath of air.

My Polish friend and I got out and walked forward along the platform to inspect the locomotive. The German locomotive which would here be supplanted by its Belgian successor was a magnificent machine, almost as big as one of the great American engines. The evidence of high velocity was legible in every line of it. What was most remarkable was the tender, a wonderful affair, the whole of which seemed to be a honeycomb of jetting pipes. One looked in through some slanting bars and saw a fountain-like display, composed of thousands of tiny little jets of steaming water. It was a marvelous machine, which bore in every line the evidence of the tremendous engineering talent that had created it.

Knowing how vivid, swift and fugitive are those poignant first impressions that come at the moment when we change from one country to another, I waited with an almost feverish interest for the approach of the Belgian locomotive. I knew in advance it would not be so good as the German one because the energy, the intelligence, the strength and the integrity which produced it were inferior, but I was eagerly sensitized to observe the exact degree and quality of these differences between the powerful, solid and indomitable race that I was leaving and the little people I would now encounter.

Presently we walked back along the platform, found our little blonde-haired lady and, flanking her on either side, began to stroll up and down beside the train. At length, observing the station clock and seeing that the moment scheduled for departure had already come, we moved quickly back towards our own coach and our own compartment.

As we approached it was evident that something had happened. There were no signs of departure. The conductor and the station guard stood together on the platform. No warning signal had been given. And, moreover, there was now evident a kind of subdued tension, a sense of crisis that made my pulse beat quicker as I approached.

I have often observed this phenomenon in life, its manifestations under certain conditions are nearly always identical. A man has leaped or fallen, for example, from a high building to the pavement of a city street. Or a man has been shot, or beaten. He has been struck by a motor car; or again, a man is dying quietly on the street before the eyes of other men. But always, the manifestation of the crowd is just the same. Even before you see the faces of the people, when you see their backs, their posture, the position of the head and shoulders, you know what has happened.

You do not know, of course, the precise circumstance, but what you sense immediately is the final stage of tragedy. You know that someone has just died or is dying, and in the terrible eloquence of backs and shoulders, the *feeding* silence of the watching men, you sense a tragedy that is even deeper. It is the tragedy of man's cruelty and his lust for pain, the tragic weakness that corrupts him, that he loathes but that he cannot cure.

And always, the manifestation of this tragedy is just the same. Even before one arrives one knows from this silent eloquence of shoulders, backs and heads that something ruinous and horrible has happened. I knew the signs too well. And now, as I hastened along beside the train and saw the people gathered in the corridor in that same feeding posture, waiting, watching, in that deadly fascinated silence, I was sure that once again in life I was about to witness death.

That was the first thing that came to me—and I believe to all of us—that someone had died. And what stunned us, what stopped us short, appalled, was that death had come to our compartment. The shades were tightly drawn, the door closed, the whole place sealed impenetrably. We had started to get on the train when this thing burst upon us. And now we saw our lady's young companion standing at the window in the corridor. He motioned quickly to us, a gesture warning us to remain where we were. And as he did it flashed over all of us that the subject of this tragic visitation was the nervous little man who had been the companion of our voyage since morning.

The stillness of the scene, the shuttered blankness of that closed compartment, were horrible. Even as we stared, appalled and horror-stricken, at that fatal curtained closet, which had so short a time ago housed the lives of all of us, and which had now become the tenement of death, the curtained door of the compartment was opened and closed quickly, and a man came out.

He was an official, a burly-looking fellow, with a visored cap, a jacket of olive green. He was a man of forty-five or more, a Germanic type with high blunt cheekbones, a florid face and tawny mustaches, combed out sprouting, in the Kaiser Wilhelm way. His head was shaven, and there were thick creases at the base of the skull and across his fleshy neck. He came out, climbed down clumsily to the platform, signaled excitedly to another officer and climbed back into the train again.

It was a familiar type, one that I had seen and smiled at often, but one that now became, under these ominous circumstances, sinisterly unpleasant. Even the man's physical weight and clumsiness, the awkward way he got down from the train, the awkward way he climbed up again, the thickness of his waist, the unpleasant width and coarseness of his clumsy buttocks, the way his sprouting mustaches seemed to quiver with passion and authority, the sound of his guttural voice, raised coarsely, somewhat phlegmily, as he shouted to his fellow officer, the sense that he was fairly panting with an inflamed authority—all these symptoms had now become, under the ominous prescience of the moment, loathsome, sinister, repellent.

All of a sudden, without knowing why, I felt myself trembling with a murderous and incomprehensible anger. I wanted to smash that fat neck with the creases in it. I wanted to pound that inflamed and blunted face into a jelly. I wanted to kick square and hard, bury my foot, dead center in the obscene fleshiness of those clumsy buttocks. And I knew that I was helpless, that all of us were. Like all Americans, I had never liked the police or the kind of personal authority that it sanctifies. But this feeling, this intensity, with its murderously helpless rage, was different. I felt impotent, shackled, unable to stir against the walls of an obscene but unshakable authority.

The official with the sprouting mustaches, accompanied now by his colleagues, opened the curtained doors of the compartment again, and now I saw that they were not alone. Two other officials were in the compartment and our nervous little companion—no, he was not dead!—he sat there *huddled*, facing them. He sat looking up at them as they bent over him. His face was white and pasty. It looked greasy, as if it were covered with a salve of cold fat sweat. Under his long nose his mouth was trembling in a horrible attempt at a smile. In the very posture of the men as they bent over him there was something revolting and unclean.

But the official with the thick creased neck had now filled the door and blotted out the picture. He went in followed by a smaller colleague, the door was closed again behind him, and again there was that vicious and ill omened secrecy.

All of this had happened in a moment while we had looked on with stupefied surprise. Now the people gathered in the corridor began to whisper to one another. In a moment our little blonde lady went over, whispered to the young man at the window and then came back, took Stefanowski and myself by the arm and led us away, out of hearing.

Then, as both of us whispered, "What is it?" she looked around cautiously again and said with lowered voice: "That man—the one in our compartment—was trying to get out of the country and they've caught him."

"But why?—What for?—What has he done?" we asked, bewildered.

Again she glanced back cautiously and then, drawing us toward her till our three heads were almost touching, she said, in an awed and almost frightened tone, "They say he is a Jew. They searched his baggage—he was taking money out."

"How much?" said Stefanowski.

"I don't know," she whispered. "A great deal, I think. Several thousand marks. They found it."

"But how—" I began. "I thought everything was finished. I thought they were done with all of us when they went through the train."

"Yes," she said, "but don't you remember he said something about not having a ticket the whole way. He got off the train to get one. And I think that's when they caught him," she whispered. "I think they had their eye on him. That's why they did not question him when they came through the train"—as indeed, I now remembered, "they" had not—"And they caught him here," she went on. "They asked him where he was going and he said to Paris. They asked him how much money he was taking out; he said ten marks. Then they asked him how long he was going to remain in Paris, and for what purpose, and he said he was going to be there for a week and that he was attending this congress of lawyers that he spoke about. They asked him then how he proposed to stay in Paris for a week and attend this congress if all he had was ten marks. And I think," she whispered, "he got frightened then. He began to lose his head. He said he had forgotten, that he had twenty marks besides, which he had put into another pocket. And then, of course, they had him. They searched him. They searched his baggage, and they found more," she whispered in an awed tone. "Much, much more."

For a moment we all stared at one another, too stunned to say a word. Then the little woman laughed in a low, almost frightened, sort of way, a little uncertain "o-hoh-hoh-hoh-hoh" ending on a note of incredulity.

"This man," she whispered again, "this little Jew—"

"I didn't know he was a Jew," I said, "I should not have thought so."

"But he is," she whispered, and looked stealthily around again to see if we were being overheard. "And he was doing what so many of the others have done—he was trying to get out with his money." And again she laughed, the uncertain little hoh-hoh-hoh that mounted on a note of incredulous amazement. And yet, I saw, her eyes were troubled, too.

All of a sudden I felt sick, empty, nauseated. That money, those accursed ten marks, were beginning to burn a hole in my pocket. I put my hand into my vest pocket and the coins felt greasy, as if they were covered with sweat. I took them out and closed them in my fist and started to cross the platform toward the train.

The woman seized me by the arm. "Where are you going?" she gasped. "What are you going to do?"

"I'm going to give that man his money. I can't keep it now."

Her face went white. "Are you mad?" she whispered. "Don't you know that that will do no good? You'll only get yourself arrested and, as for him—he's in trouble enough already. You'll only make it so much worse for him. And besides," she faltered, as the full consequences came to her, "God knows what he has done, what he has said already. If he has told that we have transferred money to one another—we may all be in for it!"

We had not thought of this. But now we did. And as we saw the possible consequence of our act we just stood there and stared helplessly at one another. We just stood there, three abreast, feeling dazed and weak and hollow. We just stood there and prayed.

And now they were coming out of the compartment. The fellow with the sprouting mustache came out first, carrying the little man's valise. He looked around. It seemed to me he glared at us. We just stood still and prayed. We expected now to see all of our baggage come out. We thought that we were in for it.

But in a moment the other three officials came out of the compartment, with the little man between them. They marched him right along the platform, white as a sheet, greasy looking, protesting volubly, in a voice that had a kind of anguished lilt. He came right by us. I made a movement with my arms. The greasy money sweated in my hand and I did not know what to do. I started to speak to him. And at the same time I was praying that he would not speak. I tried to look away from him, but I could not look away. He came toward us, still protesting volubly that everything could be explained, that all of it was an absurd mistake. And just for a moment as he passed us, he stopped talking, glanced at us, white-faced, smiling pitiably, his eyes rested on us for a moment, and then, without a sign of further recognition, he went on by.

I heard the little blonde woman at my side sigh faintly and I felt her body slump against me. We all felt pretty weak and hollow. In a moment we went on across the platform and got up into the train. The evil tension had been snapped. People were now talking feverishly, still in a low tone but with obvious released excitement. Our little blonde companion leaned from the window of the corridor and spoke to the fellow with the sprouting mustache who was still standing there. "Are—are you going to keep him here?" she said in a low tone. "You're not going to let him go?"

He looked at her stolidly for a moment. Then an intolerable smile broke deliberately across his brutal features. He nodded his head, slowly, with the finality of a gluttonous satisfaction: "*Nein*," he said, "*Er bleibt.*" And, shaking his heavy head ever so slightly from side to side, "*Geht nicht!*"

They had him. Far down the platform we heard the sudden fifing shrill of the engine whistle. The guard cried warning; all up and down the platform doors were slammed. Slowly the train moved from the station. We rolled right past him, very slowly. They had him. They surrounded him. He stood among them, protesting volubly, talking with his hands now, insisting all could be explained. And they said nothing. They had him. They just stood and watched him, each with the faint suggestion of that intolerable slow smile upon his face. They raised their eyes, unspeaking, looked at us as we rolled past, with the obscene communication of their glance and of their smile.

And he—he too paused once from his voluble and feverish discourse as we passed him. He lifted his eyes to us, his pasty face, and he was silent for a moment. And we looked at him for the last time, and he at us—this time, more direct and steadfastly. And in that glance there was all the silence of man's mortal anguish. And we were all somehow naked and ashamed, and somehow guilty. We all felt somehow that we were saying farewell, not to a man but to humanity; not to some nameless little cipher out of life, but to the fading image of a brother's face. We lost him then. The train swept out and gathered speed—and so farewell.

I turned and looked at Stefanowski. He, too, was silent for a moment. Then he spoke.

"Well, then," he said, "I think that this is a sad ending to our trip."

And we? We went back in and took our former seats in our compartment. But it seemed strange and empty now. The ghost of absence sat there ruinously. He had left his coat and hat; in his anguish he had forgotten them. Stefanowski rose and took them, and would have given them to the conductor. But the woman said: "You'd better look into the pockets first. Perhaps there's something in them. Perhaps"—quickly, eagerly, as the idea took her—"perhaps he has left money there."

Stefanowski searched the pockets. There was nothing there. He shook his head. The woman began to search the cushions of the seats, thrusting her hands down around the sides. "It might just be, you know," she said, "that he hid money here." She laughed excitedly, almost gleefully. "Perhaps we'll all be rich."

The young Pole shook his head. "I think they would have found it if he had," he said—and here he paused suddenly, peered out the window, and thrust his hand into his pocket, "I suppose we're in Belgium now. Here's your money." And he returned to her the money she had given him.

She took it and put it in her purse. I still had the ten marks in my hand and was looking at them. The woman looked up, saw my face, then said quickly, warmly, "But you're upset about this thing! You look so troubled."

I put the money back and in a moment said: *"Ich fühle gerade als ob ich Blutgeld in meiner Tasche hätte."*

She leaned over, smiling, and put her hand reassuringly upon my arm: *"Nein. Nicht Blutgeld—Judgeld!"* she whispered. "Don't worry about it. He had plenty more!"

My eyes met those of Stefanowski for a moment and his too were grave. "This is a sad ending to our trip," he said again.

And she—our little blonde companion—she tried to laugh and joke, but her eyes were also full of trouble. She tried to talk us out of it, to talk herself into forgetfulness.

"These Jews!" she cried. "These things would never happen if it were not for them! They make all the trouble. Germany has had to protect herself. The Jews were taking all the money from the country—thousands of them escaped, taking millions of marks with them. And now, when it is too late, we wake up to it! It is too bad that foreigners must see these things, that they've got to go through these painful experiences—it makes a bad impression. They do not understand the reason. But it is the Jews!" she whispered.

We said nothing and the woman went on talking, eagerly, excitedly, earnestly, persuasively, but really as if she were trying to convince herself, as if every instinct of race and loyalty was now being used in an effort to justify something that had filled her with a sense of shame and sorrow. But even as she talked her clear blue eyes were full of trouble. And at length she stopped. There was silence for a moment. Then gravely, quietly, the woman said: "He must have wanted very badly to escape."

We remembered then all he had said and done throughout the journey. And now every act and gesture, every word became invested with a new and terrible meaning. We recalled how nervous he had been, how he kept opening and shutting the door, kept getting up to pace up and down along the corridor. We recalled how he kept peering around at us suspiciously, how eagerly he had asked Stefanowski if he would change places with him when the Pole had got up to go into the dining-car with me. We recalled his explanations about having to buy passage from the frontier to Paris, the explanations he had given to the conductor. And all these things, which at the time we had dismissed as irascible ill temper or trivial explanation, now were revealed in a sequence of terrible significance.

"But the ten marks!" the woman cried at length. "In God's name, since he had all this other money, why did he give ten marks to you? It is so stupid!"

And we could find no reason, except that he had done it because he thought it might alleviate any suspicion in our minds about his true intent; or, what was even likelier, I thought, that he was in such an inner state of nervous frenzy that he had acted blindly, wildly, on the impulse of the moment.

We did not know. We never would find out the answer now. We discussed the money he had given me. The young Pole remarked that I had given the man my name and my address and that if he was later on allowed to complete his journey, he could write to me. But we all knew I would never hear from him again.

Late afternoon had come. The country had closed in, the train was winding through a pleasant, romantic landscape of hills and woods. There was a sense of forest dusk, cool darkling

waters, the slant of evening and the wane of light. We knew
somehow that we had entered another land. Our little blonde
companion peered anxiously out the window and then asked if
we were really now in Belgium. The conductor assured us that
we were. We gave the man our late companion's hat and coat and
explained the reason for them. He nodded, took them, and departed.

The woman had her hand upon her breast, and now when
the man had gone I heard her sigh slowly with relief.

In a moment she said quietly and simply: "Do not misunder-
stand. I am a German and I love my country. But—I feel as if a
weight has lifted from me *here*"—she put her hand upon her
breast again. "You cannot understand perhaps just how it feels
to us but—" and for a moment she was silent as if painfully
meditating what she wished to say. Then quickly, quietly: "We
are so happy to be—*out!*"

Out? I too was "out." And suddenly I knew just how she felt.
I too was "out," who was a stranger to her land, who never yet
had been a stranger in it. I too was "out" of that great land whose
image had been engraved upon my spirit in my childhood and
my youth, before I had ever seen it. I too was "out" from that
land which had been so much more to me than land, which had
been for me so much more than place. It was a geography of
heart's desire. It was a soul's dark wonder, the haunting beauty
of the magic land. It had been burning there forever, like the
dark Helen burning in man's blood. And now, like the dark
Helen, it was lost to me. I had spoken the language of its spirit
before I ever came to it. I had spoken the accents of its speech
most brokenly from the hour when I first entered it, yet never with
a moment's strangeness. I had been at home in it and it in me. It
seemed I had been born in it and it in me. I had known wonder
in it, truth and magic in it, sorrow, loneliness and pain in it. I
had known love in it, and for the first time in my life I had
tasted there the bright delusive sacraments of fame.

Therefore, it was no foreign land to me. It was the other half
of my heart's home. It was the dark lost Helen I had found, it

[277]

was the dark found Helen I had lost—and now I knew, as I had never known before, the countless measure of my loss—the countless measure of my gain—the way that now would be forever closed to me—the way of exile and of no return—and another way that I had found. For I knew that I was "out." And that I had now found my way.

To that old master, now, to wizard Faust, old father of the ancient and swarm-haunted mind of man, to that old German land with all the measure of its truth, its glory, beauty, magic and its ruin—to that dark land, to that old ancient earth that I had loved so long—I said farewell.

I have a thing to tell you:

Something has spoken to me in the night, burning the tapers of the waning year; something has spoken in the night; and told me I shall die, I know not where. Losing the earth we know for greater knowing, losing the life we have for greater life, and leaving friends we loved for greater loving, men find a land more kind than home, more large than earth.

Whereon the pillars of this earth are founded, toward which the spirits of the nations draw, toward which the conscience of the world is tending—a wind is rising, and the rivers flow.

The Party at Jack's

THE PARTY AT JACK'S

In 1937 Wolfe was groping again toward a form for his next novel and wrestling desperately in the struggle that ended with his severing publishing relations with Charles Scribner's Sons. Once more he turned to the short novel form, as he had done in a similar period of groping in the early thirties. In the first half of the year he wrote a rough draft of *The Party at Jack's,* and when that summer he returned to North Carolina to work in a cabin near Oteen, he set to work revising and rewriting this short novel.

Wolfe had set himself no small task in this new work. In a long letter to Hamilton Basso, he wrote: "I am working again on a very long, difficult and closely woven story called 'The Party at Jack's' . . . I suppose really a whole book could be made out of it but I am trying to do it in a story." To his agent he said: ". . . my plan when I get through is to have a complete section of the social order, a kind of dense, closely interwoven tapestry made up of the lives and thoughts and destinies of thirty or forty people, and all embodied in the structure of the story. It is an elaborate design; it has to be: it is, I suppose, somewhat Proustian but this also has to be and the interesting thing about it is the really great amount of action. This action is submerged . . ." The work of Proust's which Wolfe had in mind probably was *Sodome et Gomorrhe (Cities of the Plain).*

By the end of August he had conquered his structural problems and he declared, "I think it is now a single thing, as much a single thing as anything I've ever written." And he added, "As to the matter of action, it seems to me that the piece is crowded, although perhaps it is not apparently so. But I don't see how any intelligent reader could read it without understanding that almost everything has happened before the piece is ended." Although he moved on from this version to a further expansion of the story, an expansion which he began to think of as a full-length novel, it is the intermediate version, of which he is here talking, that his agent sold to *Scribner's Magazine*. It was published there in the May, 1939, issue, eight months after its author's death.

In *You Can't Go Home Again* the material of *The Party at Jack's* appears in the expanded, full-length novel version left incomplete by Wolfe at the time of his death and edited by Edward C. Aswell. In this long version it covers pages 196-322. It constitutes the most impressive section of *You Can't Go Home Again*, but in this expanded form it loses some of the sharp focus which the sparer magazine version has.

The version here reprinted is that in *Scribner's Magazine*, CV (May, 1939), pages 14-16, 40-49, 58-62.

From the outside the building was—just a building. It was not beautiful, but it impressed one by its sheer massivity. A mighty shape, twelve stories high, with ramparts of enduring stone, spaced evenly by a thousand windows, the great building filled a city block, and fronted on both sides. It was so grand, so huge, so solid, it seemed to be hewn from the everlasting rock itself, to be built there for eternity, and to endure there while the rock itself endured.

And yet this really was not true at all. That mighty building was really tubed and hollowed like a giant honeycomb. It was sustained on curving arches, pillared below on riddled vacancy, its nerves and bones and sinews went down depth below depth among the channeled rock: below these basal ramparts of enduring stone, there was its underworld of storied basements. Below all these, far in the tortured rock, there was the tunnel's depth.

Therefore, it happened sometimes, that dwellers in this imperial tenement would feel a tremor at their feet as something faint and instant passed below them, and perhaps remember that there were trains, far, far below them in these tunneled depths. Then all would fade away into the riddled distances of the tormented rock. The great building would grow solidly to stone again, and people would smile faintly, knowing that it was enduring and unshaken, now and forever, as it had always been.

A little before seven o'clock, just outside the building, as he was going in for the night's work, old John was accosted by a man of perhaps thirty years in a state of unkempt dilapidation.

"Say, Mac—" at the familiar words, the old man tried to move away. But the creature plucked at his sleeve with unclean fingers. "I was just wonderin' if you could spare a guy a—"

"Nah-h!" the old man snapped angrily. "I can't spare you anything! I'm twice your age and I always had to work for everything I had. If you was any good you'd do the same!"

"Oh, yeah?" the other jeered, with eyes suddenly gone hard and ugly.

"Yeah!" old John snapped back in the same tone, and then went on, feeling that this ironic repartee was perhaps a little inadequate but the best he could do on the spur of the moment.

He was still muttering to himself as he entered the great arched entrance of the building and started along the colonades that led to the south wing.

"What's the matter, Pop?"—it was Ed, the day elevator man, who spoke to him—"Who got your goat?"

"Ah-h!" John muttered, still fuming with resentment. "It's these panhandling bums! A young fellow no older than you are tryin' to panhandle from an old man like me!"

"Yeah?" said Ed, in a tone of mild interest.

"Yeah," said John. "They ought to keep these fellows away from here. They got no right to bother the kind of people we got here." There was just a faint trace of mollification in his voice as he spoke the words "the kind of people we got here": one felt that on this side reverence lay—"the kind of people we got here" were, at all odds, to be protected and preserved.

"That's the only reason they hang around this place," the old man said. "They know they can work on the kind of people we

[283]

got here and get it out of them. If I was the management I'd put a stop to it."

And having made these pronouncements, John went in at the service entrance of the south wing, and in a few moments was at his post, ready for the night's work.

II.

John Enborg had been born in Brooklyn more than sixty years before, the son of a Norwegian seaman and an Irish serving-girl. In spite of this mixed parentage, one would have said without hesitation that he was "old stock" American—New England Yankee. Even his physical structure had in one brief generation taken on that kind of special pattern wrought out upon the whole framework of flesh and bone, that is unmistakably "American." He had the dry, lean, furrowed neck of the American. He had the dry face, too, the dry mouth, a little harsh and woodenly inflexible, the lower jaw outcropping slightly, as if some conflict in the life around him had hardened the very formations of the jaw into this sinewy tenacity. His speech was spare, dry, nasal, with a kind of tartness that was really not at all truculent but that at times seemed so. He was far from being an ill-natured old man, but his humor concealed itself dryly behind a mask of almost truculent denial.

This was apparent now as Herbert Anderson came in. Herbert was the night elevator man for the south entrance. He was a young, chunky, good-natured fellow with two pink spots in his plump cheeks, and lively and good-humored eyes. He was really John's especial favorite in the whole building, although one might not have instantly gathered this from the exchange that now took place between them.

"Well, what do you say, Pop?" cried Herbert as he entered the service elevator. "You haven't seen anything of two blondes yet, have you?"

The faint, dry grin about John Enborg's mouth deepened a little as he swung the door to and pulled the lever.

"Ah-h," he said sourly. "I don't know what you're talking about!"

He said nothing more, but stopped the machine and pulled the door open at the basement floor.

"Sure you do!" Herbert said vigorously as he walked over to the line of lockers, and peeled off his coat. "You know those two blondes I been tellin' you about, doncha, Pop?"

By this time he had peeled his shirt off his shoulders, and had stooped to take off his shoe.

"Ah-h," said the old man, sour as before, "you're always tellin' me about something. It goes in one ear and comes out the other."

"Oh yeah?" said Herbert. He bent to unlace his other shoe.

"Yeah," said John in the same tone.

The old man's tone had from the beginning been touched with this dry note of disgusted unbelief. And yet, somehow indefinably, there was the unmistakable suggestion that he was enjoying himself. For one thing, he had made no move to depart. Instead he had propped himself against the side of the open elevator door, and waited there as if against his own admission he was enjoying the debate.

"Where's old Organizin' Pete?" Herbert said presently. "Seen him tonight?"

"Who?" said John, looking at him with a somewhat bewildered expression.

"Henry."

"Oh!" The word was small but the accent of disgust was sufficient. "Say,"—the old man waved a gnarled hand stiffly in a downward gesture of dismissal—"that guy's a pain in the neck! No, I ain't seen him tonight."

"Oh, Hank's all right," said Herbert cheerfully. "You know how a guy gets when he gets all burned up about somethin'. But he's not a bad guy when you get him to talkin' about somethin' else."

"Yeah!" cried John excitedly, as if he was suddenly remembering something. "And you know what he says to me the other day: 'I wonder what all the rich mugs in this house would do if they had to do a hard day's work for a livin' once in a while!' Yeah," cried John indignantly, "and him a-gettin' his livin' from the people in this house! Nah-h!" John muttered to himself. "I don't like that fellow."

"Oh," said Herbert easily, "Hank don't mean half of it—he's just a grouch."

By this time he was putting on the stiff, starched shirt front which was a part of his uniform. A moment later, squinting in the mirror, he said half-absently, "So you're goin' to run out on me and the two blondes? You can't take it, huh?"

"Ah-h," said old John surlily. "I had more girls in my day than you ever thought about."

"Yeah," said Herbert.

"Yeah," said John, "I had blondes and brunettes and every other kind."

"Just a rounder, hunh?" said Herbert. "Just an old petticoat chaser."

"Nah-h," said John, contemptuously. "I've been a married man for forty years. I got grown-up children older'n you are!"

"Why, you old—!" Herbert turned on him indignantly. "Braggin' to me about blondes and brunettes, and then boastin' that you're a family man! Why, you—"

"Ah-h," said John disgustedly, "get along with you. I've forgotten more about life than you ever heard about, so don't think you're goin' to make a monkey out of me with your cute talk."

"Well, you're makin' a big mistake this time, Pop," said Herbert. "Wait till you see 'em—these two blondes. I picked one of 'em out just for you. What do you say, pal?" he cried boisterously to Henry, the night doorman, who had just come in. "Here I get Pop all dated up with a couple of blondes and he runs out on me. Is that treatin' a guy right or not?"

Henry did not answer. His face was hard and white and narrow, and he never smiled. He took off his coat and hung it in the locker.

[286]

"Where were you?" he said.

Herbert looked at him startled.

"Where was I when?" he said.

"Last night."

"That was my night off," said Herbert.

"It wasn't *our* night off," said Henry. "We had a meetin'. They was askin' about you." He turned and directed his hard look toward the old man. "And you too," he said in a hard tone. "You didn't show up either."

Old John's face had hardened too. He had shifted his position, and begun to drum impatiently with his old fingers upon the side of the elevator. Now his own eyes were hard and flinty as he returned the other's look, and there was no mistaking the hostility instinctive to two types of personality that must always clash.

"Oh yeah?" he said again in a hard voice.

And Henry answered briefly: "Yeah. Where the hell do you suppose we'd be if everyone ran out on us every time we held a meetin'? What's the use of anything if we ain't goin' to stick together?"

He was silent for a moment, looking almost sullenly at Herbert. But when he spoke again, his tone was gentler and somehow suggestive that there was buried underneath his hard exterior a genuine affection for his errant comrade. "I guess it's O.K. this time," he said quietly.

He said nothing more and began swiftly to take off his clothes.

Herbert looked flustered but relieved. For a moment he seemed about to speak, but changed his mind: he took a final appraising look at his appearance in the small mirror, and then, taking his place upon the elevator with a simulation of fine regret, he said, "Well, O.K., O.K. If that's the way you feel, Pop, about the blondes—only, you may change your mind when you get a look at them."

"No, I won't change my mind, neither," said John with sour implacability. "About them, or about you." He pulled the lever and the elevator started up. "You're a lot of talk—that's what you are. I don't listen to anything you say." He stopped the elevator and opened the heavy green-sheet door of the service car.

"So that's the kind of a friend you are?" said Herbert, stepping out into the corridor. He winked swiftly at two pretty, rosy Irish maids who were waiting to go up, and jerking his thumb toward the old man, he said, "What are you goin' to do with a guy like this anyway? I go and get him all dated up with a blonde and he won't believe me when I tell him so. He calls me a big wind."

"Yeah, that's what he is," said the old man grimly to the smiling girls. "If he saw a blonde he'd run like a rabbit."

Herbert paused at the door and looked back menacingly at the old man, a look that was belied by the exuberant sparkle of his eyes. "Oh yeah?" he said dangerously.

"Yeah!" said John implacably.

Herbert stared fiercely at him a moment, then winked swiftly at the two girls and departed.

"That fellow's just a lot of talk," said John sourly as the two girls stepped into the car. "He lives with his mother up in the Bronx, and he'd be scared stiff if a girl ever looked at him."

"Still, Herbert ought to have a girl," one of the girls said practically. "Herbert's a nice boy, John."

"Oh, he's all right, I guess," the old man muttered. Then abruptly, "What are you folks doin' tonight anyway? There are a whole lot of packages waitin' to come up."

"Mrs. Jack is having a big party," one of the girls said. "And John, will you bring everything up as soon as you can? There may be something we need right away."

"Well," he said in that half-belligerent tone that seemed to be a kind of inverted attribute to his real good nature, "I'll do the best I can. You'd think all some people had to do was give parties all the time. It would take a whole regiment of men just to carry up packages to them. Yeah!" he muttered angrily to himself. "If you ever got so much as a word of thanks—"

"Oh, John," one of the girls now said reproachfully, "you know that Mrs. Jack isn't like that—"

"Oh, she's all right, I guess," said John unwillingly as before, and yet his tone had softened imperceptibly. "If all of them were like her," he began—and then, as the memory of that night's experience with the panhandler came back to him, he muttered angrily, "she's too good-natured for her own good. Them panhandling bums—they swarm around her like flies every time she leaves the building."

The old man's face had flushed with anger at the memory. He had opened the door on the service landing, and now as the girls stepped out, he muttered to himself again: "The kind of people we got in this building oughtn't to have to put up with it . . . Well then, I'll see—" he said concedingly as one of the maids unlocked the service door and went in. "I'll get it up to you."

Henry the doorman was just coming up from the basement as the old man reached the ground floor. John called to him. "If they try to deliver any packages out front," he said, "you send 'em around here."

Henry turned and looked at the old man unsmilingly a moment, and then said curtly, "Why?"

The question, with its insolent suggestion of defied authority, infuriated the old man. "Because that's where they ought to come," he rasped out harshly. "That's why. Don't you know the kind of people we got here don't want every Tom, Dick, and Harry with a package to deliver running up in the front elevator all the time mixin' in with all the people in the house!"

Henry looked at him with eyes as hard and emotionless as two chunks of agate. "Listen," he said in a moment in a toneless voice. "You know what's going to happen to you if you don't watch out? You're gettin' old, Pop, and you'd better watch your step. You're goin' to be caught in the street some day worryin' about what's goin' to happen to people in this place if they have to ride up in the same elevator with a delivery boy. You're goin' to worry about it so much that you ain't goin' to notice where you're goin'. And you're goin' to get hit. See?"

For a moment the old man felt something in him tremble at the unutterable passion of that flinty monotone.

"You're goin' to get hit, Pop. And you're goin' to get hit by at least a Rolls Royce. And I hope it belongs to one of the people in this house. Because I want you to push off knowin' that it was done expensive—by a big Rolls Royce—by one of the people in this house. I want you to be happy, Pop."

Old John's face was purple. He tried to speak, but no words came, and at length, all else having failed him, he managed to choke out the familiar phrase: "Oh yeah?"

Just for a moment more the eyes surveyed him with their granite hostility.

"Yeah!" said Henry tonelessly, and departed.

III.

Mrs. Jack came from her room a little after eight o'clock and walked along the broad hallway that traversed her big apartment from front to rear. Her party would begin at half past eight, but long experience told her that the affair would not be going at full swing until after nine. Nevertheless she felt a tension of excitement, not unpleasurable, even though it was now sharpened by the tincture of an apprehensive doubt. Would all be ready? Had she forgotten anything? Had the girls blundered in some way—would something now be lacking?

The wrinkled line between her eyes grew deeper as she thought about these things, and unconsciously she began to slip the old jade ring on and off her finger with a quick movement of her small, strong hand. It was the gesture of a highly able person who had come to have a certain instinctive mistrust in the abilities of other people less gifted than herself. So understood it was a gesture of impatience and some scorn, a scorn not born of arrogance, or any lack of warm humanity, but one that was inclined to say a trifle sharply: "Yes, yes, I know! Can I depend on you to do what must be done?"

By this time she had reached the entrance to the living room and was looking quickly about, assuring herself that everything was in its proper place. Her examination pleased her. Her earnest little face began to undergo a subtle transformation: in fact, it actually began to bloom, to take on somehow the look of satisfaction of a child when it regards some object of its love and self-creation and finds it good.

The big room was ready for the party: it was just quietly the way that she would have it always, perfectly itself. It was a room so nobly proportioned as hardly to escape a regal massiveness, and yet so subtly toned by the labor of her faultless taste that whatever coldness its essential grandeur may have had was utterly subdued. To a stranger the room would have seemed not only homelike in its comfortable simplicity, but even on a closer inspection, a trifle shabby. The coverings of some of the chairs and couches had become in places threadbare. On three sides of the room were bookshelves crowded with a friendly and somewhat dog-eared company of books. The warm light of the room, the crackling dance of the pine logs in the great marble hearth, all cast their radiance warmly on these worn books. And the good books glowed there as if the knowledge of their use and comfort was written in their very hue.

Everything else in the great room had this same air of homeliness and use. The gate-legged table with its pleasant shaded lamp had the air of waiting to be used. Upon the creamy slab of marble mantel there was spread out a green, old, faded strip of Chinese silk. And on top of it there was a little figure of green jade: one of those lovely figures of compassionating mercy that the Chinese made. There were a few drawings on the walls, and a portrait of herself in her young loveliness at twenty which a painter now dead and famous had made long ago.

And all these objects of a thousand different kinds were brought together in this room, into its magic and its harmony from the instinctive sources of the woman's life. It is no wonder, therefore, that the flower face of Mrs. Jack took on an added glow of loveliness as she looked at her fine room. The like of it indeed, as she well knew, could nowhere else be found, for "Here"—she thought —"Ah, here it is, and it is living like a part of me. And God! How beautiful it is."

But now, her inspection of the big room ended, she turned quickly to investigation into other things. The living room gave on the dining room through glass doors now closed and curtained filmily. Mrs. Jack moved toward them at her quick and certain little step and threw them open. Then she gasped out an involuntary little "Oh!" of wonder and delight. It was too beautiful! It was quite too beautiful! But really it was just the way she expected it to look—the *way* that made her parties memorable. Nonetheless, every time she saw it, it filled her with a wonder of new joy.

Before her the great slab of the dining table glowed faultlessly, a single sheet of walnut light. The old Italian chairs had been drawn back against the walls. This was to be a buffet supper— the guests could come and help themselves according to their taste and—well, the materials of the banquet were there. That mighty table simply groaned with food. Upon a silver trencher at one end there was a mighty roast of beef crisply browned all over. At the opposite end, upon another trencher, was a whole Virginia ham, stuck with a pungent myriad of cloves. And in between and all around that massive board was a staggering variety of relishes—almost everything that could tempt the tongue of jaded man. It was like some great vision of a feast that has been made immortal on the page of history. In these thin modern times where there is so curiously, in the houses of the great, a blight of not-enoughness, there was here an overwhelming too-muchness of everything. And yet, the whole thing was miraculously right.

After a moment's long inspection, Mrs. Jack walked rapidly across the room and through the swinging door that separated it from the kitchen. Here, too, she found a scene of busy order and of readiness. The big kitchen seemed to have been freshly scrubbed and polished till it glittered like a jewel. The big kitchen table was so startlingly white that for a moment one had a shocked illusion that it really belonged in a surgeon's office. Even the pantry shelves, the drawers and cupboards looked as if they had just been freshly scrubbed, and above the voices of the girls there brooded the dynamic hum of the great electric ice box which was itself, in its white splendor, like another perfect jewel.

"Oh this!" thought Mrs. Jack. "Oh this!—" Her small clenched hand flew up against her breast, her eyes grew bright as stars. "This is quite the most perfect, lovely thing of all! If I could only paint it! But no! It would take a Brueghel to do it! There's no one nowadays to do it justice."

And now, at last, she spoke these words aloud: "What a lovely cake!"

Cook looked up from the great layer cake to which she had been adding the last prayerful tracery of icing, and for a moment a faint smile illuminated her gaunt Germanic face. "You like him, yes?" said Cook. "You think he is nice?"

"Oh, Cook!" cried Mrs. Jack. "It is the most *beautiful*—the most wonderful—" She shrugged as if words failed her and then said humorously: "Well, all I can say is, you can't beat Gilbert and Sullivan, can you?"

The literary significance of this remark was probably lost on Cook and the smiling maids, but no one could have missed the emotion it conveyed. Cook laughed gutturally with satisfaction, and Molly, smiling, and in a brogue that could have been cut with a knife, said: "No'm, Mrs. Jack, that you can't!"

Mrs. Jack looked happily about her. Everything had turned out perfectly: it ought to be a glorious party.

IV.

At this moment the buzzer of the bell rang sharply. Mrs. Jack looked rosily, inquiringly around her and said quickly: "I wonder who—" She cast a puzzled look up at the clock up on the wall. "I think, perhaps, it's Mr. Hartwell. I'll be right out."

It was Mr. Hartwell. Mrs. Jack encountered him in the hall where he had just set down two enormous suitcases, and had seized the biceps of one arm with the fingers of the other. "Gosh!"

said Mr. Piggy Hartwell—for by such affectionate title was he known to his more intimate acquaintance—"Gosh!"—the expletive came out somewhat windily, a steamy expiration of relief.

"Why didn't you let me know you had so much to carry?" cried Mrs. Jack. "I'd have sent our driver."

"Oh, it's quite all right," said Piggy Hartwell. "I always handle everything myself." He smiled at her quite boyishly.

"I know!" said Mrs. Jack, nodding her head with quick understanding. "You simply can't depend on people. If anything went wrong—and after all the years you must have put in making them! People who've seen it say it's simply marvelous," she went on. "Everyone is so thrilled."

"Now—," said Mr. Hartwell abruptly, and walked over to the entrance of the living room, "I suppose it's going to be in here, isn't it?"

"Yes—that is, if you prefer, we'll use another room—but this is the largest one we have—"

"No, thank you," crisply, absently. "This is quite all right. Best place, I think, would be over there"—briefly he indicated the opposite wall—"facing the door here, the people all around on the other three sides . . . we can clear all this stuff away, of course" —he made a quick gesture which seemed to dispose of a large part of the furnishings. "Now, if you don't mind, I'll have to change to costume—if you have a room—"

"Oh, yes," she answered quickly, "here, just down the hall. But won't you have a drink and something to eat before you start—"

"No, thank you—nothing," Mr. Hartwell somewhat gruntingly replied, and staggered down the hall with his tremendous freight. She heard the two ponderous baggages hit the floor with a leaden thump and then Mr. Hartwell's long expiring "whush" of exhausted relief.

Mr. Piggy Hartwell was the rage that year. He was the creator of a kind of puppet circus of wire dolls, and the applause with which this entertainment had been greeted was astonishing. The last criteria of fashionable knowingness was an expert knowledge of Mr. Hartwell and his dolls. If one lacked this knowledge

he was lower than the dust, and if one had it, his eligibility for
any society of the higher sensibilities was instantly confirmed.
One could, in fact, in that sweet year of grace, admit with utter
nonchalance that the late John Milton bored him and was in fact
a large "stuffed shirt." "Stuffed shirts" indeed were numerous in
the findings of the critical gentry of the time. The chemises of
such personalities as Goethe, Tolstoy, and Balzac had been ruthlessly investigated by some of the most fearless intellects of the
time and found to be largely composed of straw wadding. Almost
everyone was being fearlessly debunked except debunkers and
Mr. Piggy Hartwell and his dolls.

To a future world, no doubt, this may seem to be a trifle strange.
And yet it was indubitably a fact: the highest intellects of the
time were bored by many things. They were bored with love and
they were bored with hate. They were bored with men who
worked, and with men who loafed. They were bored with going
abroad and they were bored with staying at home. They were
bored with the injustice all around them, with the men who were
killed, with the children who starved, with justice, freedom, and
man's right to live. Finally, they were bored with living, they
were bored with dying but!—they were *not* bored that year with
Mr. Piggy Hartwell and his circus of wire dolls.

—And the Center of the storm? The Cause of all this tumult
—what was It doing now? It was enjoying the privacy of one of
Mrs. Jack's lovely rooms—and, as if utterly unaware of the
towering position It now enjoyed in the great world, It was
modestly and matter-of-factly pulling on a pair of canvas pants!

V.

Mrs. Jack, after arranging anew a vase of roses on a
table in the hall, walked briskly toward her room. Her husband
was just coming from his room as she passed his door. He was a
well-kept man of fifty years or more. But, compared to his wife's

expression of childlike innocence, his own manner was curiously sophisticated.

He bent smoothly over her small figure and kissed her perfunctorily on one rosy cheek. It was the kiss of an ambassador; his manner and his tone, the perfect bland assurance of everything he did, were like the gestures of an old and jaded diplomat.

She was conscious of a moment's repugnance as she looked at him, but then she remembered what a perfect husband he had been, how thoughtful and how good and how devoted. "He's a sweet person," she was thinking as she responded brightly to his greeting: "Oh, hello, darling. You're all ready, aren't you? . . . Listen,"—she spoke rapidly—"will you take care of anyone who comes? Mr. Hartwell is changing his costume in the guest room —won't you look out for him if he needs anything?" She slipped the jade ring quickly from her finger and slipped it back again. "I do hope that everything's all right! I do hope—" She paused again, with a look of worried abstraction in her eyes.

"You do hope what?" he said with just the suggestion of an ironic grin around the corners of his mouth.

"I do hope he won't—" she began in a troubled tone, then went on rapidly—"He said something about—about clearing away some of the things in the living room for his show—"

Then, catching the irony of his faint grin, she laughed, shortly, richly. "I don't know what he's going to do. Still, everyone's been after him, you know—everyone's thrilled at the chance of seeing him—Oh, I'm sure it'll be all right. Don't you think so?" She looked eagerly at him with such droll, beseeching inquiry that he laughed abruptly, as he turned away, saying, "Oh, I suppose so, Alice. I'll look after it."

Mrs. Jack went on down the hall and entered her room, leaving her door slightly ajar behind her.

She regarded herself for a moment in the mirror, and her face betrayed a childlike vanity that would have been ludicrously comical if anyone had seen her. First she bent forward a little and looked at herself with a childlike innocence which was one of her characteristic expressions when she faced the world. Then she surveyed the outlines of her small and lovely figure, and arranged half-consciously the folds of her simple, splendid gown. Then she lifted her arm and hand and half-turning with the other hand upon her hip, she ogled herself absurdly in the friendly mirror.

A tremor, faint and distant, shook her feet. She paused, startled; waited; listened. A slight frown appeared between her eyes, and an old unquiet feeling stirred faintly in her heart. At times she thought she felt this faint vibration in the massive walls around her. Once she had asked the doorman a few questions. The man told her that the building had been built across two depths of railway tunnels, and that all Mrs. Jack had heard was the faint vibration from the passing of a train below her. The man assured her it was all quite safe; still, the news disturbed her vaguely. She would have liked it better if the building had been built upon the solid rock.

VI.

But now the guests were beginning to arrive. The electric *thring* of the doorbell broke persistently on the accustomed quietness. In the hallway there arose now the confused but crescent medley of a dozen voices—the rippling laughter and quick, excited voices of the women with the deeper and more vibrant sonorities of the men. One could sense and feel the growing momentum of the party. It was a mixture, smooth as oil, which grew and mounted headily with each arrival.

Mrs. Jack, her eyes sparkling with the joy that giving parties, meeting people, the whole warm and brilliant flux and interplay of life always gave to her, now left her room and moved up the hall, greeting people everywhere with a rosy, beaming face.

The whole party was in full blast now. Everywhere people were talking, laughing, bending to fill glasses with long frosty drinks, moving around the loaded temptations of the dining table

[297]

with that somewhat doubtful look of people who would like to taste it all but know they can't. It was wonderful, weaving back and forth in a celebrated pattern of white and black and gold and power and wealth and loveliness and food and drink. And through it all, like some strange and lovely flower, bending and welcoming on its gracious stem, moved the flushed and rosy face, the warm heart and the wise, the subtle, childlike, magic spirit that was Mrs. Jack.

She glanced happily through the crowded rooms. It was, she well knew, a notable assemblage: a distinguished excerpt of the best, the highest, and the fairest the city had to offer. And yet, someone was still lacking.

"Long, long into the night I lay"—thought Mrs. Jack—"thinking about you all the time."

For someone was still absent and she kept thinking of him—well, *almost* all the time. At least, so she would phrase it with that infatuation which a woman feels when she is thinking of her lover: "I keep thinking of you all the time. When I wake up in the morning the first thing I think about is you. Did you ever try to tell a story? Once when I was a child I felt sure I had to tell a story. And yet, when I began it, all that I could think of was 'Long, long into the night I lay thinking of how to tell my story.' It seemed to me to be the most beautiful and perfect way to begin a story—but I could go no further. And now I know the end. 'Long, long into the night I lay—thinking of you. I think about you all the time. You fill my life, my heart, my spirit and my being.' And that's the story. Ah, dearest, that's the story."

And so this lovely woman really felt—or thought she felt. Really, when she thought of him, she kept *thinking* she was "thinking of him all the time." And on this crowded and this brilliant evening, he kept flashing through her mind.

"I wonder where he is," she thought. "Why doesn't he come? If only he hasn't been—" She looked quickly over the brilliant gathering with a troubled eye and thought impatiently, "If only he liked parties more! Oh well! He's the way he is. I wouldn't have him any different. I think about him all the time!"

And then he arrived, a hurried but relieved survey told her that he was "all right."

Webber had been drinking just a little, the eyes were injected just a little, the speech and manner a trifle more excited than is wont, but, she saw, he was "all right."

"If only people—the people who know me—didn't affect him so," she thought. "What does he want? He is like a crazy man with doubt: he hates everyone I know, he has every kind of insane, impossible delusion—oh, he is so strange and wild and mad—and young. And he is the best! the best! At bottom he is the grandest and the best. I love him!"

As Webber entered the crowded room, Sidney Page, the novelist, who had been leaning upon the mantel talking with a handsome woman, turned, glanced at him, and then, extending his soft, plump hand sideways, said casually, "Oh. How are you? . . . Look," his tone, as always when he did something that came from the generous and sensitive warmth of his spirit, was deliberately casual. "Have you a telephone? I was trying to get you the other day. Can't you come and have lunch with me some time?"

As a matter of fact, he had not thought of it until that moment. And Webber knew that he had thought of it to put him at his ease, to make him feel less desperately shipwrecked in these glittering, sophisticated tides. He seized it desperately, with a feeling of overwhelming gratefulness and affection. He had understood the kind of man Page was from the first moment he met him, and had seen the desperate shyness, the naked terror in his eyes. He had never for a moment been deceived by the man's air of sophisticated weariness, the elaborately mannered speech. Below all the concealments of that elaborate disguise, he had felt the quality of generosity, of nobility, in the tormented spirit of the man. And now, like a bewildered swimmer in strong tides, he reached out and caught hold of it with enormous relief, as being the one thing before him in the disturbing and unfathomed currents of these brilliant lives that he could understand—he stayed there now, hung on as to a rock among the flood. He stammered

[299]

out a hasty acceptance, and Page said quickly, casually, to put an end to more embarrassment: "Good. Suppose we meet for lunch on Tuesday, then, at one o'clock, at the Meadowbrook. Do you know where it is?" He gave the address, passed quickly on to other things, introduced the young man to the woman. They made speech, the young man looked around as if searching for someone, and really to give some show of ease and purpose which he did not feel, he blurted out: "Have—have you seen Alice anywhere about?" knowing as he said the words how stiff and clumsy they must seem to be, and how absurd also, for Mrs. Jack, as anyone could see, surrounded by a group of chattering guests, was standing in the center of the room.

Almost before the words were out of his mouth, the sophisticated-looking woman had "taken him up on it." "About?" she said. "Yes, I think you'll find her about—just about there," with her cold, bright smile, she nodded in the direction of Mrs. Jack, not ten feet away.

He knew that what unfriendliness the words may have had was just the concomitant of fashion, willing to sacrifice manners to the opportunity of exhibiting one's wit, however feeble the attempt might be. So understood, so accurately appraised, why did the young man's face now flush with anger? It was absurd to feel so, and yet, as is usually the case with youth, his sense proved unequal to the welling upsurge of his feeling. For a moment, he tried to find a telling and bitter retort, but he was not apt with matters such as these, and he just stood there, looking like some baffled clodhopper and feeling ten times the clodhopper that he looked. And then, defeated utterly, he turned and stalked away.

In just a minute's time, the chip upon his shoulder, with which he had entered that great room, had grown ten times as big, and now he was not only daring someone to knock it off, he was hoping someone would. Why?

Well, of such is youth. And he was young.

At this moment Mrs. Jack saw him, and came toward him.

"Oh, hello, darling," she said, taking his hand and looking up at him with an earnest, tender glance. "How are you? Are you all right?"

Even that simple question touched some raw spot of lacerated sensitivity.

"Who said I wasn't all right? Why shouldn't I be all right?" he demanded harshly, and then, seeing her tender face, was filled with a miserable feeling that again he'd failed.

"Oh all right, all right," she said placatingly. "I just wanted to know if—are you having a good time?" she said eagerly, smiling. "Don't you think it's a nice party? You want to meet anyone?" she said, before he had a chance to answer. "You must know some of the people here."

Lily Mandell, whose sensational figure and smoldering, Slavic face had been conspicuous all the evening, now came weaving through the crowded room toward Mrs. Jack.

"Oh Alice darling," she said in a drowsy tone that also had in it a quality of yolky arrogance, "I wonder if you've heard—" Seeing the young man, she paused and greeted him: "Oh hello— I didn't know that you were here." They shook hands. Mrs. Jack's face was glowing with a rapt and tranquil joy that was almost like religious ecstasy. She put her own hands in a firm clasp upon those of the woman and the man and whispered: "My two. Two of the people that I love best in the whole world. And you must know and love each other as I do you." Her eyes misted suddenly with tears, the clasp of one hand tightened upon the closed hands of the other two, but her other hand went quickly to her breast. She turned to Lily and whispered: "If I could only tell you—" She shook her head, and whispered huskily: "The greatest—the best—" without saying what the greatest and the best might be.

VII.

"I mean!—You know!—" At the words, eager, rapid, uttered in a rather hoarse, yet strangely seductive tone of voice,

Mrs. Jack smiled and turned: "There's Amy!" Then, as she saw the angelic head with its unbelievable harvest of auburn curls, the lovely face so radiant with an almost boyish quality of eagerness, she thought: "Isn't she beautiful! And—and—there is something so sweet, so lovely, so—so good about her!"

She did not know why this was true. Indeed, from any wordly point of view it would have been hard to prove. If Amy Van Leer was not "a notorious woman" the reason was that she had surpassed the ultimate limit of notoriety years before. By the time she was nineteen years old she had been married and divorced and had a child. And even at that time her conduct had been so scandalous that her husband had had no difficulty in demonstrating her unfitness for the custody of her own child. From that moment on, she took to drink, from drink to lovers, from lovers to opium, from opium to—everything.

People had once said: "What on earth is Amy going to do next?" And really if life is to be expressed solely in terms of velocity and sensation, it seemed that there was very little left for her to do. She had been everywhere, she had "seen everything" as one might see things from the windows of an express train traveling at eighty miles an hour. People now said: "What on earth is there left for her to do?" Nothing. There was nothing. Having tried everything in life save living, and having lost the way to live, there was nothing left for her to do except to die.

And yet that auburn, that angelic head: the quick excited laugh, the hoarse and thrilling tones, the eager animation of a boy—were all so beautiful, and somehow, one felt, so good! "If only"—people would think regretfully as Mrs. Jack now thought —"Oh, if only things had turned out differently for her"—and they would seek back desperately to find the clue to her disorder —saying, "Here—or here—it happened here, you see—if only!"— If only men were so much clay, as they are blood, bone, marrow, passion, feeling!

"I *mean!* . . . You *know!* . . ." at these familiar words, Amy turned to her companions as if fairly burning with desire to communicate something to them that filled her with exuberant elation—"I *mean!*" she cried—"When you compare it with the stuff they're doing nowadays!—I *mean!* There's simply no comparison!"

During the course of this feverish monologue, the group of young people, of which Amy was the center, had moved over toward the portrait of Mrs. Jack above the mantel, and were looking up at it. The famous portrait was deserving of the enthusiastic praise that was now being heaped upon it. It was one of the best examples of Henry Mallows' early work and it had also been created with the passion, the tenderness, the simplicity of a man in love.

"I *mean!*" cried Amy jubilantly again. "When you *think* how long ago that was! . . . and how beautiful she was then! . . . and how beautiful she is now!" cried Amy exultantly, then cast her lovely gray-green eyes so full of splintered torment around her in a glance of almost feverish exasperation—"I *mean!*" she cried again—"The whole thing's obvious," she muttered. Then, turning toward Page with an impulsive movement, she demanded: "How long has it been, Steve? It's been twenty years ago, hasn't it?"

"Oh, quite all of that," Page answered in a cold, bored tone. In his agitation and embarrassment he turned away from her with an air of fatigued indifference. "I should think it was done in nineteen one or two—wasn't it, Alice?" he drawled, turning to Mrs. Jack, who had now approached the group.

"What?" cried Mrs. Jack and then went on immediately, "Oh, the picture! No, Steve—it was done in nineteen—"—she checked herself so swiftly that it was not apparent to anyone but Page that she was not telling the truth—"in nineteen four."

As a matter of fact, he knew the exact date—which had been October, 1902. And musing on the vagaries of the sex, he thought: "Why will they be so stupid! She must know that to anyone who knows the least thing about Mallows' life, the date is as familiar as the Fourth of July—"

"Of course," Mrs. Jack was saying rapidly, "I couldn't have been more than eighteen at the time—if I was that—"

"Which would make you not more than forty-three at the

present time," thought Page cynically—"Well, my dear, you were twenty when he painted you—and you had been married for two years and had a child. Why do they do it!"—he thought impatiently, "Does she take me for a fool?"

He turned toward her almost impatiently and saw an expression, startled, almost pleading in her eye. He followed it, and saw the hot eye, the fierce packed features of her youthful lover: he caught it in a flash: "Ah! It's this boy! She's told him then that—" and suddenly remembering the startled pleading of that look— so much of child, of folly, even in its guile—he was touched with pity.

"My God, here she is!" he thought. "Still featured like a child, still beautiful, still loving someone—another boy!—Almost as lovely now as she was then when Mallows was a boy."

Poor child! Poor child!—Page turned pompously away to hide the naked anguish in his eyes— So soon to be consumed and die like all of us— She was too prone to die the death upon a single death; to live the life upon the single life; to love the love upon the single love—never to save out of anything a prudent remnant for the day of ruin; but to use it all, to give it all, to be consumed, burnt out like last night's moths upon a cluster of hard light!

Poor child.

VIII.

The hour had now arrived for Mr. Piggy Hartwell and his celebrated circus of wire dolls. Mr. Piggy Hartwell wore a thick blue sweater with a turtle neck, an old pair of canvas trousers, and a pair of battered kneepads which were formerly in favor with professional wrestlers. And thus arrayed, he now made his appearance, staggering between his two enormous cases, which at length he dropped with a floor-shaking thump.

He immediately pushed back the big sofa and all other objects of furniture; pushed back the carpet and then ruthlessly began to take books from the shelves and dump them on the floor. He then fastened up in the vacant spaces big circus posters which, in addition to the familiar paraphernalia of lions, elephants, and clowns, bore such descriptive legends as "Barnum & Bailey—May 7th and 8th," or "Ringling Brothers—July 31st."

When he had finished he came back to his valises, and began to take out a great variety of objects. There were miniature circus rings made of rounded strips of tin. There were trapezes made of wire. And in addition there was a great variety of wire figures: clowns and trapeze performers, acrobats and tumblers, bareback lady riders and wire horses. There was almost everything, in fact, that a circus would need.

He got down upon his kneepads and for some time he was extremely busy with his work. At length he signified his willingness to begin by a gesture to his hostess. At the same moment, the doorbell rang and a host of new and uninvited guests were ushered in by Molly. The new arrivals were, for the most part, young people and obviously they belonged to Mr. Piggy Hartwell's "social set." The young women had that unmistakable appearance of having gone to Miss Spence's School for Girls and the young men, by the same token, seemed to have gone to Yale and Harvard and one was also sure that some of them were members of the Racquet Club and were now connected with a firm of "investment brokers" in downtown New York. All these people streamed in noisily, headed by an elegant young gentleman whose name, curiously, was Hen Walters, and who was Mr. Hartwell's bosom friend.

Mrs. Jack looked rather overwhelmed at this invasion, but was dutifully murmuring greetings when all the new people swarmed right past her, ignoring her completely, and stormed into the room shouting vociferous gaieties at Mr. Hartwell. They paid absolutely no attention to any of the other invited guests, except for a greeting here and there to Amy Van Leer, who apparently they considered one of them, even though a fallen angel.

Hen Walters greeted her quite cordially, with all the gleeful elations of his burbling voice: "Oh, hello, Amy! I haven't seen you for an age. What brings *you* here?"—in a tone that somehow indicated, with all the unconscious arrogance of his kind, that the company was beyond the pale of things accepted.

The tone and implication stung her sharply. As for herself, she had received the slander of her name with beautiful good nature. But an affront to someone that she loved was more than she could endure. And she loved Mrs. Jack.

Almost before she was aware of what she was saying, she was repeating quickly: "What brings *me* here—of *all* places! Well, first of all it's a very good place to be—the best I know . . . And I *mean!* You *know!* . . ." she tossed her head with furious impatience. "I *mean!* After *all*, I *was* invited, you know—which is more than you can say—" Unconsciously, with a gesture of protective warmth, she slipped her arm around Mrs. Jack.

"Alice, darling," Amy said, "this is Mr. Walters—and some of his friends"—but for a moment she looked at the cluster of debutantes and their escorts, and then turned away, saying with no effort to subdue her tone: "God, aren't they simply dreadful! . . . I *mean!* . . . You know!"

Meanwhile, Hen Walters was burbling to Mrs. Jack: ". . . So nice of you to let us all come in . . . Piggy told us it would be all right . . . I hope you don't mind . . ."

"But no-o—not at all!" she protested earnestly, ". . . Any friends of Mr. Hartwell's . . . but won't you all have a drink or something to eat? . . ."

"Oh, *heavens, no!*" cried Mr. Walters, in a tone of burblesome glee: "We've all been to Tony's and we simply *gorged* ourselves!"

"—Well, then, if you're sure—" she began.

"Oh, *absolutely!*" cried Mr. Walters rapturously. "But we're holding up the show!"

"Oh, Piggy," he cried to his friend, who now, cheerfully grinning, was crawling on his kneepads on the floor—"Do begin! Everyone's simply dying to see it! . . . I've seen it a dozen times myself," he announced gleefully to the general public, "and it becomes more fascinating every time . . . So if you're ready, please begin!"

Mr. Hartwell was ready and began.

IX.

The performance began, as all good circuses should, with a grand procession of the performers and the animals in the menagerie. Mr. Hartwell accomplished this by taking the wire figures in his hands and walking them around the circus ring. This took some time, but was greeted at its conclusion with vociferous applause. Then Mr. Hartwell galloped his wire horses into the ring and round and around with movements of his hands. Then he put his bareback riders on top of the wire horses, and galloped these around too. After this there was a procession of the wire elephants, etc. This performance gained particular applause because of the clever way in which Mr. Hartwell made the figures imitate the swaying, ponderous lurch of the elephants.

People were not always able to identify each act, but when they were, they applauded vigorously. There was now an act by the trapeze performers. This occupied a long time, largely because Mr. Hartwell was not able to make it work. First of all the little wire figures swung and dangled from their flying trapezes. Then Mr. Hartwell tried to make one little figure swing through the air and catch the other figure by its down-swept hands. This wouldn't work. Again and again the little wire figure soared through the air, caught at the outstretched hands of the other doll—and missed ingloriously. It became painful: people craned their necks and looked embarrassed—all, indeed, except Mr. Hartwell, who giggled happily with each new failure and tried again. At length, he settled the whole matter himself by taking one of the little figures and carefully hanging it to the other's arms. When he had finished he looked up at his audience and giggled with cheerful idiocy. And the gathering, after a brief and somewhat puzzled pause, broke into applause.

Mr. Hartwell was now ready for what might be called the *pièce de résistance* of the entire occasion. This was the celebrated sword-swallowing act on which he prided himself a great deal. He picked up a small rag doll, and with the other hand he took a long hairpin and began to work it down the throat of the doll.

It was a horrible exhibition. Mr. Hartwell kept working the hairpin down with thick, probing fingers and when some impediment of wadding got in his way he looked up and giggled foolishly. Halfway down he struck an obstacle, but he persisted— persisted horribly. He kept pressing with his hairpin while people looked at one another with distressed faces, and suddenly a gap appeared in the side of the bulging doll and some of the stuffing began to ooze out shockingly. At this manifestation some people gave up utterly. Miss Lily Mandell placed one hand against her stomach in a gesture of nausea, said "Ugh!" and made a hasty exit.

The young "society people," however, applauded everything enthusiastically. In fact, as the stuffing in the doll began to ooze out, one of the young women turned to the young man who was standing beside her, and said: "I think it's *frightfully interesting* —the way he does that. Don't you?"

To which the young man said briefly, "Eh—," an ejaculation that might have been indicative of almost anything, but which was here obviously taken for assent.

People had now begun to go out into the halls, and a few of the more cynical could be heard talking to each other ironically with little laughs. Even Mrs. Jack, who had seated herself cross-legged on the floor, like a dutiful child, squarely before the maestro and his puppets, had got up and gone out into the hall, where a number of her guests were now assembled. Here she found Lily Mandell and approaching her, with a bright affectionate little smile, she queried, hopefully: "Are you enjoying it, Lily? And you, darling"—she now turned fondly to her young lover—"are you having a good time?"

Lily Mandell answered in a tone of throaty protest and disgust:

"When he started pushing that long pin into the doll, and all its insides began oozing out—ugh!" she put a hand upon her stomach—"I simply couldn't stand it any longer!"

Mrs. Jack's shoulders shook, her face reddened, and she gasped in a hysterical whisper: "I know! Wasn't it awful?"

But now there was the sound of voices in the living room. The performance had ended and there was a ripple of perfunctory applause. The fashionable young people of Mr. Hartwell's own group clustered around him, chattering congratulations, and then, without a word of thanks to their hostess, they began to leave.

X.

The happy confusion, the thronging tumult of the great party had now ended. The guests had all departed, excepting Lily Mandell and Webber. The place had grown back into its wonted quiet, and the unceasing city now closed in upon these lives again, pervaded these great walls.

Outside, there was the sound of a fire truck, the rapid clanging of a bell. It turned the corner into Madison and thundered excitingly past the big building. Mrs. Jack went to the window and looked out. Other trucks now appeared from various directions until four or five had gone by.

"I wonder where the fire can be," she remarked presently. "It must be quite a big one, too—six trucks have driven past. It must be somewhere in this neighborhood."

For a moment the location of the fire absorbed the idle speculation of the group, but presently they began to look again at Mr. Hartwell. His labors were now almost over. He began to close his big valises and adjust the straps. At this moment Lily Mandell turned her head with an air of wakened curiosity in the direction of the hall, sniffed sharply, and suddenly said: "Does anyone smell smoke?"

"What?"—said Mrs. Jack with a puzzled air. And then, she

[309]

cried excitedly: "But yes! There is quite a strong smell of smoke out there. I think it would be just as well if we got out of the building until we find out what is wrong."

Mrs. Jack's rosy face was now burning with excitement. "But isn't it queer?" she appealed to everyone—"I mean, to think that it should be in this building—I mean—" She looked around her rather helplessly. "Well, then—" she said indefinitely, "I suppose we'd better, until we find out what it is. Oh those girls!" cried Mrs. Jack suddenly, and snapping the ring on and off her finger, she walked quickly toward the dining room. "Molly!—Janie!—Lily! Girls! There's a fire somewhere in the building. You'll have to get out until we find out where it is!"

The news obviously upset the girls. They looked helplessly at one another, then they began to move aimlessly around, as if no longer certain what to do.

"Will we have time to pack, Mrs. Jack?" said Molly, looking at her stupidly. "—I mean," she gulped, "will we need anything?"

"Oh, Molly, no, in heaven's name!" cried Mrs. Jack. "Nothing except your coats. Tell all the girls and Cook to wear their coats!"

"Yes'm," said Molly, dumbly, and in a moment she went uncertainly through the dining room to the kitchen.

Mr. Jack meanwhile had gone out into the hall and was ringing the elevator bell. The others joined him there. He rang persistently and presently the voice of Herbert was heard shouting up the shaft. "All right! All right! I'll be right up, folks, as soon as I take down this load!" The sound of people's voices, excited, chattering, could be heard down the shaft, and then the elevator went away.

Presently the sound of the elevator could be heard again as it came up. It mounted and then suddenly paused a flight or two below them. Herbert could be heard working his lever and in a moment more shouted up: "Mr. Jack, will you all please use the service entrance? The elevator's out of order: I can't go any further."

At this moment all the lights went out. The place was plunged in inky blackness. There was just a brief, a rather terrifying moment, when the women caught their breaths sharply. In the darkness, the smell of the smoke was more acrid and biting than it had ever been. Molly moaned a little and the maids began to mill around like stricken cattle. But they quieted down when they heard the comforting assurance of Mr. Jack's quiet voice: "Alice, we'll have to light candles. Can you tell me where they are?"

She told him. He went back into the kitchen and reappeared with a box of tallow candles. He gave everyone a candle and lighted them. The women lifted their candles and looked at each other with an air of bewildered surmise. Mrs. Jack turned questioningly to her lover. "Isn't it strange?" she whispered—"Isn't it the strangest thing? I mean the party . . . all the people . . . and then this"—and holding up her candle she looked about her at that ghostly company. And suddenly he was filled with love for her, because he knew the woman like himself had the mystery and strangeness of all life, all love in her heart.

The others were now gathered on the service landing waiting while Mr. Hartwell tested the bell of the service elevator. There was no response to his repeated efforts and in a few moments he remarked: "Well, I suppose there's nothing for us to do now except to walk down." Mr. Jack had apparently reached this conclusion on his own account and had started down the nine flights of concrete stairs that led to the ground floor and safety. In a moment all the others followed him.

The electric lights in the service hallways were still burning dimly. But the smoke now filled the air with floating filaments and shifting plumes that made breathing acrid and uncomfortable.

And the service stairs from top to bottom were providing an astounding spectacle. Doors were opening now on every floor and other tenants of the building, and their servants and their guests, were coming out to swell the tide of refugees which now marched steadily downstairs. It was an astounding aggregation. There were people fully attired in splendid evening dress, and people in pyjamas, dressing gowns, or whatever convenient garment they could snatch up. There were young people and there were old people. There were people of every kind and quality and age and physical variation.

And in addition to these there was a babel of strange tongues, the excited jargons of a dozen races. There were German cooks and there were French maids. There were English chauffeurs and there were Irish serving girls. There were Swedes and Italians and Norwegians. There were Poles and Czechs and Austrians, and Negroes; and all of these were poured out in a noisy tide to join in with their lords and masters, their interests all united now in their common pursuit of safety.

As the refugees neared the ground floor, helmeted and coated firemen began to come up the stairs. A few policemen came up after them and these men tried in various ways to allay any panic that anyone may have felt.

"It's all right, folks! Everything's okay!" one big policeman cried cheerfully as he came up past the members of Mrs. Jack's party. "The fire's over now."

These words, spoken really for the sake of expediting the orderly progress of the tenants from the building, had an opposite effect from the one which the big policeman wanted to produce. One of the male members of Mrs. Jack's party, the young man who was bringing up the end of the procession, paused upon hearing the policeman's reassuring words, and turned, about to retrace his way upstairs again.

As he did so, he saw that the effect upon the policeman had been alarming. The man was now stationed half a flight above him on the landing, and was making frantic gestures to entreat him to leave the building as quickly as possible. So warned, the young man turned again and hastened down the stairs. As he did so, he could hear some tapping and hammering noises from the service-elevator shaft. He paused and listened for a moment: the tapping began, then stopped . . . began again . . . and stopped again.

XI.

The space outside the great apartment building, or rather *between* it—for it was constructed in the shape of a hollow square—was now a wonderful spectacle. The sides of the tremendous building the whole way around were spanned by arches which gave the whole place something of the appearance of an enormous cloister—a cloister vaster and more modern than any other one which had been seen, a cloister whose mighty walls soared twelve flights into the air. Here, around the four sides of this great cloister, a horde of people were now constantly flooding out of the huge honeycomb. Seen so, the tremendous pageantry of the scene was overwhelming. It was really like the scene of an appalling shipwreck—like a great liner, her life gored out upon an iceberg, keeling slowly with her whole great company of people—the crew, the passengers, the rich, the poor, the mighty, and the lowly—assembled now, at this last hour of peril, in a living fellowship—the whole family of earth, and all its classes, at length united on these slanting decks.

This scene here now in this great cloister was like this—except that the ship was this enfabled rock beneath their feet, the ship's company the whole company of life, and of the swarming and unceasing city.

As yet few people seemed fully to have comprehended the full significance of the event which had thus unceremoniously dumped them out of their sleek nests into the open weather. For all of them it was undoubtedly the first time that they had had the opportunity of appraising at first hand, so to speak, unprepared, the full personnel of the great building. People who would never, under any ordinary circumstances, mingle with one another were now seen laughing and talking together with the familiarity of long acquaintanceship. A famous courtesan, wearing a chinchilla coat which her fabulously wealthy lover had given her, now took off this magnificent garment and, walking over to an elderly woman with a delicate and patrician face, she threw the coat over this woman's thinly covered shoulders, at the same time saying in a tough but somehow kindly voice: "You wear this, darling. You look cold." And the woman smiled graciously and thanked her tarnished sister; then the two women stood talking together like old friends.

Elsewhere, a haughty old Bourbon of the Knickerbocker type was seen engaged in earnest conversation with a Tammany policeman, whose companionship the Bourbon would have spurned indignantly an hour before. And so it went, everywhere one looked: one saw haughty Gentiles with rich Jews; stately ladies with musical-comedy actresses; a woman famous for her charities with a celebrated whore.

Meanwhile, the firemen had dragged in across the court from all directions a network of great white hose. Squadrons of helmeted men would dash into the smoky corridors from time to time, some would go upstairs, others would emerge from the lower regions of the basements and confer intimately with their chiefs.

As for the crowd itself, it was in ignorance concerning the cause and extent of the fire. There was, indeed, at first, save for a mist of acrid smoke in the hallways, little evidence of a fire. But now the indications became much plainer. For some time upon the very top floor of the south wing, infrequent wisps of smoke had been curling through the open window of a room in which a light now somewhat somberly was burning. Now suddenly a great billowing puff of oily black smoke accompanied by a dancing fire of sparks burst through the open window. And, as it did, the whole crowd drew in its breath in a sharp intake of excitement— the strange wild joy that people feel when they see fire. Steadily the black and oily-looking smoke was now billowing out in belching folds and the smoke itself in the room within was colored luridly by the sinister and unmistakable glow of fire.

Mrs. Jack gazed upward with a rapt, a fascinated gaze. "How terrible!" she thought. "How terrible!—but God! How beautiful it is."

XII.

The police now began to move upon the crowd and good-naturedly but firmly, with outstretched arms, started to herd them from the court, and out across the street. Mrs. Jack, her servants, and her guests went into a small drugstore near at hand, and engaged in eager chatter with many other people of their acquaintance who now filled the store.

The conversation of these people was friendly, casual, and pleasant: some were even gay. But in their talk it would have been possible to detect a note of perturbation, as if something was now happening which they could no longer fathom or control. They were the lords and masters of the earth, those vested with the high authorities and accustomed to command. And now they felt curiously helpless, no longer able to command anything, no longer even able to find out what was happening. They felt somehow that they had been caught up by some mysterious and relentless force, enmeshed in the ramifications of some tremendous web, and that there was nothing for them to do except to be borne onwards, as unwitting of the power that ruled them as blind flies fastened to the revolutions of a wheel.

And in this feeling they were right.

For, in ways remote and far from the blind and troubled kennings of this helpless group, the giant web was at its mighty spinning: deep in the boweled earth, the threads were being spun.

In one of the smoking corridors of that enormous hive, two men in helmets and in boots were talking quietly together.

"Did you find it?"

"Yes. It's in the basement, Chief. It's not on the roof at all: the draft is taking it up a vent—but it's down here"—he pointed thumbwise down below.

"Well, then, go get it: you know what to do."

"It looks bad, Chief. It's going to be hard to get."

"What's the trouble?"

"If we flood the basement we will flood the tracks, too. You know what that means."

For a moment the two men's troubled glances met and held each other steadily. Then the older man spoke shortly, and started down the stairs. "Come on," he said, "we're going down."

Far from the troubled kennings of these helpless folk, deep in the tunnel's depth there in the boweled earth, there was a room where lights were burning, and where it was always night.

There, now, a phone rang, and a man with a green eyeshade seated at the desk was there to answer it: "Hello . . . oh, hello, Mike"—he listened carefully for a moment, suddenly jerked forward, taut with interest, and pulled the cigarette out of his mouth: "The hell you say! . . . Where? On number thirty-two! . . . They're going to flood it! . . . Oh, the hell! . . ."

Far from the kennings of these helpless folk, deep in the marvelous honeycombs of that boweled rock, things began to happen with the speed of light. Six blocks away, just where the mighty network of that amazing underworld begins its mighty flare of rails, lights shifted, changed, and flared immortally: the Overland halted swiftly, but so smoothly that the passengers, already standing to debark, were unaware that anything had happened. Ahead, however, in the cab of the powerful electric locomotive, the engineer peered out and read the signs. He saw these shifting patterns of hard light against the dark, and swore: ". . . Now what the hell." Turning, he spoke quietly across the darkness to another man: "We're going in on Twenty-one . . . I wonder what the hell has happened."

On the seventh landing of the service stairs, the firemen were working ruthlessly with axes. The place was dense with smoke: the sweating men were wearing masks, and the only light they had to work by was that provided by a torchlight and a flare. They had battered open the doorway of the elevator shaft, and one of them had lowered himself down onto the roof of the imprisoned elevator half a floor below, and was cutting in the roof with his sharp ax.

"Have you got it, Ed?"

". . . O.K. . . . Yeah . . . I'm almost through . . Here it is."

The ax smashed through; there was a splintering crash, and then: "O.K. . . . Wait a minute . . . Hand me down that flashlight, Tom . . ."

"See anything?"

And in a moment, quietly: "Yeah . . . I'm going in . . . Jim, you better come down too; I'll need you . . ."

There was a silence for a moment, then the man's quiet voice again: "O.K. . . . I've got it . . . Here, Jim, reach down and get it underneath the arms . . ."

In such a way they lifted it from its imprisoned trap, looked at it for a moment, and laid it down, not ungently—something old and dead and very pitiful—upon the floor.

At this moment Mrs. Jack went to the window of the drugstore and peered out at the great building across the street.

"I wonder if anything's happening over there," she said. "Do you suppose it's over? Have they got it out?"

The cold immensity of those towering walls told nothing. But there were other signs that it was really "out." The lines of hose that had threaded the street in a thick skein were noticeably fewer, and now and then there was the heavy beating roar of a great engine as a fire truck thundered away. Firemen were coming from the building, putting their apparatus back into their trucks, and although the police would not yet permit the tenants to return to their apartments, there was every indication now that the fire was over.

Meanwhile, newspapermen were beginning to come into the drugstore to phone their stories to the papers. One of them, a rather battered-looking gentleman with a bulbous red nose, had already called the City Desk on the telephone and was now engaged in reporting his findings to the man at the other end: ". . . Sure, that's what I'm tellin' yuh . . . The police have t'rown a cordon round the building . . ."

There was a moment's pause, but then the red-nosed man

rasped out irritably: "No—No—No! . . . not a *squadron!* A *cordon!* . . . C-o-r-d-o-n—cordon . . . For Pete's sake! Didn't you ever hear of a cordon before . . . Now, get this: Lissen—" he glanced at some scrawled notes upon a piece of paper in his hands, ". . . Among the residents are included the names of many Social Registerites and others prominent among . . . What? . . . How's that?" he said abruptly, rather puzzled—"Oh! . . ." he looked around briefly to see if he was being overheard, then lowered his voice and spoke again: "Oh, sure! . . . *Two* . . . Yeh . . . both of them were elevator men . . ." Then, looking at the notes upon his piece of dirty paper, he read carefully, in lowered voice: "John Enborg . . . age 64 . . . married . . . three children . . . lives in Jamaica, Queens . . . and Herbert Anderson . . . age 28, unmarried, lives with his mother, 841 Southern Boulevard, the Bronx . . . Have yuh got it? . . . Sure. Oh, sure!" Quietly, after a moment's pause, he spoke again, ". . . No, they couldn't get them out . . . they were on the elevators, goin' up to get the tenants when the current was shut off . . . Sure: that's the idea— They got caught between the floors . . . They just got Enborg out," his voice sank lower, "they had to use axes to get in through the top . . . Sure—sure," he nodded quietly into the mouthpiece, "that's it—smoke: no, just those two . . . no, the management wants to keep it quiet if they can . . . no, none of the tenants know it . . . Yes, it's almost over . . . Sure, it started in the basement, then it went up a flue and out at top . . . Sure, I know," he nodded— "The tracks are right below it . . . they were afraid to flood the basement; if they did, they'd flood four sets of tracks. Sure, it's going down now, but it's been tough . . . Okay, Mac . . . Shall I hang around? . . . Okay," he said at length, and hung up.

XIII.

The fire was over now. The people began to stream back into the court, collecting the scattered personnel of their establishments as they did so. An air of authority and order had already been re-established. Each little group, master and mistress, servants and members of the family, had now collected somewhat frigidly into their own separate entity and were filing back to their cells in the enormous hive.

Mrs. Jack, accompanied by her husband, Miss Mandell, and the young man, went in at her entrance. There was still a faint smell of smoke, but the elevator was running again. She noticed that the doorman, Henry, took them up, and she asked him if Herbert had gone. He paused just perceptibly, and then said quietly: "Yes, Mrs. Jack."

"You all must be simply worn out!" she said quickly, with her instant sympathy. "Hasn't it been a thrilling evening?" she went on eagerly: "In all your life did you ever know of such excitement as we had tonight?"

Again, the man said: "Yes, ma'am" in a tone so curiously unyielding that for a moment she felt almost angry, wounded and rebuffed. But already her mind was working on the curious enigma of the doorman's personality: "I wonder what is wrong with him," she thought. "Oh, well, poor thing, I suppose the life he leads is enough to turn anyone sour—opening doors and calling cabs and answering questions all day long— But then, Herbert has to do these things also, and he's always so sweet and so obliging about everything!—"

And, giving partial utterance to her thoughts, she said: "I suppose Herbert will be back upon the job tomorrow?"

He made no answer whatever. He simply seemed not to have heard her. He had opened the door at her own landing, and after a moment he said quietly: "This is your floor, Mrs. Jack."

She was so annoyed for a moment after he had gone that she halted in the little vestibule, and said angrily: "Honestly, that fellow makes me tired! It's got so now he won't even answer when you speak to him."

"Well, Alice, maybe he's tired out tonight with all the excitement of the fire," suggested Mr. Jack, pacifically.

"Maybe it's all our fault?" said Mrs. Jack ironically, then with a sudden flare of humor, she shrugged comically and said: "Vell, ve should have a fire sale!"—which restored her to good humor, and a full-throated appreciation of her own wit.

They opened the door then and went in. The place smelled closed and stale and there was still an acrid scent of smoke. But by this time the maids were streaming in from the service entrance at the back and Mrs. Jack directed them to throw up the windows.

Lily Mandell who had gone into the guest room for her wraps, now came out and said good-by. "Darling, it has been too marvelous," she said, with weary arrogance. "Fire, smoke, Piggy Hartwell, everything— Your parties are too wonderful! You never know what's going to happen next."

There was an air of finality about everything. The party was over, the fire was over, the last guest had now departed, and Mr. Jack was waiting to go to bed. In a moment he kissed his wife lightly upon her rosy cheek, said good night casually to Webber, and departed. The young man was also going now, but she, taking him by the hand, said quickly, coaxingly. "Don't go yet. Stay a few minutes, dear, and talk to me."

For a moment she looked around her with an air of thoughtful appraisal. The place looked just the same as it had looked before the people came, before Mr. Hartwell and his horrible performance, before the fire, all the excitement, all the confusion. If anyone came in here now he would never dream that anything had happened. This thought was uppermost in her mind when she turned to him again.

"Wasn't it all so strange? . . . And wonderful?" she said. "I mean, the *way* it happened. I don't know—but it sort of frightens you, doesn't it? . . . No, not the fire!" she spoke quickly—"That didn't amount to anything. No one got hurt—it was terribly exciting, really—I think everyone was thrilled! . . . What I mean" —her brow was furrowed as she sought for words—"when you think of how sort of—*big*—things have got—I mean the way people live nowadays—and how a fire can break out and you won't even know about it . . . I mean, there's something sort of *terrible* about it, isn't there? . . . And God!" she burst out suddenly. "In all your life, did you ever see the like of them? I mean the kind of people who live here . . . the way they all looked, pouring out into the court . . . Have you ever *dreamed*—" her excitement as she spoke these words was almost comical, "Well, it was the most astonishing . . . the queerest . . . I mean," she said confusedly, "it's—it's—"

She paused, holding his hand, and looking at him tenderly. Then, with a rapt look on her face, like an enchanted child, she whispered: ". . . Just you and I . . . They're all gone now . . . there's no one left but you and I . . . Do you know," she said in a quiet tone, "that I think about you all the time? I carry you around inside me—*here*," she laid her hand upon her breast and looked at him like a good child who believes religiously its own fable. "Oh, do you ever think that there was ever since the world began another love like this?" she cried. "If I could play I'd make of it great music! If I could sing I'd make of it a great song! If I could write I'd make of it a great story . . . but when I try to play or write or try to sing, I can think of nothing else but you and I . . ." Smiling, she inclined her rosy little face toward his, and said: "Did I ever tell you the time I tried to write a story? But all that I could say was 'Long, long into the night I lay, thinking of how I should tell my story.' But now at night that old line of the story keeps ringing in my ears: 'Long, long into the night I lay—thinking about you all the time.' For that's the story." She came closer to him, and lifted her rose face to him—"Oh, dearest, that's the story. In the whole world there's nothing more."

He made no answer. For suddenly he knew that, for him, at any rate, it was not the story. He felt desolate and tired, weary of all the consuming passion, the degrading egotisms of possession—of desire, of passion, and romantic love—of youth.

And suddenly it seemed to him that it was not enough. It seemed to him that there had to be a larger world, a higher devotion than all the devotions of this fond imprisonment could ever find. Well, then—a swift thrust of rending pity pierced him as he looked at the rose sweetness of that enraptured face—it must be so: he to his world, and she to hers—which to the better one, no one could say—but this, at last, he knew, was not enough. There were new lands; dark windings, strange and subtle webs there in the deep-delved earth, a tide was running in the hearts of men—and he must go.

They said little more that night. In a few minutes he got up, and with a sick and tired heart he went away.

XIV.

Outside, on the now deserted street, one of the dark-green wagons of the police was waiting now with a softly throbbing motor. In a few moments a door which led down into one of the basement entrances of the enormous building was opened, and two men emerged, bearing a stretcher which had something on it that was very still, completely covered. They slid this carefully away into the back of the green wagon. In another moment two other men, bearing a stretcher with a similar burden, emerged, and this also was quietly and carefully disposed in the same way. Then the door of the wagon was securely closed.

The driver and another man walked around and got into the front seat and after conferring quietly a moment with the sergeant of police, they drove off, turning the corner below with a subdued clangor of bells. The three policemen conferred together for a moment longer and two of them wrote down notes in their little books. Then the two policemen saluted the sergeant and they all departed, each walking away upon the further prosecution of his appointed task.

XV.

At this moment, Mrs. Jack, wearing her silken dressing gown, had just gone to the window of her room, and drawn in appraisingly a good full breath of cool night air. She found it good. The last disruptive taint of smoke had been washed clean and swept away by the cool breath of April. And in the white light of the virgin moon the spires and ramparts of Manhattan were glittering with cold magic in splintering helves of stone and glass. Peace fell upon her tranquil spirit. Strong comfort and assurance bathed her soul. It was so solid, splendid, everlasting, and good.

A tremor, faint and distant, shook her feet. She paused, startled, waited, listened. Was the old trouble there again to shake the deep perfection of her soul? What rumor had she heard this night? . . . Faint tremors, small but instant, and a talk of tunnels there below?—Ah, there it was a second time! What was it?—

Trains Again!

. . . Passed, faded, trembled delicately away into securities of eternal stone, and left behind it the blue helve of night, and April, in the blazing vertices of all that sculptured and immortal peace.

The smile came back into her eyes. The brief and troubling frown had lifted from her soul. And her look as she prepared to sleep was almost dulcet and cherubic—the look of a good child who ends the great adventure of another day and who knows that sleep and morning have come back again.

"Long, long into the night I lay—" she thought—"and thought of you—" . . .

Ah, sleep.